PRAISE FOR THE COLLECTOR

"Hey Winchesters, there's a new guy in town who's as hot, sarcastic and obsessed with souls as you are. But Dante's playing for Crowley's team and he's Hell's best."
—Justine Magazine

"Witty, and so intriguing. I started reading and didn't want to stop. Victoria Scott is a fabulous new voice in YA."
—C.C. Hunter, author of the New York Times bestselling series SHADOW FALLS

"Dante Walker is the kind of guy I wish I'd met when I was seventeen. And the kind of guy I'd kill if my daughter brought him home."
—Mary Lindsey, author of ASHES ON THE WAVES

"He's mouthy, he's arrogant, and he's here to reap your soul for the bad guys, but you still can't help but love Dante Walker, loud and proud, from page one. His is one of the most unique voices I've read in a while and I could not put the book down!"
— Heather Anastasiu, author of GLITCH

"Victoria Scott's smokin' hot paranormal debut, The Collector, left me breathless at every turn with its sizzling anti-hero."
—Mindee Arnett, author of THE NIGHTMARE AFFAIR

"Dante Walker's bad—swaggering, sexy, cocky, charming, soul-collecting, bone-deep, anti-hero bad. And Victoria Scott's witty, dark debut The Collector is so very, very good."
—Eve Silver, author of RUSH

THE LIBERATOR

A DANTE WALKER NOVEL

❧VICTORIA SCOTT❧

Entangled Publishing, LLC
2614 South Timberline Road
Suite 109
Fort Collins, CO 80525
Visit our website at www.entangledpublishing.com.

Edited by Liz Pelletier

Ebook ISBN 978-1-62266-017-9
Print ISBN 978-1-62266-016-2

Manufactured in the United States of America

First Edition September 2013

*For Mom, who showed me the magic books possess.
And for Dad, who taught me perseverance.*

"And throw them into the fiery furnace.
In that place there will be weeping and gnashing of teeth."
—Matthew 13:50

I was once a collector. I worked for the devil himself. If you sinned when I was around, I'm the piper you would've paid. But then I met a girl. She was everything I wasn't—kind, honest, virtuous. And in the end, though it was my job to drag her soul to hell, I sacrificed everything to save her from demons like me.

Today, they say I'm born again. That I have a second chance as a liberator. But let me tell you something…I'm no angel. Never have been, never will be. I'm just bad, baby. Maybe because of the way I was raised, or maybe it's good old-fashioned genetics.

Or maybe it's because deep down, I like the way being bad feels. Pow!

—Dante Walker

IMMORAL

"Some rise by sin, and some by virtue fall."
—William Shakespeare

1

I AIN'T NO ANGEL

Real men don't cross their legs.

In an emergency situation, like if you need to adjust your junk, a dude can place ankle to knee. But that's it. There shouldn't be any danglage. I shouldn't see one leg lying limply over the other, and I definitely—*definitely*—shouldn't see you bounce your dangling foot.

The guy in front of me is breaking this Man Rule. And about a dozen others.

He's wearing black-framed glasses I'm sure he doesn't need and a Burberry scarf that's as phony as he is. Even worse, he's sipping champagne from a friggin' crystal flute.

And he's talking to *my* girl, Charlie.

And making her laugh.

Music from the party throbs and echoes off the basement walls. I'm not sure how I got here, and I'm certain I don't know how Charlie ended up on the other side of the room with Guy In Touch With His Emotions. Raising a bottle to my lips, I watch as the guy uncrosses his long legs and recrosses them.

His tampon must be killing him.

I know perfectly well why this dude is moving in on Charlie. She's completely beautiful. But I can't complain. I'm the one who did this to her.

A month ago, I was given an assignment from Boss Man, AKA, Lord of the Underworld, to collect Charlie's soul. Like the champ I am, I pulled out all the stops to complete the job. Why wouldn't I? I was a collector from hell, after all, and there was a huge promotion on the line. So I offered Charlie something she couldn't refuse, something in exchange for her soul—*beauty*.

My past is working out real well for me right about now.

A girl struts by slowly, drinking in my appearance. *I know, fancy face. I'm effin' hot. But you're blocking my view.*

I raise a hand and flick my wrist, dismissing Ogling Girl. She rolls her eyes and clicks away in Payless heels.

When my eyes return to Charlie, they nearly pop from my head. Feminine Man has his arm around the back of her chair and is leaning in way too close. I take a moment to see how Charlie reacts. She isn't leaning into him, but she's not leaning away, either.

Time to break this crap up.

I try to stand but immediately stumble back into my chair. *Oh, man,* I think, *I'm plowed*. Steadying myself, I try again to stand. This time I'm successful. A guy near me holds his hand out, and I slap him a high five.

Then I cross the distance between Charlie and me. She looks up, and her mouth curves up in a cautious smile.

"Hey," D-bag says. He looks at me like *I'm* the one interrupting.

"Oh, hey," I say. "Did you want me to come back when you're done with my girlfriend?"

"Dante," Charlie says, sensing I'm about to blow.

I place my hand on her shoulder and give her a gentle squeeze, but my eyes never leave his face.

The dude looks at Charlie, then up at me. "Relax. We weren't doing anything." His words are innocent, but there's an arrogant tilt to his chin that I want to crush.

"Of course you weren't," I say. "Why don't you get yourself something to drink?" I nod toward the other side of the room. "Over there."

The guy stands up and steps in close, the smell of his cologne burning my nose. He nudges those black-rimmed glasses, and I consider jacking them, since I'm having a hard time seeing straight.

D-bag looks down at Charlie and smiles wide. "Hope I run into you again, Charlie," he says. "We have a lot in common."

I rub my jaw to keep from breaking his. The old demon in me wants to crack his skull for even looking at Charlie, but I know it'd cause a fight between me and her, and I won't risk that. Nothing is worth hurting her again.

Charlie stands and twines her arm around mine. Her lips brush my ear, and goose bumps rise on my skin. "Careful, Dante. I'm not your property." She pulls back and smiles, though I can tell she's still a little peeved. Her head falls to one side. "Besides, you can't kill them all."

I turn my head, looking into her blue eyes. They're bright and alert and unlike my own, which I'm sure are bloodshot as hell. "I can try." I cup her cheeks and pull her mouth close.

She kisses me for a moment, then jerks backward. Her hand covers her lips. "You've been smoking."

"Yeah, so?"

"I thought you were going to stop." She wraps her arms around herself, and my heart tugs at the distance between us.

"Why would I stop?" I ask. "I'm already dead. It's not like it's going to hurt me."

"But you're an angel now," she retorts.

"Please," I say, but the gold cuff around my ankle reminds me she's right. Big Guy, AKA Lord of the Heavens, gave me another chance after I died saving Charlie from hell's collectors. He said I could be useful as a liberator on Team Heaven, but he's wrong there, 'cause I ain't no angel.

I grab a bottle of tequila from the table and take a swig as a bunch of drunk chicks bump into me. At once, tequila races down my throat and the front of my shirt. I pull the bottle away and brush off my dark red jacket.

"Damn it," I snarl.

Charlie shakes her head. She's disappointed I didn't turn into Golden Boy following my rebirth as an angel. But I can't help it, because deep down, I'm still a demon.

She pushes the jacket off my shoulders and folds it over her arm. The look in her eyes crushes me. It says that even though I'm not behaving like an angel, she accepts me anyway. "We should get out of here," she says.

"Why? Because of that guy?"

"No, because…"

"Because you think I'm drunk." I nod like I've nailed it. "Girl, I'm stone cold sober."

Charlie laughs and shakes her head. Then she reaches into my jacket pocket for the keys to Elizabeth Taylor, my candy apple–red Escalade. She jiggles them in front of my face. "Come on, I'm driving."

I pull her close and breathe warm air onto her neck. "You saying you want to take me home?"

She leans into me. "That's exactly what I'm saying."

"Then by all means," I bellow. "Take me home and have your way with me."

Charlie shushes me as people stop and stare. I flip them off nice and hard and allow my girl to drag me outside.

"Get in," she says, pointing to Elizabeth Taylor.

I bow like she's my queen and I her simple servant. Then I climb into the passenger seat and blast Rob Zombie as Charlie drives toward her grandmother's house. I glance over when I notice her going for the Skittles in her pocket, and sigh with pleasure that some things never change. For the first time, I wonder if there's a story behind those way-too-hard, way-too-brightly-colored candies.

Pulling into her driveway, she kills the music. The two-story white house is covered in red-and-white Christmas lights that I strung up, even though I insisted I don't do such things. Grams usually does the job but couldn't hack it this year. She's has been sick for a while now, and though she's tried hard to hide it from Charlie, I'm pretty sure her adopted child knows full well what's happening, even if she won't acknowledge it.

"Want to stay here while you sober up?" Charlie asks, taking my hand.

"Girl, I told you, I'm—"

"Stone cold sober." She rolls her eyes. "Right."

I form my hands into guns and fire them off in her direction. "Smart girl."

She shakes her head. "Drunk boy."

I hop out of Elizabeth Taylor and walk toward the house. Then I decide crawling on my hands and knees would be more convenient. I drop down and instruct Charlie to mount my back and ride me like a horse.

She does it without hesitating.

I fall in lust all over again.

Outside her grandmother's house, Charlie pauses. "Meet me in my room, okay?"

I stand up and give her a soldier's salute. Worrying Grams will catch my ass, I throw on shadow—my ability to become invisible thanks to the cuff on my ankle. Then I head toward the lattice beneath her window. Twice, I fall off and land in the bushes. When at last I'm victorious, I shake off my shadow, and Charlie slides the window open so I can crawl inside.

Her bed is a beacon for my drunk bones, and I stumble toward it and collapse. Sitting beside me, Charlie pushes the hair from my forehead. She leans over and blows a cool breeze across my neck. Within seconds, my entire body is on fire. I push myself up and look at her.

It's been six weeks since hell put a target on Charlie Cooper. Five weeks since I collected her soul. Even now, I carry it with me. I place a hand to my chest, remembering. Charlie wraps her hand around mine and closes her eyes. I imagine she's remembering, too. I wonder if she feels the same thing I do about her soul. That somehow it feels *off*. I tell myself it's because it's *her*; she's destined to do great things, so of course her soul would feel different. But sometimes, I'm not so sure.

Admitting this is hard, because one of the most esteemed parts of my old job as a collector was knowing when you'd absorbed a soul, and when you'd successfully deposited it in hell. A soul doesn't feel like a brick inside your chest—quite the opposite, actually. A soul is feather light, and the subtle variations between how one soul feels and another can lead to confusion. But collectors take pride in sensing a soul inside their body. It's like a surgeon guiding a blind hand toward where they know an injury lies. The sensation, that *knowledge*, isn't solid, but it's there, nonetheless.

But with all the souls I've carried, all the variances I've felt—it's never been like this.

I often wonder why I can't simply return her soul to her body, but Valery says it's unsafe. That it must be stored with Big Guy where it's untouchable. Though why we don't do that immediately is beyond me.

Watching Charlie, my breath catches. Her blond hair falls in waves over her shoulders, and her skin has a glow only happiness brings. Someday, this girl will save the world. Her charity and her work will bring about Trelvator: a hundred years of peace. But right now, alone in this room—she's mine.

I kiss her closed eyelids, and they open to reveal two blue gems. I take her lips in mine, slipping my tongue inside the warmth. I feel her body respond to my touch. Before she can protest, I wrap my arm around her waist and in one solid movement sweep her beneath me.

Parting her thighs with my knee, I lower myself down. Those blue eyes stay locked on my face, and I see her pulse quicken along her neck. I press my lips to that spot and hear her breath rush out.

"Charlie," I whisper.

She responds by running her fingers through my hair and pulling me closer. They slide up and down my back like she's tracing the lines of my dragon tattoo.

Kissing her, I lose my friggin' mind. I yearn to be closer to her, to show her just how close we can be. But I also want it to be perfect for Charlie, because if anyone deserves a perfect first time, it's her.

"Dante," she says quietly, but I already know. She's not ready, and I don't blame her. I haven't exactly been the ideal boyfriend these last few weeks.

I start to lift myself up but stop. I can't help kissing her one more time. I push my mouth over hers and, reaching down, pull her thighs up and press my hips down harder. She moans, and the sound touches my lips, rousing me. I'm reconsidering my earlier conviction about being patient—when a sound crashes through the house.

Charlie grabs onto my elbow and we both listen.

It comes again, louder.

"The door," Charlie says. "Someone's at the door."

I roll to my side, and Charlie jumps from the bed and leaves the room. I follow after her, watching as she *thump-thump*s down the stairs. When her hand reaches for the knob, my mind screams.

"Wait," I yell-whisper. Though I'm fairly sure collectors wouldn't bother knocking, it still bugs me that someone's outside her house past midnight. I jog down the stairs and pull Charlie behind me. Only then do I open the door.

There's a flash of red as a woman turns and faces me.

Valery.

The spitfire twenty-something with bright red hair is a liberator. She helped me rescue Charlie from Rector, head of the collectors, but would just as soon castrate me as admit we're friends.

"Thought you said you and Max were going on vacay," I say.

"Postponed." Valery starts to stride into the house, but I grab her wrist.

"No," I say, glancing upstairs, where I know Grams is sleeping. "If you want to talk, let's go outside."

She shrugs her slender shoulder and sashays out the door. When Charlie heads after us, Valery holds up her hand. "I've got to speak to Dante alone, sweetheart."

I wrap my arm around Charlie and pull her close. "Anything you have to say to me, you can say to her."

Valery looks at me for a long time. "Fine."

She reaches into her purse and pulls out a long white envelope.

"Oh, *hell*, no," I say as a chill races down my spine. "Get that crap away from me."

"What'd you think? That He'd look the other way while you partied your ass off?" Valery shoves the envelope against my chest. "You haven't sealed a single soul for heaven, Dante. You were practically begging for an assignment."

Beside me, I can almost feel Charlie brighten. She's been praying for something to get me off my sin spiral. And now her wish has been granted.

I cringe and step away from the envelope like it has chlamydia. "Tell Big Guy I'll take a pass."

"Actually, this comes with a message from Him." Valery glances at Charlie, then back at me. "You're on probation."

"Probation?" I say, laughing. "Ooh, I'm friggin' terrified."

And I am. Terrified. Because I'm a badass, but he's like…you know…*God*.

"You have two options," Valery says, ignoring my mockery. "You can either complete this assignment or turn in your cuff."

My hands curl into fists. "Wow, those are generous options. So I can do His bidding or I can die a final death? Real nice."

Valery shrugs. "You didn't leave Him much choice." She holds the envelope out again, and this time I take it. In my drunken state, I imagine it burns my hand. Maybe it does. Who knows?

"Max says hi," Valery finishes before heading to her car.

Charlie's eyes are round with surprise. We both knew I worked for Big Guy now, but I don't think either of us was prepared for *this*. She recovers quickly, reaching up on her tiptoes and nuzzling my neck. "This will be great, you'll see," she says. "Come back in when you're ready." She kisses her fingers and presses them to my lips. Then she goes inside and closes the door behind her.

I stare down at the envelope in my hand. For several minutes, I just stand there, drunk and swaying and panicking about what it'll say. Then I snap the hell out of my trance and pull myself together. How bad could it be?

I tear the envelope open, rip out the sheet of paper, and start reading.

And then I laugh.

Because there's no way in hell I'm going to cold-ass Denver to liberate a girl named Aspen.

⇥ 2 ⇤

SUMO WRESTLER

Valery is climbing into her car, a black Mercedes S500, when I realize there's something else inside the envelope. I reach in and pull out a pair of small, curved ivory things that look like horns. One is slightly larger than the other, and both confuse the hell out of me.

I call out to Valery, "Hey, Red."

She turns and looks at me, making a face like she's simultaneously asking me what I want and cursing my existence.

"What are these?" I hold up the horns.

"How should I know?" She shrugs. I think she's about to drop down into her car, but she pauses and glances over the top of the hood, the look in her eyes softening. "They're from your father."

Valery disappears from view, starts the engine of her Mercedes, and pulls away. I had more questions for her, questions she's dismissed for weeks. But right now they don't seem so important. Not when I'm staring at the horns in my palm. *From my father*, she'd said. *My father, who died in a car crash minutes before I did. The guy I've seen only once since.*

As I think of him, my chest feels like it's on fire. He's given me these two crescent-shaped things, and I have no earthly idea what they are. The fact that he left *anything* for me blows my mind. Doing this, it's like he cares. Thinking of my dad also reminds me of my mom — of how Rector was dating her in order to learn more about me, and to show me he could get close to those I care about. My dad told me he had that issue nipped in the bud. I'm not sure how, but if there's one thing I know, it's that Pops will make sure that bastard doesn't get near her again. Game over.

Overhead, I hear a knock. Glancing up, I spot Charlie standing in the window, her slight figure framed by the glow of a lamp. I grip the ivory horns and slip them into my pocket. All I want to do is keep Charlie Cooper safe, because even though her soul was taken by collectors, that doesn't mean the same guys won't come for her body, too. But protecting her seems impossible when no one will tell me what the H is going on.

I don't understand why I can't turn Charlie's soul in to heaven yet.

And I really don't understand why every time I ask Valery about these things, she acts like I just told her I'm rubbing bellies with her mom. Like *I'm* the jerk for asking questions.

Charlie waves from her window, and I raise my hand. She motions for me to come up, and I want nothing more than to do just that. So I push my questions aside for now and head toward her room. She's sitting on the bed, and despite the thoughts clogging my head, my body reacts to seeing her there. She's wearing this white, lacy gown that chicks usually only wear in movies, and she looks so innocent, I could scream. I want to protect this girl from all the terrible things in the world, but at the same time, I want to do all kinds of terrible things *to* her. Most involve the bed she's sitting on. Or the floor. I'm not picky.

"Are you going to do it?" she asks, pulling her blond hair over her shoulder.

"Ravage you? Yes."

She smiles, but her eyes fall to the floor. "You know what I mean."

I cross the room and sit next to her, fighting the impulse to tear that sweet-as-cream nightgown from her body. "I don't want to think about it."

I look at her, and she meets my gaze. I expect to her say that I must. That I don't really have a choice. But instead, all she says is, "Then don't. Just go to sleep." Her grin widens. "With me."

My eyebrow hitches up.

She laughs. "That's not what I mean."

But it's too late. I scoop her into my arms and cover her body with mine. Before I press my lips over her mouth, I stop and look at her. Really look at her. With my thumbs, I brush the hair away from her cheeks. Then I run my eyes over her face, her neck, her delicate shoulders. She looks like a doll. And even though she's perfection now, I remember the way she was—her thick glasses, her crooked smile, her cheeks that blazed red when she was excited. It's ridiculous, but sometimes I miss those things.

I lean down and kiss the space between her collarbones. Then I brush my lips across her neck and move toward her ear.

"Dante," she whispers. I stop instantly because I already know what she needs.

Lifting my head, I see I'm right. There are tears in her eyes, and I think I might lose my mind when one slips down the side of her face toward the pillow. "It's okay," I say gently. I move behind her and wrap my arms around her waist. Then I pull her against me and let her cry.

I let her mourn the loss of her friend, of Blue, who died at the hands of a collector.

Charlie is like this many nights. During the day she's fine, but once she's curled up in bed with time to think, Blue finds a way to slip into her head. Probably doesn't help that Annabelle, her remaining best friend, has been on lockdown by her parents.

Valery's presence always sets Charlie off, not that we've seen that much of her lately, either. But when all of us *are* together, I think it's hard not to remember who else was there that night.

The truth is I mourn Blue's death, too. I never really liked the guy...until the end. Until I realized he was friggin' Clark Kent, an undercover Superman who would risk his life for Charlie's.

It was then I understood we both just wanted the same thing—Charlie's happiness.

• • •

When I open my eyes, the sun is trying to murder me. It's shining on my face and making my head pound. Or maybe it's my hangover that's giving me the headache, but nonetheless, me and the sun, we're not on friendly terms.

"Mmm..." Charlie murmurs beside me. My arms are still wrapped around her waist, and I suddenly realize I must have crashed out in her bed last night. If Grams wakes up and finds me here, she'll run me a bath and toss in the toaster.

"Morning, babe," I say as quietly as I can.

"Morning, hot stuff," a distinctly male voice says from behind me.

I whip around, my heart racing, and find Max sitting in a chair across the room. "You look so hot when you first wake up." He raises a hand to his hair. "Got that whole sexy bedhead thing going on."

Charlie doesn't even move from her place, but I feel her laughing against me. "Your friend is kinda creepy, Dante," she manages.

"Max, what the hell are you doing in here?" I ask, pulling the covers farther up even though I'm—regretfully—fully-clothed.

"Real question is, why did I wait so long to join you guys?" he responds, standing from his chair. A mischievous smile crawls across his face.

"No," I say, trying to appear as serious as possible. "Don't even think about it, dude."

Max starts running in place, his smile widening until he looks deranged. "Ready or not!" Before I can stop him, Max races toward the bed and dives on top of us. "Oh! Oh, it feels even better than I imagined." He rolls back and forth across us as Charlie laughs and I wonder why I'm friends with such a raging idiot.

With all my strength, I grab Max's shirt and roll him toward the edge. He falls off the side, his arms pinwheeling. There's a loud *thud* and then nothing.

I wait for several seconds then lean over to look for him. Max is lying face down on the floor, his arms and legs curled like a dead spider. "You're not really hurt," I say.

"I think…I think you gave me spina bifida. You need to call someone."

"That's a genetic disorder," I say with a sigh, collapsing back onto my pillow. A second later, he raises his head very, very slowly over the side of the bed. It's one of the more unsettling things he's ever done. "Max, is there a purpose to this visit?" I ask. I want so badly to act like he's annoying me. But he knows, and I know, that we both love this game: the one where I act like he's a pain in my ass, and he acts like a damn circus clown.

He stands up, crosses the room, and plops back down in the chair. "Valery sent me."

I throw an arm across my eyes. "Of course she did." Beside me, Charlie moves to get up and I immediately reach for her. She squeals and wiggles out of my grasp.

I watch as she walks around the bed and ruffles Max's hair. Max pants like a dog. It's a bit disturbing, since he's twenty-eight and

Charlie's seventeen. She eyes me with a grin. "I'll make waffles."

My face lights up.

"Yes," she continues. "And bacon."

I look at Max and nod toward Charlie. "That's my girl."

"Damn straight," he says.

"I'm still making breakfast for your birthday," I call after Charlie. Then, looking at Max, I say, "Charlie's going to be legal soon."

Charlie stops at the door and points to another door across the hall, to the room where her sick adoptive mother, or Grams, as we call her, sleeps. She raises a finger to her lips, and I nod in understanding. *Don't wake her*, Charlie's saying. But what I'm wondering as she leaves is, does she realize just how sick Grams really is? Charlie isn't stupid, and I think she knows something's off. But I still don't know if she understands the whole truth, that Grams isn't getting any better. There are days when I want to tell her, but Grams had a relationship with Charlie long before I did. And I'm trying to respect that. Besides, it's not like Charlie has given her Grams full disclosure about who I am. So maybe secrets are common between them.

Max leans back in the chair and twines his fingers behind his head. "So, dude. We need to talk about this assignment business."

"How about instead we talk about why you didn't go on your honeymoon," I say. "You *postponed*? You, who have dreamed of trapping a woman on a secluded island since you were eleven?"

Max sucks in a breath and looks away. His eyes narrow like he's pained, but then he turns back with a quick smile. "We decided to do a big wedding, after all. None of this 'quiet affair' shenanigans anymore. Then we'll honeymoon."

"Good man," I say. "It's bad manners not to throw your friends a party when the opportunity presents itself."

"Speaking of parties…" Max puts his forearms on his knees and leans forward. "Heard you've hit up quite a few of them lately."

"You going get on my case, too?" I ask.

"Seriously, D. You know you're my bro, but you've got to slow down on the crap storm you're spinning. I know you're a demon at heart; so does everyone else. You don't need to prove it, right?"

I look at him, my lips pressed together. I know he's looking out for my best interests, but he doesn't know what's going down in my head. How I feel like I don't belong anywhere anymore. I'm not a demon, and I'm certainly not an angel, even if Big Guy did strap a liberator cuff around my ankle. I've never lived the kosher lifestyle, and now I'm supposed to fly to Denver, teach this random girl how to live a pure life, and, somewhere during all that, liberate her soul to heaven piece by piece? Give me a break. "I do what I do, Max."

"I hate you." Max straightens in the chair. "But I love you, too. In, like, a completely sexual way."

"Are you even supposed to be here?" I ask, ignoring his last comment.

He shrugs one shoulder. "You've had enough of people questioning your extracurricular evenings, I've had enough of people questioning my presence."

"The difference is," I say, "I'm not risking the collectors finding us."

Max winces like I've hurt him, but it's the truth. The collector cuff he wears could lead the other collectors, including Rector, straight to our doorstep. Not that it matters. My cuff is sending enough of a signal on its own. And they'd know where to find us, anyway. I tried to get Charlie to go into hiding, but she refused to leave after the collectors, including myself, ascended on Peachville. She lived in this big white house before everything happened, and she lives here now. Her words, not mine. I think it's because of Grams. Because she doesn't want to make her guardian move.

It's strange that liberators and collectors are now active enemies.

Before I met Valery, I didn't even realize liberators existed. But after that night in the forest when Rector took Charlie's soul, the line was drawn. Now we're divided. The liberators want to keep Charlie's body safe so she can lead us into a hundred years of peace, and the collectors want… We don't know yet.

I realize there's no reason to make Max feel like he's doing anything wrong. "Look. If they were going to return, they would have already. They know they lost. I collected Charlie's soul, and Rector sure as hell would've come after me, except he killed Blue. Because the collectors aren't allowed to hurt humans, they're probably lying low to keep from starting a war with Big Guy. So for now, we're good. You're good."

"We need to discuss this Boss Man title," Max says. "Needs a good rebranding, don't you think? I mean, he's not really our boss anymore."

I rub a hand over my jaw and feel stubble there. It still amazes me that I can do things like grow facial hair when I'm technically dead. "*Ex*-Boss?" I suggest.

"Lame," Max says. "The Warden?"

I let out a sharp laugh. "Not bad. He is oppressive." Rubbing my hands together, I think harder. "I've got it."

"Give it to me," Max says, his face lighting up with excitement.

"Lucille. It's like Lucifer, but with a touch of femininity."

I expect Max to laugh, but he doesn't. Instead, he gets real serious and moves to the edge of his seat. "Dante?"

"Yeah?"

"If I told you Lucille was easy, would you believe me?"

"I would."

Max laughs and starts to say something, but I hold up my hand to stop him. I'm not sure I'm right until I raise my nose in the air and take another whiff. Then I close my eyes in ecstasy. Bacon. "It's ready." When I open my eyes, I notice Max looks ready to bolt from his chair. "Don't even think about it."

He jerks like he's going to race me down the stairs. Or tackle me. I'm not sure which, but I'm ready for both. I flick my finger just to screw with him, and he leaps to his feet.

Me. He's definitely barreling *toward* me.

We lock arms like sumo wrestlers and grunt like the pigs we're fighting for.

"There's...probably enough...for both of us," Max growls through the strain.

I push my weight into him, knowing there's no way he's winning this ridiculous battle. And a battle it is. Because I'd fight to the death for crispy, fatty bacon. "Then stop fighting me... you...moron."

"Okay," Max says nonchalantly, and at the same he time moves to the side and makes a break for the stairs.

I fall forward from momentum and hit the ground. Then I go to take off after him, thinking I can still make it to the kitchen first—when something catches my eye. I turn toward Charlie's bedroom window, and my face scrunches up with confusion.

When I move closer, my confusion switches to alarm. The something that caught my eye is a dude I've never seen before. He's staring up at Charlie's window, and something tells me he's been there awhile.

Before I can think, I turn and run.

⫷ 3 ⫸

LURKER

I see Max in my peripheral vision as I hit the bottom of the stairs, but I can't see his face. All I'm focused on is getting outside and finding out who's creeping around Charlie's place.

"Beat you, jerk-off!" I hear Max say as I whip the door open.

I don't close it behind me; I just barrel through and head toward the street. Stalking down the walkway, I glance left and right. I spot him striding away from Charlie's house. He's about six feet tall and has a bright blue baseball cap on. I'd know the miniature "C" logo on the back anywhere, because it was born in my hometown in honor of my favorite team—the Chicago Cubs.

"Hey, lurker," I yell out, my pulse racing. "Stop."

The guy doesn't turn to look over his shoulder. He doesn't speed up. He just keeps on walking. I half think I'm out of my mind, that I used to be this guy who was chill about everything, and now suddenly I'm this roided-out freak show chasing guys down the street. But I was *chill* before I met Charlie. I was *chill* before I started caring about someone other than myself.

Now I'm *this* guy.

"Dude, can you not hear me?" I ask, louder. He's only a few yards away when he turns a corner and I lose sight of him. I jog, then sprint, toward the curve in the road. My heart picks up, and I breathe harder. For five weeks I've been on edge, waiting for something like this to happen. Now I've caught a guy spying on Charlie. I don't sense dargon—the material our cuffs are made from—but maybe it's because I'm too panicked. I try to calm myself down and focus, but it's hard when I'm sprinting toward a creeper who's out of sight. The bend in the road is near, and I move even faster, sweat pricking my brow. I turn the corner—

And slam into the enormous guy.

He reaches out and grabs my shoulders. "Whoa, bro. Watch where you're going."

With adrenaline coursing through my veins, I go for the dude's midsection. I take him to the ground and pin his shoulders to the pavement. Then I get close to his face and snarl, "Who are you?"

"No, who are *you*?" The guy, who looks to be my age, says through labored breaths. "You're the one who just tackled me."

"I'm the guy who's going to bury you if you don't tell me what you were doing outside her house." I shove his shoulders back toward the asphalt to drive my point home.

"Outside her house?" he says like he's confused. Then understanding relaxes his features. Or maybe it's that he just came up with a convincing lie. "Oh, crap. Must be Easton. My brother. Was he wearing a blue baseball hat?"

I ease up a little, because yeah, he was. My eyes rake over the guy beneath me, and I decide this wasn't the same person who was watching Charlie. *This* guy is even taller and broader than…Easton. "He was looking up into my girl's *window*," I bark, my muscles still balled up with tension.

"Look, can you let me up?" he says. "I'm not trying to fight you."

I look the guy dead in the eyes and I don't like what I see. His open palms, his half smile—he's trying almost *too* hard to show he's not a threat. But I can't keep him pinned down forever, as much as I'd like to, so I get to my feet and yank him to a standing position. "Talk."

After brushing off his dark blue shirt, he offers his hand. "I'm Salem."

I glare at his hand until he pulls it back and shoves it into his pocket.

"Look, my brother is harmless," he says, rolling his shoulders. "He was in a car accident a couple of years ago, and it's messed with his head."

Salem's jaw works like he's upset, but I'm not sure he is. Glancing over my shoulder, I ensure Charlie is nowhere in sight.

"Before the accident, Easton had a girl," Salem continues. "And sometimes he gets confused. But he won't be a problem. I swear."

I look the guy, Salem, up and down. "Six foot one, I'd say. Dark hair that falls below the ear." I lean forward a bit. "Green eyes that seem *shifty*."

"What are you doing?" Salem asks, and I see a spark of anger in his stance. It's the spark I knew he was hiding.

"Memorizing your face," I answer. "So that if I ever see you or your brother near her house again, I can welcome you back." I punch the word "welcome" so he gets my point.

Salem smiles, but there's a flash of darkness in it. "You won't be seeing us again."

I stare at him for a long time, then nod, because what else can I do? And if I'm wrong that this guy is bad news, then I really am morphing into a paranoid sociopath. Spinning around, I head away from him. I try my damnedest not to turn back and glare. Turning back would imply I'm insecure, and I need this guy to know I'm not afraid of him.

When I near Charlie's house, I notice she's standing in the doorway with a spatula in her hand. Despite being on edge, I can't stop myself from grinning. I feel like such a chick around her sometimes, like I'm seconds away from buying a tiara and starting my period.

"What's going on?" she asks. I expect her to look worried, but instead she looks strong. Her head is tilted back, and her shoulders are squared. It's like she's been ready for this. Like she's been waiting to step in and take control. Charlie must weigh a buck twenty, but right now she looks fierce.

Her body language is so freaking hot; I want to eat her alive.

I contemplate not telling her about the guy. I don't want to upset her, but the assurance in her eyes tells me she can handle it. "There was someone out here," I say. "He was standing in the street looking up at your window."

"Did you sense anything? Another cuff?" she asks. I shake my head, and her shoulders relax. "Then come inside and eat some damn bacon."

My eyes widen. "You just cursed. That was very unladylike."

"Get inside," she says, a hand cocked on her hip.

I'm trying hard to look unconcerned, but I can't forget what I felt around Salem—like something was off about him and his brother. But Charlie's got a point. I didn't sense a cuff, and collectors can't survive without them. So chances are, it's just some jerk who saw a pretty girl and wanted to stop and stare. Still, as I'm walking by her to go inside, I turn and look back over my shoulder to double-check that they're both gone.

"It's fine," she adds softly. "I'm fine."

I stop suddenly and take her face in my hands. "I'll never let what happened to you that night—"

"I know," she says.

I let go of her and move inside, but before I can get too far, she pops me on the butt with her spatula. In a flash, I sweep her into my arms. She squeals, and I dip her close to the floor and kiss her long and deep on the mouth. When I finally pull my lips from hers, my blood pumping hard, she looks at me and says, "We have company."

I look up and see Valery and Max standing near the kitchen table. Righting Charlie on her feet, I take a couple of steps toward the redhead. Then I hook my thumbs under my new kickass red belt with the skull belt buckle. Said belt is supposed to take the edge off the fact that Rector stole my favorite kicks. It doesn't quite work. "Your timing is perfect, Val," I say. "Too late to be of any help."

"Help with what?" she says, readiness overtaking her stance.

I jab my thumb toward the door. "Two guys. One staring up at Charlie's window. The other claiming it's just his nutcase bother."

As Max watches, Valery races to the doorway and looks out. Then she glances back at me, her face creased with worry. "Did you sense a cuff?"

I steal a look at Charlie. She raises her eyebrow as if to imply she's not alone in thinking I'm overreacting. "No," I admit. "No cuff."

Valery swings around and saunters back toward the kitchen. Max never takes his eyes off her. "We can't afford to draw attention to ourselves right now, Dante."

"There was a guy watching my girlfriend," I say, spitting each word.

"Are you so surprised by that?" she asks, and for the first time, I feel a little like an idiot. Before, I wondered if *maybe* I was visiting Looney Town. Now it's like I *know* I did.

"Still don't want random dudes hanging around like dogs in heat," I mumble.

"Something tells me you took care of it," Red says, checking herself out in a nearby mirror. "Besides, you've got bigger things to think about. Like your assignment."

"Come to strong-arm me, Red?"

"No, came to confirm you're intoxicated again. Imagine my surprise," she says in her typical slow, even way. "Must be strange with all that blood in your alcohol stream."

I look to Max for back up, but he's biting his lower lip and looking at Valery with such intensity that I wonder if he's stroking out. "Max?" I say.

"Hmm?" he answers, eyes still on Valery.

"A little help?"

He finally manages to look at me. "Sorry, D-money. You're on your own." Max stands up and leaves the room.

I glance at Valery. "What'd you do him, Red? Threaten to withhold your parasitic love?"

She straightens. "When are you leaving for your assignment?"

"This again," I say, sighing.

Valery sits down at the table. "I understand your reservations for leaving."

"Do you?" I growl.

She looks me dead in the eye. "Yes, I do."

As much as I tease Red about her relationship with Max, I do believe the two care about each other. So yeah, maybe she does get how I don't want to leave Charlie. But what I don't tell her is that there's more than just leaving Charlie that makes me hesitate. Being a liberator—pretending to be someone who does *good*—doesn't feel right. I've never been good, and I don't play nice. So the idea of my being this person who saves people doesn't fly.

Just thinking about it turns my stomach, though I can't put my finger on why exactly.

I need a drink.

I head to Gram's stash and pull out a bottle of dusty champagne. "Mimosas?"

Valery's chest deflates, and for one moment, I feel guilty. I may pretend to hate Valery, but she helped save Charlie's soul, and I'm grateful for that. But I can't be who she's asking me to be, so I pop the cork off the bottle and listen to the fizzle of the happy juice inside. Pouring myself a glass, I risk a glance at Charlie. She's putting syrup and butter out on the counter and shoots a smile my way. I recoil seeing the faith in her eyes. A part of me feels like I'm just waiting for that faith to fade, like I'm testing it. But somehow, she never stops believing I'll be the person she thinks I am.

If only I could be like *her*.

It's easy to admire Charlie. But how she's able to accept me so easily, so freely—that's something I'll never understand.

Max returns to the room. "Not that I was eavesdropping—okay, maybe I was, but Val's right, D. You've got to do this assignment."

I look at him, fight setting my muscles ablaze.

"You'll be back before you know it," he adds. "And really, what else can you do? If you don't go, Big Guy will give you the slip."

I glance from Max to Valery. She nods. I'd wanted to avoid this conversation, figured if I kept myself in a haze for the next few days, the topic would somehow disappear. But apparently this is an intervention, and I've got to get on a plane or pick out a cemetery plot.

"Who did you even get the assignment envelope from? I'm sure Big Guy handed it to you himself, right?" I say it mockingly, but I'm half hoping Valery says that she *did* get it from God himself. That he has that kind of interest in me. But even as I think this, I know I'm kidding myself.

"Kraven gave it to me," she answers.

Pow! My interest is piqued. "Home boy with the white wings?"

She shrugs like it's not a big deal, like we all haven't been beating our brains as to how a liberator sprouted wings the night Blue died. Valery, Max, and I have spent many nights trying to figure out how to do the same thing, yet we've gotten nowhere. Our objective might be a lot easier if Valery would do what we've been asking her to do, which is to *ask* Kraven about how he summoned his wings.

I hang my head and groan, rubbing my temple with the hand that isn't holding the champagne bottle. The answer on what to do about this assignment should be easy. I know it should. But it isn't. When I look up, Charlie is standing before me. "Charlie?"

"Do what you think is right, and don't worry about anything else," she says.

I squeeze my eyes shut against the sound of her voice. It's so sure, so soothing. I don't want to be away from the sound of her voice. I don't want to be away from *her*. Charlie is my happily ever after.

When I remember this, that this assignment is only a blip of time, and that it's the only way to ensure we aren't apart for the long haul, I know I have to go. I wanted to ignore my new placement as Big Guy's soldier. I wanted to live my life as Dante, not as a liberator. Not as something I will never really be.

But for Charlie, I'll pretend to be anything.

I squeeze the ivory horns in my pocket and pull in a long breath. "I'll go," I say. "But only if we have one hell of a send-off."

Max pulls out his new phone, the one he hasn't shut up about for the last six days, and pushes a few buttons. Pulsing music fills my ears, and I raise the bottle in the air. "That's what I'm talking about."

Max dances in place, Charlie hands me a plate of bacon and waffles, and Valery comes to stand beside me. She takes the champagne from my hand, holds it up even higher, and says above the music, "To Aspen."

Then she puts the bottle to her lips and drinks.

CONNECTION

The day flew by in a blur.

Grams woke up a few minutes after our makeshift party started. She didn't seem too upset, though. Just came downstairs, sat in her nearby oversized love seat, and nursed her water bottle. Of vodka. Max and I acted like morons and insisted Valery, who was now sober, chauffer us around in her Mercedes. We hung our heads out the window and howled at the afternoon sun, and later, the moon. Charlie sat between us as we cruised Peachville, Alabama, stopping here and there to complete dares, and capturing the idiocy with Max's new phone. We also stopped at The Wireless Hut so Valery could buy herself a cell and, in a moment of coolness, buy Charlie and me phones, too. I would have done it myself, but I couldn't since I was now cut off from my hell-issued AmEx Black Card.

When we get back to Grams's place, I say good-bye to Max. He hugs me, slaps me hard on the back, then pulls on his shadow and vanishes from sight. I turn to Valery. "Thanks for the phone."

"I enjoy helping the needy," she says.

I scrunch up my nose. "I am many things, but needy isn't one of them. Though speaking of, when am I getting my new card? Is it all blue and sparkly to represent the heavens?"

"You'll get it tomorrow, once I get you to the airport."

Groaning, I hook my arm around Charlie. "What time?"

"Seven in the morning," Valery answers.

I shake my head. "You did that on purpose."

Valery smiles and waves before she disappears inside her Mercedes. As she drives away, her windows down, I can hear the clatter of empty bottles clinking against one another in the backseat.

Charlie squeezes me around the middle. "I had fun today."

My eyes close as I breathe her in. Whoever said "like attracts like" had their head stuffed up somewhere dark and stank-like.

I bury my head in the side of her neck and lay my lips on the warmth there. My stomach tightens as I feel her hands roam over my back and across my sides. She moves them farther down until her fingers dig into my pockets. Then she pulls me closer. "Stay again tonight?"

I raise my head. I'm not sure how she can even question this. There's no place I'd rather be. When I even think about how I'll be away from her—in Denver—my insides revolt. I can't imagine spending my days wondering where she is at any given moment and questioning whether she's safe. "Course I'll stay."

I expect her to smile, but instead her eyebrows pull together in confusion. "What's this?" she asks, wiggling her fingers deeper into my pocket.

Restraining myself from saying the dirty thing that's on my mind, I step back. She withdraws the ivory horns my father gave me. In all the talk of whether I was going to Denver, and then celebrating—err, mourning—my decision, I'd forgotten to tell her what else was inside the assignment envelope.

A rush of excitement races over my skin at the chance to talk about my father. "My dad sent them for me." Charlie's mouth falls open. "My thoughts exactly."

"What are they?" she breathes, her full pink lips stretched into a smile.

"Beats me." I pour both of them into her outstretched hand. It's a difficult transaction considering I'm hopped up on enough bubbly to intoxicate a tractor.

Charlie rolls them around in her palm. "Kind of heavy," she says, rubbing her thumb over them. "And so smooth."

"I just don't understand why there wasn't anything about them in the assignment," I say. Charlie drops the horns back into my hand, and we both stare at them, bewildered. "You know what might help me figure it out?" I add in a whisper.

Charlie leans close, her eyes widening slightly.

I nod my head toward her room. "Taking you upstairs."

She throws her head back toward the night sky and laughs, and I can't stop myself from staring at her throat. At the soft, sun-kissed skin that travels from her jaw, to her collarbones, to her chest. "You're bad," she coos.

"The baddest." I circle one arm beneath her shoulders and the other behind her knees and pull her up into my arms. It's a Don Juan move, if I do say so myself, but it's not quite perfect, because I end up dropping one of the ivory horns in the process. I try to lean over to grab it while keeping hold of her, but Charlie insists I don't have the proper motor skills to do both. Finally, in an attempt to help a dude out, she reaches her arm down and snatches it.

"Success," she yells, punching her fist into the air.

And then something happens.

Something *electric*.

A current fires through us, and I drop Charlie to the ground. She hits the driveway pavement.

"Are you okay?" I ask. "I didn't mean—"

But then I stop, because there's this sensation between us that I can't wrap my head around. Charlie gets to her feet slowly, her eyes locked on mine as she moves. We stare at each other, breathing fast.

"Can you feel it, too?" she murmurs.

I lick my lips and nod.

"Are you doing it?"

I shake my head but don't speak. I can't. I'm too overwhelmed by what's happening.

"I can…," she starts. "I can *feel* you."

Closing my eyes, I try and gather myself. But even with my lids clamped tight, nothing changes. I can sense Charlie. It's like I know where she is without even seeing her. "How is this happening?" I ask, finding my voice.

"Maybe we drank too much," she offers, though when I open my eyes again, I can tell she doesn't believe that.

"It feels the same way it does when I sense a collector or liberator nearby." And suddenly, understanding pours over me. I open my palm and look down at the ivory horn in my hand. Charlie sees me eyeing my horn, then looks down at her own.

"Amazing," she says. I meet her eyes, and she smiles. "Your dad did this. Maybe he meant for you and me to share them."

My eyebrows knit together as I try to process this.

"So that even when you're gone," she continues, "we're together."

I grip the horn like it's a lifeline, because it is. I fight the emotion rolling through me. My father did this for me. He knows how I feel about her. I take Charlie's face in my hands and pull her mouth to mine. I may be leaving for Denver tomorrow morning, but in a way, I'll always be here with her.

And as long as I have that, this assignment will be cake.

❧ 5 ❧

A LITTLE MORE LIKE ME

When Valery calls from outside Charlie's house at the crack of dawn, I am not pleased. She, on the other hand, looks like a kid on Christmas morning. Like she can't wait to see the angry look on my face.

Throwing the strap of my Louis V. bag over my shoulder, and rolling a matching suitcase behind me, I head toward her Mercedes. My Escalade is still parked out front. I hand the keys to Charlie, who's walking beside me.

She grips them in her hand. "No way."

I laugh despite feeling like the sun is trying to karate kick my brain. "All yours until I get back."

Charlie throws her arms around my middle, making me grunt. I turn away because I don't want her to see how I feel like screaming. How getting on a plane to Colorado makes me want to tear my damn eyes out.

"Hey, sunshine," Val says after I put my bags in the trunk and crawl in the backseat. I nod and refrain from cussing her out. It's too early for cussing, even for a gangster like me. Charlie climbs in beside me and lays her head on my shoulder.

"Max still asleep?" I ask.

"Like a hibernating grizzly," Valery answers, and I'm glad she knew the answer to my question.

"Hey, Valery," Charlie says, "I like your trench coat."

Red turns around in her seat. "Really? Been waiting for an excuse to wear it." She nods toward the window at the fat purple clouds and the barren trees. "Not quite cold enough to warrant it, I don't think. Even in December. But I'm making it work."

"Can we go?" I ask. Valery glares at me in the rearview mirror as I pluck the gold-framed shades hanging from my shirt and slip them on. "Now, please?"

"You're despicable," she says, but she puts the car in drive, anyway, and heads toward the airport.

"How am I paying for my goodies in Denver?" I ask. "Papa needs play money."

Valery reaches over, keeping her eyes on the road as she digs through her oversized, satin purse. "Glad you reminded me," she says. "Here."

I take the card from her and turn it over. "Pull over."

"Why?" she asks. "What's wrong?"

"I'm going to be freaking sick. That's why." I flick the card back into the front seat. It hits the windshield and plunks to the floor. "My name is Dante Walker, and I do not carry Discover cards. Discover is for senior citizens and *budgeters*." I say the last word with a shiver.

Valery manages to reach down and find the card. Then she throws it into my lap. "You're a liberator now, which puts you on a *budget*."

"Oh, hell, no. I may have agreed to this assignment, but I'm used to a certain level of sweet, sultry excess," I say. "Plus, why would I be on a budget while you're driving a Benz?"

"It was a bonus for doing my job well." Valery straightens her turquoise necklace. "Don't be so dramatic, Dante. It'll do you good to see what it's like on the other side."

I stick the Discover card into my back pocket and instantly feel like I'm covered in fleas and soot. Like I just got done cleaning some fart stain's chimney, and I'm right about to beg for more porridge.

Valery's phone vibrates in her purse. She yanks it out. In the rearview, I watch her face change from delight at limiting my spending to alarm.

I sit up straight. "What is it?"

She glances at me in the mirror, and her face relaxes. "Nothing. You may be surprised to learn I have a life outside of toting you around." Red may be trying to pass off the text she read as something innocent, but when she punches the accelerator, I'm not so sure.

. . .

When we get to Birmingham Airport, my stomach is in knots. Charlie's hand never leaves my knee, but I can hardly look at her. Somehow, between last night and today, I lost my confidence in being separated. I still have the ivory horn in my pocket, and I know she must have hers, because I can feel it. But it doesn't seem to be enough.

Valery parks, and we walk toward the check-in area, the three of us. I'm not sure why Red feels the need to tag along for this part. Probably wants to make sure I follow through with my assignment.

The airport is bustling even at the crack of Sunday morning. Beneath the fluorescent lights, guys in business suits and kids with candy cane–stained faces hurry past, headed to who cares where. The sounds of rolling suitcases is deafening, only broken up by sporadic announcements by an airport attendant who sound like he's moments from taking his own life. Ah, Christmas cheer.

There's a horrendous snack stand with turd-colored coffee and flaky danishes that probably shouldn't be flaky. But I'm hungry.

I bypass the line and smile to myself when the peeps behind me mumble complaints. Telling their families and friends about "this dick in the snack line" will be the highlight of their day.

When my gut is reasonably satisfied, and there's not much left to do besides check my bags, I turn and look at Charlie. "Hey, uh…," I start. "Think I can talk to Valery for a sec?"

Charlie looks a little surprised but nods and smiles, anyway. "Just make sure I get the final send-off." She motions toward some benches along a wall a short distance away. "I'll be over there." I want to tell her I know, that I'd sense her there even if she hadn't told me. But I just walk over to Red, who was trying to give us space.

"Before I do this—" I begin.

"You're not doing *me* any favors; this is your rear on the line."

"Before I do this, I have some questions. For starters, I want to know if we've heard any word about Blue's death, and about whether Big Guy's going to seek vengeance."

I can't be certain, but I think I detect the corner of Valery's mouth quirk upward. "It's been handled."

"Yeah?" I say, grinning and throwing punches in the air. "Did we send someone in to tear crap up? Show 'em not to mess with the big dogs?"

"So you're a big dog now?"

"Always have been, girl. *Ruff.*"

She shakes her head. "I don't think he wants war over what happened. But you never know. Things are shaky right now."

"This is all from Kraven?"

Valery purses her lips as a man with a sad toupee nearly barrels into her. "Yes, from Kraven."

"He who has all the answers," I say, tucking my thumbs beneath my belt buckle. "Okay, what about Charlie's soul? When can I turn it in?"

The hint of a smile I saw before vanishes. "Charlie's soul is a special classification. He has to be sure they're prepared for it."

"And in the meantime I'm supposed to carry it around with me? How can that be safer than *anywhere* up there with Big Guy?"

"Do you have a problem carrying it?" she asks, stepping closer. "Because if you do, I'd be happy to take the burden."

"No," I snarl. "No one touches it but me." Glancing up at the harsh lighting, I say, "It's just that her soul feels different than it should."

"You expect it to feel like all the others?" she asks, straightening her spine.

I know she's probably right, but I needed someone else to challenge my thought that it *should* feel the same. Looking over at the benches, I glimpse Charlie on her cell, though I can't imagine who she's talking to. Her blond hair falls over one side of her face, and she neatly tucks it behind her ear. She's right there, so close I could get to her in a heartbeat, but already she feels too far away for comfort.

"What if something happens to her while I'm gone?" I say. "What if the collectors return to finish what they started?"

Valery does something out of character. She puts a hand on my shoulder. "If the collectors ascend anytime soon, it's not Charlie they'll be coming for."

I know what she's saying. It's something I've thought myself in the last few weeks, but never wanted to accept. "If I have her soul inside me, then it's me they want."

Valery hesitates and nods. Then she drops her hand from my shoulder and glances over at Charlie. "They won't hurt her. Not yet. Not when they don't have her soul. Because if they kill her now, her body and soul go to us."

I shake my head. "It sounds like you're talking about cargo."

"You know that's not what I mean."

"If you knew they might come for me, why didn't Big Guy send me on assignment away from Charlie right off the bat? Why wait until now?"

"Arrangements had to be made first." Valery pulls a cigarette from her purse and lights it. I'm pretty certain she can't do that here, but meh, what do I care?

"What kind of arrangements?" I ask.

Blowing out a puff of smoke, Valery looks past me. "I can't discuss them with you."

Rage rushes through me. "Then how about I stick around until you do tell me? Screw this assignment."

Valery's eyes connect with mine. "You'll go. You'll go because you know you shouldn't have stayed. Because you know as much as you want to protect her yourself, you're doing more damage by being nearby."

I squeeze my eyes shut and pull in a deep breath through my nose. She's right. I know she's right. But it doesn't sting any less to leave. "You'll watch after her," I say to Valery, more as a statement than a question.

"With my life."

I yank Red into a hug. I didn't consciously think to do it, and Valery immediately stiffens in my arms, but eventually she relaxes and pats me awkwardly on the back.

"Get off me, fungus," she says into my shoulder, but her words hold no venom.

Releasing her, I look back at Charlie. Valery heads toward the benches, and Charlie moves toward me. When she gets closer, she wraps her arms around my neck and pulls my face to hers. As her mouth touches mine, she says, "I have a surprise for you."

"I hate surprises," I say.

"Even surprises that could kick your ass all over a court?" someone says from behind me.

I grin against Charlie's mouth, then turn and see Annabelle standing nearby. Her short black hair and straight-as-Hugh-Hefner bangs make her look like that chick from *Pulp Fiction*. But her body is far from Uma Thurman's. No, Annabelle's built like a brick house… if a brick house married an Amazonian warrior. "I see you broke out," I say.

"Nah, I burned the whole damn place to the ground." Annabelle holds her fist into the air like she just led several thousand prisoners out of Alcatraz. Then she pulls me into a hug that nearly severs my spine.

"What were you in for again?" I ask when she releases me.

"First degree meets B and E, holmes," she answers in her best street voice.

Charlie laughs. "Yeah, that or sneaking out to meet Bobby."

I raise my eyebrows at Annabelle. She bites down on her bottom lip and sways side to side like a schoolgirl. "Very naughty, Annabelle," I say. "I do approve."

Annabelle places a hand on her hip. "What can I say? I'm a desirable woman," she purrs. "Anyway, came to see you off. Char tells me you're going to save a damsel in distress, but you'll be back in a few days."

"That's the story."

"Then I'll leave you two to suck face." Annabelle waves over her shoulder.

Watching her go, my shoulders tense. Because I know what comes next: the part where I tell Charlie good-bye. I'm trying to think of the right thing to say when Charlie lays her hand on my arm and looks at me with the most perfect smile. "Want to see something?"

I nod, but I can't get over how happy she seems. It's like my leaving doesn't even bother her. I hear a man calling something else over the speakers as Charlie reaches down the front of her shirt and pulls out the ivory horn. It's attached to an old-looking silver chain.

"My grandma gave me this chain when I showed her the charm." Charlie grips the horn in her palm. "She was the one who found the small hole at the top."

Narrowing my eyes, I pull my own horn out of my pocket and look it over. Sure enough, there's a tiny hole drilled into mine as well. "Cool," I say.

Charlie's smile falters. "I'm going to miss you."

"Are you?" I ask, my voice raspier than I intended.

Her face falls. "Of course I am," she says. "Why would you ask me that?"

I shrug. "You seem pretty cheerful about this assignment."

Charlie's face brightens again, her blue eyes shining. "That's because I know you're going to do great." She tilts her head, grinning. "Because I know you're a good person, and you can do good."

Something in me snaps. I know it's probably the fear that she won't be truly safe while I'm gone, but it's also that I'm afraid what she's saying isn't true. "Maybe I don't want to be good, Charlie. Maybe I want to be me." I lean down and get in her face, beat my chest with a closed fist. "Maybe I'm bad to my core. And maybe I wish you were a little more like me."

She's going to flip me off. I just know it. I've screwed up this good-bye, and now she's going to tell me to jump out of the plane at thirty thousand feet. But instead she sucks in a breath like I've gut-punched her, and her eyes fall to the floor.

"Charlie . . ."

"You and I are going to be fine," she says in a voice so calm it almost scares me. Her eyes flick up. "You hear me? You don't want to leave because you're afraid to be away from me. Of how you'll be when I'm not around to influence your behavior."

My brain nearly splits open, because she's right. I've been rebelling against becoming a liberator, and the only thing that's kept me from becoming the Dante Walker I was when I was alive is her. I'm afraid I can't be a good person.

Charlie puts a hand on my chest. "I care about you. I'll care about you wherever you are in this world." She smiles. "And Denver isn't so far away."

I pull her against me and hold her tight. I have an assignment to complete. And what's more, I have to learn how to be a liberator. I've been putting off my transition from demon to…whatever…for too long. But I guess now is as good a time as ever.

When I'm starting to feel a little better, I raise my head to look at Charlie. But when I do, I spot Valery on her cell. The action alone isn't what grabbed my attention; it's the look on her face. There's a deep line between her eyes, and her lips are pulled tight. It seems like whoever is on the other end is telling her something huge. Dodging the huge crowd rushing by, she takes a few steps in our direction.

I lean forward as much as I can without alarming Charlie.

"…the twin scrolls," Red says into the phone. "Yes, I understand she's important. …leaving now. And once he's there, Charlie will be safe. Right." She nods and glances over at us.

I look down at Charlie. "Did you hear what I said?" she asks.

I cup her cheeks in my hands and nod. I don't want her to think I'm ignoring her, but I need to hear what else Valery is saying. Red may have said that she trusts me, but I'm not sure the feeling is mutual.

"Why can't anyone read them?" Valery says, and I rejoice at having caught a full sentence. "…matter now. Yes, I'll meet you at the Hive." She pulls the phone away from her ear and pockets it. I try to keep a poker face when I look back at Charlie.

She must realize I'm distracted, but she doesn't show it. In fact, Charlie looks a bit distracted herself, like she's lost in thought. I contemplate asking Valery what that was all about, but the knot in my chest tells me whatever she was discussing is important, and if she were going to divulge anything, she would have already, which means I need to keep the fact that I overheard her conversation a secret.

Valery has pushed me to take this assignment, not that I really had a choice. And now I suspect that it may be for more than liberating this girl, Aspen. Maybe my going *will* keep Charlie safe, and not just because it separates me—who the collectors may come after—from Charlie, but because of something bigger. I'm not sure what that thing could be, but I'll find out. In the meantime, I'm going with my gut. And my gut says to get the hell out of Alabama.

Wrapping Charlie in my arms once more, I touch my forehead to hers. And then I press our lips together. A rush of energy and longing fires through my body as our mouths connect. My hands crawl up her back, and I pull her closer. In return, she wraps her arms around my neck and stretches up on her toes. I barely touch my tongue to hers, and a clap of thunder sounds in my chest. We're in public, people brushing past us every few seconds. But each time I hold her like this, *kiss* her like this, there is nothing else. "I'll miss you, angel," I whisper. Then I release her and walk away while I still can.

From over my shoulder, I hear Charlie mumble, "I'll miss you, too."

But her words sound strained, like she's lost in her own head.

⪦ 6 ⪧

ROAD RAGE

An hour into the flight, I still can't stop thinking about Valery's conversation. Who was she saying was important? Aspen? What are the twin scrolls? And what the H is the Hive?

These thoughts swirl in an unproductive circle in my head. But before I decide to let them go, I vow to ask Max to do a little snooping for me. It's a risky decision, because he might go running to Valery. But I'm betting on "bros before hos" and all that.

I'm about to wave the flight attendant down to order a Bloody Mary when I catch sight of a fidgety girl one row back. She looks to be about seven and is leaning over this ancient guy—trying to see out the window—in a seriously invasive way. It's like the girl doesn't even see him at all. And this geezer looks like he's sick and tired of being invisible to everyone.

The girl tips over, and Death Walking shoulders her into place. No biggie. She just pushes across him again. The man glances around like he's searching for her parents, but he doesn't find them. After shouldering the kid back into place again, the man barks, "You're being very rude."

The girl sits back instantly, her eyes as round as quarters. "I'm sorry," she says with an oversized grin. "I'm trying to see if it's true."

The man sighs. "If what's true?"

"If you can really see aliens from up here," she answers, pulling her navy vest closed.

People around the man chuckle, and though I'm fighting a smile, my lips win out and jerk upward. I bite the inside of my cheek, waiting to see how the guy responds. At first, he doesn't. He just looks at her like she's slow. Then he glances back out his window.

I turn around in my seat and face forward, wondering how people do this. How they sit in coach and don't purposely choke themselves out with stale peanuts. A while later, I check out the old man and girl again from sheer boredom and realize they've switched places. A laugh bursts from my throat and the woman next to me gives a worried look. I ignore her and study the man that's watching the girl. He seems pleased to see her grinning at the postcard-sized window. As the girl presses her nose to the glass, he points past her at something. The girl giggles and gives him a light shove.

I bet that's how Charlie was as a kid.

All changing people for the better and shit.

In that moment, I think about what I could do right now. How Charlie has this power to make people better, and I have the power to reward them for it. When I think of it this way, it doesn't seem quite so overwhelming. I'm not a liberator, not really. And I'll never be as good as Charlie. But I did decide to accept this assignment, and since I'm already doing stuff I'm uncomfortable with, I might as well go all out.

I roll my eyes and groan. Then, with my lips pulled up in disgust, I release a seal the way I did when I was a collector. Just like normal, the man's soul light flicks on. But instead of a red seal appearing from my chest, a blue one does.

Curling my hands into fists, I try not to rip my seat from the floor. *Red* is my color. Always has been. So I don't know what Big Guy thinks he's doing up there. As the seal moves toward Old Man, I try to calm myself. My jeans are blue. And no one looks better in a pair of kick-arounds than me, so maybe blue's not so bad.

Old Man's got quite a bit of soul light left. In fact, he only has a few black stamp-sized sin seals. My seals usually attach to soul light. But this blue one doesn't do that. Instead, it floats toward an existing sin seal and lands directly on top of it. And just like Valery's pink, glittery seals, it begins to break down the sin. It's a strange sensation watching my seal doing someone a solid instead of the other way around.

Even though I know it's ridiculous, I feel sort of feel like a traitor.

I sigh, remembering the collector I used to be. And even though I'm totally forcing it, I can't help but fire a hand in the guy's direction and say a weak, "Pow."

· · ·

After we land in Denver, I head toward the rental car stand. Valery texted me while I was in the air and said she'd reserved a vehicle under my name.

The anticipation is killing me.

I show the rental car dude my Discover card and—I swear on my mama's soul—his nose scrunches up in revulsion. He holds the card with the tips of his fingers and types something into the computer with his other hand. Then he thrusts my card back at me. I'm surprised he doesn't reach for a wet nap to rid his hands of my general poorness.

"One of my guys will meet you out front," he says without making eye contact. I shove the card back into my pocket and hold my middle finger within three inches of his face. He doesn't look up.

Out front, I wait with my luggage nearby, hoping beyond hope that Valery done me good. But when I see a lime-green Kia Rondo pull up around the corner, I know my hoping was in vain. I also know that somewhere out there, Red is laughing so hard she's crying. That she's picturing my face in her mind, wondering if *now* is the moment I'm seeing my ride.

The guy behind the wheel jumps out of the driver's side. "Dan Walker?"

"Dante," I correct him. "My name's Dante."

He shrugs like it doesn't matter.

I point to the green car as he hands me the keys. "Let me guess… Eight horsepower and cloth interiors nice enough to spread any woman's legs."

The guy turns and walks away. He's an important person with important places to be. Way too important for a peon like me.

I crawl inside my Panty Dropper and start an engine that sounds like it belongs in a Power Wheels. Then I crank the plastic stereo and head out onto the road to find my assignment, resentment boiling in my veins.

Cruising along I-70, I expect to see mountains stretching toward the sky. But from a distance, they look more like boobs in training bras, like they've got a ways to go before they're *real* peaks. Rolling the window down, I breathe in through my nose and smell pine. Then I roll up the freaking window, because it's cold as balls outside. I think about what I packed and wonder if I have enough warm clothes for this kind of ungodly weather.

Everything outside my big-timin' car is coated in a sheet of white. As the afternoon sun shines down on it, it kind of…sparkles or whatever.

Charlie would love this.

I'm headed toward the address Valery texted me with pure,

unfiltered excitement. I'm sure my lodging will be just as awe-inspiring as my vehicle. Though I've been driving for half an hour, I still don't see the turn I'm supposed to take. And at some point, I decide I've gone too far. I check my rearview, wondering if I can view the exit.

But the only thing I see is a black sedan way too close to my tail.

I speed up, cursing the aggressive driver, but he stays with me.

"All right, Dick Slap," I mutter "Let's calm the hell down." Tapping my brakes, I watch in the mirror to see if he gets the message.

He doesn't. In fact, he speeds up and gets closer to my bumper.

Too close.

And that's when my frustration becomes alarm. My shoulders tense, and my mind whirls with who this could be. Gunning it, I concentrate as hard as I can but don't sense a cuff. The only thing I do sense is Charlie at her house. I'm not sure who she's with, or what she's doing, but she's there. And my gut says Valery is there, too, keeping her safe.

Knowing this makes it a lot easier to do what I'm going to do next, which is to confront this guy.

I punch the accelerator and head toward the next exit, throwing my signal on early enough so that if he wants to follow, he can. Sure enough, as I pull off onto the access road, I catch sight of the black sedan doing the same thing. Fine by me Spotting that creeper, Easton, outside Charlie's house yesterday still has me fired up. I'd like nothing more than to let off a little steam.

Pulling off onto the thinnest road I can find, I start to slow down, ready to give this guy a piece of my mind. But before I can, my bright green car lurches forward.

"Son of a bitch," I yell. "He just hit me."

I'm thinking it's an accident on his part. That this guy is pissed that I cut him off and only wanted to hassle me, not *hit my car*. But when I look back, I see that he's accelerating. And then the dots connect. This guy doesn't just want to startle me, he wants to *hurt* my ass.

My arms tighten on the wheel as I gun my Kia Rondo. The Kia makes this awful high-pitched whizzing sound that has absolutely no growl. If my heart weren't racing, I'd find it hilarious. But right now, I'm afraid this lunatic may have a death wish…or a carving knife. So it's not funny. Not at all.

Jerking the wheel to the right, I speed up, slamming my foot on the accelerator. My stomach clenches as I peek in the rearview and realize I'm not going to outrun this guy. All I can think as this is happening is, *where are the damn cops when you need them?*

My head flies forward as my car is slammed again from the back. I drive faster.

Tiny houses and empty fields fly by, and I begin to panic over when this road will end. And what will happen when it does. Never have I felt so out of control. Even that night in the forest with Charlie and Rector, I had my body to rely on—my legs to run, my fists to fight with. But now, now I'm just some cornered chump in a busted-up car.

Thinking this, my panic turns to anger. Who does this guy think he is? I'm Dante Walker. I've died twice and am still walking around earth like a champ. And this dirt bag with a rage issue is ramming into me because he's had a bad day?

I don't think so.

Hitting my brakes, the black sedan pummels into me. The driver's horn blares and doesn't stop. The sound rings in my head. But I don't care about that *or* the fact that my muscles seem permanently locked. All I care about is showing this chode exactly who he's messing with. Throwing my door open, I step out. If he has a gun, so be it. I'll take it in the chest like the animal I am.

I jab my finger at his tinted windows. "Get out of the car."

Though I can't see what the guy looks like, I do see him look over his shoulder at something. Following his gaze, I see that there's another car headed toward us. He may think that's going to help him, but he's wrong. This guy's had his fun; now it's my turn.

Prepared to tear him out of the vehicle, I yank on the passenger door. The door is locked. No matter. Tilting my head, I give the guy a cold smile. Then I jerk my fist back and throw it through the window. Glass explodes.

Right as I'm leaning down to get a look at who's inside, dirt kicks up from his back tires, and he peels away. The only thing I catch sight of before he's gone is a branded tattoo on his right bicep. "Coward," I scream, even though it was me fleeing only a few minutes ago.

Moments later, a silver SUV pulls over. A woman in her mid-forties rolls down the window, her face worried like she isn't certain she should be stopping. "Everything all right?"

Still fired up, I nod and stare after the sedan's taillights. "I'm fine," I manage. "Thanks for stopping." Looking back at the woman, I furrow my brow. "It was nice of you to check on me." Most people would've driven right past, especially a woman alone in her car.

She smiles, though I can tell she's still a little nervous. "It's no problem." Looking at my car, she adds, "Do you need a ride?"

I wrap my bloodied knuckles in my shirt and return her smile. Sometimes good people are pretty cool. "Nah, the car's still running." I nod toward the Kia and its barely audible motor.

The woman exhales like she's relieved. "Okay, then. Take care."

"Wait." I grab onto her open window before she leaves, and the motion startles her. Then I flip her soul light on. Just as I expect, this broad's soul is squeaky clean. Only a few seconds, that's all it takes to release a blue seal. Then I remove my hand from her vehicle. "Never mind. Forgot what I was going to say." She takes off, completely unaware that she just offered a ride to a guy who's technically dead.

Sealing as a liberator wasn't as unnerving the second time around,

I decide.

After the broad is gone, I calm myself down and crawl inside my beat-up car. Then I stare forward in a daze. What the hell just happened? And who the hell was that guy? Just some dick with an anger problem, most likely. But it still sits wrong in my stomach.

He wasn't a collector, I tell myself. *That's all that matters.*

I've been in Denver for all of an hour, and already I'm calling attention to myself, as Valery would say. Maybe I'd better not mention this to her judgmental ass. She'd be all, "Why are you the only one this crap happens to, Dante?"

Breathing in deeply, I rub my hands over my face a few times. Then I turn my car around and head toward the highway.

"These mountain people are batshit," I mumble.

My phone vibrates in my pocket. When I pull it out, I see it's a text from Charlie.

WISH U WERE STILL HERE.

You and me both, I think.

❖ 7 ❖

CIGARETTE HALO

After settling into my charming abode of a hotel, AKA the Holiday Inn, where they have luxuries like free ice and shower caps, I head toward Aspen's house. It's the last and final address Valery texted me, and I'm so looking forward to meeting this charming girl.

No.

Glancing down at my phone, I wonder if I have enough time to call Charlie before I get to where I'm headed. But then I see my turnoff and decide I'll talk to her once I get my bearings. Besides, I want to wrap this assignment up quick. The faster I complete this job, the faster I can get home to Charlie.

As I think this, Valery's words come back to me: "*...as much you want to protect her yourself, you're doing more damage by being nearby.*" I also think about what Valery said at the airport. That *she* is important. But my question remains: *was she talking about Charlie, or Aspen?*

I shake the thought from my head and look for Aspen's address. I'm on the right road but don't see any houses. Flipping through my texts, I realize what Valery sent isn't really an address at all. It's just a street name. Idiot. How could she forget the freaking house number? And how could I have headed out without thinking to check for one? I start to text Red back when I spot something. A house. Or maybe I should call it a hotel. Or a castle. Because a *house* doesn't spread over the land this way, like it's devouring everything in its path.

I suddenly realize why this place doesn't have a number: the street was created for this house alone. Because a house this big needs an entire street to itself. The exterior of the home is covered with dark red and black brick, and the abundant English windows are made of diamond-shaped glass. Sheets of ivy crawl up the walls like a gremlin's fingers, and twisted, barren trees surround the property. And everything, every last part of the house and grounds, is draped in a blanket of snow.

Though the fresh powder has a virginal appearance, the place still looks like Boss Man—err, *Lucille*—could call it home.

As I approach an oversized iron gate, I notice there's one of those box things where you have to ask permission to enter. I narrow my eyes because I've never asked permission for anything, and I'm not about to start.

Almost like the gate reads my mind, it slides open, groaning and clicking as it moves.

Pausing for only a beat, I punch my fist lightly on the steering wheel. Then I head down the flagstone driveway, navigating a near-totaled lime-green Kia Rondo toward this completely sick mansion. But I'm not sweating it, 'cause I know this chick will take one look at me and remember it's what's inside the car that counts.

When I'm only a few yards from the door, I stop and throw the car into park. It only took about six and a half hours to get this hunk of metal from the iron gate to here, so I'm feeling pretty good about myself. After grabbing my chocolate-brown corduroy jacket from the seat, I kill the engine and step out. I've put zero thought into how I'll recognize this girl, or what I'm going to say when I meet her, but I'm a master at winging it, so whatev.

Walking toward the entryway, I square my shoulders and run a hand through my hair. *It's showtime.*

I put a little swag in my step—and stop when the front door flies open.

A girl my age bursts into view and rushes down the sidewalk. We're more than twenty feet apart, but I can see her clearly. She's got long black hair and fair skin. Her body is fuller than Charlie's, and she's taller, too. There's an alarming gracefulness in the way she moves. *Like a serpent,* I think.

She dressed in a long black coat, yellow leggings, and black ankle boots—a fashionista with a touch of Goth. A man appears in the doorway, and when she turns and flips him the bird, I notice her hands are covered with black fingerless gloves.

"Get back here," the man yells. "Aspen, this is the last time. I swear to God, this is it."

The girl, Aspen, throws her head back and laughs. Then she turns and rushes toward the driveway. When she finally notices me, her wild green eyes spark like they're lit from within. She stops, looks me up and down. Then she glances over my shoulder.

"That your...car?" she says, punching the last word with what sounds like repulsion.

"Sure is," I say without missing a beat. "Want to get out of here?"

Aspen glares back at the man, who I decide must be her father, and cocks her head toward the Kia. "I'm driving."

I toss her the keys and climb in the passenger seat. Then I grab hold of the oh-shit bar and hang on as she screeches away from the house. Glancing over at Aspen driving my car like she's in a freaking video game, I decide "winging it" still works. And that maybe I should write a book for all those uptight managers with their pocket planners and pinched assholes. "Where we going?" I ask.

Aspen digs a pack of cigarettes out of her jacket pocket. She lights one and searches for the button to roll down the window.

"It's manual," I tell her.

She jerks the cigarette out of her mouth. "What the hell does *that* mean?"

"Means you have to crank it with that handle. Are you serious?"

Aspen spins the lever in a circle until the window inches down. Then she looks at me. "Who are you? What were you doing outside my house?"

My mind spins. I'm not prepared for these questions, but it's cool, 'cause I got an answer that always works. Cocking my head, I give her my best sexy eyes, complete with a lazy half-smile. "Do you care?"

Her eyes run over my face, my body. She shrugs. "Not really."

I expect her to swoon, to get all girly on me. Not that I'm trying to go down that road. I would never do that to Charlie. Ever. But it's just my *look* usually garners a certain reaction. And Aspen, the way she said "not really" was more like she doesn't care about *anything*.

A few minutes later, we pull up to what seems like an apartment building, but it looks too nice for that, so I decide maybe they're condos. The walls are made entirely of uninterrupted glass, and the building is about ten stories high. Aspen parks and gets out of the car, tipping her head for me to follow. When she does, I notice there's a small diamond stud in her nose. Classy.

We walk through a long hallway, mirrors and crystal-covered light fixtures sprinkled throughout. When we step into an elevator, Aspen pushes the button for the ninth floor. Then she looks at me, cigarette smoke swirling around her black hair in a halo. "Tenth floor is reserved for corporate pricks."

I'm not sure why she felt the need to explain this, but I just nod. Then I try *the look* again.

Nothing.

As the elevator creeps upward, she glances at me with passive interest. "What's your name? And this time, why don't you try answering instead of giving that stupid" —she waves her hand near my face— "look."

I nearly gasp. No girl has ever called me on my crap before. I'm a little thrown off, but recover quickly. If she wants to play this nothing-fazes-me game, I'll be her huckleberry. Because no one can pull indifferent like I can.

Opening my palm, I flick my fingers toward her. "Cigarette."

She raises an eyebrow but retrieves her pack and gives me one. I light my cig with her lit one and blow the first delightful lungful of smoke up over my head. Sticking my hand out, I say, "Dante Walker."

Aspen eyes my hand, then shakes it. "Nice jacket," she says as the elevator doors finally slide open. "Armani?"

"Naturally." I take a drag. "How old are you?"

"What's it to you?"

"It's not."

She steps out of the elevator, letting her eyes run over the rest of my outfit, which costs enough to save the penguins. For the first time, her mouth quirks upward. "I'm seventeen, *Dante.*"

Following behind Aspen, I decide she definitely doesn't seem *important.* I also find myself wondering why I'm always sent to collect girls who are seventeen. Can't someone mix it up? Assign me to a granny or a kid? I also wonder why Aspen's adopted me so quickly. But as a personal policy, I try not to question when a good thing lands in my lap, so I just seal my mouth shut and keep up.

Aspen raps once on door 917 and lets herself in. The condo is made of light: bright stone floors, cream-colored walls, white furniture, and floor-to-ceiling windows along the back wall, and in the corner, sits the one of the most emo-looking kids I've ever seen.

My assignment *click*s across the stone floors in her high-heeled boots and plops down on a white leather couch. The guy in the corner watches every move I make, which isn't hard. I mostly stand near the sprawling kitchen and try to look casual.

Aspen flips her wrist back and forth between me and the guy. "Lincoln, this is Dante. Dante, Lincoln."

Emo kid Lincoln rises from his chair like a panther and crosses the room. He gets right up in my face and looks at me with one open eye. "I'm going to ask you a question, and I'm going to know if you're lying."

"Calm down, Lincoln," Aspen says, even though she hasn't moved and sounds unconcerned.

Lincoln steps closer, and the copper rings in his eyebrow twitch. "Can I trust you?"

I laugh because I don't know what else *to* do. "Yeah, man. You can trust me."

"Liar!" Lincoln yells. "He's lying."

"Lincoln," Aspen barks, her voice raised. "He's with me. He's cool."

The guy pushes his greasy black hair behind his ears. Then he looks down, his eyes still wide and crazy. "Sorry, dude," he says when his head pops back up. "Gotta be careful." His camo jacket swooshes as he makes his way back to his chair.

I raise an eyebrow at Aspen.

"His dad is up there in the government." She holds her cigarette above her head, and I notice her nails are painted yellow. "No one knows what he does exactly, but he's, like, in defense or something. The guy's never here, and Lincoln's sister and mom live in South Dakota. So we get this pad to ourselves mostly."

I glance at Lincoln, who's staring out the window like he's looking for a sniper. The back of one of his hands is covered with a tattoo that spells out "jackrabbit" — whatever that means — and he's got more ink peeking out from the front of his shirt, almost like it's trying to crawl up his neck.

Aspen finishes her cigarette and snubs it out. Then she stares at me until I meet her gaze. "So, D-Dub," she says. "You like to party?"

⋊ 8 ⋉

FIREFLY

Aspen makes a phone call. Half an hour later, she announces it's time
to go. I'm already starting to feel a bit restless. When *Lucille* gave me
my assignment to collect Charlie, there was a deadline. And Valery
insinuated the same was true for this one. So far, I've blown two days
stalling and traveling. Now that I'm finally here, I'm not sure how to
proceed. This girl's obviously got some issues, and I guess my job is to
reel her in and show her how to live *right*. I have no idea how to do
that when I can't figure out how to do that myself.

Still, I'll have to work something out if I want to keep my cuff and
return to Charlie.

"You ready to roll?" Aspen asks. "They're downstairs."

I don't know who *they* are, but I know for now, my best plan is
to just observe Aspen. To see what's going wrong in her life, and then
somehow work through that. So I nod. "Let's do it."

Aspen gives a quasi-smile as Lincoln rushes forward like he's
guarding us from some unseen enemy.

When we get outside, my heart cries. It *weeps*. In front of me is
a car so beautiful it deserves tears. It's a black-as-death BMW 760i

complete with 535 horsepower, night vision, and a TwinPower Turbo V-12 engine. Pow! I consider taking it from behind, but decide to treat her with respect just this one time.

Lincoln, Aspen, and I climb into the car as the last of the sun disappears behind the snow-capped mountains. A tall girl in the passenger seat throws us a wave, and the guy behind the steering wheel turns and grins at me. "You a friend of Miss Lockhart's?" he asks. His teeth are bird-shit white, and his blond hair spikes up around his head like a cartoon character's. He's got a Miami tan and an L.A.-sized ego, and I don't like him one bit.

"I am," I answer. "How fast this baby pick up?"

"Zero to sixty in four-point-five." Blond dude turns back around in his seat and pulls away from the curb.

The engine growls like a damn lion.

And I totally get wood.

• • •

Music bumps from all corners of the room as the party rages. For the millionth time, I check my phone. I've texted Charlie repeatedly since we arrived, but she hasn't answered a single one of them. I fight the panic attack building in my chest, telling myself that Valery and Max are with her, and I have nothing to worry about.

Across the room, Aspen is drinking fast and hard. It's not like she's doing it to have fun. It's like she's doing it to lose herself. Her dark hair falls in her eyes, and she leaves it there. A hoard of guys circles around and watches her every move. In this dark room—bodies pulsing to the music—Aspen is like a firefly, capturing people's attention, then blinking out from view. She raises a long, thin arm into the air, and those around her join in a toast. She yells something I can't make out.

Lincoln strides over and leans against the wall nearby. "It's those two," he says.

I lean closer, trying to hear him over the music. "Say what?"

He nods toward Aspen. "She's always been a little like this. But ever since those two showed up, she's gotten even worse."

I follow his gaze and finally see who he's talking about—the guy who drove us here with the white smile and spiky hair, and the girl who rode along. The chick stands tall, her brunette hair pulled into a ponytail that ends just above her rear. I hadn't paid attention to her before, but now I do. As I eye the pair, my skin buzzes with alarm. The others, they stare at Aspen because they want to know her, want a piece of her. But these two, they watch her like she's an experiment. Like they just put beer in a dog's water dish, and now they're sitting back to see what happens.

My brow furrows, and I survey them closer. There's something off about their stature. I hadn't noticed it when I was in the car—my mind was on the Beemer's interior—but now that I'm watching the duo, I understand why Lincoln doesn't like them.

"How long have they been hanging around?" I ask Lincoln.

He digs his hands into the pockets of his camo jacket, jingling something. God knows what he's got in there. "Not too long. A few days. But you see the way she is. She picks up new friends like they're strays in an alley. Most people, she just ignores." He tips his chin toward the group around Aspen, the ones she looks right through. "But then with others, it's like she swallows them into herself." When I glance back at Lincoln, he's staring at me. "Everyone takes something from her. Money. Sex. Happiness." His hands ball into fists. "What will you take?"

I'm thrown off guard by Lincoln's question, and I don't know how to answer. So I don't. I just look back at Aspen, my thoughts of the strange pair who drove us here forgotten. Aspen crawls onto a table and raises her gloved hands into the air. All around, people push in toward her. They want to be closer. They want to touch her, to *be* her. Someone else watching this might think she's a girl who has everything: beauty, cash, an industrial-strength attitude. In her eyes, there's a lust for life. It's what seduces her onlookers. They note the way she does what she wants, *says* what she wants. But I see beyond her eyes, and I know the truth. I know that behind the green irises and potent personality, there's emptiness.

Aspen nods toward me with an even emptier smile. Then she wraps her arms around herself and lets her head fall back.

She dances on the table, high above everyone else.

Pulling in a breath, I flip on her soul light. Just as I suspected, the remaining glow is barely noticeable amidst the standard black sin seals, and even a few colored collector seals. I wonder how she got the latter. But with her resources, she's probably traveled the world. And something tells me Aspen enjoys hitting locations where collectors do good business—places like Las Vegas and New Orleans and Miami.

Watching her, I have no idea how I will complete this assignment. What's more, I'm afraid this girl could easily lure me into her lair. Because this life she's living, I know it all too well.

She looks at me, and a shiver races down my spine.

How do I liberate a girl who is exactly like me?

• • •

As I'm walking back to my hotel room, I'm still trying to process this assignment. I expected Aspen to have some issues, but nothing this extreme. It's like she's gone from this world, like she's already dead.

I could hardly get Aspen home tonight without incident, so I have no idea how I'll get her to wake up from this self-destructive lifestyle. I wonder if Lincoln could be a comrade in this mission. He seems to care about her, which could help my cause, but he's also wary of me.

My mind turns to the two people who drove the BMW, Gage and

Lyra, when I unlock my hotel room and go inside.

Then I forget everything else. My room is trashed.

The bedside lamp is lying on the floor. The contents of my suitcase are spread across the room. Towels are hanging from the curtains. A wastebasket is upturned on the desk. And everywhere I look are tissues. My room looks like a practical joke between friends, but I don't have any friends in Denver.

Walking into the bathroom—and stepping over my six-hundred-dollar Olga Berluti shoes—I spot something written on the mirror.

Can you hear me now, liberator?

I stumble back and nearly fall into the bathtub. Grabbing onto the towel rack, I right myself. Then starbursts of anger dance before my eyes. Someone is messing with me. I don't sense anything now, but I know it's a collector. How else would they know I'm a liberator?

The question is, which collector? Is it Patrick, the scrappy bastard always eager to find favor with Lucille? Or maybe Kincaid with his beady all-seeing eyes? I consider Anthony—a gorilla of a collector—and decide it couldn't have been him. It wouldn't be Zack, either; he doesn't have it in him to harass me alone. There's one other collector it could be, but even thinking his name causes my throat to tighten.

Rector, Rector, my mind taunts.

Racing from the room, I grab my cell phone and call Charlie's number.

"Come on, pick up. Pick up," I mutter.

Panic fires through my body when her voicemail kicks on.

As I listen to her recorded message, I pull the ivory horn from my pocket and concentrate on where she is. Not at home, but not far from there, either. I can't get a read on her emotions and curse the horn for not giving me more. Since I've already left two messages tonight, I push end and glance at the clock: 1:28 a.m.

I pace the wrecked room, wondering how quickly I can get a flight back to Alabama. I punch Valery's number into my phone and beat my fist against my thigh as it rings.

She picks up, and her voice is muffled with sleep. "What do you want?"

"A collector has been in my room," I bellow. "Where's Charlie?"

I hear a faint *click* and gather that Red is switching on a lamp. "Charlie is at a party," she says. "Max is there. I just spoke with him. What do you mean, a collector has been in your room?"

I glance around the floor, at the clothing and socks and boxer-briefs strewn about. "Someone threw all my crap around and left a note on the bathroom mirror."

"Well, what does it say?"

"It says, 'Can you hear me now, Liberator?'" I drop down onto my bed. "Are you sure Charlie is all right?"

"I'm positive," she answers. "About the note…" Red trails off like she's thinking. I expect to hear a note of alarm in her voice, but it isn't there. "I wouldn't worry about it."

"Come again?" I say. "I don't think I caught that last bit. It sounded like you said, 'Don't worry about it,' which I *know* isn't right."

Through the phone, I hear Red sigh. "Look, sometimes I'm going to tell you to take action. And other times I'm going to tell you not to worry about it. Right now, don't worry. We'll handle this."

I look around for the hidden camera, because this has to be some kind of freaking joke. "So, you guys just want to slap some liberator dargon on me and dole out pointless assignments? Well, let me tell you something, princess. I don't roll that way."

"You didn't roll that way when you were a collector," Valery says evenly. "You work for Big Guy now, and there's a certain rank among us, just like there was in hell."

"And my rank is…?"

"Bottom feeder," Red says. "I'm going to bed now."

"How can you be so dismissive? There was a collector in my room. A *collector*. We haven't seen these guys in over a month, and now they're back. Above ground. They know where I am. And they've probably come to steal back Charlie's soul. Is any of this registering?"

There's a long silence on the other end of the line. "Charlie is safe. I assure you. Finish your assignment so we can discuss you returning to Peachville."

"*Discuss* me returning?" I roar. "Oh, I'm returning, Red. I'm coming back, and when I do there's—"

"Dante, stop," she interrupts, her voice suddenly authoritative. "I want you to listen to me very carefully. It's crucial that you liberate this girl. Do you think Big Guy would ask you to take on this assignment after everything that happened to Charlie, and to the human, if it weren't important?"

So she was talking about Aspen when she was on the phone at the airport. "That human that died helping us," I say. "His name was Blue."

"I'm going to bed," Valery answers. "I've said too much."

"You haven't said anything useful whatsoever. Tell me why Aspen is important!" I wait for an answer before realizing—

Valery's hung up.

Shaking with fury, I throw the phone across the room. Then I tear the blankets from my bead and hurl them toward the wall. Next, I grab the heavy overturned lamp and fling it at the television set. The shattering sound it makes upon impact sends a wave of satisfaction rolling over me.

I kick a shoe into the glass window.

I tear a fugly painting from the wall.

I yank the mattress from its frame and overturn it.

My girlfriend, who is thousands of miles away, isn't answering my calls. I have no idea how to get a girl like Aspen to *come to Jesus* or why she even matters. And now Valery tells me not to worry about the collector who's been. In. My. Room.

I send the desk onto its side, then look for something else to throw. But there's nothing left. And though my dead heart is pounding with rage, I know this isn't helping. I rip my shirt over my head and stride back and forth across the room bare chested.

A thought snaps into my head. I stare forward, but my eyes don't focus on anything in particular. I'm thinking…thinking.

Or maybe it's more like *remembering*.

Remembering the way Rector's black, leathery wings sprouted from his back. And the way Kraven's white, glowing ones hung in the air behind him. I don't know why I visualize their wings now. Max and I have pondered them a million times over the last several weeks, and though the issue of wings didn't seem to surprise Valery, I suspect she doesn't know how they work.

I've tried in the past to conjure my own set of wings, deciding if Kraven and Rector had them, maybe I did, too. I was never successful, though. But then again, I never tried while I was like *this*, while every nerve ending felt like it was on fire.

Growling like an earthquake, I throw my arms open wide and call out for wings. I roar, my entire body quivering. Sweat drips down my chest. Dark hair falls into my eyes. My muscles scream in pain. A burning smell fills my nose. But still I summon what I believe must be there.

And suddenly, two things happen.

My phone starts ringing, and a loud sound thunders through the room.

❧ 9 ☙

CHARLIE'S NEW DRESS

Cocking my head, I realize the booming sound is someone knocking on my hotel door. But I don't care about that. All I see is Charlie's name lit up on my phone display. Racing across the room, I grab my cell and accept the call.

"What's up?" I try to come off as chill, but instead sound like someone crotch-kicked me. "I've been calling."

Smooth, ass clown, I think. *Real smooth.*

I'm new to this whole caring thing. I quickly realize that I'm not that good at it, that I've kind of skipped over affection and jumped right into Lifetime-movie-stalker.

"Heeeey, Mr. Walker," she sings.

One hundred percent drunk. That's Charlie. I know because I'm sober. How is this happening?

Some persistent bastard keeps knocking on my door, so I cross the distance and swing it open. A woman stands on the other side, her face Bloody Mary–red. She points a finger the size of a cornhusk in my face. "You need to be quiet," she hisses.

"Oh-kay," I snap back. Then I slam the door before she can add anything else and go sit on the overturned mattress. "Charlie," I say into the phone, "are you all right?"

She laughs. "I'm doing *real* good. Annabelle and I went to a Christmas party."

I have no idea why, but I get a sinking sensation in my stomach. "Oh, yeah? Have fun?" is what I *actually* say, but what I really want to ask her is, "Why are you going out? Shouldn't you be missing me? Also, since when did you start liking parties? Thought you preferred movies at home and shit?" Because honestly, it was always me dragging her to parties, so what changed?

"I did. It was so much fun," Charlie purrs. "How's the assignment going? What's Aspen like? Is she…is she pretty?"

I'm relieved that she seems concerned about Aspen. I guess even someone like Charlie can get jealous, because even though she's absolutely stunning now, sometimes she forgets to see herself that way. And sometimes I miss the old Charlie's quirky beauty.

I'm about to reassure her that my eyes are only for her when a voice rings in the background—Annabelle, I think. "Did you tell him how you almost killed yourself?"

I leap to my feet. "What's she talking about?"

"Nothing," Charlie responds, her mouth too close to the receiver. "At the party we were seeing who could hold our breath the longest underwater. And guess what? Guess what happened?"

"You won?" I say. I can picture her smiling face in my mind, so it's hard for me to be upset. But I don't like the idea of Charlie playing let's-almost-drown-ourselves while intoxicated. And what the hell were they even doing swimming in December?

"Yep," she says. "And he said I couldn't."

I swear on all that is red and bacon-y, if she says Max is the one who challenged her, I'll tear out his scrotum. "Who said you couldn't?"

"This guy, my new neighbor. The party was at his house."

My blood freezes in my veins. "Charlie, what's this dude's name?"

She pauses on the other end of the line, and I'm just about to start throwing things again. But I remember Man Hands knocked on my door and asked me to be quiet, so I don't.

"His name is Salem."

The desk chair flies into the wall with a loud clatter. So much for restraint. I glance at the door and expect to hear the beefy woman knocking again, but the sound doesn't come.

"Charlie, that guy's brother was the one who was creeping outside your window," I say as evenly as I can.

"Yeah, Easton." She announces this like we're discussing Tupperware. "Look, Salem told me all about your run-in. He said to tell you he was really sorry about what happened. He kept asking me where you were. Said he wished you could've been there so he could show you his brother is a good person." Charlie grows quiet, and I can tell she's biting her nails. "They're really cool, Dante. When you get back here, I bet the three of you will be friends."

"I don't want you anywhere near those guys," I say through clenched teeth. It's all I can manage, because now I'm remembering the way Salem looked at me with challenge in his eyes. And now he's getting Charlie drunk and telling her to hold her breath underwater and playing Nice Guy. Well, I'm calling him on what he is—a sleazer.

"Okay, first, they really are nice people." Charlie's voice gets louder. "And third, I do what I want."

I don't tell her that she actually only named two things, not three. And I don't jump on a plane to Alabama and tie her to the bed like I'd like to (for numerous reasons). Instead, I squeeze my eyes shut and say, "I know. It's just those guys—"

"Those guys were hanging out with Max all night. He liked them. He said so."

This actually does cause me to hesitate. Because I trust Max, I really do. And if he was around those dudes and didn't sense anything off about them, then maybe I actually am looking for danger in the wrong places. Maybe I need to concentrate on the collector who was in my room tonight instead of the fact that two guys invited Charlie to a party.

One of which I caught staring up at her window.

Okay, okay. I hold my hand up like I'm negotiating with myself. *I'm letting this go.*

"You look so hot," Annabelle slurs in the background. "Can't believe you actually wore it."

It's the freaking Fourth of July in my head right now, explosions detonating left and right. But I bite my lip and remain calm. "You get a new outfit or something?"

"He can hear everything you're saying," Charlie tells Annabelle.

"Good. Everything I say is magical," Annabelle responds. "Can he hear me when I say, 'Screw Bobby!'?"

Charlie laughs before returning to our conversation. I can almost taste blood by the time she answers me. "Bobby was kissing another girl tonight. He and Anna are over." Her voice goes from sad to excited in the space of a breath. "And yeah! I went shopping. Got a new dress."

"—that'd fit an American Girl doll." Annabelle howls with laughter.

"I bet you look hot," I say. And it's the truth. I can picture her now, all legs and hips and big, innocent eyes. I bet she looks like Little Red Riding Hood, attracting all kinds of wolves.

"I look pretty good," she slurs.

"Try *amazing*," Annabelle interjects.

"Amazing," Charlie says, "I look amazing. And you look beautiful, Annabelle. Bobby's an idiot."

I adore her confident words, even if I know they add up to a lie. She's never been comfortable with her appearance, and I can't think of anything that would've made that change.

Briefly, I think about mentioning the collector who was in my room but decide against it. I don't want to scare her, and I know Valery and Max have her safety covered. For now, the best thing to do would probably be to get off the phone and call it a night. Then maybe call her again in the morning when I know she's sober. But even as I think this, I know it'll be hard to get off the phone. I *know* Charlie, which means I know she'll want to keep talking until the sun comes up.

Charlie yawns through the phone. "Hey, I better run. Got to get some shut-eye before school tomorrow."

My mouth drops open. *She's* got to run? Trying to maintain what pride I have left, I recover quickly and say, "Yeah, I'm pretty beat, too." And then, because my heart starts to race at the thought that she's actually about to hang up, I add, "Hey, how many days you got left before winter break?"

I already know the answer to this question, and Charlie pauses like she *knows* I know. "Just this week. Then it's Play Day every day."

"Play Day, huh?" I say. "I don't like the sound of that one bit." ·

Charlie laughs lightly. "Good night, Dante."

I squeeze my eyes shut. "Good night, angel. Tell Annabelle I'm sorry about Bobby. Guy's a douche."

"Wait," Charlie says, as if I were about to hang up the phone, which I wasn't. "You know I miss you, right?"

Rubbing a hand over my face, I grin. "That's good to hear. I miss you, too."

Charlie hangs up, and I sit with the phone pressed to my head for several seconds before leaning back on the naked mattress. Thoughts of Salem and Easton try to wiggle their way into my mind, but I shove them aside and think of Charlie.

Gripping the ivory horn in my fist, I concentrate on the feel of her lying in her bed. I think of the way she looks when she laughs, and the way her skin smells. And with a knot in my chest, I think of how tonight she sounded like someone else entirely.

Despite the surge of anxiety I felt earlier, I cling to Valery's assurance that for now, all is well.

My eyes slip closed, and I fall into a deep sleep.

❊ 10 ❊

HERE I AM TO STAY

On the ride over to Aspen's house, I think about the collector who paid me a visit last night. There's not much I can do but keep my guard up. Not like I can go running around Denver trying to sense a cuff nearby. Dumb.

So instead, I focus on my assignment. I focus on the fact that Valery said Aspen was important, though that could mean a thousand different things. I know it's not her fault that I've been sent to liberate her, but right now, I'm feeling resentful. After all, if she had her shit together, I'd be back with Charlie. So yeah, I'm not a happy camper this morning. But a job is a job, and no one can pull tricks like I can to get crap done.

It's painfully early as I cruise through Aspen's gate and head up the drive, but I've got to catch this girl before she heads off to school. After killing the engine and striding up her walkway, I stop and admire myself in the glass door. Looking mighty fine, if I do say so myself: red v-neck, dark denim, designer combat boots, and enough testosterone rolling off me to satisfy Nicki Minaj. Pow!

I knock once on the ten-foot tall door and wait until a little window opens. A guy cocks an eye at me like this is *The Wizard of Oz* and he's Emerald City's damn gatekeeper.

"How's it going?" I ask him, stuffing my hands into my pockets. "I'm here to pick up Aspen for school."

The door swings open, and an older dude with Aspen's green eyes stares back at me. He's a burly guy, the kind with a barely visible neck. And he isn't doing himself any favors with his too-tight dress tie. "Who are you?" the guy says, and I notice his voice sounds a little like how I imagine an alligator might talk, all throaty and showing way too much tooth.

"Dante Walker." I stick my hand out because parents love that crap, but this guy only nods his head toward something behind him.

"She's upstairs," Crocodile Man says. "I'm going to work, so no funny business."

I want to tell him not to worry, that we need to head out, and I'm a guy who likes to take my time when performing "funny business." But I decide against this and instead move aside as Aspen's dad brushes past me toward the garage. I take this as my cue to enter his humble abode, so I walk inside and shut the door behind me.

My eyes bug out of my head, because even though I was raised on the green, I've never seen this kind of excess. The place looks like a pic that'd pop up on Google when you typed in "Americans Who Prosper from Child Labor." Glancing down, I notice the floors are Italian stone, the real kind. The kind that crack and soak up anything that spills but shows others how much more money you have than them.

There are also pops of designer wall paper in all the right places. Poor people think wallpaper is out, but that's because they're a generation behind the wealthy. And always will be. The rich will always say to themselves, "What do the poor people hate today? Ah, yes. Wallpaper. Good. Let's *embrace* that, then."

Crawling toward the top floor is a pair of sweeping stairs that'd make any Disney princess weep with joy. I imagine if most girls saw them, they'd run out and buy every wedding magazine they could get their simple hands on.

Not Aspen, though. I've only spent one evening with her, watching her, and already I know she's never pictured how she'd look in a wedding dress.

For some reason, I assume Aspen's room is probably upstairs, so I ascend quietly. When I get to the top, I stop and glance both ways down a gold-and-white hallway. I choose to turn left and am soon rewarded by the sound of heavy base.

At least the girl's got an ear for music, I think as I stroll toward deep, screaming vocals.

I push the cracked bedroom door open the rest of the way and find a girl who looks every bit like Aspen but is half her age. The girl child's eyes grow large when she sees me.

"Aspen," she calls, and I notice the alarm in her voice.

Holding my hands up, I try to look innocent. "Sorry, I was actually just looking for — "

Pain shoots up my spine as I'm slammed into a wall. Aspen's face is inches from mine, her forearm pressed against my neck. When she recognizes me, she lets up, but not much. As she cuts off my oxygen, I can't help noticing she's wearing fingerless gloves again; yesterday's pair was black, and today's gloves are bright green.

"What do you think you're doing?" she snarls. "Who the hell *are* you?"

"D-Dub in the flesh," I manage, thinking this girl might do well in the WWE. She certainly has the charm for it.

Aspen glances at her sister, who's moved closer. And the look she gives her baby sister tells me everything I need to know; Aspen would do anything to protect her. "Don't come out of your room, Sahara. My *friend* and I are going to have a little chat."

Sahara nods, her big, vulnerable eyes still enlarged.

Aspen grabs my upper arm and leads me down the hallway. I could easily overpower her, but I let her do her thing, since it's mildly amusing.

After my prison guard has pushed me into a bedroom covered in reds and blacks, she turns on me. "Look, I was a little messed up yesterday, so I let it go that I didn't know who you were. But I'm not now," she states. "Let's start with what the hell were you doing in my sister's room?"

"Such salty language," I *tsk*, trying to refrain from yawning, because seriously, this girl is boring me.

Aspen steps closer in an attempt to intimidate yours truly, but that so isn't happening.

"I came to see you, not her," I offer, remembering I have to befriend this girl for the sake of the assignment. "I didn't know which room was yours."

"Now you do," she says, breaking eye contact. I decide the gesture means she's nervous, which tells me even though she's acting all Fearless Woman, I must make her uncomfortable. And that means, my friends, that it's time to spew lies.

"Aspen, listen, your dad and my dad work together. I was sent over to make nice with you so that Pops will get a leg up. But I'd rather saw my own arm off than be his damn pawn. So I decided instead I'd come over and make your life hell." I grab the cigarettes from her nightstand, pull one out, and light it. "I've since decided I don't fucking care enough to do even that."

One corner of Aspen's mouth quirks upward. "Such salty language."

I grin and offer her a cigarette from her own pack, knowing Charlie would not be pleased to see me full on smoking. But hey, she's out partying, right? Aspen takes the cigarette. "Shouldn't we be off to the playground?"

"We're out for winter break." Aspen sits on her bed and stares out the window, taking long pulls on her cigarette. I follow her gaze and notice the mountains look larger from here. Less like titties and more like mom boobs. I plop down on a black suede chair in the corner and admire the silver studs along its curved back. It's very Adam Levine.

Aspen glances back at me and the small diamond in her nose catches the light. "So you hate your old man?"

I already know Aspen despises her own dad. I mean, maybe I'm wrong, but something tells me when you flip your parent the bird, you're kind of over them. Remembering this, I say, "If I could use him as shark chum, I would."

Aspen laughs hard and clean, like there's nothing holding her back. "I feel ya."

Blowing a perfect ring of smoke into the air, I inspect her room closer. Part of bringing this girl in means knowing what would motivate her to live a purer lifestyle. And there's no better place to start, I decide, than studying her natural habitat.

Her bed is queen-sized, even though she could easily fit three kings in here. And her floor is covered in black carpet, which I'm certain she picked out. A miniature crystal chandelier hangs from the center of the ceiling, and all along the walls are splashes of red and white. Near the soaring window is an enormous black leather beanbag. Overall, the room is designed for a rock star and looks similar to a deck of playing cards.

I can't help thinking Charlie would like the bold red. That maybe this is the room she'd actually like to have, even though everyone would rather picture her in something pink and sparkly.

Eyeing the area near the beanbag, I notice there are little trinkets on the window ledge. I stand from the pimp chair and move across the room. Aspen sees what I'm headed toward and leaps to her feet.

"Those are mine," she says, and I'm surprised at the possessiveness in her voice.

Ignoring her, I edge closer. They're music boxes, I realize. Well, not boxes, actually. More like just the little mechanical parts of music boxes, all silver cords and string. On the side of each device is a little crank. I want to turn one so bad, but suddenly I feel like my hands are too big. I glance at Aspen who's standing close by, her face lined with worry. She flicks her cigarette into a chrome trash can like she never wanted it in the first place. "Do these actually play anything?" I ask.

Her eyes glare past me at the trinkets, and I note the blue eye shadow smudged over her lids. I wonder why she wears it, because Mom—who also has green eyes—always said the shade was blasphemous.

"Yeah, they work." Aspen steps around me as if she's guarding them. Then, maybe because she can tell how badly I want to pick one up, she chooses one from the back. Then she rolls it between her gloved hands and gives me a long look. It's like she's silently conveying how much these things mean to her, though she'd never say it aloud. Glancing away, she holds it out to me, trying hard to act like she doesn't care if I crush it under my heel.

I take it from her and then, balancing my cigarette in the corner of my mouth, I crank the miniature lever. Music ticks out from the gadget and I can't help but laugh. It's freaking awesome. I have no idea why, but it is. Aspen turns away and goes to get another cigarette. She lights it and curls up on her bed like a compressed coil, like if I make one wrong move, she'll fire across the room. "Why do you have these?" I ask around my cancer stick.

She shrugs. "Why not?"

I spin the lever a few more times and then put the gadget back exactly where it was. Then I glance around the room again, looking to see what else I can find. This time my eyes land on a checkerboard.

At first I think it's décor, considering her room is splashed with reds and blacks. But the board and pieces are blue and yellow, and look way too intricate to be intended for actual play. Still, I know better than anyone that rich kids' toys are always extravagant. Even crap like board games. I reach for a yellow checker.

"Stop!" Aspen yells, leaning forward. "Just…just stop touching things." My arm freezes in midair, and a chill shoots over my skin. Most people would assume she's just some spoiled brat who can't share. But when I see the fear hidden in her eyes, I know better.

"What are you worried about, Aspen?" I ask quietly. And for once, I actually care what comes out of her mouth. I know Aspen likes to party, but before, I thought this was about a girl whose daddy didn't pay attention. Now I'm not so sure.

My eyes rake over her dark hair, the small diamond stud in her nose. I watch her hands clench and unclench, and I zone in on her fingerless gloves.

Aspen toys with a small silver chain around her neck. It's an unconscious action but one I notice all the same. There isn't a charm on her necklace. It's just an empty thread, like whoever bought it forgot the most important part.

I take a small step closer. "Aspen?"

In a flash, she's on her feet. "Don't give me that look. I'm warning you. Don't you *dare* look like you feel *sorry* for me." She jerks a finger in my direction. "I have everything. And I certainly don't need some poser acting like I'm the one who needs help."

Poser? my mind screams. *Moi?* But then I remember I'm wearing high fashion while driving a busted-up Kia.

I consider letting this go, but I've never backed down from a challenge. And this girl, she's tossing 'em around like it's the freaking summer Olympics. In three quick steps, I close the distance between us. I grab her upper arms and jerk her so that she can't avoid my eyes. "You're real good at pushing people away, aren't you?" I growl around my cigarette. "Push, push, push. That's Aspen." My eyes search her face as I reconsider what I just said. "Push them away or pull them closer, right? So close they can't even see you clearly anymore." Cigarette in hand, I put my mouth right next to her ear. "I don't get pushed around easily, doll. And there's only one girl I let pull me in."

Aspen spins her arms in a quick circle, then throws her hands into my chest. "Get off me!"

I stumble backward, and we stare at each other, breathing hard. There's absolutely nothing sexual between us. It's just two screwed-up people seeing each other for the first time.

"I'm not going anywhere," I tell her. I have no idea why I say this. It just comes out. But once I say it, I know it's true. I don't care about saving Aspen. Not really. Even if Valery does insist she's important to Big Guy. But I won't leave her alone.

Aspen mutters something under her breath.

"Speak up," I bark.

"I said, 'you will.' *Everyone* goes away." Her stone skin relaxes, like she's just realized what she said.

"Nah, screw that." I stub my cigarette out in a red ash tray. "I ain't got nothing else to do."

Aspen laughs. It's riddled with nerves, but it doesn't change anything, because now we're both smiling like idiots.

"Can I come out now?" a small voice asks.

Aspen and I spin around to see her sister, Sahara, standing in the doorway. She appears to be about eight years old, and I notice she dresses the way Aspen does, all black with a pop of one other color. Sahara slinks into the room when Aspen doesn't immediately tell her to leave. She goes to stand in front of her older sister, and Aspen wraps her arms around her shoulders.

"This is Dante," Aspen tells her sister. Her eyes bore into me, like she's warning me not to say anything about our super-strange moment.

"Pleasure to meet you." Sahara holds out her hand like a businesswoman, and I offer my own in return.

"Nice grip," I tell the girl. "You could be a race car driver."

Sahara laughs and looks up at her sister. The muscles relax in Aspen's shoulders as she watches us interact, and I can't help but think Sahara seems pretty freaking cool.

"Want to see my new dress?" Sahara asks me.

I rub my chin like I'm deep in contemplation. "Depends on whether you want an honest opinion. 'Cause I'm going to give one."

"Okay." Sahara moves toward the door, smiling like the world is hers to hold.

I meet Aspen's eyes, and she nods. Then she brushes past me toward Sahara's room, and I follow close behind. The three of us trail down the hallway, and I can't get over how odd this is. How moments ago Aspen and I were speaking in code about her messed-up life. And now we're hanging out with her little sister like we're best buds. But that's the thing; Aspen can change her tune in a heartbeat. It's what I always prided myself on, too, how I could put on different faces depending on who was in the room.

Aspen and I are so much alike, showing the world what we want them to see and hiding everything else away.

Watching Aspen touch Sahara gently between the shoulder blades, I realize she has something I never had—someone to cling to. A sibling. I don't have one, but I've always wondered what it'd be like.

A wave of dizziness rolls over me, because suddenly I understand why I said I wouldn't leave Aspen. Because she's just like me. She and I could have been related.

She could have been my sister.

⇥ 11 ⇤

HELL IN HIS EYES

Aspen and I spend the morning hanging out with Sahara. It's amazing how easy it is to just kick it when there's a kid in the room. It's even easy to forget that last night, a collector was in my room. And that he may still be lurking around, despite Valery's assurance that there's nothing to worry about. Or that I have no idea why Aspen is important to Big Guy.

At some point, Lincoln drops by. He scurries around the house like he's looking for explosives then settles into a chair in Sahara's room and paints his nails black.

"That's pretty manly," I tell him when he shows us the finished product.

"It's black," he responds, like this makes any difference.

"Right." I raise an eyebrow at Sahara, who laughs. She moves toward me like a cat, like she wants to be closer, but also wants me to come to her. I take two quick steps and scoop her up. She's eight, not exactly a featherweight anymore, but she's light enough. Her dark hair sprays out as I spin her in a circle. Then I set her down and tickle her until she can hardly breathe.

No mercy for the weak.

Glancing over at Aspen, I expect to see her laughing along with her sister. But instead, she's staring at the floor with a blank expression on her face. I feel Lincoln studying me and meet his gaze. His forehead is lined with worry, but he doesn't say anything.

Aspen's head snaps up. She tilts her ear like she's listening for something. When the doorbell sounds, I realize it must have been what she heard. She lifts herself off Sahara's bed and makes for the stairs. Lincoln and I exchange another look, then we both get up to go after her. I don't need whoever this is breaking her concentration. Hanging out with her sister does something good to Aspen, and if I'm going to liberate her soul, keeping her around Sahara may be my best bet.

I don't know how long turning a person good will take, because I've only ever turned them bad. Convincing someone to embrace their sinister desires isn't so difficult, but convincing them to forsake those desires may take much longer. I'll have to be a shining example of purity (not easy) and show her how beautiful life can be when you're living it clean (kill me). All in all, because I am amazing at All Things, I think I can have this wrapped up in about a week or so.

Aspen reaches the bottom of the stairs and opens the mammoth door. It grinds on its hinges, and I spot Gage and Lyra standing outside. Great. Just what I need is these two snaring her with their jellyfish tentacles.

Gage leans his head inside and sees Lincoln and me on the banister. "What's up, guys?" he says, all smiles and charm like he's Boy Wonder. He looks back at Aspen and says something I don't catch. She nods and gazes up at Lincoln.

"Hey, will you stay with my sister while I go out for a while?"

"No," he retorts, the chains on his camo jacket rattling. "Just stay here with us, Aspen."

Her eyes slide over to me. I can tell she wants to ask me to babysit but doesn't fully trust me yet. Not with her sister. "Come on, man," she says, her sharp green eyes returning to Lincoln. "I'll do your hair when I get back."

I glance at the guy next to me, my brow furrowing. Then I notice the blond roots growing from his scalp. "Don't cave," I tell him. I don't know why I'm so wary of Aspen going off with Gage and Lyra other than what Lincoln told me. How Aspen is worse around them. And also maybe because I see the way they look at her, like she's part of some agenda they have.

Lincoln shrugs a thin shoulder and mutters, "She's gonna go no matter what. I don't want Sahara to be alone." He narrows his kohl-lined eyes and calls down, "Don't leave me here forever."

Aspen blows him a kiss and starts to slink through the door.

"Uh, hold on there, princess." I descend the stairs, keeping my eyes locked on Gage. "I'm coming, too."

"I don't think so," Lyra snaps.

I hold my palm up to her face and speak to Gage. "I'm coming, or Aspen stays here."

Gage laughs hard, his neon teeth flashing. "She's a big girl. If she doesn't want you along, then you're not coming."

Aspen's jaw is set like she's pissed I'm acting this way, but there's something else in her glare—another challenge, maybe. "He can come," she says. Her mouth pulls into a smile, but the gesture doesn't reach her eyes.

"Splendid." I grin at Gage just to piss him off real nice. Then I turn back to Lincoln. I don't know much about the paranoid, Goth-clad dude, but he seems to care about Aspen, which I may need. And if I'm being honest, I guess I appreciate it, too, because Aspen needs someone to care. I nod in an attempt to tell him I got this, but Lincoln just watches Aspen walk out the door before heading back to Sahara's room.

When I turn back around, Gage meets my stare. "Ready to roll, pretty boy?"

I cringe, because "pretty boy" is what Max calls me. *Max*. Not him. I'm going to try and give Gage the benefit of the doubt, but we need to get off on the right foot. "Name's Dante, asshole. Next time you call me something other than that, I'll put you in the ground. Got it?" I slap him on the arm like we're pals and brush past him.

Behind me, I hear Gage laughing, but I'm not sure it's authentic. If it is, we could end up being friends. Crazier things have happened.

Aspen has already lodged herself in the backseat of the BMW 7 series—or the Regulator, as I've named it—and has pulled her knees to her chest. She bobs her head to the angry music Lyra's flipped on, and I feel the beat rush into my veins.

"Don't you have a car?" I ask Aspen as I slide in after her.

She nods her head toward the garage. "Old Man took the keys."

As we pull away from Aspen's fortress-of-a-house, my eyes cling to the garage, because if this is the casa Aspen calls home, I'd kill to know what her sleigh looks like. I look back at her to ask what she's packing in there, but she's already lost to the music, her eyes glassed over.

Gage turns around from the driver's seat and grins at me. "Buckle up, *Dante*."

Lyra cranks the volume, and Gage steps on the accelerator.

He drives fast.

And it feels good.

• • •

A half hour later, we pull into an overgrown neighborhood that probably keeps Kool-Aid and ramen noodles in business. Gage turns behind a small blue house and into an alleyway. After throwing the car into park, he looks at me in the rearview. Holding a finger to his lips, he winks.

I contemplate popping him in the eye but decide to let his douche lord move slide.

He climbs out of the car, and the rest of us follow along. When we get to a garage immediately outside the alleyway, he turns and faces us. "You guys ready to get stupid?"

Aspen wraps her arms around herself. "Just show us what's inside," she deadpans.

Gage glances around and rolls the door open with a rattle. Inside are three motorcycles that lock way too tight to be in this part of the city. I don't know much about rides with only two wheels, but already my blood is pumping, because I appreciate anything with an engine.

Lyra walks inside, her long brunette ponytail swishing back and forth. She's dressed in all white—white blouse, white leggings, white heels—which makes me think she didn't know about Gage's idea. But it doesn't stop her from turning around and saying with a smile, "Bad."

Gage walks past us and throws his leg over a yellow Suzuki that reads *Hayabusa*. Without missing a beat, Lyra gets on behind him and grabs onto his thighs. "Geezer won't even know they're missing," Gage says. He pops his chin toward the other bikes, his gaze steady on me. "Two more bikes, two more players."

My head pounds with excitement because this is the old me. I'm the guy who'd *borrow* some anonymous person's pride and joy without thinking twice. But I can't be that person anymore. Because I'm with Charlie, and she believes I can be one of the good guys. Gripping the horn in my pocket, my mind flashes to where she is—

—and a bolt of anger fires through me. Because Charlie isn't at home. And she's not at school. But she is somewhere *near* her house, which means she's probably spending her lunch break at Salem's house.

My body floods with concern, but then I remember how she stuck up for him and his brother. I also remember that Max and Valery are both around, protecting her from doing anything unsafe.

So she's just there…hanging out.

My mind snaps to attention when I hear the snarl of an engine kicking on. "If you're coming, you better hurry the hell up," Lyra sings.

Aspen straddles a storm cloud–colored bike with an exhaust pipe as wide as my biceps. She starts the engine like she's done this a million times, though the rigidness in her frame tells me otherwise. She looks at me through the gap in her helmet, her riotous eyes flashing. "Sure you ain't got nothing else to do?"

She's quoting what I told her earlier. And I know what I need to do is get her off that bike, because crap like this earns seals for hell, not heaven. But that growl rolling off the twin bikes—oh, shit, that *growl*—it creeps in; it slinks through all the openings in my body and smothers my resolve. Without thinking, I touch a finger to the skull on my red belt. It's cool and reassuring beneath my skin.

My eyes land on the third bike. It's cherry freaking red. And it's calling my name. I move forward and—gripping the chrome handlebars—I mount her. Then I start the engine, pull on a helmet, and close my eyes in ecstasy. When I open them, Gage is smiling at me—

And in his eyes is something I've only seen in hell.

The sight should scare me. It should tell me to get off the damn bike and get Aspen out of here. But for the first time since I left Charlie, my head isn't back there with her, it's here and in the now—a beast between my legs, an empty road begging to be plowed, and a dare in Gage's eyes I'm not about to abandon.

Throwing my head back, I howl at the open sky like an animal.

Then I release the brake and thunder out into the afternoon sun.

The last thing I see before my eyes lock on the road is a flesh-colored tattoo peeking out from beneath Gage's sleeve. And I swear on all that is unholy, I've seen it somewhere before.

⊰ 12 ⊱

I WANT HER

After racing on the bikes for several hours, we finally return them. The owner still doesn't know they're gone, so no harm done, I figure. We leave them in the garage and jump into The Regulator. Then we hit up Mickey D's before swinging by Aspen's house to get Lincoln.

Gage lays on the horn as he stuffs French fries into his mouth. "Come on, shithead."

I almost laugh, but the sound dies in my throat, because I like Lincoln. And I can't tell whether Gage does. For some reason, I doubt it. It feels like we're all here for Aspen, like we all want a piece of her just like Lincoln said, and that makes us competitors. Still, I like to think Lincoln and I are on the same train. So yeah, I don't laugh.

Lincoln comes strolling out of the house, surveying the battlefield like a soldier at war. Finding it free of enemy fire, he climbs into the backseat, squishing Aspen between us.

"My dad home?" Aspen asks, touching a finger to her empty necklace.

Lincoln glances at her, then up at Gage and Lyra. "Yeah, he's here. With Sahara. He sends his well-wishes."

Aspen laughs and tells Gage to get us out of here.

He does.

Ten minutes later, we roll up to another party. "You Denver peeps enjoy the frosty beverages, no?" I tell Aspen.

She gives a small shrug but smiles. "We do it up. Don't be J."

I get out of the car, and everyone follows suit. "I'm not jealous of your whack job city with your whacked-out drivers trying to run me off the road."

"Say what?" Aspen says with genuine surprise, and maybe a little concern, stretched over her face.

"Never mind," I mumble, because I'm busy watching Gage whisper to Lyra about what I said. Freak shows.

Lincoln shivers and shoves us both toward the house. "Can we get inside, please? My man ornaments are going to shatter out here."

I wrap Lincoln's head under my arm and lead us inside. In response, he elbows me in the crotch, and we both crumble to the ground right inside the entrance.

"Idiots," Aspen says, but I can tell she's happy we're getting along. As she glides into the room, people stop what they're doing. They offer her a drink, they remove her mink coat, they orgasm as they note her green Jimmy Choo heels. I'm familiar with the way she allows herself to be consumed by them. *It feels good*, I remember. *Like it doesn't matter that Mom doesn't give a crap or that Dad's always gone.*

I grab a beer from the kitchen and drain it in one long take. Then I flop down on a sketchy-looking, pastel-colored couch, which is about the nicest thing up in this joint, and snatch my phone from my pocket. My back stiffens when I see I have a text.

Let it be from Charlie.

Since I arrived in Denver, I've only gotten the one text from her, and even that one sounded off. I need something to remind me she's still my girl, that we're still *us*, but when I check to see who the text is from, my heart clenches like a fist. It's Annabelle, and it's only a single line:

CHECK OUT UR HOTTIE!

My fingers tingle when I see there's a pic attached to the message. Tapping the icon, and thinking I'll scream if my phone moves any slower, I wait for the image to download.

And then I see sweet Charlie.

Except she doesn't look so sweet.

She looks sexy. She looks *dangerous*. And maybe she is, because I'm about to have massive coronary failure eyeing the skirt she's wearing. "What the hell?" I mutter.

"Damn. That your girl?" Lincoln's leaning over my shoulder, ogling Charlie's physique.

I lower my phone and make sure Lincoln meets my glare. "You got two seconds to divert your eyes before I remove them from your skull."

He laughs, runs a hand through his greasy hair. "My bad. Just window shopping."

"Well, don't." I get up from the chair and head outside and into the cold. I don't care that Gage and Lyra are once again feeding Aspen enough booze to drown a life jacket. I don't care that it's my job to seal her soul for heaven. All I *do* care about is getting a better look at the picture of Charlie.

Standing in the snow, wrapped in a cloak of darkness, I study Charlie: her laughing face, her wide blue eyes. And that damn skirt. It looks like something she wore to a party a few weeks ago when she was proving a point, a night that ended with my carrying her out of a barn. But this time, it looks like she's embracing her new figure. Like she's finally figured out she's got one, and she's damn well going to flaunt it. I don't blame her. If I'd spent seventeen years with an average body, I'd be eager to flash my goods. But this is *Charlie*. She's better than that. Right?

I rub my thumb over her picture and jerk as my phone starts ringing.

It's Charlie.

For some idiotic reason, I glance around like I'm searching for someone to tell me what to do. I feel like I'm back in high school when I was alive, like I'm one of those cheerleader chicks who used to be all, "Oh, my gawd. He's calling! What do I do?! Should I pick up?"

I shake my head—what the hell *am* I doing?—and push accept. "'Sup?" I say, going for cool and calm and the exact opposite of how I feel.

For a long moment, Charlie doesn't speak. The silence makes my chest tighten like I swallowed a freaking porcupine. "I miss you," she says finally, her voice soft.

It doesn't seem like it.

You've barely called.

Salem seems more important than I do.

"I miss you, too," I say. "I wish I were there." Charlie is quiet again. So quiet I start to think she'll hang up. I don't understand what's happened between us. I don't get why we were perfect two days ago, and now I feel like I'm going to explode if she doesn't say something. "Is everything okay?" I say, surprising myself. "I mean, between us."

"Of course," she responds. "Why would you ask that?"

If she thinks everything's fine, then I don't want to dwell on it. Instead, I try to steer the conversation forward. "No reason," I say. "How's everything at home? You only got—what?—four more days until school's out for winter break?"

"Three, actually. Last test is Thursday morning." I hear a clipping noise on the other end of the line and imagine Charlie biting her nails. "But I've been having fun even with school in."

My stomach plummets. "Yeah? That's cool. What have you been doing?"

"Lots of stuff. Annabelle and I went to a swimming hole even though it was super cold. It was really fun. No one thought I'd jump off the cliff, but I did."

"Jump off what?" I nearly shout. "Why are you jumping off things, Charlie? Don't do that. Don't jump off things."

"It wasn't a big deal. I'm just having fun."

"Were you with him?" I ask. "Were Salem and his brother there?" Charlie is quiet, and even though I hate myself for asking, I hate it even more that she's admitting what I already knew. "Let me guess, he's the one who dared you to jump."

"He doesn't treat me like I'm breakable," Charlie snaps.

I have no response for this, because I know that's how I treat her. But it's because I care about her. I care about her so much, it makes me sick. I should tell her this, but all I can picture is Salem encouraging Charlie to drink, or hold her breath underwater, or leap off the side of a cliff. And I picture the way he celebrates with her when she does these things. Like he's this fun dude, and I'm some paranoid schizo who's killing the party.

"How's the assignment going?" Charlie asks. Her voice is back to being soft. It's like she's struggling between two sides of herself, and I want so bad to point this out, but I can't, because the same thing is happening to me. I'm not doing crap about my assignment. I haven't sealed Aspen's soul a single time. In fact, all I've done is lose myself in her world, a world I've known much longer than the one Charlie's shown me.

"I'm going to get this assignment done quickly," I say, though the words sound like a lie leaving my mouth.

"I wish you were standing right next to me, Dante," Charlie says suddenly.

"Then don't hang up."

Charlie's laugh sounds like bells ringing. "Annabelle just got back."

"So?" I say. "So make her wait. Make her leave. Whatever. Just stay on the phone."

"We've got plans," she says. I can tell she's doing that thing again, fighting two sides of some internal argument.

"Cancel them." I look over my shoulder at the house to ensure I'm still alone. "This isn't like you, anyway. Going out every night when you have finals."

"How would you know?" she demands. "You've barely known me two months."

Her words shoot holes through me, because she's right. I haven't known her long at all. Our relationship moved quickly, so quickly that I've often wondered whether the strong connection we felt or the couple of times we exchanged *I love you*s were triggered by the threat of the collectors, or maybe even the conflict I experienced over whether to defy Lucille.

Ever since I left, I haven't stopped thinking about how neither one of us has said *I love you* since the day I woke up with a liberator cuff around my ankle. Each time we're together, we can't keep our hands off each other. But maybe that's lust. Maybe it's admiration. How do I know if we were ever really in love if I've never experienced these feelings before now? "I know you," is all I whisper. "I know you, Charlie."

She pulls in a long breath, and it feels like she steals it right from my lungs. "I miss you," Charlie repeats. I think she's coming back to me, that she's going to tell me we can talk as long as I want. But then I hear Annabelle's voice.

"Okay, got the juice," Annabelle says in the background. "Let's get on the road, girl! You talking to D? I sent him a picture of your naughty self. Hey, Dante, Valery and Max are going out with us tonight! We'll be good. Your girl's got to run."

Charlie sounds like she's battling Annabelle for the phone. Finally, I hear Charlie say into the receiver, "Call you later."

"Be safe," I say to dead air. Feeling like I just got kidney punched, I trek back inside, barely feeling my fingers from the cold. Snow crunches under my shoes, and when I land inside, I brush them off on a doormat that reads, "Wipe your paws" and has little animal prints on it.

When I glance up, my eyes meet Aspen's. She must see something on my face that concerns her, because she rips away from Gage and Lyra and the rest of her leeches and comes to stand beside me.

She doesn't ask what's wrong. She just puts her drink in my hand and touches the bottom gently, nudging it toward my mouth. Her eyes never pull away from mine. It's like she knows something big is wrong with me, but doesn't know how to handle it. So she offers what she'd want in the same situation—a chance to forget.

I stare down into the amber liquid and think about Charlie. Think of how I need to make headway on this assignment and stop screwing around. But then Aspen says, "Drink some. It'll make it better."

She doesn't know what's wrong with me, doesn't care. She's got her own issues to wrestle. But she knows the booze I'm holding will make my worries fade into the distance. And she's right. I don't know how to handle feeling like the only girl I've ever cared about is vanishing, being replaced by someone I don't recognize. But I do know this. I know how I'll feel when I turn this cup upside down and feel the bite of liquor rushing down my throat.

So I do what I know. Just for tonight, I let go of my unease and find myself again. And never, not once, do I leave Aspen's side. She makes room for me. In her eyes, I can see that she's grateful. That she thinks maybe I'm going to stand by my word and stick around. And not for the wrong reasons, either. She doesn't want anything from me except for me to stay. And I don't want anything from her except to remember how I used to be—free, wild…

Alive.

As the sun appears from behind the mountains, Aspen throws her arm around my shoulders like we've been friends for as long as the sun has risen. "If you could have anything, Dante, anything at all, what would it be?" she slurs.

Even with my thoughts muddled by alcohol, my answer comes out clear and quick. "Her. I want Charlie."

✥ 13 ✥

FIELD TRIP

For the next two days, I stay in Aspen's fog, trying hard not think about the girl I miss in Alabama. On a few occasions, I encourage Aspen to spend more time with Sahara, thinking maybe her baby sister will do my job for me.

It doesn't work.

Instead, I spiral further away from the man Charlie had somehow pulled out of me and lose myself in my old lifestyle. Somewhere in the back of my head, I know I'm a liberator. That I only survive because of the dargon around my ankle. I wonder at times how much longer Big Guy will let me slip by. I've heard he's a vengeful leader, so it can't be long.

I wake up on my fourth day in Denver to someone pounding on my door. I imagine it must be Man Hands returning, and that maybe I was loud again last night. My throbbing head tells me that if I was, I wouldn't remember it.

Pulling open the door, I find Aspen dressed all in black except for hot-pink fingerless gloves. She flashes by me, and as she does, she admires my tats—the dragon spread over my back and the tree growing up my arm and branching over my shoulder. Other than that, she gives my half-dressed torso the same attention she'd give a number-two pencil.

She studies the room and then caves into herself like maybe she's just discovered where all forms of influenza come from. "Thought you said your dad had a condo."

Did I say that? I can't remember if I did. Thinking fast, I decide to play the sympathy card. I cast my eyes toward the floor and turn away. "Asshole's been gone awhile."

Aspen looks at the furniture around her, which I've put in some semblance of order again. "Parents can be pricks, huh?"

I nod, thinking the less I say, the better. Though I would like to ask how she knew where to find me.

"Get dressed." Her mouth pulls into a smile. "We're going on a field trip."

"I'd rather stick my head in a meat grinder," I respond. But in actuality, I'll go wherever she goes.

Because she's my assignment.

Because I fucking hate being alone.

"How'd you get here?" I ask.

"We have these magic yellow cars in Denver that take you places for cash." Aspen starts throwing my things into an overnight bag, wrinkling her nose—and her nose *ring*—at some of my fashion choices, which I find highly insulting.

"That shirt you're so disgusted by cost a hundred dollars," I tell her.

"No wonder it looks like crap," she says. My jaw drops, because I'm not used to this. *I'm* the rich one. *I'm* the one with nice crap everyone wants to have. But not around her, I guess. Aspen is like me if I drank a steroid-crack milkshake each morning. "Terrible clothes or not, we're getting out of town. I need a break from this place."

She glances at me from the corner of her eye like she's anticipating a rebuttal. "You're the one who said you don't have anywhere else to be."

Ten minutes later, Aspen is driving my pimp car out of Denver like there's an F5 tornado on our heels. And a half hour after that—so she says, I was crashed out—we pull into a town that belongs on a postcard. That is, if the postcard had yellowed thirty years. It's like all the tightly lined shops and paved roads used to be a sight to behold, but now it's a place people say "will come back around."

Aspen turns onto a dirt road and slices a path between the fir trees. It's only then do I think to ask where we're headed. For the last few days, I've followed Aspen blindly. I used to be the one people followed. But like many others, I've been trapped by Aspen's web, allowing myself to be drained by her needs.

"Where we headed?" I ask. "And why didn't Lincoln come?"

"This is my family's place." Aspen all but spits the word *family*. "Lincoln said he'd stay behind with Sahara. Someone's got to watch her while Dad's off doing whatever."

I glance at Aspen, watching as her knuckles tighten around the steering wheel. "Lincoln is good to you. Have you guys ever gotten dirty?"

Aspen laughs. "Lincoln? No. We've been friends since we were kids. Been through war together. Literally if you're asking him."

"He *is* pretty skittish," I say. "Bet that military father of his loves Lincoln's piercings."

Aspen doesn't say anything, just shakes her head.

I drop the subject and dig my cell out of my back pocket. It hasn't vibrated since we left, so I know there won't be anything from Charlie. Still, I'm dying to talk to her, even if our conversations have become increasingly strained. For the record, if Salem and Easton would stop talking her into doing stupid crap, we'd be fine.

My face warms when I see there are nine missed calls, and four voicemails, from her.

"What's wrong?" Aspen asks.

"My girl has called, like, a million times." I can't help the grin splitting my mouth. She called. She called *a lot*. And my damn ringer was off. I tell myself everything is fine with our relationship, otherwise she wouldn't have called that many times, even if it was at like two in the morning. Like always, I contemplate whether something bad happened, but realize if that were the case, someone other than her probably would've called. And I'm trying to trust her more.

As Aspen pulls up to a snow-laden cabin that must have been built for Zeus, I try retrieving my voicemails. The reception is crap, though, and her messages are too broken to understand. I reach into my back pocket to get the horn my father gave me and grip it in my palm. But I don't get a good read on where Charlie is. It's almost like I'm only feeling my own horn here in Colorado. Frustrated, I glance over at Aspen.

"Can you take me back into town?" I say. "I can't get my voicemails."

"Why don't you calm down, D-Dub. I know you're menstruating, but everything's going to be fine. Once we get inside, I'll explain all about maxi pads, personal hygiene, and the feel of a man's penis." Aspen grabs our bags from the trunk and heads toward double arched oak doors. The way she skitters up the stairs, it's like she's nervous about something, like she's waiting for something big to happen.

I grit my teeth and crunch through the snow behind Aspen, knowing I'll probably only make it another half hour before I forfeit the last of my manhood and go searching for a signal. Though I'm not sure why Aspen brought me here, I'm glad. Being away from Gage and Lyra and all the parties will help me focus on finishing this assignment. And if I'm being honest, this place is pretty kickass.

A wraparound porch hugs the two-story cabin, and the exterior is built to look like it was made from logs and mud alone.

More like slave labor and cold hard cash, but whatev.

The interior is more of the same: rustic-meets-rich-folk in the form of an antler chandelier, bearskin rug, dark leather sofas, and plaid chenille throws. Walking through the place, I spy six bedrooms and enough washrooms to bathe Snow White's seven dirty-ass dwarves.

After my exploration, I sink down onto a couch and watch as Aspen lights a fire. My mind begins ticking away, thinking it's now or never. I've enjoyed losing myself in this girl, but I know where my heart lies, and after seeing how many times Charlie called, I know I want nothing more than to get home to her. I decide my best chance is to be aggressive with Aspen. Maybe bring up Sahara. Ask what kind of example she thinks her little sister deserves.

I'm all set to start my rant when there's a knock at the door. Aspen jerks like a startled fawn then races across the room. Remembering who I am, and that a collector is still out there somewhere, I jump to my feet. "Who is it?" I ask her.

Aspen freezes right before she reaches the door, like she's thought of something. "I don't know."

She turns and stares at me, her face giving nothing away. I move quickly and stand in front of her, blocking her body with mine. "Get back," I hiss. Then I turn the handle, pull the door open—

And see Charlie Cooper smiling back at me.

Aspen slaps me on the back, "God, you should see your face! What the hell did you think was out there?"

I hear her words, but I can't think of anything else besides Charlie. She stands perfectly still, her long, slender arms hanging loose by her sides. "Dante," she breathes.

I don't hesitate a moment longer. Scooping her into my arms, I pull her against me. She's so close, but it isn't enough. To touch her is beyond words. Even when we were apart, I carried her soul inside me. But now I have her body, too. And the sensation is enough to make me dizzy with pleasure.

I set her down and run my hands over her cheeks, her neck. I stare at her face and memorize it. We've only been apart for four days, but already I'd forgotten just how amazing she is. "My Charlie," I whisper. Forgetting every strained moment between us, and all the reckless things she's done, I lean down to press my lips to hers.

But before I can kiss her, Annabelle crashes onto the doorstep, an oversized Nike bag slamming into Charlie and me. "You didn't think I'd miss out on the fun, did you?"

Charlie laughs and wraps her arm around my waist, looking now at Aspen. "I can't thank you enough," she says, but I don't miss the way she eyes Aspen, sizing her up.

I can barely grasp the fact that Charlie is here, much less what she's saying. Following her gaze to Aspen, I say, "You did this?"

Aspen smiles at me but keeps a wary eye on Charlie like she might regret her decision. "I asked you if you could have anything…" She shrugs like it's nothing. "Though I don't know how you two do long distance. Blows."

I grin at Aspen, and before I do anything else, I seal her soul so damn hard, I almost feel drowsy. She deserves it, too. Because Aspen doesn't like being alone, and she probably realizes that if Charlie's here, my attention will switch from her to my girlfriend. But she did it, anyway. She flew Charlie and her best friend up here because she knew it'd make me happy.

"So what's going on?" I say to everyone, so happy I'm delirious. "Winter break at the cabin, the four of us?"

"Well…" Charlie responds. The way she says that one word makes my muscles tighten. Eyeing the horn lying against her chest, I realize it wasn't my own charm I felt earlier, but hers. Because she was here. Because she *is* here.

"Just be chill, okay, D-Town?" Annabelle glares at me like she's ready to wrestle if I argue with whatever she's talking about.

But I *don't* know what she's talking about.

Until I see them.

Behind Annabelle, I notice two guys strutting toward the cabin. One is wearing a blue Cubs hat, and the other is throwing me a sly smile, a smile I'm about to break off his damn face. My hands close into fists, and as Charlie tugs on my arm, I head out to meet them.

"There's more," Charlie pleads. "I tried calling you."

She keeps tugging on me, but it's like a butterfly trying to block a bull. I swore I'd try to trust Charlie, but this Salem guy has been playing with her life, influencing her to play dangerous games. And now it's time to pay the fucking piper.

"Wait, listen to me," Charlie says. "Listen to me. You're not going to believe—"

But she doesn't finish, because someone new steps directly into my view.

Charlie stops talking.

My heart stops beating.

The guy looks over my shoulder at Aspen and grins. "Damn, that girl is hot," he says.

Blue says.

⇥ 14 ⇤

BLUE ISN'T BLUE ANYMORE

I stand frozen as Salem and Easton pass by to go inside. Blue continues staring at me, a huge smile plastered on his face.

"How is this…?" I say, trailing off. "I thought you were…"

"Duh-duh-duh-dead?" Blue laughs, his eyes shining with pleasure. "Is that the word you were looking for? You thought I was *dead*?"

I glance behind me, ensuring no one heard him admit he's a walking corpse.

"Don't look so surprised." He stuffs his hands into his pockets and leans back on his heels, looking up at something. "You're not the only *special* person who's walked the earth."

And then the answer comes to me. Dropping down to the ground, I rip the leg of his jeans up. "Ha!" I thump his cuff, somewhat embarrassed I hadn't sensed it before now. "Dead man walking, am I right?" Leaping to my feet, I throw my arms around Blue. I can't help it. I thought the dude died out there, and now he's here, sucking air like a politician. "Wait." I pull away and look him in the eye. "You *are* a liberator, correct?"

"Of course!" Blue's chest swells with pride, and I notice it isn't as small as it used to be. Just looking at him, my body buzzes. I can't seem to wrap my mind around the fact that this is real.

Turning to Charlie, I notice she's trying to cover her smile. So is Annabelle. But Salem, Easton, and Aspen just look lost, which is good. I don't need my assignment or the twin dipshits knowing what's going on.

"I'll be right back," I tell Charlie, reaching in to squeeze her hand. She nods before I pull the door shut behind me and drag Blue off the porch. Though the snow sparkles in the morning sun and my nose fills with the smell of fir trees, I can't seem to relax. Because Blue, who I used to think was six feet under, is standing right in front of me. And that can't be good.

"Why did Big Guy make you into a liberator?" I ask. I've got a string of questions for this dude, and I'm not sure why this is the first.

"More manpower," he responds with an air of professionalism. "I guess."

"More manpower for what?"

Blue shrugs. "Beats me."

Thing is, it doesn't look like the question beats him. It looks like he might know exactly why. But I've got way too many other questions to argue. "How long have you been a liberator?"

He grins. "A few days after I croaked, but I didn't get assigned until about a week ago."

"Assigned?"

"Yeah. I was sent to watch her once you were shipped off to Denver." Blue looks back at the cabin. He's talking about Charlie. The thing I don't understand is why he's got that faraway expression on his face. Then I remember how hot the guy was for her when he was alive. Guess even after death, some things don't change—one of those things being my ability to kick his ass if he hits on her. Though judging from the size of him, it might not be as easy.

"You look different," I say. And now that I've vocalized the thought, I realize exactly how much has changed about Blue. He's got muscle, facial hair, and his curly hair looks less wet dog and more rock star. "You get a liberator makeover special?" I laugh because I'm joking, but his face reddens like I've hit the money. "No. Seriously? You asked to look this way?" I'd heard of collectors making special requests of Lucille before they got cuffed, but always figured it was a myth. Now I'm not so sure it *was* a myth, or that it applied only to collectors.

Blue steps closer. "Seems to me Charlie may have another option when it comes to boyfriends."

My eyebrows furrow because I *know* this guy didn't just challenge my ass.

The corner of Blue's mouth jerks up like he's got a bomb he's about to drop. "Can you hear me now, liberator?"

Those words ring through my head like a gunshot. "You! You were the one who left that message on my mirror!"

"I don't mumble anymore, collector."

"I'm not a collector anymore, pipsqueak." I can't help matching Blue's grin, because even though Blue's threatening my relationship, I'm happy to see he's grown a pair.

Blue rolls his shoulders like he's not sure how to say what's on his mind. "We've got to talk about something."

I glance back to make sure no one's there, because whatever he's about to spill sounds serious. When I turn back around, Blue is rubbing a hand over his jawline, which is crazy, because last I saw he barely had a jawline.

"That Salem guy and his brother, Easton?" Blue says. "I don't like them."

Finally, something the two of us agree on that isn't my girlfriend. "Yes. That! Why hasn't Val or Max gotten Charlie away from them?"

I ask. "By the way, do Red and her bed-buddy even know you're here?"

Blue nods. "Valery knew I'd be assigned before I did. Max found out right before the trip. So did Charlie. Kind of difficult to sport shadow on a plane."

I think back to how many times Valery insisted Charlie was safe, that they had everything taken care of. I guess Blue being assigned to watch my girl was what she meant. It creeps me out that Blue's been following Charlie, *watching* her, without her even knowing. But it was for her protection, I suppose. This also explains why Charlie called me nine times this morning. She must have found out about Blue and couldn't wait to tell me. I grin thinking about this, then stop when I realize Blue is staring at me. And that he still hasn't answered my question about Salem and Easton.

"So why are we letting these skid marks near her?" I ask.

Blue presses his lips together. "At first we thought that the more humans hanging around her, the better. The collectors don't want to chance hurting anyone else. So if she's surrounded by humans outside of school hours, all the better, right?"

"And now?" I ask, feeling my fists tighten. Red and Max may have thought these jokers would help their cause, but I never liked the brothers to begin with. The sooner I can get rid of them, the better.

"Now we're discussing it," he says, "weighing the pros and cons. On one hand, Charlie's whole goal on earth is to continue her charity and do good in people's lives. She likes helping questionable characters, and we can't run them all off. On the other hand, these guys are dicks."

I nod my head and turn my palms up as if to say, *exactly*.

Blue loses his professional composure and sighs. "They keep pressuring her to do crap that…crap that…"

"Crap that most people our age do?" I offer, sharing his frustration.

"Yeah," he says, meeting my eyes.

I groan. "Who even invited them? Not Charlie."

"No clue," he says. "Maybe Annabelle. But why wouldn't Charlie invite them? Aspen stressed that she should bring whoever she wanted. And doesn't it just seem like Charlie to extend an invite to new friends?"

"I still don't understand why we don't run them off. Surround her with other humans, ones that don't influence her to do idiotic things."

"Like rappelling into an underground cave?" Blue offers.

"You better be lying." My blood burns at my temples.

Blue grits his teeth. "I wish I were. It's like they're some adrenaline junkies, and Charlie's just going along for the ride."

I spin on my heel, headed toward the house. I don't care about anything right now but keeping Charlie safe. And if I have to pummel these guys to do that, I will. Blue grabs my arm before I've made it three steps and jerks me back, but it barely slows me down. I mean, Blue is bigger than he was, but he's doesn't have two hundred pounds of muscle spread over six feet, two inches.

"Calm down," Blue clips. "We'll watch them. Tonight, we'll watch them. And if either of them suggests Charlie do something stupid, we'll pummel their asses."

I stop dragging Blue and hesitate. From over my shoulder, I say, "I get to throw the first blow."

Blue laughs. "I can agree to that. Just lay off the protein shakes, Hulk. They put cow piss in that stuff."

I turn around and study Blue for a long time. "You really here?"

"In the flesh," he says.

"You gonna go after my girl?"

"Bet on it."

I laugh, and a puff of air blooms from my mouth and into the cold afternoon. "Let's get inside before your needle dick gets hypothermia."

As Blue and I move toward the house, I catch him looking at me from the corner of his eye. His face is tight with worry, making my stomach flip. I grab his shoulder. "Is there something else you're not telling me?"

Blue bites his bottom lip. Then he shakes his head. "Nope."

"Blue?" I say, squeezing his shoulder tighter.

"Dude, stop freaking. If there was anything else to say, I'd say it." He smiles, and I relax slightly. "Let's get inside. My needle dick hurts something awful."

Deciding to trust Blue for now, I follow him inside and immediately seek Charlie out. She's sitting behind Aspen, braiding her hair. Aspen glances at me like she's not sure how to handle Charlie being so kind, and I wonder if Charlie isn't being nice to compensate for how she eyed Aspen when she got here, like she was ready to throw down to keep her man if need be.

Regardless of why she's being nice, a warm sensation grows in my chest watching Charlie care for Aspen. It almost seems like by caring for Aspen, she's caring for me, though I have no idea why.

Annabelle, who obviously isn't pleased at sharing her bestie, glares at Aspen.

I turn my attention to Salem and Easton, who are spread out on the couch. And then I shoot toward them. Blue thinks I shouldn't confront them, but that doesn't mean I can't remind them who's watching after Charlie now.

I slide in between the pair and turn my head back and forth, grinning just to piss them off.

"Can I help you?" Easton says.

I whip my head away from Salem and stare at Easton. *That* was not what I expected. Easton glares at me for a long moment, and just as I'm about to pop him in his mouth—vow to Blue be damned— Easton throws his head back and laughs.

"I'm sorry," he says, dark eyes dancing. "I was just messing around."

I still want to hit him.

He puts his hand out. "My brother said you caught me looking up at Charlie's window. Man, I'd probably kill someone if they'd done that to my old girlfriend." His eyes glaze over and the smile slides from his face. "I get confused sometimes."

Watching his shoulders droop, I almost feel bad for the guy. But I'm not ready to cut him any slack just yet. "How often do you get confused?"

He winces like I *did* hit him, and then I do feel bad. "Let's just say I'm not real popular with the ladies."

"It's okay," Charlie says from across the room, pulling a rubber-band thingy around Aspen's braid. "It wasn't a big deal. Right, Dante?" She glares at me, and all I can think is how much I want to kiss her.

I glance over at Salem who's looking around the cabin like a kid in an ice cream shop. "Place is so cool," he mutters.

And just like that, I consider that these guys might actually be harmless, and that they're probably not out to *get* Charlie. More like they're a couple of daredevil junkies without a lot of brain cells to spare.

Aspen stands up and moves away from Charlie, reminding me of a nervous cat who's been kicked one too many times and no longer trusts this level of kindness. "I've got an idea for tonight," she says, tilting her head to the side so that we have a better view of her diamond nose ring. "Friend says there's a rave going on down here."

"A rave?" I say. "What is this, the nineties? Do people do that stuff anymore?"

Aspen rolls her eyes, and then for some reason she looks at Blue. "You in?"

Blue's eyes widen to the point of nearly exploding, proving he's not quite as newly confident as he let on. "Me? Yeah, that sounds good. I mean, that could be fun."

"Cool," she says. Then she lights a cigarette and moves to the kitchen.

I get up and stride toward Charlie, no longer able to keep my hands off her. Pulling her to her feet, I wrap her in my arms and press my mouth to her neck. "Can't believe you're really here," I whisper against her skin.

Charlie suddenly tenses in my embrace. "Hey, Aspen," she says, stepping back from me. "Why don't we start prepartying now? Why wait?"

My heart burns like a falling star. It's not from what she said, though her words alone make me cringe. It's that she pulled away. I was holding her against me, and she actually stepped back.

As Charlie all but skips toward Aspen, and Aspen retrieves a bottle of something scandalous, my mouth drops open. I thought I had one girl to keep out of trouble. One. But now—as I watch Charlie reaching for the bottle, and asking where the music's at—I realize I've got *two*.

I'm a stunner.

A champion.

But I've only got two eyes, and I can't keep one on each girl. Even I'm not that good.

As Aspen blasts Modest Mouse, and Charlie grabs her hands to dance, all I can think is, *Ah*, hell, *no*.

Blue looks every bit as worried as I am. And Annabelle just looks pissed off.

And Salem. Well, Salem sends a shiver racing down my back. Because he's staring at Charlie and whispering to his brother like everything is going perfectly. The dude catches me staring, and I straighten.

Then I see it, that gleam in his eye I saw the first time I met him. It tells me he's hiding something. It says that between Charlie becoming someone I don't recognize and Salem eyeing her like she's an objective, tonight isn't going down without someone getting knocked the hell out.

15

PEEKABOO

For the rest of the afternoon, Charlie confuses me. I'll pull her close, and she'll collapse against my chest like it's her home, then tear away and make herself another drink. I'll lay a trail of kisses along her collarbone, working my way up her throat toward her mouth, and she'll turn away before our lips connect.

If she's trying to kill me, it's working.

Once, I tried leading her into a corner to discuss what the hell is going on, but she just released a drunken laugh and said everything was fine. But I know it's not. I see it in her eyes, like she wants nothing more than to accept my affection and to return it—but she won't allow herself the luxury.

When the sun finally sets, the seven of us split up between my lime-green Kia and Blue's rental sedan. I get the pleasure of chauffeuring the two brothers, who stare at Charlie from the backseat and whisper. Glancing at them from the rearview mirror, I reach over and grab Charlie's hand. She lets me hold it, and relief rushes through my body. But I can't completely relax, not when I'm trying to hear what Salem and Easton are saying.

I follow Aspen for twenty minutes before we pull behind what looks to be an abandoned Walmart. Music emanates from the building, and I wonder just how long it'll be before the cops bust this place. Then again, seeing how many broken-down storefronts surround the area, I wonder if anyone actually ever passes by here.

Charlie releases my hand and gets out of the car. Once I kill the engine, I rush toward Blue. "The brothers whispered the whole way over here." I step in close so they don't hear me. "It's setting me on edge, dude."

Blue glares at Salem and Easton, then looks back at me. He breathes out through his nose like he doesn't want to admit what he's about to say. "They've been acting different since we got here."

"How so?" I ask as Annabelle takes pics with Charlie on her camera phone.

Blue shrugs. "When we were back in Peachville, they acted normal. Like they were just some—"

"Idiots?" I offer.

He nods. "Yeah. Exactly. Even on the plane, they were harmless. Just a couple of fuckwads playing with the barf bags."

Aspen waves for us to hurry up and mimes that it's freezing. I hold up a finger. "When they were acting normal, was Max there?"

"Yeah," Blue says. "So?"

"So maybe they play chill while people are watching."

"Maybe." Blue throws a light punch into my shoulder. The action is strange considering how turtle-like he was in life. "Look, collectors can't walk the earth without a cuff. And we don't sense anything, so that means we're cool. Like I said before, Valery thinks it helps having Charlie surrounded by humans, so we watch them like we agreed. And the second they screw up"—Blue smacks his fist into his palm—"pop goes the weasel."

He's got a point. There's not really anything we can do now. We're all on edge knowing I'm harboring Charlie's soul inside my body, and that the collectors could return any moment to try and steal it back. The thing is, that may never happen. Lucille may decide to forget about Charlie's soul and instead concentrate on how to disrupt Trelvator—the hundred years of peace her volunteer work will bring about—as soon as it begins. Makes sense. It'd be a lot more underhanded to lay low and spring up when Big Guy doesn't expect it.

So yeah, chances are Blue and I are letting our imaginations run away with us. Salem and Easton make me nervous, sure. But I can't risk harming an innocent human and having my cuff removed. Because if I'm not here on earth, I can't protect Charlie, should something happen.

Turning back toward the enormous building, I see everyone has gone inside except for Charlie. Even Blue has stopped debating things and is headed toward the door.

Charlie smiles at me, and my feet move toward her before I even know what I'm doing. She's dressed in black tights, knee-high boots, and a short dress with long sleeves. She looks so good, it makes my body ache. I wonder when she got the outfit. I wonder *why* she got the outfit.

She stretches her hand out to me, and her smile widens. For once, I don't question what's happening between us, I just accept her offer and go inside.

The music inside hits me like a summer heat wave. It washes over my body and makes me feel heavier, like I'm rooted to the ground when I wasn't before. Glancing down at Charlie, I realize she's watching me closely. I run my thumb over her cheek.

And she lets go of my hand.

Frustration drowns every other thought I have. The only thing I can focus on now is Charlie moving toward Aspen, who's already found a spot in the limelight. As red and purple lights slash across the dance floor, and a DJ slams tracks between the bouncing bodies,

Aspen dances on a small table. Guys stop what they're doing and stare. She doesn't look back at them, just throws her hips back and forth and gives pieces of herself to anyone who asks. I've seen this before. It's nothing new. What I haven't seen is my own girlfriend climbing onto a table to join the spectacle. Aspen makes room but keeps a cautious eye on her.

Every muscle in my body flexes as I watch Charlie, hair splashing around her, one arm punching the air, eyes closed as she matches the music's tempo. Her birthday may not be for a few more days, but she's certainly dancing and partying as if it's tonight.

When I see a guy in a white v-neck try and get her attention, I decide I've had enough. *Nothing* will stop me from getting Charlie off that table and away from all the surrounding testosterone.

Nothing except Annabelle.

She steps in front of me, a thin red straw between her lips. "Where you going, buster?"

"To get Charlie off that stage." I snarl, trying to step around her.

Annabelle lays a hand on my chest. "Hold up, Romeo. I know you want to be all romantic and show her just how amazingly jealous and petty you are, but have you stopped to think about *why* she's up there on that table?"

"Yeah, it's Salem and his twin taint. They're changing her."

Annabelle frowns in confusion. Then her face relaxes into an expression of contempt. "Oh, man. You're more full of yourself than I gave you credit for." She takes another sip of her drink. After she swallows, she says, "I mean, you really think you can do no wrong."

I glance at Charlie. Easton's moving toward her. He's shorter than his brother but still built like a linebacker. He runs a hand through his dark hair, then steps closer to the table Charlie's dancing on.

"What are you talking about, Annabelle?" I ask. But I'm not really paying attention anymore, because I spy Salem lurking in the corner, watching his brother and talking into his cell phone. His eyes are wide, and each time a purple-red light flashes across him, I see his eyes grow larger, more excited.

"Charlie is doing all of this because of you," Annabelle says. "Because of what happened—"

I don't hear anything else she says.

A storm explodes in my chest and crashes through the rest of my body. Because Easton just handed a drink up to Charlie. And when he did, I saw something peek out from the bottom of his shirtsleeve—a branded tattoo in the shape of an "A."

The same one I spotted on the guy who rammed into me with his car.

The same one I saw on Gage when he straddled the Suzuki.

They're connected.

All of them.

My pulse pounds in my ears as I brush past Annabelle and crash toward Charlie like an avalanche.

MONSTER

"We are each our own devil, and we make this world our hell."
—Oscar Wilde

16

KNOCKOUT CHARLIE

I don't make eye contact with Easton, I just pull Charlie into my arms and race toward the back of the warehouse, searching wildly for Blue.

Charlie takes one look at my face and seems to know something has happened. Her head whips side to side, searching for the cause of my panic. Blue sees me when I'm a few feet away, and his eyes widen. He rushes forward.

Placing Charlie down, I nudge her toward Blue.

"Take her," I tell him. "Get her out of here now." I ready myself to force Blue if I have to, but he doesn't hesitate. Grabbing Charlie's hand, he makes for the door, snaking between dancing bodies.

Spinning around, I search for Aspen and Annabelle. If these flesh-tattooed guys are connected, I know they're probably here for either me or Charlie, but I won't leave the other two girls behind. One is Charlie's best friend, who happens to be a friend of mine, too. And Aspen, well, the moment I saw that tattoo on Easton's arm, I remembered the world I live in is divided by good and evil, and that you can't hide from either. Aspen is my assignment, and if I want to

play for Big Guy's team, I have to liberate her soul. Plus, Aspen is…
Aspen. I can't leave her.

But when I search for Aspen on the table, or Annabelle in the
crowd, I find neither. Now I'm wondering if Blue's made it to the car.
Except I didn't give him the keys.

Damn it!

Vowing to return for the girls, I sprint toward the door Blue and
Charlie left through. As soon as I blast outside and into the winter
night, I spot Blue shielding my girlfriend with his body. Easton and
Salem creep toward him like hyenas, their eyes cold and calculating. I
had hoped we would have time to slip away before the brothers knew
I was onto them, but I guess I screwed that up when I sprinted away
from Easton with Charlie in my arms. Watching them now, I expect
them to sneer. I expect them to hurl insults and divulge their plan.
But they don't. They just skirt closer to Blue and analyze the situation.

Two against one, they seem to decide. *Because there's no way
Charlie can defend herself.*

I slink along the edge of the wall, pulling on my shadow so I can't
be seen. Blue appears to gauge the distance between Easton and
him, between Salem and him. If he waits too long, he won't stand a
chance. To fight, you need room. I hope he knows this. Remembering
the way he was in life—a skinny, mumbling Eeyore—I can't imagine
he does.

But he strikes out like a bolt of lightning, flashing toward Easton
and hitting him once along his jaw. While Easton recovers, Blue
charges toward Salem and slams into him like an eighteen-wheeler.
My chest explodes with pride at how quickly he rebounds and fights
the two brothers. Still, even though he's blowing my freaking mind, I
know he won't be able to hold them off for long. Attacking without
a fear of dying grants you a certain advantage, but that doesn't mean
you can't be overtaken.

I barrel toward Salem. He looks in my direction the moment before an invisible fist connects with his stomach. Down he drops. I shake off my shadow so Blue can see I'm here. Once he does, he concentrates his attention on Easton. The two kick and tear like dogs along the ground, while I drag Salem up and we battle on our feet.

Salem gets two clean shots into my side and face after I turn to check if Charlie's safe. I spin on the eldest brother and wrestle him to the wall.

"Blue, wrap your hands around Easton's throat," I yell. "Squeeze until he stops fighting, but don't kill him."

"Leave him alone," Salem snarls, writhing against me. I manage to hold him in place and hope that behind me, Blue is overpowering Easton.

He must be, because soon after I hear Blue say, "Having trouble breathing?"

"Remember, Blue, not too much," I say, taunting Salem. "Just make sure his brother here answers my questions."

"Got it." His words sound strained, and I know I may only have so long before the brothers break free.

"First question," I say, leaning toward Salem. "Who the hell are you?"

"Screw you."

"Blue, can you squeeze a little tighter?" I say.

There's a short pause before Blue answers with, "Ooh, he doesn't like that one bit."

"Who are you?" I repeat to Salem.

The elder brother glances over my shoulder, and his brow furrows. "You know my name, prick," he says.

"What does that tattoo on your brother's arm mean?"

Salem's eyes snap to mine. I can see the surprise swimming in them.

"Dante?" Charlie says.

"It's okay, angel," I tell her. "We're just getting to know these guys a little better." I shove Salem harder into the wall. "What does the tattoo mean?"

"I don't know what the hell you're talking about," he growls.

"Blue?" I say like a question.

Salem thrashes around like a snared wolf. I grab his shirt and rip. Buttons plink off as I tear the material down.

"What are you doing?" Salem yells.

Finally, I see the flesh-colored tattoo—the brand—I knew I'd find. It's a circle with an "A" in the middle, the sign of anarchy if memory serves. "*This* tattoo." I yell, tired of not getting answers. "Tell me what it means!"

Salem looks at his brother and grinds his teeth. "We all have them. It's a brand. Means we're part of the sirens."

"What the hell is that?"

Salem shakes his head and glares at me. "I don't know, man," he says. "These guys came to us and said they'd fix us up if we did what they asked."

"Fix you up how?" I fire.

"Money. Crap we need." Salem presses his lips together and closes his eyes for a moment. "Money my *family* needs."

"Who asked you to do this? What were their names?" A chill spreads through my body anticipating his response.

Salem opens his eyes and seems to think. "I don't remember."

"Not good enough," I say. "Blue?"

"Stop hurting him, damn it." Salem tries to land a knee into my groin, but I turn my body in time and slam him back against the wall.

"Answer me or your brother gets buried." I look him dead in the eyes, make him see I'm not playing.

"I swear they didn't give us their names. But there was this one guy. He stood near the back. Weird dude. He only talked a few times, but the way he spoke, it was like he was from the sixteen-hundreds or something, saying his words all proper and shit." Salem pauses like he's remembering something else. "He had on these ugly-ass red shoes."

I suck in air between my teeth, because now I know. Rector is back. *The collectors* are back, and they're using humans to do their bidding. The hair on my arms prickles when I remember the way Rector transformed the night he kidnapped Charlie. The way his body and face warped into something closer to demon than human. It made me question how much humanity was left in him, if any. "What did they want you and your brother to do?"

Salem glances at Charlie, and I'm pretty sure I'm seconds away from ripping his throat out. "They said to find her." He nods toward Charlie. "And to…"

"And to what?" I ask quietly, fighting the impulse to scream.

Salem looks at me. "To get her to hurt herself."

I yank my fist back to break his jaw but hear a loud smack before my hand connects with his face. Glancing to my left, I see Charlie shaking her hand out, her face flushed with fury.

I barely have time to process that my girlfriend punched Salem in the face before Blue calls out. I spot Easton backing away from Blue along the ground and getting to his feet. His eyes seek out Charlie, and like a rabid animal, he charges toward her.

Cocking my arm, I rush forward and land a shot clean into Easton's temple. Salem slams into my back at the same time that someone yells from beside us.

Even from the ground, I can see it's Aspen and Annabelle piled into Blue's rental car. Aspen's window is rolled down, and Annabelle is reaching behind her to throw open the back door. Though I'm laid out, I watch as Blue grabs Charlie's hand and races toward the car. He gets her inside and turns back toward me. Salem yanks me to my feet, and a fully recovered Easton plows his fist into my stomach. I double over and groan, wondering how the hell I'm going to get out of here. Not really caring if I do as long as the others are safe.

I plan to wave Aspen on, to tell them to get out of here *now*. But when I look up, I see Blue churning toward the brothers like a tsunami. He slams into Salem, who's holding me upright, and it's just enough time for me to lay into Easton. I only hit him once, then grab Blue's shoulder and run for the sedan.

"Start driving, start driving," I yell to Aspen as we race toward her.

She pushes down on the accelerator, just enough to get the car moving. Seconds later, I dive into the backseat and nearly land on top of Charlie. Blue smashes into me, and Aspen peels out of the parking lot, fishtailing on ice as Blue yanks the door shut behind him.

When I feel the tires hit the road, I breathe a sigh of relief.

"Is anyone badly hurt?" I direct the question to everyone, but I'm looking at Charlie, wrapping my arms around her, touching each place I can to make sure she's whole. She presses against me, and our eyes never waver.

No one says anything for a moment.

Finally, Blue exclaims, "Holy crap."

"Right? That mess was crazy," I say, still looking at Charlie. A bubble of laughter builds in my chest, though I know it's more from nerves than actual humor.

"No, look," Blue barks, pointing behind us. "Isn't that your rental car?"

I turn to look and catch sight of my lime-green Kia Rondo zipping toward us.

"That damn car," I mumble. The assholes must have gotten my keys during the scuffle. When I reach into my back pocket, I find that's not the only thing I lost—my ivory horn is gone. "Aspen, you're going to have to step on it."

Aspen glances in the rearview mirror. "Believe it or not, that POS may be able to outrun us."

I jerk around to look at her. "You've got to be kidding me. That car couldn't outrun a wheelchair."

"Actually, it has a similar engine as this car, and it's lighter. So yeah, it could."

"Just drive, woman," I snap, noticing how fast their headlights are gaining on us.

Aspen doesn't say anything. When I turn back around, I notice her gloved hands are gripping the wheel tighter than before.

"What are we going to do?" Annabelle whispers.

Aspen switches on the radio and flips the stations until she finds what she's looking for.

"What are you doing?" I yell. "Stop messing around."

Heavy, grinding rock blasts through the speakers as Aspen pushes the car faster. "We can't outrun them. Not even with me driving. But we can keep pace for a while. Long enough."

"Long enough for what?" Charlie says. Her voice is even and controlled, and I can't help staring at her, wondering how she can be so calm.

"To get back to my house," Aspen says.

"The cabin? " Blue asks.

"No." Aspen turns the volume up.

"We're going to drive all the way back to Denver?" I ask, watching the headlights behind us, steady in their pursuit. "That'll take almost an hour."

"It won't take near that long," she says over the music. "And in the meantime, you guys can tell me what I'm running from."

17

GONE

The car rushes forward as Aspen awaits our response.

Blue and I stare at each other, and finally, he shrugs. So I tell Aspen what we are. I tell her about Trelvator, and how these guys want to steal Charlie's soul from me, and that I came to Denver on assignment to liberate her soul.

I tell her everything.

At first she doesn't believe us. Then Blue shows her his shadow, and when his body vanishes, Aspen nearly runs off the road. In retrospect, it may not have been our most brilliant plan.

"I feel like I'm going to be sick," Aspen says when I finish talking.

"Just keep driving." I look behind us and notice the headlights of the Kia Rondo are still visible. But despite Aspen's earlier doubt, she's managed to put some distance between the two cars.

"So these guys want Charlie's soul?" Aspen clarifies.

"Yeah," I say. "But when we asked them, they said their orders were to get Charlie to hurt herself, which doesn't make sense, because if the collectors don't have her soul, then why would they risk her dying before they got it back?"

Blue glances at me, worry creasing his brow. He looks away before I can question his expression.

"Maybe they thought if she got injured, I'd return to Alabama, and they'd snag her soul then. 'Course, that doesn't make sense, because they could come after me here in Colorado."

I say all this while staring at Blue. He turns even farther toward the window until it seems like he's trying to hump the passenger door.

Every muscle in my body clenches as I say, "The only other explanation would be if I didn't actually *have* Charlie's soul."

Blue turns and meets my glare.

"And that Salem and his brother," I continue, "*were* trying to get Charlie to kill herself. Because if they already have her soul, that'd be a great way to bring in her body next. No blood on their hands, nothing Big Guy can complain about, and hell gets what it wants—an end to Trelvator and a big screw-you to the god who ordained her birth." I finish my speech but keep my gaze locked on Blue's face. Despite a lump building in my throat, I manage to squeeze out, "How am I doing here?"

Blue holds my stare for a moment longer. Then his eyes drop to the floor.

I press back against the seat. Dark spots swim before my eyes, and the only thing that keeps me from losing it is Charlie's hand wrapped around mine.

Concentrating on breathing, I say, "I don't have her soul."

"I wasn't supposed to tell you," Blue says.

"When did you find out?" My free hand curls into a fist. Though I'm shocked to hear the truth, I always wondered about the sensation of Charlie's soul inside me. I knew something felt off. Souls are difficult to detect inside a collector's body once collected, but I always thought I'd perfected the skill of *knowing*. Flashing back to the airport before I left Alabama, I remember Valery making up lame excuses for why

I couldn't check her soul into heaven yet. I suppose being misled and wishful thinking went a long way in this situation.

I also suddenly remember the night I faced off with Rector and the other collectors, how Rector briefly pressed his chest to mine before fleeing.

How could I have been so stupid?

My anger needs an outlet, so I turn to Blue.

He licks his lips and hesitates like he's afraid to say the wrong thing. "Valery told me right before I came here. She said my assignment had changed. That I was supposed to keep Charlie safe and…"

"And what?" I growl.

Blue eyes the back of Aspen's head. "And ensure you finish your assignment."

I grab him by his collar, thinking I'd very much like to tear his cuff off with my teeth.

"Valery said it's imperative that you liberate Aspen's soul," Blue fires out, his eyes wide. "She used that word, *imperative*. She also said that Big Guy needs you for something important. Something huge. And once you complete this assignment, he'll know he can trust you. "

"And how am I supposed to do that when these guys"—I jab my thumb toward the car speeding after us—"are trying to kill off Charlie?" The moment I say this last line aloud, I let go of Blue. Because now all I'm thinking is that *Charlie* is in the car. And that *Charlie* is probably just now learning all of this.

I turn toward her and notice her eyes are focused on nothing at all. She's gripping my hand so hard, I can feel my pulse in my palm.

"Charlie?" I whisper. "Did you know?"

She shakes her head no but doesn't look at me.

"Don't worry, I won't let anything happen to you." I try to tilt her chin so that she faces me, but she holds still. "Do you hear me? I'm not going to let them lay a single finger on you. So help me, even if I have to—"

"Let me out," Charlie whispers.

"What?" I say.

"Don't be stupid," Annabelle adds through clenched teeth. Guess she's also pissed at Blue for keeping secrets from us.

"Let me out," Charlie says again, louder.

I grab her other hand and press both between my own hands. "You don't understand. They were trying to get you to *kill* yourself. And now they might just do it themselves. So, no, you can't get out of the car. I won't let you."

Charlie looks directly at me, and in her eyes I see a blue fire raging. "I won't sit here while the rest of you risk your lives for me," she says in a voice I've never heard before. She sounds daring, reckless even. "Let me out of this car."

And in that moment, I'm afraid Charlie will get her way. That she'll throw herself onto the rushing pavement if it means her friends are safe.

It's Aspen who speaks next. "Can it, chick. If you're really able to bring a hundred years of peace to this hellhole, then this isn't just about you. Got it?"

Charlie's head whips in Aspen's direction. She stares at her for a long time. And finally, after I feel like I'll burst if she doesn't react, she turns slowly toward her window.

From the corner of my eye, I see Aspen slump in the driver's seat, like she'd been holding her breath and just now released it. "Imperative," she whispers.

"Is it just my imagination," Blue asks, "or are they catching up to us?"

I look out the rear window and decide that, yeah, it does appear they're closer. "Aspen, are we—"

"We'll be there in five minutes." Aspen grabs her phone and texts something. It's a miracle she can do this while driving nearly a hundred miles an hour. It's a miracle this POS rental car can even *go* a hundred miles an hour. She puts her phone away, and, true to her word, I notice soon after that we're nearing her house.

But there's a problem. Before, we had empty roads to sail along. Now we're entering the city, and even at one o'clock on a Friday morning, there are other cars Aspen must weave between.

"Here's how it's going to work," Aspen announces. "At the entrance of my family's house, I'm going to haul ass out of this car, and Blue, you're going to jump in my seat and drive."

"You're ditching us?" Annabelle says.

Aspen glances at her. "Would you blame me?"

Annabelle shakes her head, her face white.

Aspen smiles. "We're almost there. Blue, you ready?"

Blue looks over his shoulder. "They're really close."

"Don't worry about that," Aspen says. "I've got it covered."

I look at Blue. "I'll drive," I tell him. "You just sit tight." I don't know what Aspen plans to do, but I know I need to get Charlie out of here, and if Aspen wants to jump ship she'll do it eventually. I can't stop her. I didn't really expect her to bail on us, but she got us this far after knowing we lied about who we were. And that's more than most people would do.

As we get closer to Aspen's street, a truck parked right outside the entrance comes into view. Aspen slows just enough to make the turn, and when she does, Lincoln sticks his head out the truck window. Guess that answers the question of who Aspen was texting earlier.

Lincoln releases some sort of war cry, and I only have time to notice the lunatic grin on his face before we race past. Then he kicks his truck forward and blocks off the street.

I laugh watching this, though I'm kind of worried what Salem and Easton might do to him. Then again, maybe he can take care of himself. In fact, I'd put money on Lincoln winning almost any fight. When you got enough psycho in you, it isn't hard.

"Get ready," Aspen yells. "We're almost there."

And then we're stopping.

Aspen lunges out of the car and races toward her house.

Before I can make a move, Blue shoves me back and leaps into the front and presses on the accelerator.

"Damn it, Blue," I say.

But he's not hearing me. He turns the car around for some unknown reason, and since this private street is only one way, he punches on the gas to greet Salem and Easton once again. But before we get going too fast, Charlie jumps out of the car.

Blue slams on the brake and even Aspen turns around in confusion as Charlie rushes toward her. Her concern quickly changes to acceptance, though, and she waves us on. "Get out of here," Aspen calls out.

Blue hesitates long enough for me to open the door, because there's no way I'm leaving Charlie behind.

"Trust me!" Aspen screams.

And Blue does.

The car lurches forward, and I'm thrown back in my seat. I nearly lose my fingers when the door bangs shut.

"Stop driving, asshole!" I yell.

Even Annabelle looks like she's not sure if he's doing the right thing. She also looks too scared to speak.

"Stop the damn car," I repeat.

Blue sets his jaw. "We have to take out Salem and Easton."

I think fast. "Yeah, okay. Let Annabelle out. We have Lincoln now," I say, even though Blue doesn't know who Lincoln is. "We three can overtake them."

Blue shakes his head and the speedometer rushes upward. "No. We're going to plow right into them."

"What?"

Annabelle slams her palms onto the roof. "I don't want to die. I can't die. I've never been in love. I've never even had sex. I can't die sexless."

Blue nods. He nods so hard, I'm sure he must pull a muscle in his neck. "We're going to take them out. Right. Now."

Lincoln's truck and the Kia Rondo are pushed together like they're kissing. Black smoke blossoms out from behind the truck's tires, and I realize Lincoln is trying to force their car back. I consider grabbing the wheel to get Blue to stop. But then I think about Charlie and Aspen back there, safe, and how I don't want them touched by these guys. Also, how I wish Annabelle were safe with them, too.

"Let Annabelle out," I say calmly.

"Yeah, let me out," Annabelle says, her voice shaking.

"No," Blue barks and drives faster.

"Blue!" Annabelle says. "Please. Please, I don't want to do this. I don't want to—"

"Turn right," I scream. "Don't hit them, Blue. There's an opening on the right side. Take it! Take it! Blue, trust me like you did Aspen. Take it! Now!"

Blue hesitates, then jerks the wheel to the right just in time. We brush past Lincoln's truck and blast through the black clouds. And seconds later, from outside the back window, I see what I saw before—

A car.

A *different* car.

It's sleek. It's yellow.

It's a Ford Shelby GT 500.

And it's driving toward us, growling like a fucking grizzly bear. Aspen is behind the wheel, and Charlie's in the passenger seat.

"Pull over," I yell.

Blue screeches to a halt. We scramble for the sports car, opening doors and closing them.

Aspen slams on the accelerator.

And we're gone, baby.

We're *gone*.

⇒ 18 ⇐

KISSING A DEMON

We drive for several hours before we're sure we're not being followed, and before our nerves are calmed. Then Aspen pulls into a hotel and rents us rooms for the night—or morning, really.

We decide we'll sleep for a few hours, then get back on the road. We're headed for Peachville because we can't think of anything better to do than to find Valery and Max. Power in numbers and all that. Annabelle encourages me to call Val but I know Blue already has, and I don't feel like dealing with Red tonight.

Now, as I fall back onto my bed, the weight of everything that's happened fills me like lead. All this time I never had her soul. Big Guy had to suspect the collectors would come for Charlie's body next. So why send me on assignment? Blue said my assignment, liberating Aspen, is vital. He said I'm being tested for something big. But what could be more important than keeping watch over Charlie?

Charlie.

I've barely had a single moment alone with her since she arrived at Aspen's cabin. And even though I'm exhausted and starving, all I want to do is be alone with her. But first, I need to talk to Aspen. Once I make sure she's going to stick around, I can focus on Charlie.

Outside Aspen's room, I wait for her to open the door. But she never does, even after I've knocked several times. Then I shake my head, because I know exactly where she is.

I walk across marble floors to the elevator and take it to the first floor. And there—in the corner of the bar, surrounded by a cloud of smoke—is Aspen. As I get closer, I notice she's swiped a blue bottle from behind the counter and has it clutched beneath the table. I slide in next to her.

"Care to share?" I say.

Aspen hands me the bottle without speaking. I take a small sip, and my chest warms. Handing it back to her, I let my hand linger on hers. But she still doesn't turn and look at me.

"Everybody wants something from me." Aspen squeezes her eyes shut. She's wearing the blue eye shadow again. "That's what Lincoln always tells me."

"Aspen—"

"But my soul?" she says, wincing. "You want my *soul*?"

I take my hand away. "It's for heaven. Most people want that."

Aspen's green eyes flash. "That's not the way it's supposed to work, dead people walking around sealing souls. You're supposed to live, and then you go in the dirt." She swallows and looks down at her cigarette. With her mouth turned down and her brow lined with thought, she looks more like a woman than a seventeen-year-old girl. "How does it work? Have you sealed me already?"

I nod. "Once. When you flew Charlie up to see me. That was selfless." I run my hands over my jeans. "I could do it again now. It'd be right after what you did for us back there. Getting us away from Salem and Easton like that? It was amazing."

"Don't you dare," she snaps.

My back stiffens. "Aspen, you want to go to heaven when you die, because the other alternative isn't good. Trust me."

"Just don't." Aspen takes another drag, then stubs out the cigarette in a plastic ashtray. She looks in my direction. "You can't walk away from the things you've done. If you're a bad person, you stay bad. There's no redemption for the wicked, Dante Walker."

I pull away from her, stung silent. Then I pull in a long breath, because everything has suddenly become clear. "What did your father do to you?"

Her eyes flick up. "Screw you."

She rises to get up from the table, but I grab her wrist. "Why do you keep those music boxes?"

"Because I like them," she retorts, pulling back.

I hold tight. "What about the checkerboard?"

Her eyes burn with anger, scorching my insides. I can almost feel heat where I touch her wrist.

I glance at the necklace she wears, the one without the charm. "Did he give you that necklace?"

Aspen rears back and slaps me hard across the face. I let go of her wrist. She spins on her heel to flee, but she only gets a few feet before slamming into Charlie.

Charlie's several inches shorter than Aspen, but right now she looks regal. Aspen stops, her chest rising and falling rapidly, but she doesn't try to dodge Charlie. She just stands there, waiting.

And I do, too.

Slowly, Charlie reaches out. The look on her face isn't one of sympathy. It's one of compassion. Her fingers find Aspen's hands. When I look again, Charlie's removing Aspen's fingerless gloves.

Moving on silent feet, I glance over Aspen's shoulder. Fury detonates inside my body when I see her exposed palms. They're covered in circular pink scars. Almost like someone burned her with cigarettes.

"Did he do that to you?" I growl.

My heart drops like a stone when I notice she's crying.

I step closer, but Charlie holds her hand up. Then she wraps her arm around Aspen's waist. "Let's go to sleep,"

As the two of them move away, I stand dumbfounded, my jaw hanging open like a caveman.

When they disappear around the bend, I think about what I saw. If her father really did that to her, I hope his soul fries in hell. I press my lips together and think about my assignment. It doesn't seem so strange that Big Guy sent me to liberate her now that I have an idea of what she may have gone through at home.

The problem is, I still don't know if I'm the right person for the job.

But who else would understand her the way I do? I think. *We're the same, both wanting parents who see us.*

Though after witnessing the marks on her hands, my own demons don't seem as big anymore. And while her torment is evident, it still doesn't answer the question of why Big Guy wants her to be helped more than every other teen suffering abuse.

I wait a bit longer before making my way back to my room. When I get there, I find Charlie outside my door. I close the distance between us and place my hands on her hips. This time, she lets me pull her as close as I want.

"Is she okay?" I ask. Charlie nods against my chest. "Did her dad do that to her?"

She glances up. "She says he's better now. That he got confused after her mother left."

A snarl builds in my throat. "*Confused*, my ass. I'll kill him."

"She doesn't need vengeance," Charlie says. "She needs someone to care. That's all."

"Lincoln cares," I spit. "People care. She doesn't need that shit stain."

"Leave her alone for now." Charlie squeezes my hand. "Let's go inside."

My anger vanishes when she says those words. Because even though I want to drive back to Denver and leave a body count, I miss my Charlie. I miss her smile and her eagerness to believe the best in people. And I miss her body beneath mine.

Opening my hotel door, I move inside, never letting go of Charlie's hand. It's like I'm worried if I do, she'll pull away again. My heart picks up for a different reason than when I was thinking about Aspen's dad. Because now all I want to do is talk to Charlie. To ask her what's been going on with us. Never did I think this would happen to me, that I'd be the one begging a girl to open up. But emotions turns even a dope cat like me into a dipshit.

I guide Charlie toward the bed. She sits down while I pace in front of her. I seem to do that a lot since I met Charlie Cooper—pace.

Pace like an animal.

Pace like a mad man.

"Why did you get out of the car?" I try to keep my voice even. "When we got to Aspen's? Why did you jump out? You knew that'd scare the crap out of me. You can't do that."

"I knew she wouldn't leave us." Charlie folds her hands in her lap. She looks dignified. And I feel scared shitless. Scared that she doesn't care about me like she used to, which is why it was so easy for her to jump out of the car. Scared that the *I love you*s we exchanged before came too soon.

"How did you know she wouldn't leave?" I demand. "You couldn't have."

Pace, pace, pace.

"I did," she insists. "I couldn't leave her alone."

"What about me? You left *me* alone!" Charlie doesn't say anything, so I keep railing, my voice growing louder with every word. "What if something had happened to you? It's supposed to be you and me. Charlie. Not you and Blue, or you and Aspen. It's supposed to be us. Don't you care about *us*? Don't you care about *me*?"

Charlie stands up and heads toward the door.

"Don't you dare walk out that door," I tell her. I try to sound strong, but my voice shakes. And my legs shake. *Everything* shakes. Because I need an answer from her, and if she leaves now…

Charlie stops. Quietly, so quietly I almost don't hear her, she says, "I can't be who you want me to be."

"What?" I stand frozen, relieved she said something, anything.

Charlie remains silent for several moments. "At the airport, you said you wished I was more like you." She pauses, and I wrack my brain trying to remember what she's talking about. When I *do* remember, my stomach clenches. "I tried, Dante. I met new friends, people I *thought* were friends. I did things I wouldn't normally do. I danced when someone asked and drank when someone offered." She turns around so that we're facing each other. "I dressed differently, I never left a dare unfulfilled, and I thought about myself before others. Instead of watching old movies with Annabelle, I watched the sun rise after partying all night. I became someone I'm not. And I did it all for you." Charlie lets out a long breath. "But I resented you for it. Because the truth is, I don't want to be more like you. I just want to be me. I won't change, and you're always going to want—"

"Stop."

Charlie's mouth stays open, but she doesn't say another word.

"What I said before I left for Denver…" I trail off, because I don't want to screw this up. "I don't want you to change. Since the moment I met you, I knew you weren't like me. You were better. You *are* better. You're the person I wish I could be. Your whole life…it means something. It means something so big that angels and demons are buzzing around you, trying to take some for themselves. You care about people besides yourself. Like, you *really* care. Not because of how it makes you feel, but because of how it makes them feel." I step closer to Charlie. She doesn't move away.

"I love the way you are, Charlie. I love it so much it tears me apart. I think about what would happen if I didn't have you in my life—*you*, the girl you were when I met you—and I feel like I can't breathe." I trace my thumb over the dip below her bottom lip. "All my life, all I've ever wanted was to *take*. But with you, all I want is to give you everything—every creature in the sea, every star in the sky…my own beating heart. I love you, Charlie. Just the way you are, I love you."

I don't care if it's too quick to say those words, or if she ever really felt the same way. Screw it all.

I kiss her.

Her lips move against mine, hesitantly at first, then with hunger. My heart hammers when I grasp that she's not going to pull away this time. I place both hands around her waist and pull her closer. I lose myself in the taste of her lips. Her hair spills over her shoulder, and I breathe in the sweet blossom smell as I trail kisses down her neck. Charlie circles her arms around my neck and leans into me as a fire builds in the pit of my stomach. I feel her fingers digging into my back, and a low moan escapes my mouth as she brushes her hands over my chest, my hips, and just below the waistband of my jeans. Every place she touches me—every place where my lips touch her skin—bursts alive. My hands move up her waist to the top of her back. I press nearer so that I can almost sense our hearts beating in time.

Moving to her ear, I whisper, "I love you, Charlie. I love you."

I can't stop saying it—

Each time I kiss her.

I love you.

Each time her fingers move up the base of my neck and into my hair.

I love you.

When I lift her off her feet and move toward my bed.

I love you.

Charlie lies back on a blanket of white. Her blond hair creates a halo around wide, blue eyes, pink mouth, cream skin—

Open arms.

A lump builds in my throat when I lower myself onto her, parting her thighs. And for a moment, I'm not sure I can do this. It never seems right. The timing is always off. But when Charlie takes my face in her hands and meets my gaze, every uncertain thought fades away.

"If I had a soul," I say. "I'd give it to you."

Charlie pulls me closer so that our lips almost touch. She lays a hand on my face, and her eyes swim with affection. "You may not have my soul, Dante. But you will always have my heart."

And then it's over.

My life as I knew it is over.

Her shirt slides off easily over her head, and my entire body burns in anticipation of feeling her in this new way. With trembling hands, I undo the button on her jeans and guide them off, stopping to kiss the tops of her knees, the insides of her ankle. Charlie leans up and pulls off my shirt, and in slow, gentle movements—in between kisses in new, sensual places—the rest of our clothes fall to the floor.

Charlie slips beneath the white blanket. I join her, my breath coming deep and quick.

I pause over her, staring down at this girl I met months ago with her wide smile and crystal laugh. And her heart. I press my lips to her chest and lay a kiss where I feel it thrumming.

"I'll love you forever," I hear her whisper.

And even though I've said it a hundred times. A thousand. I say it again.

"I love you, angel. Forever."

With my heart overflowing, and a tear slipping down Charlie's cheek—

We are together.

❖⫷ 19 ⫸❖

FOREVER

When I wake up, it's midday. The sun is slipping through the curtains, casting a soft glow over Charlie's bare skin.

As I watch her sleep, curled into the blankets, love seeps from every pore in my body. I hesitate for a moment, taking in the sight of her, safe and blissful, before placing my lips against her shoulder. She makes a small sound and rustles beneath the sheets.

My heart feels as if it's outside my body as it remembers last night. I've never experienced anything like it. It's nowhere near my first time being with a girl, but it's the first time I've been more concerned about the person I was with than how things felt for me. Even now, I can't help worrying about how she'll feel this morning. I may have lost the horn my father gave me, but it's okay because now Charlie and I are connected in this incredible way. I only hope she doesn't regret that connection.

"I need pancakes," I hear Charlie mumble.

I laugh too loud, relieved she seems normal. Laying my arm across her slight frame, I curl my body around hers and breathe in. I can smell the orange scent of her shampoo on the pillow beneath my head.

It's enough to drive me mad with lust all over again.

"Was I not clear about the pancakes?" she says.

Chuckling, I kiss her once, twice on the ear, then move to find her something to eat. As I start to get up, she grabs my hand.

Her eyes connect with mine, and an easy smile glides across her face. "I'm okay."

"I wasn't worried," I say. She raises a single eyebrow, and I know she doesn't believe me. She shouldn't. "You really are all right?"

"Me and you, Dante." She leans back on the pillow. "Just like you said."

"You wanted bacon, correct?" I say, tugging on my jeans.

"Dante."

"A crispy, heaping pile of it. Check. I've got my phone if you need me." I head toward the door, ready to harass whoever I need to in order to feed my woman. But I can't help pausing before I leave the room. "I meant what I said last night, Charlie. *Forever.*"

"Forever," I hear her echo quietly. And then right as I walking through the doorway, she asks. "Dante, do you like the way I look now? I mean, better?"

I step back into the room and make sure she meets my gaze. "You are breathtaking, Charlie. You are stunning now, you know that. But you were stunning before, too. Not everybody could see it, but sometimes that can make a girl so much more appealing. The beauty who doesn't know she's beautiful. The girl everyone seems to ignore, but to the right person she's like this…like this beam of light. You were a beam of light, Charlie," I say. "I'm just sorry it took me so long to see it."

Charlie smiles so big, my heart aches. I hate myself for not telling her this sooner.

"I'm out of Skittles," she says, grinning. "Go and fetch me some, prince."

And so I do.

The door clicks shut behind me. I head toward the elevator, then to the lobby. Though my heart seems to be back in the room with Charlie, I can't stop the concern that creeps in as I move farther away from her. Not just about what happened between us last night, and the question she just asked, but because of what's out there, lurking.

Those people, the sirens, they could be hunting us at this very moment. Before, Salem and Easton's goal was to have Charlie kill herself and call it an accident. Now what? Will they do the job themselves? What about Gage and Lyra? Maybe they know about this Big Something that Blue says Big Guy is testing me for. Perhaps they even know why He wants Aspen so badly. Why else would they have lurked around Aspen, influencing her to sin? They wanted me to fail my assignment. And what about the siren who tried running me off the road? That was all kinds of jacked up.

Dwelling on all this reminds me that I need to check in with Max. See if he's found anything out. For the past few days, all I've done is lose myself in Aspen, embracing her lifestyle instead of helping her. But now I've got to be on my game, and I need all the help I can get.

Digging my phone out of my pocket, I find a quiet corner and call Max's number. As it's ringing, I wonder what it would be like if I lost my phone and someone came across it. They'd have themselves a nice speed-dial list of demons and angels.

I'm smiling to myself, remembering just how amusing I am, when Max picks up.

"Bro," he says, and it sounds like it took everything he had to speak that one single word. I want to ask him if he's all right, but know it's business first.

"The collectors have recruited humans to work for them," I blurt.

Max doesn't say anything.

"Max?"

"You're kidding." His voice perks up. "Are you for real? How do you know?"

I explain everything to him and he *oh, snap*s and *oh, shit*s several times.

"Okay, I'm going to call Val," Max says. "We've got to get to you guys."

"Don't worry about it. I'm calling her now." I pause a beat. "Hey, have you been keeping an eye on her like I asked?"

"Like an eagle, dude. Like a freaking bald-assed eagle."

"So have you learned anything?" I ask. "Like something she's hiding?"

"Oh, that," he says. "No, not really." I realize Max just basically admitted to stalking his own fiancée. "Oh, wait. I heard her saying something on the phone the other day. Something about *stoles*, whatever that means."

"Stoles?" I say, confused. Then I remember something. "Do you mean *scrolls*?"

"Oh, yeah. Scrolls." Max clears his throat. "Twin scrolls. It was something about one being in heaven's possession and the other being in hell. Apparently no one can read what they say. I think, like, Lucille and Big Guy can read them, but that's it. So the rest of us are in the dark about what the H is going on. Which is awesome."

Twin scrolls that can't be read by anyone other than the kings— the thought makes my skin crawl.

"Anything else?" I ask.

"Valery barely talks to me," he mumbles.

I rub a hand over my face. Max is my best friend, but when humans are trying to hurt or kill Charlie, I don't really have time for his love life concerns. "Max—"

"I know. We'll talk later. Not over the phone," he says. "Too painful."

"Call me if you hear anything else." I roll my eyes. "And try to stay cool about Valery, man. You guys will be fine."

"You think?" he says, his voice sounding very much like an eight-year-old girl's.

"Got to go, dude."

Max grumbles and hangs up the phone. Seconds later, I'm ringing Red. I woke up ten minutes ago, but already I feel like we need to get moving. I can't be stagnant when the collectors and sirens are out there. Red picks up on the second ring.

I fill her in on everything that's happened, and just like Max, she agrees we need to get to one another.

"We thought about booking a flight to get home faster," I say. "But we didn't want to be stuck in one place too long."

"No, that's good," Valery says. Her voice is almost back to normal, though I can picture the worry lines etched across her face. No one expected this. The collectors returning? Sure. But them playing with humans? Lucille is obviously getting less wary of igniting war. "I'll call Kraven and get you guys back here quickly."

"The dude with wings?" I ask, enjoying the fact that Red used our nickname for ex-Boss Man even though it's out of character for her formal fashion.

"Yeah, Dante. The dude with wings."

"He going to fly us out of here on his back?"

Valery doesn't respond to that. She doesn't like talking about Kraven's ability to wing out. Probably because she doesn't know how he does it, or why he can do it when she can't. "I'll get back to you soon."

"Hey, Red," I say. "Thanks for telling me about Blue. That was swell of you."

"Charlie wanted to tell you herself," Valery explains. "Besides, I wasn't very pleased with him after he paid you a visit in Denver."

Well, that's something. At least Valery was pissed that Blue screwed with me by writing creepiness on my hotel mirror. Ass. Though it would have been nice if she'd admitted she knew it was him when I expressed concern that night. Or if she had, I don't know, told me she knew I didn't have Charlie's soul.

"You know, I guess the sirens are after me, right?" I say, testing her. "I mean, they just want Charlie's soul back."

Valery doesn't say anything.

"Hello?" I say, sarcasm dripping from my voice. "Did our connection go bad or something?"

"Blue told me you know," Valery finally says. "Look, Dante, we just found out ourselves. Kraven paid you a visit a few nights ago and reported back that you didn't have her soul. But we didn't want to say anything until we were sure the collectors had it."

I don't ask when Creeper Kraven paid me a visit, or how they finally figured everything out. I don't care. "You should have told me. The second you suspected, I should have known."

"I wasn't allowed to. There's structure among the liberators," she says. "I've told you this before, but you have no idea how bureaucratic it can be."

"Angels and red tape, who knew?" I growl, my temper rising. "You know what? Maybe I'll take Charlie and run. If the sirens found us, it won't be long before the collectors do, too. If you guys won't keep me in the loop, then it's time for me to work alone. And let me tell you, my gut says to get Charlie out of the country without an assignment or a new liberator tagging along."

"Listen to me," Valery snaps. "Aspen's safety is Charlie's safety. Understand?"

"No, I don't understand that at all!"

Valery sighs. "Look, I promise I'll try to keep you more in the loop. I know you care about Charlie, and you've made a lot of changes that prove it."

Guilt sits in my stomach like a hot coal. Because how much have I really changed when all it took was for Charlie to be out of sight for me to revert back to my old ways? "It's okay," I say, finding it hard to speak. "I know Big Guy can't divulge everything, but you've got to tell me this: what are the twin scrolls?"

"Who told you?" Valery barks.

"Who cares?" I respond, happy to have surprised her. "What are they?"

Red pauses. "I'm not supposed to—"

"Yeah, yeah. Hierarchy and bureaucracy and paperwork and all that crap. Just forget it; I'll figure it out on my own." I'm being difficult, but I'm also giving Red an out, because I really don't want her to get slapped around for not playing Honorable Liberator. I know she respects the system, and nothing I say is going to change that.

So it surprises me when Valery speaks next. "The twin scrolls are two separate documents, both with the same exact verbiage, created centuries ago," she says, her voice hesitant. "When Lucille was cast out of heaven, and he stole the dargon which made our cuffs, he also stole one of the scrolls. I've been told he can read it, but that none of the other demons can."

My mind whirls. I can't believe Valery knows that Lucille stole the remainder of Big Guy's dargon. I figured that was a story only I knew, but I guess Big Guy is more generous with the information.

"What Lucille doesn't know," Red continues, "is that whatever was written on the document he stole was *meant* for him. God knew he'd steal it, and it was intended as a last-chance sort of thing."

"Last chance?"

"Right. God decided he wanted Lucille to know about his plans for humankind's future. His thinking, if I understand this correctly, was that if Lucille allowed God's plans to continue without interrupting them, then he would be allowed back into heaven."

"Why would Big Guy give him that chance?"

"Because he's merciful."

"Because he's *vengeful*," I respond. "Because he can't wait to kick Lucille back down when he fails."

"One day, you'll get it, Dante," Valery says. "But I'm not going to try and convince you how amazing he is."

"Oh, so you've met him?"

Nothing.

"Didn't think so."

"I've got to go." she says. "I'll talk to Kraven. We'll get you back here. Just take care of yourself."

I hang up, and only after the line is dead do I realize Valery told me to take care of myself. Not Annabelle or Aspen or even Charlie. Myself. I'm not sure how Big Guy operates, but some of his liberators are pretty cool, I decide. And maybe that means something.

Stuffing the phone in my pocket, I see Blue walking toward me. I'm still furious that he kept the secret of Charlie's soul from me. I mean, Valery has her recent promotion to protect, so I know she doesn't want to mess anything up. But Blue? He's a new liberator like me. I thought we were friends. Kind of.

As he gets closer, I forget about my anger and instead remember what took place in my room last night. If he knew about Charlie and me, how would he react? It doesn't matter, because I'd never tell him, or anyone else for that matter. That moment was between us, and I don't want to share a single piece of it.

"Hey," Blue says, wiping powdered sugar off his mouth. I glance down and see a package of mini doughnuts in his hand. Guess some things never change. "I wanted to apologize for not telling you about Charlie's soul. I almost told you outside Aspen's cabin."

"So why didn't you?"

Blue's gaze falls to the floor, and some of my irritation dissipates. He runs a hand through his curly hair. "I'm trying to believe in Big Guy's plan."

"That's it?" I say. "That's all you got?"

Blue's head snaps up. "If he has a plan that includes keeping Charlie safe, then I'm all in, no matter who gets hurt in the process. *She's* my priority. Got it?"

I raise my hands. "All right, Casanova. Keep your dick in your pants." Some dudes would be insecure that Blue felt the need to protect their girl, but I'm relieved. If anything were ever to happen to me, he'd die before he let something bad befall Charlie. He's already died for her once.

Blue grins. "We cool?"

I bump his fist. "We're cool. But next time I'll pop you in the mouth, foreskin." Glancing around, I say, "Have you seen Aspen? We need to get a move on."

"I was just thinking that," Blue says. "I'll go get Annabelle and Aspen up and meet you down here in ten. Cool?"

I nod, and he starts to walk away. Then I remember something. "Hey, where'd you get the doughnuts?"

He cocks his head toward the front of the lobby. "Vending machine."

After draining the contraption of mini doughnuts, glazed cinnamon rolls, and Skittles, I head back toward my room. I open the door as quietly as I can and find Charlie curled in the bed, snoring softly.

I smile to myself...until I remember.

Until I remember that her soul is gone. For some reason while standing over the bed, my arms filled with junk food, I remember with painful clarity that it's my fault. That I'm the reason she collected sin seals, and the reason she forfeited her soul so that Rector, the head collector, would spare my life. The collectors and sirens are trying to kill Charlie, and it's my fault.

My heart aches inside my chest.

I did this to her. But I will undo it.

No matter what it takes, I think. *I will get her soul back.*

Brightly colored packages fall to the floor. Something is happening, something *horrible*. A ripping sensation spreads over my back, and my ears ring. My entire body feels like it's turning inside out, like my ribs are pushing their way through my spine. And I can smell something burning. It *burns*.

I faintly grasp that Charlie is beside me, calling my name, but I can hardly hear her. Someone is screaming. *I'm* screaming.

Wrapping my arms around my body, I fall to the floor. I roll to my side and cry out. Charlie runs from the room. The pain still comes, faster, stronger. Bones snapping. Muscles tearing.

I'm being torn apart.

I scream until my lungs explode, until I can't breathe.

⚜ 20 ⚜

LOOK AT HER GO

My mind repeats the mantra over and over.

Stop-stop-stop!

And then, suddenly, the pain is gone.

Blue rushes in with Charlie at his heel. He grabs my arm and tugs me to my feet. A wave of dizziness sweeps over me, but other than that, I'm fine.

"He was screaming," Charlie says, her voice shaking. She wraps her arm around my waist, and the two of them lead me toward the bed. I sit down.

"What happened?" Blue asks. He holds a hand to my forehead like he's my mom. I slap it away.

"I don't have a fever, idiot," I say. "I just…"

I just what? Almost broke in half? Spilled my guts onto the swirly carpet? Deep in my mind, I know what just took place, but I don't want to say anything. Not now. Not until I'm sure.

"I just had a cramp," I say, realizing how ridiculous it sounds.

Better than, *I think wings just tried to shoot out of my back.*

Charlie eyes me in a way that says she isn't buying it. But she doesn't push me, either. "Just tell us you're okay."

"Screw that," Blue interrupts. "Tell us what the hell you were screaming about, because I'm pretty sure it wasn't a cramp."

For the next several minutes, he asks the same question, and I repeat the same answer—I had a cramp. It's strange, but the only person I want to talk to right now is Valery. And I trust that she'll stay true to her word and get to us soon.

"Let it go, Blue," I growl. "I'll talk to Valery about my muscle spasms."

Moments later, Annabelle and Aspen enter, bickering about who knows what. "They've been at each other's throats all morning," Blue offers, though he's still watching me uncertainly. I wonder if, like Max and me, he's thought about Rector's and Kraven's wings. I'm not sure. But if he has, he may suspect what I just experienced. Thankfully, he seems to be letting it go. Me, on the other hand, I'm having a full-blown panic attack and trying hard to hide it.

As Annabelle calls Aspen some sort of name—that sounds something like *hussy*—Charlie disappears into the bathroom. She returns with a wet towel and runs it over my brow. The towel reminds me of when a collector knocked Max out with a fire extinguisher, leaving him to spend the night with a hotel towel pressed to his head. That was the same night I told him that I was going to go against Lucille's orders to collect her soul.

"We need to go." I get to my feet and wobble for a second. Charlie grabs my arm. "Aspen, you got your keys?"

Aspen gives Annabelle one final repulsed look before facing me. "Yeah, I got them."

"Then let's head out." I try to play it cool, but inside, my heart still pounds.

As we walk toward Aspen's car, Blue keeps an eye on me. He

seems genuinely concerned, and I can't say I hate knowing he cares. But all I can think about, regardless of who is worried about me, are those damn wings. I want them, but I don't want to experience that torture again. For now, to calm my twisting stomach, I try to think about something else. About Charlie. About Valery telling me Aspen's safety is Charlie's safety. About Grams and her water bottles full of vodka. Whatever.

It doesn't really work. Not as we crawl into the car and buckle up. Not as Aspen heads east toward Alabama. Not even when night tumbles in through the windows.

And much later, when we're leaving a shady diner after grubbing down, I'm still thinking about it.

Charlie squeezes my hand, and even though every light in the oversized parking lot is burned out, I know every curve of her face well enough to still see it perfectly.

"You've been quiet," she says.

I grip her hand and pull her closer. In front of us, Annabelle and Aspen argue over whether black-and-white movies are amazing or archaic. Blue walks a few feet behind like he's waiting for the pair to transition from verbal zingers to hair pulling. He wants a front-row seat for that show, and I don't blame him.

"I know what happened back there," Charlie says. "I know why you were screaming."

I stop midstride.

She curls herself against me and wraps her arms around my waist. Staring up at me, she moves her hands to my shoulder blades. Her fingers run over the place where I felt the most pain, but now all I feel are goose bumps raising along my skin. I close my eyes against her touch and lean my head down toward her neck.

"Are you afraid?" she asks. "That it'll happen again?"

Yes.

"No," I say, my voice gruff.

Behind me, I hear the sound of car doors being opened and know that soon the Three Stooges will break up our moment. But for now, I let Charlie soothe me and try to do the same for her.

When the sound of Aspen's voice finally rings out, it doesn't surprise me. What does surprise me is her tone. Behind Charlie, I notice four figures neatly hidden in the shadows.

I hold Charlie tighter, slowly turning our bodies so that I'm between them and her. Bending down, I take her heart-shaped face in my hands. I press my lips to her honeysuckle mouth—

And then I push her back toward safety and explode toward the shadows.

Blue is there a second later, his fist connecting with Gage's stomach.

I hit Salem once before the other three—Easton, Gage, and Lyra—are on me like cockroaches. I punch and kick and receive a burst of adrenaline when Charlie screams. One glance in her direction tells me Annabelle's holding her in place, and though Charlie is fighting to get loose and help our cause, Annabelle is much stronger.

Thank Big Guy for that.

Agony detonates from all sides of my body as the four sirens throw their fists into my muscles, my bones. At some point I hear the crack of my cell phone in my pocket and know it's DOA. Blue tries to help fight, but it isn't enough. We're two against four, and we'll be lucky if we can get the three girls out of here unharmed.

Remembering Charlie's life may be on the line, I ignore the pain and focus on one siren at a time. The first person I see is Lyra. I pause for only a beat before pulling my arm back, because I'm not above hitting a chick if she's trying kill Charlie. But before my hand connects, Lyra gets laid out.

I mean, she gets—

Laid.

The.

Fuck.

Out.

Standing over her, causing everyone to stop and stare, is Aspen. With fury dancing in her green eyes, and a touch of red glowing against her dark clothing, she looks very much like a black widow ready to strike.

"Get that bitch," Gage yells to Easton, and the way he says it, with such urgency, it's like Aspen was their target all along.

Blue tries to stop him when he rushes by, but Easton's suddenly Adrian Peterson, spinning like a ballerina and finding an opening. Before I can warn Aspen to get back, he's on her.

And then *he's* laid out, too.

Aspen's hands are raised like she's Bruce Lee, like she can't wait to slaughter the next person who's dumb enough to come at her. And all I'm thinking is, *how is this chick able to fight better than I am?*

While Salem is distracted, I throw a punch into his gut and bring him to the ground. He's back on his feet in seconds, and now he and his brother, who has recovered, are on me. My back hits the concrete, and pebbles dig into my skin as Easton whips his leg into my ribs. From the ground, I see a silhouette over the brothers' backs. It's Aspen; she's back for more.

She chops the side of her hand into Salem's neck, and he drops like a fallen tree. Easton whirls around and goes for Aspen's throat. No matter. She just spins her arms in and out, deflecting his hands and throwing her fist into his kidney.

"Hope you piss blood for a month," she spits.

Next, she lands a kick on Lyra's side before returning to Gage. She's like a tornado, taking out everything in her path with controlled rage.

Blue pulls me to my feet. As soon as I'm up, I move to help Aspen, but he blocks me with his arm. "Look at her," he says, wiping blood from the corner of his mouth. "She's amazing."

I hesitate, watching this girl with fingerless gloves among four sirens, beating them back with the same effort she might use to paint her nails. She doesn't even need our help. And Blue's right—she's amazing.

Charlie finally gets away from Annabelle and races toward me. I meet her halfway and hold her back with even more strength than her best friend used.

"We've got to get you out of here," I say, eyeing Annabelle, hoping she understands I mean for her to take Aspen's car and go. "We'll get Aspen and be right behind you." Spinning around, I see Blue has joined the fight again, and adrenaline floods through me. "Go," I tell Charlie, trying to push her back toward Annabelle.

"Like hell I will," Charlie yells. Like a rabbit struggling against a coyote, she somehow breaks free and bounds toward Aspen.

"Charlie!" I charge after her until I hear the sound of a car approaching. I imagine it's the owner of the diner, or the cops. How long have we been fighting the sirens? It feels like hours but has probably only been a couple of minutes.

A green 4Runner rips across the parking lot. Someone leaps out of the driver's side.

Max!

Max gets to Charlie before I do. He reserves none of the gentleness I bestowed her before. Instead, he throws the tiny girl over his shoulder and rushes toward the SUV.

"No, wait," I call out, relief rushing over me that he's really here. My best friend is here. "Take Aspen's car."

He glances at the Ford Shelby. "Oh, damn," he says before changing course and running toward the car. He corrals Charlie into the back, and Annabelle gets in the front.

"Blue," Max calls out. "Get in the car."

Blue looks at Max and then goes right back to pulling Lyra off Aspen.

"Blue, now!" Max thunders. His voice holds a ring of authority I've never heard before.

This time Blue listens. He jumps in the back with Charlie.

Now it's my turn to get Aspen. I sprint toward her. After throwing one last right hook into Salem's temple, she dashes away, yanking the keys out of her pocket and tossing them to me as she runs.

Aspen jumps into the back, and Max dives over Charlie's, Aspen's, and Blue's laps. They groan from the weight as I start the engine and slam on the gas. In the rearview, I see the four sirens jogging behind the diner, probably headed to Gage's BMW.

"What's the plan, Max?" I ask. "We probably don't have long."

"Take the freeway east for six miles, exit at Lancaster, and take a right," he instructs from the backseat. "There's a plane waiting."

I nod. "How the hell did you find us?"

"The tracker in your phone, duh." Max giggles like a child from the backseat.

"My damn phone had a tracker?" I growl, glad it's gone now. "Who did that?"

"Dude, seriously?"

And yeah, I guess he doesn't need to say anything else. Valery is the one who insisted Charlie and I get phones, and that she'd buy them for us. I roll my eyes and decide to let it slide, considering Max just got us out of there safely.

I take the exit and pull into a small landing area. There's only one small plane, painted creamy white with a maroon racing stripe. The side reads, BUCK'S PLANE CORP.

I throw the muscle car into park and get out. Soon the six of us are loaded onto the plane, and Buck himself is zooming us down the runway. Aspen stares through a window at the car we're ditching, and a ball of guilt bubbles in my chest. She's left behind many things for us—her sister Sahara, her friend Lincoln, and a damn fine car. I'd like to seal her soul as a thank-you but decide to respect her wishes and let her be.

I turn to Charlie. She puts a hand on my leg, and I give a weak smile as the plane lifts from the tarmac and into the air. Behind us, Blue is drilling Aspen with questions. *Where did she learn to fight?* and *Can she teach him those moves?* And a bit quieter, *Is she okay? Is she sure?*

I focus on the ground rushing by beneath us and ponder the same questions. But more than anything, I wonder why the sirens fought Aspen like there was nothing more important than taking her down. I study Aspen, this girl that's surprised me more than once.

Who are you?

Glancing back at the runway, I don't see Gage's car or any sight of the sirens. And for some reason, that bothers me more than if I did.

21

FADE

Outside the window of the private plane, the clouds are even with the wings. It's always my favorite part of a flight, where it looks like you could step outside and take a nap on spongy softness.

When Charlie drifts to sleep, Max moves closer. It's the first time I've really looked at him since we took off minutes earlier. Worry creases the space between his eyes, and his mouth is turned down. I motion for him to take the seat on my other side.

"What's wrong?" I whisper, not wanting to wake Charlie.

Max shakes his head. "It's Valery."

I should have known. Max just busted us out of a dire situation James Bond style, and he's worried about a girl. Still, he's my dude. And if he needs someone to listen, I want to be there for him, regardless of what else is happening.

"Talk to me." I lean back against the head rest and give him my full attention.

He looks down at his hands. "We were supposed to get married, right? But I guess Valery got notice that she couldn't shack up with a collector. Doesn't matter that I haven't been an active collector in what feels like forever. No, all they care about is where I got my cuff."

I put a hand on my friend's shoulder. "So much for free will and all that. I mean, really. That's a load of crap."

"That's what I said. I mean, look at you and Charlie. Why is that allowed?" Max raises his head. "Thought things were supposed to be different on the other side. I always heard Big Guy didn't discriminate and was forgiving and stuff."

"So what are you going to do?"

He shrugs. "What can I do? Val says we need to take some time. That maybe Big Guy will see that I'm not going to return to my old ways, even though that means Lucille will tear me to shreds if his guys find me. But I didn't know *take some time* meant we weren't even going to touch each other. It's like we're not even engaged anymore."

Guilt hits me like a thunderbolt. I've been so caught up in Charlie that I've neglected a friend who's needed me. "Hey, I'm here, right? I know I haven't really been available, but I'm here now." I bump his shoulder with mine. "Is there anything I can do?"

Max presses his lips together. "Nah, man. It's cool of you to offer, though."

I expect Max to appear less burdened after talking about Red, but he doesn't. In fact, it appears as if he's still holding something back.

"Max?" I ask. "Is that all that's bothering you?"

His eyes flick to where Charlie's sleeping. He bites his lip.

I straighten in my seat. "What? Tell me."

Max glances once more at her and then leans in. "I was going to tell her as soon as she woke up. Her grandma—err, Grams—she's not doing well."

My stomach drops. "She's always been sick."

"She's worse," Max says. "It's like she was waiting for Charlie to be gone."

"How bad is it?"

Max's gaze falls away, and my insides twist. This can't be happening. Not with everything else going on. Not when Charlie needs the familiarity of home and those who love her. Plus, I like Grams. For an oldie, she's freaking awesome. And I don't want...

"Have you guys taken her somewhere?" I ask. "A hospital or something?"

Max sighs. "She won't go. And quite frankly, she seems tired of Valery and me stopping by. She thinks we're a part of Charlie's volunteer organization—that Hands Helping Hands thing—so she's been nice. But I think she's ready for the visitors to stop. Some lady came by and has been staying with her."

"Irene?" I ask, remembering Charlie telling me about her Grams's friend.

"Yeah, that's her name. Irene was running interference this morning, wouldn't let us see her even once."

My nails dig into my palms. How am I going to tell Charlie this? I glance at her and try to keep my hands to myself. She needs to sleep. She needs to have this last bit of peace before her world is crushed.

• • •

Every nerve in my body is firing when we pull up outside Charlie's house. *We shouldn't be here*, I think. Not when the collectors and sirens are ready to strike. What's more, ever since I learned the true whereabouts of Charlie's soul, I've been obsessed with stealing it back. It's the only offensive action I can think to take. Though just considering returning to hell makes my bones ache. I remember the stairs leading down into the mouth of hell, and what's behind them, and I shudder.

I shake my head. Charlie needs this moment with her Grams, and I won't be the one to tell her she can't have it. And if I'm being honest,

I want to see Grams, too. When I think about how *much* I want to see her, it scares me. It's been years since Dad died in my arms, and I don't know how I'll handle it if Grams dies, too.

Though neither Max nor I have breathed a word, I sense Charlie knows something's up. Aspen and Annabelle aren't at each other's throats anymore, and with Blue staring blankly out the window, it seems like everything has stopped.

I step out of the silver Tahoe Valery picked us up in, and Charlie gets out after me.

After rolling down the window, Red says, "I'm going to take everyone back to the hotel Max and I are staying at. You guys should pack some of Charlie's things. We're sitting ducks if we stay here too long."

Then Valery looks at Charlie with sad eyes. I have to make a face at her to stop being so damn obvious.

When the Tahoe pulls away, Charlie wraps her arms around her waist. "Everyone knows, I guess."

"Knows what?" I manage to say.

"That she's dying."

My jaw drops open, and Charlie spins to face me.

"Don't look at me like that," she says. "Do you think I'm stupid? Do you think I don't know she's sick? That I don't hear the way you guys whisper every time she comes in the room?"

"Angel—"

"Don't call me that! There are no angels here tonight."

Her words are a cold slap. But they also make her more real, more reachable. Charlie has always been *better* than the rest of us, but in this moment, she seems less like a child sent to save the world, and more like a woman losing the only family she has.

Charlie takes my hand, and we head inside. Irene meets us at the door. The woman has to be less than five feet tall, and with her black beehive, she totally reminds me of the chick in that old movie *Poltergeist.*

Irene points at me but looks at Charlie. "Who's this?"

"My boyfriend," Charlie answers, her eyes on the staircase that leads to Grams's room.

I get the slightest rush hearing Charlie call me her boyfriend. It reminds me that she'll have someone after her Grams is gone. Since I'm immortal, she'll *always* have someone, even when she's the old woman in the bed.

This last thought is jarring, thinking of Charlie leaving this earth. Will I be able to see her…after? Though it's something that won't take place for decades, it already has my mind reeling. An equally disturbing thought is the one where Charlie ages, and I remain forever seventeen. How will it ever work for us?

"She's upstairs," Irene says before pulling Charlie into a quick hug. "She's not well, sweetie. Say nice things to her."

Say good-bye, is what she means.

Somewhere between stepping out of the Tahoe and entering this house, I built a wall around myself. I will not feel. I will not care.

I will not let this hurt me.

If I can keep telling myself these things, then it won't be so bad.

Irene excuses herself and shuffles into the kitchen. As Charlie and I ascend the stairs, I concentrate on the sound of Irene rattling dishes. It's easier to think about what's behind me than about what's waiting in Grams's room.

Charlie pauses outside the door, and I hook my thumbs into my belt, fidget with the skull buckle. I think about what I should say. *It's going to be okay* or *She could get better* or *Everything happens for a reason.*

Each adage sounds like horse crap in my head, so I can't imagine what it'd sound like out loud. Instead of speaking, I press a kiss to Charlie's temple and open the door for her.

The inside of the Grams's room smells sour. My first thought is an anxious one, because there's no way Charlie can't smell it, and I know it's going to upset her. We edge closer to the narrow bed and find Grams resting on her side. She's facing a window on the opposite wall and has her back to us. I imagine she's looking out the window, just taking in the night sky, maybe thinking about what to make for breakfast when the sun rises.

But I know better.

Charlie touches Grams on the shoulder, and the slim lump beneath the quilt stirs. Slowly, she rolls over. Her face is the color of old bread.

"Hey, darling," she mumbles, "and Man Child."

Hearing my old nickname sends affection through me. I note the pill bottles sitting on her nightstand and wonder what she has taken, and how many.

"Grams," Charlie says, her voice breaking over that one word. There's a chair near the bed. Charlie drops down into it. The two take each other's hands, and I glance away. A part of me feels like I shouldn't be here, like I'm an intruder.

"I should call someone," Charlie says.

Grams manages a small smile. "So beautiful."

Charlie's head dips, and I remember that I should be doing something, anything. I move closer and rub my hand over her arm.

"Why are you comforting *her*?" Grams asks. "I'm the one who's dying."

My head whips in the old woman's direction, and I find she's still smiling. I'm happy to see her this way, but part of me wants to scream. "What can I do?" I whisper.

"Exactly what you're doing." Grams winces, and something in my chest cracks. Her blue-gray eyes meet mine. "Keep doing exactly what you're doing, you understand me, Man Child?"

I nod and squeeze my eyes shut. I know what she's asking of me, and it's a request I can easily fulfill, because I'll always be here for Charlie.

Charlie glances up, and when I see her face streaked with tears, my internal barriers nearly crumble. Grams is dying. *Grams*. The woman who loves Charlie the way I do, perhaps more, if that's possible. The person who adopted an orphaned girl and insisted they treat each another like biological family.

"Her soul?" Charlie whispers.

The muscles in my back clench. I know what she's asking, but I'm afraid. Afraid of what I'll see, and of whether I can do anything about it. The last time I checked Grams's soul light, it was partially obscured by sin seals. That was months ago. Could things have changed?

"What are you talking about, Charlie?" Grams's eyes slip closed as she speaks.

Gathering what resolve I have, I flip her soul light on.

And breathe a sigh of relief.

There's no change. Her soul light has numerous sin seals, but plenty of light still shines through. In fact, I see a couple of pink liberator seals over some of the sin seals. I almost smile, imagining Valery sneaking in what she could. "Her soul will go to Judgment," I say gently.

Charlie jumps to her feet. "That's not good enough."

Soft snoring wafts from the bed, telling me Grams won't hear the rest of our conversation. "I can't…" I start. "I don't know what I could do for her now. It's okay, Charlie. Most people go to Judgment. She's lived a good life, and she'll be rewarded for it."

She shakes her head. "No. No, you're going to make sure of it. I won't let her go without knowing."

What Charlie's saying is almost too much to bear. Because the one thing I need in order to seal her soul for heaven is something she doesn't have—time.

I open my mouth to tell Charlie there's nothing I can do, but I can't find the words.

Charlie meets my stare for a long time. Then she turns and leaves the room. I hear a sob break from her throat before the door shuts.

Then it's just me and Grams.

I sit down in the chair and reach for her hand. When I give her hand a gentle squeeze, Grams's eyelids flutter before closing once again. I should be unsettled to be alone with this old woman who's dying. I should feel out of place. But when Charlie left the room, it's like she took my heart with her. Now I'm empty.

Grams grips my hand, and I look down at our overlapping fingers. "Can you hear me?" I ask.

Nothing.

I swallow. "I'll do what you said. I'll be there for her anytime she needs me."

When Grams doesn't respond for the second time, I get up to leave the room.

"At least I know she'll be taken care of," Grams mutters.

My emotions threaten to overwhelm me, but I remind myself that I'm not really here. That no matter what she says, it doesn't hurt, because I don't care.

I don't care.

"That's right," I respond. "I'll always take care of Charlie."

Then I do leave, because there's nothing left to be done. If it were up to me, I'd call for an ambulance. I'd make Grams fight for her life so that I could have more time to ensure her soul is liberated. But from looking at her, I know she's past the point of getting well again.

And she's Charlie's Grams, not mine. If the woman wants to be warm in her bed, then she should at least have that.

When I get downstairs, Irene tells me Charlie is in the backyard. I move to go after her, but Irene blocks my path. "Give her space."

I consider pushing past her, but something tells me the woman is ready to throw down. So I let it go and make a place for myself on the couch. Irene strolls back into the kitchen to do whatever it is she's doing in there. I stare off into space, wracking my brain, trying to think of something I could have done differently.

It isn't until much later, while Charlie is still outside, that the smallest glimmer of an idea tickles my brain.

I'm on my feet in a flash.

Bounding up the stairs even faster.

⛄ 22 ⛄

MAYBE I SHOULD BELIEVE, TOO

I burst into Grams's room, not even attempting to be quiet.

"Wake up," I say. "Please."

The blankets rustle, and I help her along, pulling them down toward her feet. She's wearing a purple silk nightgown that makes it seem like she prepared for this moment. Like she said to herself, "I'm not going out underdressed. Bring me my finest robes."

I'm shocked at how frail she's become. She's always been thin, far thinner than any woman over sixty should be, but now she's a wisp.

"Grams, you have to wake up." I give up trying to rouse her with my voice, and instead give her shoulders a firm shake. This is her soul we're talking about, after all.

The movement does the trick, because before long, her eyelids drift open. "Man Child," she says, her lips tugging upward.

I sit down into the chair. "Tell me what you meant earlier."

"Hmm...?"

"When you said, 'At least I know she'll be taken care of,' what did you mean?"

She doesn't say anything, and I'm afraid she's fallen back asleep. "Grams?"

"I meant you'll be there for her," she says, her eyes meeting mine. "You said so."

My heart drops. "Is that all?"

She nods. "And the house, of course. She'll have that, too."

I grin. "Her inheritance. You have a will, and it leaves everything to her. Is that right?"

"It isn't much," she says. "The house, my car. A bit of money at First Peachville Bank. The rest will come from my life insurance."

Charlie told me her Grams once did makeup for the stars. It must have netted her a good income for her to have paid off the house and car and still have enough for retirement.

"Grams, I need you to listen," I say. "I'm going to ask you to do something that you may not want to do."

She looks at me expectantly, her thin lips parted. "Where's Charlie?"

I eye the medicine bottles near her bed again. "I know this is hard, but it's really important that you try and focus. I don't want to have to press when you're not well, but…" I shake my head. "Have you ever thought about what will happen after…after this is over?"

She works her jaw.

"You may not think there's an afterlife. But I do. In fact, I *know* there's an afterlife. For you, for me—for all of us." I fill my lungs and plunge forward. "I need you to believe what I'm telling you. I need you to believe it so much that you're willing to prove it."

She looks at me, her eyes narrowed. Finally, after I've convinced myself she won't answer, she asks, "How would I prove it?"

I smile. I can't help it. This may not work, but at least she's not tossing me out. "You say you have a will, and that it leaves everything to Charlie."

Grams nods, but I can tell she's getting tired. Her eyelids droop, and her mouth falls open wider.

"Why did you leave everything to her?" I ask.

Grams closes her eyes. "Because she's my Charlie."

"Because you love her," I say.

Grams smiles.

"What if I asked you to give it to someone else?"

Her eyes pop back open, alert this time. She narrows those blue-grays at me. "Why are you saying this?"

My pulse pounds, but I push on, hoping she'll continue to listen. "You're leaving everything to Charlie because she's given something back to you—love, companionship. Whatever. But if you were to leave everything to someone you'd never met? Well, that would be charitable in a big way. Huge."

Maybe enough to tip the scales during Judgment.

"You're trying to take my money," she accuses, pulling back in the bed. Fear rushes through me that I'm losing her. I want to show her my ability to shadow, or maybe my cuff, something that will convince her of who I am and what I'm trying to accomplish. But I can't. Because then it wouldn't be the same. She has to do this on her own—on faith.

I ignore her accusation. "If you believe in an afterlife, if you want to spend an eternity where Charlie can eventually join you, then do this. Believe when I tell you there's life after this one, and that you can live it well. Do this, Grams. Please."

She looks at me like I'm crazy, and my insides tie themselves into knots as I await her response.

When she turns away from me and faces the window, I know I've lost her.

But then.

Then she says something—

"What would you have me do?"

My heart threatens to break open, but I seal it tight. *Don't let anything in or anything out,* I remind myself. *Then it won't hurt.*

I glance around the room and find paper and pen. "I'm going to tell you what I'm writing, okay?" I tell her. She doesn't say anything, so I start writing and reading aloud. "*This is the last will and testament of...*" I stop and look at Grams. My face flushes in the dark. "What's your full name, Grams?"

She takes a labored breath. "Mary Ann Geraldine Carpenter."

"That's a good name," I say with a smile. "*This is the last will and testament of Mary Ann Geraldine Carpenter. As my last request, I would like to leave my entire estate including, but not limited to, my home, vehicle, furniture, and any money, to someone in dire need—to be chosen by my adoptive daughter, Charlie Cooper.*"

Grams watches me. She doesn't smile, but she doesn't turn away, either. "I like that last part. About Charlie choosing who it goes to."

My legal contract is completely phony, but that doesn't matter. I just need to make Grams believe it's real. "Will you sign it?" I ask. "I'll take care of her. She won't want for anything. You can trust me."

Grams stops watching me and glances away. Her eyes find the ceiling, as if looking for a sign there. "Did Charlie ever tell you that before she met you, she was thinking about shutting down her charity?"

My stomach twists.

Grams raises a hand to the base of her throat. "She wasn't sure if it was really helping anyone. And I guess no one new had signed up in several months. But then you came along, and suddenly that girl thought she could change the world. Every second you weren't here, she was working on that charity. Hanging flyers, making a God-awful website, calling local businesses to see if they'd partner with her." Grams looks me dead in the eye. "You made her believe again, so maybe I should believe you now."

Every wall I'd put up, every protection I had in place to guard my heart, shatters into jagged little pieces. I can't stop *feeling*. Can't stop hearing what she just told me. Tears slip down my cheeks as Grams reaches for the piece of paper. She signs and hands it back. Grams is a good woman. Someone I care about. And as sorrow hits me like a wrecking ball, I realize I don't want her to go. Not now. Not ever.

Yet there's nothing I can do.

Except.

I stand from the chair and let my head fall back. Then I reach down, down into myself—further than I thought possible—and I tear away a seal and jerk it out. I nearly cry out from pain as it leaves my chest. When I look down, my vision is blurred with tears. But I can still make out the blue seal floating toward Grams's torso.

Her face lights up when she sees it.

She sees it!

Warmth floods the room as her soul light flips on. Nearer and nearer the seal floats, and when it finally attaches to her soul, the room explodes in brilliance. I gasp and stumble backward as the blue crawls, destroying every last sin seal and wrapping her soul in an embrace.

Her soul cracks away from her body in a rush, like it's eager to escape, and blazes into my body.

I fall back onto the floor.

The sensation—it's overpowering.

Liberating a soul doesn't feel the same as collecting. No. This feels different. It feels like *bliss*. Every day, I've resented getting assigned to liberate Aspen's soul. But now I know with overwhelming certainty that I will complete the task. I want this same freedom for her. I want to feel her soul—heavy, tortured—spring from her body with vigor.

"Mary Ann," I breathe, my voice breaking on her name.

She looks at me from her bed. I don't know what I expect her to say. She saw what I did. I mean, she *saw* it. So I can't imagine what's going through her head, or what questions she'll have. But when she speaks, she only has one request. "I want to see my granddaughter."

⤝ 23 ⤞

THE HIVE

The next day, when both hands on the clock pointed straight toward the sky, Mary Ann Geraldine Carpenter died.

Charlie was inconsolable at first, but she was also comforted that Grams was taken at high noon. "She liked her lunch hour," Charlie said afterward. "Sometimes we skipped breakfast, and most times Grams ordered in for dinner. But lunch? If we were both home, Grams loved cooking the 'high meal for highborn girls.' Sometimes she'd make hot tea and swear we were both English."

Now, sitting beside Charlie in the church pew, I fumble with how to feel. I don't want this pain for Charlie, but it helps to know Grams's soul is where it belongs. Though Charlie hasn't mentioned it, I know she realizes what I did, and I also know it's helped her cope.

I run my hand over the back of Charlie's head, and her eyes slip closed. My touch seems to bring her comfort, so I never take my hands away. When the pastor gives the eulogy, I trace circles over her back. When several of Grams's friends speak from behind the podium, I squeeze each of her individual fingers, all ten of them, over and over. And when finally the organist begins playing, and people around us whisper the word *cancer*, I run my fingertips over the back of her neck.

I do all of this for her.

But I also do it for myself. Because seeing Grams in a coffin is destroying me.

Hours later, when Grams has finally been laid to rest, Charlie and I walk hand in hand toward a black sedan. Valery and Max are in a car behind us, and Annabelle, Aspen, and Blue keep their distance in a vehicle a few yards back. After I've tucked Charlie into the seat, Valery makes a motion for me to join her. I don't want to leave Charlie, not now, but I also realize every moment we spend in Peachville is a risk in itself. It's a wonder the collectors haven't descended on us already.

I duck my head into the sedan. "I'm going to talk to Red for a minute. Will you be okay?"

Charlie stares ahead, her face absent of makeup, her slight frame shrouded in black. She nods.

I run my hand over her hair once, then I shut the door and make my way toward Valery and Max. While walking in their direction, Aspen catches my eye. It reminds me that I have questions for her. Questions like, *Who the hell taught you to fight?* But that's a mystery for another time.

When I get nearer to Valery, I notice her eyes are puffy and swollen, though her mascara-junk is pristine. Max touches Red's arm like he's trying to console her, but she doesn't reciprocate.

"I'm sorry about Charlie's guardian," Valery says.

"Why are you saying that to me?" I respond. "She wasn't *my* family."

Red purses her lips. "I know you cared about her."

I glance back at the car Charlie is in and shrug. "We need to get her out of here." My chest aches saying this aloud. Like Charlie, I don't want to go anywhere. Because it feels like if we leave, it's really over. Grams is really gone.

Valery nods. "What do you want to do, Dante?"

"You're asking me?"

She turns her palms up.

I run a hand over the back of my neck. Should I tell her what I'm thinking? What I'd really like to do? Or should I keep it to myself so she doesn't interrupt my plan? Eyeing the newly etched gravestone to my right, I decide to trust Valery the way Grams did me.

"I want to get Charlie's soul back." I straighten. "I'm *going* to get her soul back."

Maybe I'm mistaken, but I imagine I see the corner of Val's mouth twitch upward.

"Won't Rector have already turned her soul in downstairs?" Max puts in.

Red meets my gaze. "Probably so."

I swallow what she's saying...what I already suspected. "Her soul is in hell."

Valery doesn't even blink. "Yes."

"Then that's where I'll go." I say the words, but I'm not sure I really think about what it will be like—the beast with the gaping mouth or the room of nightmares.

"What?" Max gasps.

"Good," Valery says, clearly smiling now.

Max looks at his fiancée—ex-fiancée?—like she's lost her freaking mind. "Am I the only sane one here? What are we even talking about? We keep Charlie safe. She does her job on earth and lives a long life. That's the deal."

"And then what?" I bark.

Max flinches. "And then she'll—"

"And then she'll join her soul in hell for all eternity, Max."

He sighs and shakes his head. "So that's our only option? We send you, my best friend, into hell where they'll slaughter you on sight?"

"We'll prepare him," Valery says.

"Yeah? How's that?" Max is pacing now, running his hands through his hair.

Valery looks me in the eye. "At our training facility—at the Hive."

I remember overhearing Red mentioning the Hive at the Birmingham Airport, but I have no idea what it is. Doesn't matter. It sounds like we're on the same page, and that's all I need. "Will this place help get me into hell unnoticed? Our shadow doesn't work down there, you know."

She raises an overplucked brow. "They'll help you," she says. "Just get Charlie packed, and I'll meet you at her house in a half hour."

I motion toward the car a few lengths back, where Aspen, Annabelle, and Blue linger. "What about them?"

"Aspen will come, too, so you can complete your assignment," she says. I don't tell her that I'd demand she come, that after liberating Grams's soul I can't imagine not doing the same for Aspen. "Blue also," Valery continues. "He's one of us."

"And Annabelle?" I ask.

"She has no place there, Dante. She's better off far away from us until everything is safe."

I shake my head. "Annabelle has to come. She knows too much. The collectors could use her to get to Charlie."

Valery's face falls like she hadn't thought of this. Then she glances at Max. He shrugs. "Bring her then," she says with a hint of defeat. "I'll talk to her parents. Reference a school field trip or something."

Wet grass squishes under my heel as I turn and head toward Charlie. For once, I don't waste time asking more questions. I just want to make progress. As I slide into the seat next to my girlfriend, I wonder how much to tell her. *Just enough*, I decide. Secrets in a relationship are never good, even I know that, but if she knew I wanted to steal her soul back from hell, she'd flip. So I tell her we're headed to some place called the Hive, another one of Val's mysteries. And that we'll be safe there.

She agrees to go. Or rather, she doesn't protest.

My arm slips around her shoulder, and I pull her against my side. Charlie lays her head on my shoulder, and I kiss the crown of her head. Her hair is cool beneath my lips. Even in Alabama, winter has made a full appearance, and though there isn't snow like there was in Denver, the air still has a cold bite. I run my hand over the top of her head and then over her ears, trying to warm her body. Then I tell the driver we're ready.

We take off toward Charlie's neighborhood, where an empty house waits.

Happy holidays.

• • •

Later that evening, after packing everyone's things and catching a flight to Oregon, we're nearly at the Hive. Valery, Max, Charlie, and I are in a black SUV in front, and Blue, Annabelle, and Aspen follow along behind us. Our two matching vehicles make us look like we're Mafiosi, and if we hadn't had such a gut-wrenching morning, I'm sure Max and I would be cracking jokes.

Red steers our car down a dirt path that's crooked as the devil's backbone. When I spot the place Valery says is the Hive, I'm not sure how to react. In my head, I'd imagined a vast fortress-like home, one with a massive gate and soaring doors and guards in uniform. Maybe a moat too, because that'd be totally kickass.

Instead, I see a house that's enjoyed one too many lines of freebase crack. The entire estate is enormous, but that's the only part that meets my expectations. Gables rise up in sporadic spots like zits, and the entire place is a painter's canvas: one piece blue, another yellow, another green, and a small area in the back shaded deep purple. Dozens of lights dot the outside, as if the owner is afraid guests might pass the house altogether and drive straight into the sea.

The oddest thing though, isn't any of these quirks. It's that the place looks like someone strung several different houses together to make one. A castle made of cardboard.

"I'm almost afraid to ask, but who lives here?" I ask, leaning forward to get a better view.

"Dracula," Max answers. "Count Dracula with Alzheimer's."

"This place was built recently," Valery interjects. "It had to be put together quickly."

"Looks like the high-class craftsmanship of carnies." I glance at Charlie. She's staring out the side window, not paying attention to where we are. I grip her knee, and her head jerks in my direction. She smiles, but the gesture slides off her face as soon as she realizes what she's doing. It's like ever since Grams passed, she won't allow herself to be happy. Like if she does, she'll be admitting life can be good again. And she's not ready for that yet.

Valery pulls closer to the mansion and throws the SUV in park. We file out of the vehicle, Charlie last. The seven of us gaze up at the house. I can smell the ocean in the distance. The salt wraps around my body, making my skin feel tight, and already I want to shower. I can do big cities, and small cities, and the even the occasional mountaintop is cool. But oceans are ridiculous. They take up way too much space in this overcrowded world and are filled with creatures that have several sets of teeth, like one row of man-eating teeth isn't enough. And just to add insult to injury, all that water isn't even drinkable. If you ask me, the ocean is kind of a prick.

Max leads the way toward the front door, even though he made it clear during the trip that he's never been here before. In fact, he made it clear about a hundred times. I don't think he's pleased that Valery never told him about the Hive. That makes two of us, but I'm trying to accept that Red can't share everything she knows. *Trying* being the key word.

When we get to the main door, Max raises his hand to knock.

"That won't do anything." Valery pulls a skeleton key from her purse. After a quick snapping sound, she pushes the door open. We file past her and into an entrance area with a black-and-white tiled floor that's covered with dust. *Built recently*, my arse.

When I look up from the grimy floor, my jaw drops.

There are seventeen doors in total, and it seems the room's sole purpose is to confuse guests when deciding which to take. Some doors are three stories up, with narrow, winding staircases stretching toward them. Others are wide and sit along the floor, so short I'd have to bend to enter. Similar to the exterior of the house, each door is painted a different color. The overall impression reminds me of a carnival funhouse.

"Before we go any farther, I need your phones," Valery says. "They have trackers in them, and we don't want anyone picking up the signal. It was a gamble we had to take before, but not now."

"It was a gamble *you* had to take," Blue mumbles, slapping his cell into her palm. I guess I wasn't the only one who didn't know Valery was tracking our asses.

Charlie hands over her phone, and then Red turns to Aspen and Max. "Phones," she demands.

I can't help but laugh when Aspen and Max look equally shocked.

"How on earth did you bug my phone?" Aspen asks with a note of approval.

At the same time, Max says, "Woman, you're so hot."

"If you guys don't have phones," Annabelle interjects, "how am I supposed to call my parents? My mom will come looking for us. With a shotgun."

Valery pulls on a green-and-white earring shaped like a ladybug. "I've informed her that there will be times when she can't reach you. After all, college prep classes take a lot of studying. And with senior year fast approaching, parents need to become accustomed to their children being independent."

Annabelle balks. "*That's* what you told them? There's no way they bought that! Then again, my mom would eat that up, wouldn't she—me spending my winter break studying?"

After dismissing Annabelle's disbelief, and ensuring she has us all in proper hostage fashion, Valery spins on her heel, approaches a set of rickety stairs, and climbs. She arrives at a green door on the second story and then slides in the key.

"What is this place?" Aspen asks.

I spin around and look at her. She almost surprises me standing there, her diamond nose ring winking in the dim light. Ever since Charlie arrived in Denver, it's been hard to concentrate on anything else. My cheeks warming, I remember our last conversation ended with Aspen's hand whipping across my face. I still recall how I felt in Grams's room, and I'm determined to liberate her soul. Assignment or no, I want to ensure her afterlife is secure. She meets my gaze and doesn't look away. I can't tell whether she's forgiven me for pushing her about her father.

Someone's hand slips into mine. Charlie. My heart leaps at seeing this small sign of life, and I waste no time gripping her fingers, reminding her that I'm here.

Valery doesn't answer Aspen. She just opens the door, and we follow behind. On the other side are more doors, and when Valery opens yet another one, there are even more behind that. Each room holds the obnoxious scent of fresh paint, and I wonder how often the doors are painted.

Altogether, there are three sets of doors beyond the entrance, all various colors distracting the eye. *Like a poisonous flower*, I think. When we move through the last door, I'm relieved to find a large open room. The smell of paint is gone, replaced by a faint lemon scent. The ceiling has thick white beams, and the floor is constructed of aged wood. In the center of the room is a long table with fourteen chairs. And at one end, facing us with knowing eyes, is someone I've seen before. He looks to be about twenty years old but carries himself like a king.

"Kraven," Valery says.

The guy rises and strides toward us, his shoulders squared. He's dressed all in white, which is pretty bold, even for an angel. "I had started to worry," he says. He sounds exactly like he did the night Rector attacked. His voice is alarmingly calm, like nothing has ever frazzled him.

He sounds like I did before I fell for Charlie.

"We stayed in Peachville a few extra days for…" Valery's eyes dart toward Charlie.

"Right," Kraven answers.

I keep staring at Kraven's shoulders, disappointed that I don't see wings peeking above them. Do they come out of his back like they almost did for me? If so, how does that even happen?

Kraven looks at each of us in turn starting with me. His eyes linger on my face for a long while, like he's considering what to say, if anything. After a moment, he moves to Charlie. "How are you?" he asks. His tone is so sincere that I decide I may not hate the guy. Not that I ever did, but I do have a serious case of wing envy. I mean, Max and I have been talking about this dude ever since That Night.

Charlie nods, and I wrap my arm around her waist. Kraven studies my arm there, but I don't remove it. If he has issues with PDA, his conservative ass can look elsewhere.

Next, the dude in white moves to Aspen. He looks at her with disinterest. "The assignment?" he asks.

Valery nods. "Yes. Her name's Aspen."

Aspen tilts her chin up like she's not about to be dismissed, but Kraven doesn't notice; he's already moved on to Blue. *Not much to see there*, he must decide, because he quickly steps away from Blue and closer to Max.

"Why is he here?" Kraven asks. Though Cyborg Guy doesn't show much emotion, even I can tell he's pissed to find a collector among us.

"He doesn't work for them anymore. And he knows too much," Valery says, stealing my line from earlier. "We were afraid the collectors would use him to learn information about Charlie."

"Can we trust him?" he asks.

Max straightens. "You can trust me."

Kraven pushes his shoulder-length blond hair behind his ears. Then his gaze comes to a rest on Annabelle. Anna barely acknowledges him. Not at first, anyway. Not until his hands curl into fists and he says, "Another human?"

Annabelle meets his glare and, God love her, cocks a hand on her hip. "And?" She does a little head bob, and I can't help the laugh that bursts from my chest.

Kraven continues to stare at Annabelle.

He doesn't blink. He doesn't speak. He just stares.

"Dude," Annabelle says, breaking the silence, "you're totally creeping me out."

Kraven finally looks at Valery, awaiting an explanation. "Same situation as Max," Red says. "She knew too much."

"*Why* did she know too much? Him I understand." Kraven jerks his head toward Max. "But *her*?"

"Excuse me," Annabelle says. "I don't know how you liberators roll, but on earth we have friends. And Charlie? She's the best I've got. So yeah, she told me about you guys. Get over it."

My breath catches. I always knew Annabelle had some balls, but I never knew they were gold plated.

Kraven's eyes rake over Annabelle.

She stands her ground.

Something passes over his face, unreadable. Then he strides away from us.

Annabelle glances at Valery. "What's up with Crazy Face?"

The sound of Kraven's voice crashes through the room. "Training starts at oh-seven-hundred. I suggest you get some sleep."

⇒ 24 ⇐

CLOSER

Valery guides us down several hallways and flights of stairs until I'm sure I could never get back to the great room. There are people at every turn—humans. I suspect they don't know about liberators and collectors and sirens. It probably isn't hard to find employees willing to leave questions unanswered as long as they're offered an easy job with good pay, though it's startling to know collectors aren't the only ones engaging humans in our earthly endeavors.

Red unlocks yet another door. "There's a lounge room here," she says, waving her arm. "And bedrooms that branch off of it."

I'm beginning to understand why they call this place the Hive. It's a honeycomb of rooms, doors, and hallways, and probably serves to protect its inhabitants. "Hey, Red," I say. "How are you guys so sure the collectors don't know about this place?"

She turns and faces me, her high heels tapping against the wood floors. "They probably do. No matter where we built, they would find it. So we did what we could and designed it so that only a few people would know their way around."

I cross my arms over my chest. "So if someone breaks in, they're more likely to get lost than cause trouble."

"That's the idea."

Blue collapses onto a leather couch. I know the feeling; I'm exhausted, too. The rest of the lounge room is sprinkled with dilapidated chairs, oversized ottomans, and more couches. Nothing matches, but it all appears comfortable. I notice there aren't any windows, and that I haven't seen a single one since we stepped foot inside the house.

As Annabelle and Charlie curl up on a love seat, I continue to drill Valery. "You said this place was created recently, but how recently?"

Red shrugs. "I'm not really sure. I was given blueprints to memorize a few weeks ago and told a training facility was being constructed. I think it's part of something…bigger."

"This place?" I ask.

She nods.

I think about what Blue said, that Big Guy has huge plans for me, and that Aspen is a test to see if I can be trusted. Could this house, the Hive, also be a part of this plan? If Valery thinks so, then I could believe it.

"I'm going to bed," Red announces. "I'll wake you for training in the morning." She glides toward the door. *Click, click, click* go her heels. Max follows behind her like a stray and Red pauses at the door. I watch Valery to see how she'll react. Her eyes travel over his face, and then she leaves, but not before cocking her head in the direction of the hallway.

Max bounds after her.

After the couple makes their exit, I find a huge beanbag thingy and plunk down. The Styrofoam shells give a satisfying crackle as they settle around my oversized frame. Above my head is a single blinking string of multicolored Christmas lights. The liberators really go all out to celebrate JC's b-day.

Aspen is sitting next to Blue, and Annabelle and Charlie face them. With Valery gone, we all just kind of stare at one another. What do we say when we've never had a conversation without sirens trying to kill us?

Blue cranes his neck to look at Aspen. "Dude."

Her eyebrow quirks upward. "Yes?"

"Where did you learn to fight like that?"

Annabelle snorts, and Blue glances at her. "What?" he asks.

She shifts next to Charlie, pulling one of her long legs beneath her. "That's what you want to talk about right now? Not, *where the hell are we*? Or, *Does this place have rabies*? Or even, *What is up with that freakazoid, Kraven?*" Annabelle pulls her finger up. "No, no. Blue just wants to know about Aspen's nunchuck skills."

"Um, I don't own nunchucks," Aspen says.

Blue looks at her. "Maybe you should."

"That's ridiculous."

"Where'd you learn to fight like that?" he presses.

Aspen bites her bottom lip. "Lincoln."

Blue laughs. "Now who's being ridiculous?"

She sighs. "Not the president, asshole. My friend. His name is Lincoln. His dad is in the CIA or FBI or some crap like that. He taught him self-defense." Aspen shrugs. "So then Lincoln taught me."

"It'd be a lot cooler if it'd been ole Abraham who taught you," Annabelle says.

Charlie laughs. We all look at her. "Am I not allowed to laugh?" she asks.

Our hands suddenly become extremely interesting.

"Come on," Charlie adds. "It was a joke. Stop treating me like I'm an invalid."

Aspen stands up. "In that case, why don't you get off your rear and do something?"

I'm out of my seat in a flash. "Aspen," I say, a note of warning in my voice.

Aspen reaches her hand out to Charlie. "I'm starving. Help me find something to eat, O Savior of the World."

My heart leaps when Charlie grins and takes Aspen's hand. The two head toward the door like a pair of misfits.

"You're going to get lost," Annabelle warns.

Aspen doesn't turn around. "So come with us."

Annabelle rolls her eyes. "Fine, but only because you'll bring back crap food if I don't." She rises from the love seat and shoves herself between Aspen and Charlie so that she can be closer to her best friend—and maybe to remind Aspen that Charlie already *has* a best friend.

I glance at Blue. He sighs and then gets up to follow them.

"You, too?" I say.

Blue shrugs. "You want to try and convince them not to leave? Go for it. Otherwise, we might as well make sure they get back okay."

Annabelle and Aspen whip around together.

"Like we need your help," one says.

"Just stay here," the other barks.

You'd think Annabelle and Aspen would get along a little better considering they both scare the crap out of me.

Blue and I trail after the girls, and exactly forty-seven minutes later, we make it back to our room with stomachs full of junk food. Annabelle punches a victorious arm into the air and tells us to *eat it*, even though she got us more lost than anyone. After making a big show of yawning, she and Blue wander off to bed, her through one door and him through another. Aspen looks at Charlie and me for a moment after they leave.

"It's good you two have each other," she says. Then she leaves the room in search of sleep.

Charlie glances up at me. "I like her."

"You like everyone."

"Do not," she rebuts, grinning.

My black heart sings, seeing her smiling and eating and playing normally, but I know she's far from happy. And realizing how hard this day has been for her tears me up inside. I run my thumbs over the side of her cheeks and step closer. "How are you doing?"

Her gaze falls.

Instead of pushing for an answer, I take her hand and guide her toward a door in the far corner. Together, we spill into a small room with humble furniture: a queen-sized bed with a patchwork blanket, an oak nightstand, and a cushioned bench. I spot another door and assume it's a bathroom; probably one we'll share with Annabelle who's one room over.

Charlie lets go of my hand and climbs into bed. Her hair falls over her neck, which I know bugs her. At one point, she reaches up to nudge her glasses like she sometimes does. But the glasses aren't there anymore post makeover. Still, I find the gesture reassuring, like the Charlie I fell for, the girl who wore bad glasses and purple jeans, is still in there.

The bed groans as I lie down next to her, and I brush the hair from her neck. I lean down and kiss the bare spot. I don't expect Charlie to respond, not after what she's been through today. But I want her to know she's not alone, and that I'll be here to kiss any wound that needs healing.

"Your birthday is coming up," I whisper near her ear. "I'm going to do something amazing for you." I'm not sure why I bring this up, maybe to remind her that there are days to look forward to. And that no matter how chaotic things become, I'll fight to ensure she retains some normalcy.

Charlie curls into a tight ball. "I just want her back."

Hearing the pain in her voice, I've never felt so useless. I will take out any siren who tries to harm her. I will fight my way into hell to reclaim her soul. I will risk my life and everything I have to keep her safe.

But I don't know how to protect her from this.

Charlie drops her shoulder back so we're facing each other. Then she reaches up and cups her hand around the back of my neck.

Our lips connect.

She pulls my body nearer, and warmth wraps itself around us. My hand slides from her arm, to her hip, my fingers taking in every rise and valley of her silhouette. Slipping my leg between her knees, I tug her against me. Charlie's palms skim up the back of my shirt. Her fingers dig into the muscle beneath my dragon ink. Deep in my gut, a primal instinct awakens. I didn't expect this from her. But I understand it. She needs me close, close enough to remind her she's alive and that she won't lose someone else she cares about.

This is something I can do.

As her fingers swim through my hair, I move on top of her. I reach down, hook my arm beneath her knee, and press down. Her mouth comes away from mine, and she trails her lips down my neck to the place between my collarbones. She moves to my ear and nibbles. The sensation drives me absolutely bat shit. Before I can think, I'm tugging our clothes off.

Charlie buries her head in my neck and pulls me tight, tight enough to lose herself in this moment. Our stomachs press together, and her skin feels like silk beneath me. Sliding my hands beneath her back, I curl my fingers around her shoulders.

And then I'm the one pulling her closer.

Closer.

⊰ 25 ⊱

DEFENSE

I wake to the sensation of being watched. When I glance at the foot of the bed and realize it's not my imagination, I spring to my feet.

Two women stand shoulder to shoulder, outfitted in brown knee-length dresses. They don't speak; they just stare.

Charlie stirs from the bed, and I rush to shield her with my body.

"What are you doing?" she says from beneath me, her voice muffled.

"Charlie," I say, "there are two chicks with bad fashion sense standing in our room."

She whips her head around and gazes over my torso at them. "Hello."

The women turn and leave in unison.

I glance down at Charlie. "Well, if that wasn't the freakiest crap I've ever seen, then my name isn't Dante Walker."

She gives a half-hearted smile. "Is that your name? I'd forgotten."

I'm tempted to tickle the life out of her, but instead decide I'd better address the stalkers in the lounge area. After climbing from the bed, I find my jeans and tug them on, keeping an eye on the open doorway. From outside, I can hear Blue speaking. His voice sounds casual, like we're all just hanging out at a beach house on vacay.

When I slip outside the bedroom, I find Aspen and Annabelle sitting on the floor, their legs stretched beneath a coffee table. In front of each of them is a plate with the World's Largest Omelet.

Aspen stuffs another bite into her mouth before she sees me. "Protein," she says around her food. "Because we're training today."

I don't tell her that I doubt *she's* training today, even though they should totally let her, since she's *important* and all. I'm more relieved she's speaking to me at all. Instead, I focus on the two women who stand near a wall, their arms loose at their sides.

Looking at Blue, I ask, "What's with the robots?"

He shakes his head, his eyes narrowed. "I don't know. They have cuffs, though." I glance at the women's ankles and see he's right. "I'm not eating that stuff," he says. "Not until Valery says it's safe."

My gaze moves from Blue to a plate in front of him. I shrug as I pick it up and settle down on a yellow chair, fork at the ready. "Pussy."

Charlie makes an appearance in the doorway. Her hair is disheveled, and her eyes dance around the room. She almost looks guilty.

Blue stops what he's doing and studies her. His narrowed eyes narrow farther, and his mouth tightens into a thin line. Then he glares at me. His stare blazes like actual fire, and I do the thing where I pretend not to notice him watching.

One of the women carries a plate to Charlie.

"Oh, thanks," she mumbles. "Have you eaten already?"

The woman glances nervously at the other lady behind her. Then she turns back to Charlie and nods once.

I'm halfway through my omelet when Valery strides into the room. "It's time to go. Annabelle, Aspen, you two will stay here. The rest of you can follow me."

"Bunch of bullshit," Annabelle says.

"Over my dead body," Aspen clips.

The two girls glance at each other. They seem to realize they've been agreeing on a lot lately but aren't ready to admit it to themselves.

Blue, Charlie, and I follow Valery through the maze. Even after sneaking around the place last night, I have no idea where we are. A man and two young girls, all with blue dishes in their hands, pass by us. They pretend we aren't even there, so I return the favor and keep walking.

After a few minutes—and mere moments before I scream from claustrophobia—we spill into an enormous room. Well, maybe *enormous* is an overstatement, but the room does look huge.

Walking toward the farthest wall, I understand why. The entire back area is one solid sheet of glass. Beyond it, the ocean spreads out like a blanket. I can hardly see the cliff's edge from up here, and the effect makes it seem as if I'm floating on water.

"Line up," someone orders.

Kraven appears through a doorway, dressed all in white again. I wonder if the dude owns stock in Clorox. I head toward the back of the room, stepping over spongy mats as I move. Blue and Charlie stand on either side of me, and the three of us wait to see what Mr. Clean has to say.

He glides across the room, and with the ocean behind him, he looks a lot like Jesus—walking on water and crap. I resist telling him this.

And Valery says I don't know how to behave.

Kraven's chest inflates. "At the Hive, there are six sectors of training you must complete. Failure to pass even one sector means losing your status as a liberator."

My head whips toward Valery. Her eyebrows knit together like this is news to her.

I raise my hand like a respectful pupil. "Uh, excuse me. You're telling me if we flunk out of Hive school, we'll have our cuff removed?"

Kraven continues, dismissing my question. "In the first sector, we'll cover self-defense. You'll have three days to master basic skills, and at the end of those three days, you'll be administered a test."

My raised arm drops to my side. "Hey, Miami," I say. "Did you not hear me? I asked for a little clarification."

His eyes meet mine. "I didn't ask if you had questions, and from here on out I will not answer them. But to clarify this one topic, Dante Walker, yes. If you fail a training sector, your status as a liberator will be revoked. There are too many angels in heaven who'd love to wear that dargon of yours. So if you don't respect the rules, you will be replaced."

"And when did this new *rule* get established?" I sneer.

Kraven shoots me a look, one that says he's seriously done taking questions. Well, that's fine. He can ignore me all he wants, because I can play that game all day long. I move to leave the room, but before I make it two steps something stops me. *Charlie* stops me. Her blue eyes are wide and attentive, like she can't wait to get started. I have no idea whether Kraven will actually let her train, but seeing her reminds me of why I'm here.

I have to rescue her soul from hell.

And this training could help me do that.

Maybe Kraven does know a thing or two about fighting. I guess I could give the rat bastard a chance. It might be fun, now that I think of it, to put him in his place. Mr. Kraven is big enough, but not many guys are built the way I am. And what's more, I know how to throw around every inch of muscle I've got.

I raise my hands in defeat. "All right, let's hear what you've got."

For the next four hours, Kraven repeats several moves. Blue

and I try our best to pick up on them as Charlie stays near the back, mirroring our motions. Kraven never tells her she should learn the defense tactics, but it's obvious he knows she's watching. I'm thankful, to be honest. It wouldn't hurt for her to know a few things just in case. She may never be able to attack a collector, but maybe she can learn to hold him off until help comes.

"Stop using brute strength," Kraven orders me for the millionth time. "Use what I taught you. Don't deviate."

He comes at me from behind and wraps his forearm around my throat. Just like he showed us, I kick my heel back into his knee and then throw my elbow into his stomach. He releases his hold.

"That would have been good if you'd focused more on your heel and elbow, and less on pulling away from me," he scolds.

Blue picks up the moves well, but when it comes time to execute them, he panics. Maybe Kraven is right. We're better at attacking than freeing ourselves. In retrospect, I'm not sure how Blue or I would have fared against numerous sirens if caught alone.

Kraven wipes sweat from his brow. I'm surprised he sweats at all. "What you need," he says, "is motivation."

The blond liberator nods toward someone behind me, and an arm circles my neck. My head cracks backward. The arm is slender, so I know he's pulled Valery into this stunt.

"Traitor," I manage, even though she's cutting off my air supply.

Kraven narrows his eyes at me, and his pupils dilate until there's only darkness. Then he rushes toward Charlie and wraps his hands around her throat.

With speed I didn't know I possessed, I throw my head back into Val's forehead. Then I stomp on her Jimmy Choos. She releases me with a yelp, and I fly toward Charlie. Kraven may act like he's here to help us, but anyone who touches Charlie like that is an enemy.

I'm an arm's length away when Charlie kicks Kraven hard

between the legs. Then she swings her arms up and out, breaking his hold on her neck. He drops like a boulder.

I stagger to a stop and stare.

She breathes hard for a moment, and then meets my gaze. "I did it."

I grin like an idiot. "Damn straight." The smile slides from my face when I notice Kraven's on his feet again. He moves toward the middle of the room as if nothing happened, as if he didn't just wrap his gnarly hands around my angel's throat.

"He wasn't squeezing," a soft voice says.

I spin around and find Charlie gazing up at me. She places a hand on my chest, nods her head to assure me she's fine, and then steps away, her eyes back on Kraven.

The liberator claps his hands. "Again."

. . .

Blue and I practice moves on each other through lunch and into the afternoon. When we bitch about empty stomachs, Kraven ignores us. Eventually I give up on the thought of food. If he can go without, then so can I.

Late in the afternoon, Blue successfully blocks one of my blows. He hoots and dances around the room. I'll admit learning this crap feels good. Empowering. I steal a glance at Kraven to see if he noticed Blue's achievement.

But his eyes are locked on a closed door.

"Miami, did you see Blue go?" I ask. Yeah, I asked another question, but my boy deserves a little credit.

When I realize Kraven still hasn't moved, my pulse quickens.

"What's wrong?" I ask.

Kraven holds his hand up to me and keeps his gaze on the door. Then he steals toward it, slinking like a fox. When he gets closer, he steadies himself, pulling in a deep breath.

The door flies open beneath his hand.

Aspen and Annabelle tumble into the room.

The two girls get to their feet, fighting the urge to laugh. Seeing them, I feel laughter bubble up inside me too. Blue and Charlie also wear smiles. Even Red can't hide her grin.

Kraven, however, is not amused.

"What do you think you're doing?" he says. I can tell he wants to yell, but that's not his style. He's more the totally-creep-you-out-by-remaining-calm guy.

Aspen straightens her spine. "Just seeing if you know your stuff, old man."

"Rest assured, I know my stuff," he replies. "And I'm hardly an old man. We're nearly the same age, girl."

"Jerk," Annabelle chimes in.

Kraven turns to address Annabelle.

When his gaze doesn't waver, she takes a small step back. "What are you looking at?" she asks in a small voice.

Kraven studies her for a long time, just the way he did last night. "Nothing," he says at last. Then he turns on his heel and heads back toward Blue and me. "The two of you will return to your rooms at once."

When he whirls back around, his eyes land on Annabelle. "I said *now*." It's the first time I've heard any venom in his voice, and it's clearly directed at Annabelle alone.

"You shouldn't talk to them that way," Charlie says, stepping forward.

Kraven continues to glare at Annabelle.

"No, it's fine," Annabelle says with a note of hurt. "I'm not special enough to be here. Isn't that right, *liberator*?" She spits the last word, then leaves.

Aspen points a finger at Kraven. "You're a dick."

I could be mistaken, but I think Aspen just took up for Annabelle. Maybe this awkward moment was the beginning of the two girls forging a bond. At least that'd be something.

"After that bit of pleasantry, I'm officially done for today," I announce.

"We are *not* done," Kraven says.

"Correction, we're quite done. When you act like a dick weasel to my friends, I'm gone." I'm not sure if I'm out of line by calling Annabelle and Aspen my friends, but it feels right. I head toward the door, hoping Charlie and Blue will follow. I also hope I'm headed in the right direction.

When I feel Charlie take my hand, my heart leaps. And when Blue throws his sweaty arm around my shoulder, it's almost too much.

All I think as I leave the training room is, *Yeah, these are my friends. Real friends.*

And then, *So this is what it feels like.*

⊰ 26 ⊱

DINNER IS SERVED

Blue, Charlie, and I return to training for the next two days. I can tell Kraven is trying to be more empathetic, but we still call him Cyborg behind his back. Every night, though we return to our rooms broken and bruised, I'm the first to admit that it's damn fun learning defense. And that I can't wait to move on to something new.

Valery has been good about checking in on us. She explained that she's continuing her training in other parts of the estate, and that she'd already passed the self-defense sector. Guess that's where she was when she was supposed to be on her honeymoon. Knowing she's training elsewhere also tells me there are other liberators up in this joint, because all I've actually seen is Kraven and the two mute chicks who deliver our food.

Speaking of food, where are those broads? They're usually here by now.

Annabelle kicks her legs up onto a busted-up coffee table in our small lounge area. "I just don't understand why Cyborg hates me so much."

"Because you threaten him," Aspen says. "Because he's afraid of strong women."

Blue shakes his head. "No, that guy isn't afraid of anything. He doesn't pack that gene."

"Bet he's afraid of this." Charlie raises a bicep into the air and flexes. Beneath her fair skin, a muscle the size of a golf ball pops up.

We all laugh at this.

Charlie acts offended.

She's been in better spirits lately. Part of it is being distracted. The other relates to something she told me two nights ago after our first day of training. She said that her Grams was with Big Guy now, and that the money she left behind will help Charlie take Hands Helping Hands to a new level. *Maybe He took her for a reason*, she whispered in the dark. *Maybe it's time for the charity to grow, and He needed to guide these resources into place.* She melted into me. *Besides, who wouldn't want my Grams at home with them?*

I remember her words and try to believe the smile on her face now. It doesn't appear as forced as it did three days ago, but it still looks strained. The couch squeaks beneath us as I wrap my arm around her waist and tug her against me. She nuzzles her face into my neck.

"Get a room," Annabelle says.

"Yes, ma'am." I jump to my feet and swoop Charlie into my arms, then I carry her toward our room like a caveman. She laughs and slaps at my chest.

I'm about to set her back down when the main door swings open. It's Red, Max at her side.

"Kraven has invited you to join him for dinner," Valery announces.

I put Charlie down. "Miami wants to eat with us? What's he serving—human hearts?"

Aspen barks out a laugh as Valery rolls her eyes.

For the first time, I notice what Max is wearing. "What's up with the penguin suit?"

"I look damn good, son." Max brushes his lapels. "Better than you're going to look."

My eyes jerk toward Valery. "What? It's, like, black tie?"

In response, Red moves out of the way and the Mute Chicks shuffle in. Their arms overflow with gowns and suits and bags full of Big Guy only knows what. I decide I have two choices: fight the wardrobe requirement using my mad self-defense skills, or suit up like the hustler I am.

I choose the latter.

Blue heads toward one of the women to dig through the choices, but I block his path before he can get there.

"Nah, man, I get first dibs," I say.

"You think so?"

As Blue and I wrestle to the floor, the girls step forward and gracefully accept the dresses. Then they make a beeline for one of the rooms, the Mute Chicks following after them. Not sure why a pretty dress makes even the fiercest girl get all squeal-y. When Blue and I finally glance up, we realize we're alone with two suits and some fresh toiletry stuff.

I shove Blue off me. "You're a barbarian."

Blue and I get ready in about ten minutes. We wait for a lifetime for the three girls to emerge. We bitch and we moan, and we sound like a pair of old women at bingo night.

But when the girls finally appear, it's all worth it.

My gaze goes immediately to Charlie. Her slight body is accented by a black bodice that makes the blood burn against my skin. Beneath the bodice is a pink layered skirt that looks like something a ballerina would wear. Black heels wrap around her calves and lace up all the way up to her knees. When my eyes travel back up, I notice soft pink makeup shimmers above her eyes and along her cheeks, and the remaining ivory pendant my father gave me lies against her chest.

She really does look like an angel…avant-garde.

"Charlie," I breathe.

She smiles and points to Aspen, who's standing beside her. "What about *her?*"

Aspen is also killing it in a navy thigh-length dress with sleeves that billow out toward her glove-covered hands. With nude pumps and a diamond-encrusted band around her head, she looks half hippie, half high fashion. When I notice Blue's mouth hanging open, I elbow him in the ribs.

"What?" he says, acting innocent, but he's already back to ogling Aspen.

"Where's Annabelle?" I ask.

Aspen inspects a bracelet around her wrist. "She won't come out, keeps saying she looks like a tomato."

"Annabelle," Blue shouts, "get out here so we can make fun of you."

With my empty stomach speaking in tongues, I brush past Aspen, press a lingering kiss against Charlie's temple, and enter the room.

"Let's move it, girl. I've starv—"

Annabelle turns and faces me.

And I forget what I was saying.

Charlie will always be the love of my life. No one else could ever make me feel the way she does. But tonight Annabelle has stolen the show.

She's dressed in a fire-engine red gown that hugs all the right parts of her body. An emerald necklace lies against her chest, and a matching ring hugs her finger. Her hair is styled in its usual manner, a dark bob with hard bangs across her forehead. But her eyes are different. They're shadowed in charcoals and blacks, and they're lined with a heavy hand. At the corner of each hazel eye, the eyeliner sweeps up.

Annabelle looks like an Egyptian princess.

No, a queen.

I place a hand on her arm, but she won't meet my eyes. "Annabelle, you look incredible."

"I look enormous." She jerks her chin toward Charlie and Aspen, who are busy talking to a bumbling Blue. "And they're so *perfect*."

"Stop," I tell her. "Don't do that. You're one of the most badass chicks I've ever met, and you're going to be afraid of a dress that puts you on display? Girl, you were *born* to be on display. Look at you!"

Annabelle smiles with one side of her mouth. "I don't look like a tomato?"

"You look like a beauty." I take her arm and guide her toward the lounge area. "Now rock that shit."

Ten minutes later, Valery returns to collect us. She's wearing a silver gown, and as we head toward the great room, she has to slap Max's hand away every few seconds. Though it doesn't escape me that each time she lets his touch linger before batting it away.

As we walk like cattle to the slaughter, Charlie twists her ankle, Blue stutters trying to talk to Aspen, I make fun of Blue's stuttering, and Annabelle loses an earring. Aspen is the only one who acts like a refined adult, which both surprises me, and doesn't.

When we spill into the great room, Kraven is there waiting. He stands from the end chair and waves an arm toward the table. "Please, take a seat."

The Mute Chicks pull out our chairs as Kraven instructs them to serve the first course.

"Why don't those chicks talk?" I ask when they're out of earshot.

"Dante," Charlie chastises, but I catch the hint of a smile.

Kraven pushes his hair behind his ears, something he does way too often. "They've taken a vow of silence."

"Why?" I ask.

He unfolds a black napkin and lays it over his lap. "Where is the other human?"

I narrow my eyes at him. He avoided my question, but that's not what has my attention. Kraven—he's nervous. But what about?

"Dropped an earring," Blue answers. "She's coming."

Kraven studies Blue, and then his eyes widen at something different. I follow his gaze and spot Annabelle standing in the doorway.

Seeing her there alone, my stomach clenches. We should have waited for her. She was nervous about being around Kraven after their exchange the first day of training. But it turns out I have nothing to worry about. Annabelle raises her chin, drops her hands to her side, and strides toward the table like Cleopatra herself.

Kraven is suddenly on his feet, watching every step she takes. Only when she's seated herself at the opposite end of the table does he lower himself back down into his chair.

"That dress you're wearing..." Kraven says to Annabelle. Her eyes rise, meeting his stare. "It's quite expensive."

Annabelle makes a face. "Don't worry, I'll give it back. You're the one who wanted to have this ridiculous dinner."

We all turn and look at Kraven because this here is entertainment at its finest.

He opens his mouth to respond, but just then three girls close to our age enter the room with silver trays. They lay down white dishes filled with lobster bisque that locks so good, my stomach aches. Next comes a spinach salad with raspberry-walnut vinaigrette. And then the main course: stuffed prawns, garlic rice pilaf, and roasted asparagus sprinkled with goat cheese and sautéed grape tomatoes.

As we eat, Valery forces conversation. We do our best to join in, but mostly we watch Kraven and Annabelle to see if they'll talk some more trash. Every once in a while, someone brings something up that's an obvious attempt to make them argue. It's sad, really, because we like Annabelle, but we're stir-crazy, and this is the most fun we've had all day. Plus, Kraven seems to be on better behavior tonight, so no harm done.

A man who's dressed like an old-fashioned butler clears our dinner plates and chauffeurs in miniature dishes that look like dessert. What I want to know is where they're hiding the cooks. Because I'd like to human traffic them to Peachville, assuming we ever make it back there.

As an older woman sets a fresh plate in front of me, something catches my eye. It's Kraven, rising from his seat like if he moves too suddenly, his chair will explode. At first I assume Annabelle has done something heinous, like used the wrong utensil for her spiced-chocolate tart.

But it's not that at all.

It's men—three of them—snaking into the room with blades in their hands.

⫷ 27 ⫸

SPY

Valery springs into action, rounding the table and grabbing Charlie. She pushes her away from the men, using her body as a shield. Kraven lunges toward Aspen and does the same. Even Max has come alive, snatching Annabelle from harm's way. The house staff scurries from the room on mouse feet.

Then it's just me and Blue.

My pulse pounds so hard in my head that my hearing dulls. With as warped as this house is, how did they find their way in? One of the guys with a shaved head tosses his knife to his other hand and moves closer. That isn't what scares me, though. It's that his eyes are locked on Charlie. When I realize what he's come for, and that this guy is a siren, I lose my mind with rage.

This place is supposed to be safe. But it's not. Valery said it herself, *no matter where we built, they would find it.* Well, I'd done enough running. These dudes are human.

And I'm immortal.

Born Dante Walker, reborn a demon—

Today a liberator who's about to put these guys down.

Lunging toward him, I keep my hands up, protecting my eyes. Then I land a solid blow into the guy's arm that holds the knife. He nearly loses it, but not quite. I'm about to go in for another hit when dizziness overtakes me. Then I'm looking up from the ground.

There are three of them, I remember.

Behind me, I can hear Charlie's voice. My head is still foggy, so it sounds like she's screaming from behind a closed window. But remembering she's here drives me to regain my composure, and before I'm knocked out a second time, I slide to the right. Then I throw my fist into a siren's ribs and hear a dull crack. From the corner of my eye, I notice Valery shoving the girls through a doorway, leading them somewhere safe. Max flanks behind her, alert and at the ready. Seeing Max reminds me I only have to fight the sirens off long enough until Max or Red—or hell, maybe even Aspen—can return to help.

I land a strong kick into the next guy's knee, and he drops to the floor. Then I spin on the other siren and attempt to throw my fist into his gut. I don't make the connection, though, because the siren I kicked is already up, and now he's got his arms under mine, restraining me. *Where's Blue when I need him?* A quick glance tells me the answer. He's busy defending himself against the third siren.

Defending.

In a flash, I remember what Kraven taught us. On instinct, I'd been using some defense. I had to. But I hadn't thought to apply the new tactics I'd learned.

Now I do.

The siren behind me restrains my arms, but I still have access to other body parts, starting with my foot. I slam my heel back into the siren's knee and then bring it down on his shoe. He groans and loosens his grip. As soon as he does, I collapse to the ground in a heap. He doesn't expect this, so he stumbles and falls with me. His arms pull away, and I jump to my feet. But I'm only free a few seconds before the second siren goes for my throat. I deflect his hands and pull a Charlie, kicking him straight in the junk. He stops reaching for my throat, instead cupping his manhood and crumbling to the floor.

But now the guy behind me is up again. He heads toward Blue like he's done with our fight. I'm about to stop his advance when Bruised Balls grabs me again. Now Blue is stuck defending himself against two sirens.

As I deflect an attack from Bruised Balls, something causes me to pause.

Where is Kraven?

We've only been fighting the sirens for a few seconds, but he should have been here. A thought fires through my mind. I shuffle back from the siren who faces me and hold up my hand. He hesitates, his brow creased with confusion. Glancing at Blue, I notice the two sirens take turns attacking and restraining him. But neither inflicts much damage to the liberator.

"Stop," I say.

Bruised Balls sneers and circles closer, like he's not about to listen.

"No, really. All of you can just stop. I get it," I say. "This is our test."

The sirens stop and look toward the back of the room. Kraven stands watching, his arms crossed over his chest. I expect him to start clapping or some crap. But he doesn't. He just opens his mouth and says, "Thank you for your assistance, liberators."

The sirens—err, liberators—slap one another on the back and head toward the dining table, laughing like old friends. They pick over our dessert as Charlie, Aspen, and Annabelle burst into the room. Charlie's eyes are wide and frantic, as if she's expecting a bloodbath.

She rushes toward me and lifts her hands to my face. "Are you okay? What happened?"

I pull away because I'm angry, though not with her. I should have sensed the liberators' cuffs when they entered the room. I should have been paying attention. But that's the loophole with the cuffs. We can sense them, but only by concentrating all the time. It's a bit like listening for a bird outside your window in the middle of the night; at some point you get tired and fall sleep. "What happened is this was a test to see if we'd mastered the self-defense sector."

"The hell?" Annabelle says. "That's a pretty shoddy tactic."

I'm certain her words are targeted toward Kraven, but that's not who responds. Instead, one of the liberators in disguise turns around. "Damn, Kraven. No wonder you've got the human without a cause hidden away. Girl's *hot*. I'd like to get my hands—"

"Enough!" Kraven yells.

We all stop and stare at Kraven, who I somehow doubt has ever shouted. Not like this. He seems to realize his mistake, but it doesn't stop him from glaring at the liberator who wants himself a piece of Annabelle. Kraven's face is so red, it rivals the severity of Anna's dress. He looks away from the liberator and toward Annabelle. Then he strides from the room.

Annabelle's breath rushes out in a gasp right as Valery and Max reappear.

"Oh, it's over?" Valery says.

"You knew this was a test?" Aspen accuses.

Red waves her hand. "'Course."

Max stares at her in awe. "You amaze me, woman. I'm not sure whether to be impressed or afraid of how good you are at keeping secrets. Maybe just turned on." He tries to grab for Valery, and a smile plays on her lips.

One of the liberators, the dude with the shaved head, licks his fingers, says something to a guy across the table, and heads in the same direction Kraven went.

I pull Charlie close and whisper in her ear. "I'm going to ask how I did. Will you distract them?"

She nods and whirls in a circle. "Valery. I don't…I don't feel so—"

She slumps to the ground. I have to march away before my grin blows her story.

Her fainting spell does the trick. Valery and everyone else in the room rushes over to see what's wrong with Trelvator Girl. As for me, I slip across the room and spill into a wide hallway. Moving like a ghost, I catch up with Kraven and the liberator who followed him.

What I told Charlie was the truth; I want to know how Blue and I did. Especially after he threatened that my cuff was on the line, not that he'd have a prayer of taking it from me. But I also want to know if I can find out anything new. Like why Big Guy has decided we need a training pad, besides the obvious threat of collectors and sirens. But why train us to fight instead of training us how to recapture Charlie's soul? Valery insinuated they'd help teach me how to descend into hell. But thinking back on our conversation at the graveyard, I remember she actually said, "They'll help you."

But help me do what?

Red said the collectors and sirens could find us anywhere, so why not go on the offense immediately? What are we buying time for? I know how she'd answer that question: *to train you so you're better prepared to face them*. But with the number of secrets floating around, I want to be sure that's all there is to it.

I take a few more steps toward the pair of liberators and listen. Right away, I recognize Kraven's smooth calm voice in comparison to the other guy, who speaks much quicker

"It's not safe yet," Kraven says.

"But the guys are getting restless," the other dude replies. His voice has a slight accent to it, like any second he's going to suggest we *throw another shrimp on the barbie*. "We've been locked up in here for three weeks. We've completed training. Just give us a few hours to go outside and try them out."

"Are you so eager to leave your post?" Kraven says. "Have you forgotten the commitment you made? I gave you a choice. I gave you all a choice. And you chose protection."

The Aussie dude groans. "Wasn't much of a choice when the alternative was to become a mute house slave."

"But it *was* a choice. And they've only agreed to stay quiet until the words on the scroll reveal themselves."

The guy doesn't respond right away, giving me time to mull over what's been said. The liberators who pretended they were sirens... they're here to be protectors, probably for Charlie. And I guess the two women liberators chose to help around the estate instead. I wonder why.

"Listen, Neco. We have to remember what else we're harboring here."

The other liberator, Neco, raises his voice. "I know. That damn scroll. You only remind us every day. A lot of good it does anyone."

"You have to believe," Kraven replies.

"Believe what? That the words are going to magically appear? It wasn't meant for us. I don't know why God even gave it to you. Probably just to mess with our heads."

"Watch your tongue," Kraven says, his voice deepening.

Neco hesitates. "Can you at least tell me whether they're still out there?"

"Of course they are. They haven't gone anywhere." Kraven sighs. "They've set up on the side of the cliff as if we don't know they're there."

"Just another reason we should leave. Draw them out, fight them before they have a chance to attack."

I don't hear anything else. I'm already storming back toward Charlie. *They* are out there. Kraven admitted as much. Sure, Valery warned us it could happen. But there's a difference between saying they might know we're here, and that they're actually parked outside.

My mind spins as I move faster. Who exactly are *they*? Are there sirens out there, hidden among the cliff face? Or are they collectors?

Where is Rector?

The last thought needles into my chest until I can hardly breathe. When I make it to the great room, everyone is gone. Maybe they took fainting Charlie back to her room. Good. I can talk to her in private there. But what will I say? I hate keeping secrets from her, and I remember the promise I made after the night she was taken, that I would never lie to her again. But my plan is to steal Charlie's soul back. And she'll never agree to that. She'll insist I'm trading my life for hers.

And that's exactly what I will do if I must.

But not tonight.

Tonight I'm finding that blasted scroll.

28

THE SCROLL

Later that night—after we've all discussed the test ad nauseum and then slunk off to bed—I prepare myself to sneak out.

Charlie is asleep next to me, her bottom lip working like she's having a conversation with herself. I want to lean down and kiss that chubby lip, but I know it'll wake her. And then I'll want to kiss other areas on her body, too.

So instead, I slip out from beneath the covers and pull on jeans and a T-shirt. The lounge area is vacant when I step through our doorway, and so is the hallway outside it. We don't have a clock in our part of the house, and my phone is dearly departed, so I'm not sure what time it is, but it feels like just after midnight.

All the hallways look different from one another, which helps me to remember which ones I've already been down. But it does nothing to tell me where this scroll is. For all I know, it could be in Kraven's bedroom, beneath his pillow.

Wouldn't that be lovely?

Still, I have to take the chance that I can find this thing. From what I understand, there are no words on it. But something tells me

I have to try. The sirens are going after Charlie and Aspen, and this is the only clue I have that may provide me answers to protect them both.

After what feels like two hours of creeping through the warped mansion and dodging staff members who soundlessly patrol the area, I'm no closer to finding the scroll. But I have decided this would be a nice place to hide a body, or maybe do a haunted house. It's creepy as shit in here.

I stop and lean against a wall, thinking. Roaming around the place isn't helping. This is something I'm going to have to puzzle through to get anywhere. So I ask myself, *what is the safest room in the house?*

My first response is to say with Kraven. That's what he'd say. But if the place was designed specifically to protect those inside it, wouldn't the middle be safest?

That's tornado speak.

And it leads me directly to my target, the great room.

Adrenaline courses through me as I kick off the wall. I pass through seven rooms and travel down four hallways before I make it there. Once I've arrived, I do the only thing I can think of: I scour the place. I look everywhere for a hiding spot, including beneath the long dining table, but don't find anything.

When I've all but given up and I'm about to cave into the temptation to rejoin Charlie in bed, I gaze up. The rafters are empty. But then I remember that when Valery brought us into the Hive for the first time, we ascended a flight of stairs, which means there's a level beneath this one. I sweep my eyes across the floor.

I see something.

It's just a square of wood that's grain doesn't match the rest, but I'll take it. Kneeling down near the spot, skull belt buckle digging into my stomach, I run my fingers along the edges until I find a place to slip a nail under. The board moves a centimeter. An inch.

And then it's gliding open, far enough so that I can peer inside. There's a light down there, but I can't make out anything else. As a chill runs over my body, I lower myself into the basement-type area. I drop to the floor with an echoing *thud* and then pull myself upright.

The area isn't big, maybe fifteen feet by fifteen feet. Hardwood floors cover the ground, just like in the great room. And all along the perimeter is warped wallpaper that doesn't match—orange and yellow flowers along one side, and damask on another. A single light buzzes overhead, shining down on a small black box.

I approach the box slowly, holding my breath. My heart jackhammers in my chest because even though I'm a big dude who's fought his fair share of demons, I don't particularly enjoy being trapped like this.

I focus on Charlie. I think about how she probably looks in bed right now, a little bowling ball on the edge of the mattress, making room for my long limbs. I bet she's talking to herself extra hard right now.

The thought brings a smile to my face as I come to stand in front of the box. The box that isn't underground. Because *I'm* not underground.

"What are you hiding?" I ask it as I squat down.

I slide my hands along the edges, searching for a way to open it. Disappointment eats away at me when I find a keyhole near the back. Of course it'd be protected by a lock. But I'm not about to leave without searching the area. When I don't find the key after twenty minutes, I move to Plan B.

Holding the box in one hand, I hurl it at the wall.

It shatters open.

"Damn straight," I tell it in a whisper, even though I'm not sure why I'm whispering, because if I was going to wake someone up, it's already done.

I scramble forward and then freeze. Beneath the box's carcass is a sheet of gold paper curled into a tight roll. I lick my lips, imagine what I'll do if it doesn't reveal anything—I've already broken everything there is to break—and then reach down to grab it.

It unfolds easily. At first I don't see anything. It's blank, just like I knew it'd be.

But then I turn it over.

There are words. But only a few of them.

Whoever is able to read this is the Secret Carrier. Keep this knowledge hidden in your heart until the time is right.

Be patient.

The Secret Carrier. My top lip curls up, because what am I—five years old? But on the inside I'm dancing my ass off. Me! I'm the Secret Carrier! I don't know what the hell that means, but it's probably up there with Trelvator Girl. Maybe even bigger.

I knew my ass was special.

No one can read the words except the kings, they said.

Guess what that makes me? Pow!

I drop the scroll to the floor, because my chest is three times as big as it was a moment ago. I need more space to be so awesome. There isn't time in my busy schedule to be holding scrolls. Maybe someone should hold it for me. I'm the Secret Carrier, after all.

Reaching overhead to the space I dropped down through, I start to pull myself up. I'll let whoever finds this think there was a break-in, because I'm not ready to let on that I can read the scroll. Maybe I never will. Because that's what it said, right? Be patient.

As I'm about to wiggle up through the hole, something catches my eye. It's a fold in the wallpaper that looks off. I mean, everything looks off. But this appears to be done intentionally.

I let my arms drop and move toward the corner. Then I reach up and pull back the paper. It comes away easily. I have to squint to see, because the only light is on the other side of the room, whereas this spot is dark as sin.

As the paper peels back, the area brightens. A little at first, and then brighter and brighter until I'm shading my eyes instead of squinting.

Something flutters to the floor.

A scroll—the *real* scroll.

I bite the inside of my cheek, then snatch it off the ground. The paper feels weightless in my hand, like if I let go, it'd fly away instead of float back down. I flip it over. Then I flip it again.

Nothing.

It doesn't say a damn thing.

My pride deflates like a limp penis.

• • •

At seven a.m. the next morning, I'm about as pleasant as a freshly castrated bull.

The first scroll was a decoy, set up to drive the reader into silence and to make them stop searching for the real thing. But the other one, that was real. Too bad it didn't say dick. After realizing I wasn't going to find anything out, I'd replaced the real scroll and returned to bed.

And now I can't wait to get to Kraven. Because I haven't forgotten what he said last night: "*They* are out there." Which means Charlie is too close to harm. Way too close. I have to get her soul back soon, but it's a delicate balancing act. The longer I stay at the Hive, the more I learn how to survive on my quest. And I have to survive. At least long enough to hand her soul off to Valery or Kraven or whoever can turn it in.

On the other hand, every minute I waste here is another minute I'm taking a risk. A risk that they will find a way in here and get to her. Then they'll have everything. Her soul. Her body.

And then what?

Is she gone forever?

I can't think about that. Because I have a plan and I need to focus. Ever since I arrived at the Hive, things have been in Kraven's control. But that's about change.

When Valery arrives, I'm ready for her.

"I'll be the only one attending training today," I announce.

"Whaaa?" Blue stands up, his mouth stuffed with a flaky crescent.

I don't take my eyes off Red. "I mean it, Valery. Take me to Kraven. Just me." I square my shoulders, raise my chin, and wait.

She must realize I'm serious, because she nods. Conversation explodes behind me as I follow her out, but I just close the door and keep moving. I don't have time to explain.

When we get to the training room, I ask Valery to leave. Her mouth pulls into a half smile, like she's somehow proud that I'm making demands. I don't understand this in the least, but I accept it.

She turns to go, and a few minutes later, Kraven saunters in. He's wearing white pants and a white sleeveless shirt. There's a green belt cinched around his waist, and I'm a bit thrown off because I thought Miami was allergic to color.

"We need to talk," I say.

Kraven inspects the training room. "Where is the other liberator? Sector two training starts today."

I lose my focus for a moment. "So, we passed the defense portion?"

Kraven opens his arms as if to say, *you're still here, aren't you?*

A smile hangs stupidly from my face. Then I shake it off, remembering why I wanted to speak to Miami alone. I straighten my spine until I can't stand any taller. I may need a chiropractor after this. "I know the Hive is surrounded."

"It's hardly surrounded."

"So you admit it." I jab a finger in his direction. "They're out there."

"There's nothing to admit. You already knew."

I bring a hand to my hair and pull, trying to think this through. "Are they sirens?"

Kraven nods.

"You know about them," I say. It isn't a question.

"Valery told me. They're soulless, you know. They were collected the moment they agreed to work for demons, even if they didn't really know who they were partnering with. It's *what* they agreed to do that matters."

"The collectors have Charlie's soul. We don't have it." I'm sure he's already aware, but I need to hear him say it.

His gaze turns to the glass wall, to the ocean beyond it. "I know."

"I'm going to get it back." I close the distance between us so that we're an arm's length apart. "I don't have time for this training sectors crap. You need to show me how to break into hell, steal her soul back, and return with it."

His raises an eyebrow at hearing my plan, which for him is the equivalent of tearing off his clothes and running around buck naked screaming, "Oh, man! Oh, crap! You just blew my effing *mind*!"

"You're going to go after her soul?" he clarifies.

I shrug like I do this crap every day. "Yep, I'll take a tank full of weapons and blow them all to pieces if I have to."

"You will do no such thing," Kraven snaps. "Weapons were born of sin, and you will not use them. If you do, I can guarantee you won't be wearing a cuff any longer."

This certainly screws with my plan, but on the off chance I make it back, I'm going to need my dargon to keep kicking. I hold up my hands. "All right, don't get your panties in a wad. No weapons. I'll just use *these* guns."

I show him my biceps.

Kraven ignores me and rubs a hand along his jaw. "Your current assignment is very important. You can't abandon that mission."

"Her name is Aspen, Cyborg. And I'll liberate her soul as soon as I return. Hell, I may not even have to work that hard. Girl's turning a corner, I think." I pause. "Do you know why Aspen is so important to the dude upstairs? You must not since you aren't training her."

"We have protocol. The sectors are placed in a certain order for a reason," Kraven says, following his own train of thought. Nothing new to see here, guys. "You won't survive in hell without the training."

"Tell me you can teach me something valuable, and fast, or I'll leave tonight."

Kraven snaps his teeth together. "I can teach you things, but you have to commit to the timeline. Three days for each sector, five sectors remaining. I need two weeks. *You* need two weeks. And that's without adding on Amplification, which you'd probably want to—"

"That's too much time," I growl. "Try again."

"I need two weeks, or I can't—"

I hold up my hand and, amazingly, he stops talking. Our eyes meet. "We're done here."

Every nerve in my body pulses as I stride toward the exit.

"Wait," Kraven says.

I keep moving.

"Wait!" he yells.

I'm almost gone when he breaks.

"I'll show you," he whispers. "I'll show you how to summon your wings."

With my face still turned away from him, I smile. *That* is exactly what I was waiting for.

DESCENT

"Demons exist whether you believe in them or not."
—Emily Rose

⊰ 29 ⊱

OUTSIDE

I spin around and face Kraven. "How fast can you teach me?"

He turns his hands palm up. "That's the beauty of it, Dante. That all depends on you."

The way his voice rises, I can tell he likes this. That the ball's in my court. I roll my head from side to side like Evander Holyfield, like I'm to go twelve rounds. "Bring it, Cyborg."

Kraven eyes me. "Think you're a big man? Think you got what it takes?"

"Damn straight."

He steps toward me. "Let me tell you something. There are eight liberators, all who have trained to summon their wings. What's more, those cuffs have seen a lot of ankles. Yesterday's liberators aren't always today's. You know how many of them have learned what I have?"

I curl my hand into a zero and hold it up, because I know where this speech is headed.

He surprises me and holds up a single finger. "One other liberator besides me."

Laughter bursts from my throat. "Oh, ho! Someone else is as awesome as you? Bet that twisted your panties right up."

Kraven's lips form a tight line. "You're not ready to learn."

"I am," I say, swallowing my laughter. "I'm totally ready to wing out."

He circles around me like a wolf, analyzing my build. "You could be strong enough."

"I am strong enough." My voice drops an octave. "I've already almost done it a couple of times."

Kraven stops in front of me. "Let's avoid fictitious tales while we're training, yes?"

"You don't believe me?"

He sighs so long I wonder if he's got three lungs instead of two.

"I'm not lying, Cyborg," I tell him. "It hurt like hell. Felt like something was trying to tear its way out of me. And it burned."

Kraven cocks his head to the side. "I don't believe you, Mr. Walker. But that doesn't matter. What matters is you try to summon them now."

I close my eyes and try to focus on growing Hercules wings. I'm doing a pretty good job imagining how wicked cool they'll look when Kraven interrupts my thoughts.

"I didn't mean right this second," he says. "First you have to clear your head."

I keep my eyes closed. "Head clear. Check. What's next, sensei?"

Kraven's bare feet shuffle against the training mats. "Clearing your head doesn't happen that quickly. You need to be sure you know who you are."

"Name's D-Dub. Pleasure."

"You need to be sure you know, without a doubt, that you are a liberator. That you are ready to leave behind your old lifestyle. Are you harboring any old demons, demon?"

My eyes open. His face softens, and the lines around his mouth relax. He grips the back of my neck. "Everyone has a past, Dante. Have you let yours go? Are you changed?"

Heat creeps across my skin. He asked me a question, so why can't I answer it?

Because I know what lies in my heart. And I'm not ready to let it go.

Kraven walks to the glass wall. His back is to me. "Do you call yourself a liberator?"

My muscles relax. This is an easier question, one I can answer. "That's what I am."

"Is it?"

"What are you, my therapist?" I roll my shoulders to try and loosen up. This sudden change in topic is messing with my head. It's like he's already gotten in there, like he can read my mind or some crap.

"I wasn't always a good man," Kraven says.

"Are you now?"

Kraven turns around. His dark eyes look past me. "I did terrible things, unimaginable to me now. But I repented. I embraced a new life. And because God is merciful, I was forgiven." Kraven touches a hand to his chest. "Look at me now, a liberator."

I don't believe Kraven ever did terrible things. He's so Rule Book. But maybe that's what made him do those things. Maybe he didn't like it when others wouldn't abide by his rules. Could that be why he rarely shouts, rarely even raises his voice? Perhaps his demon was his temper.

"I never did terrible things." My stomach rolls saying this aloud. I'm not lying exactly, but the words are heavy leaving my mouth, like I don't believe them myself.

"So you were a saint?" Kraven asks, his lips quirking upward. "That's how you came to be a collector?"

My hands tighten into fists. "It doesn't matter. It's in the past."

"Wrong. In order to summon your wings, you have to dig deep inside of yourself. And if there's something there that isn't resolved, it'll never work."

I bite the inside of my lip. "Then how did Rector use his wings?"

Kraven averts his eyes. "His wings are not the same as ours. He uses all that darkness in him—all that blackness—in order to call them. You don't want to do that. You don't want to awaken that side of yourself."

Don't I?

"I don't have anything to let go of," I snarl. "So what's next?"

"Again, if you don't follow the steps, this will never work."

I grit my teeth so hard my jaw aches. "Listen to me, Kraven. I'm tired of your sectors, and of your steps. Show me how to summon my wings or I'm out of here." My heartbeat throbs in my ears. "No. You know what? I don't need this. What I really need is time. And every second I'm here, I'm risking the sirens breaking in."

"Do you know why you were chosen to be a collector?" he asks suddenly.

My heart leaps, because it's a question I've never truly known the answer to.

"Lucifer believed you were strong, intelligent, manipulative. He believed you'd faithfully follow orders that satiated your own selfish desires. And more importantly, Lucifer knew that out of all the fallen souls in hell, that you in particular would never consider yourself redeemable. Six cuffs built for six people who fit that exact description. You were one of those six, Dante."

"How do you know this?" I say in a near whisper.

Kraven turns on his heel and moves away from me.

"And where exactly are you going?" I ask.

"Follow me."

The SOB must be confident I'll do as he asks, because he gets farther and farther away without checking to see if I'm behind him. I drop my head back and stare up at the ceiling. Then I groan and jog to catch up, thinking about what he said, wondering if it's true.

It's true.

We trek through the house without a word. When he reaches an orange door, he unlocks it and spins around.

"Ready?" His grin sweeps from ear to ear.

"For what?"

"To play."

Kraven shoulders the door open, and sunlight slams into us. I shield my eyes from the sudden brightness. When my vision adjusts, I gaze across the horizon. We're in the back of the mansion, patches of snow dotting the ground. A chill creeps in beneath my long-sleeved shirt and jeans, and the smell of salt fills my nose. There's an empty expanse of dead grass and beyond it nothing except the ocean. But how far down is the water? Twenty feet? Thirty?

A hundred?

Kraven glides toward the cliff without hesitation. He doesn't even have shoes on, the freak. I follow after him not because I think it's the best idea, but because my racing pulse demands it. I want to be here. I want to find the sirens.

I want to pick a fight today.

I've been cooped up in that house for four days. Today is day five. The sun feels good on my neck, even if the cold bites at my nose and ears. I fill my lungs. Once. Twice.

Walking after Kraven, my blood surges. Yes, I want this. This is what I was reborn to do. Screw strategy, screw process. Just show me the fiend that wants to hurt Charlie and I'll tear out his beating heart. Then I'll eat it.

Kraven gets right up to the edge of the cliff, so close I think he might leap off. I'm so hopped up on adrenaline that part of me wants him to. Would I jump after him? See if I can fly without wings?

He spreads his arms out wide, and the wind rolling off the ocean tangles in his blond hair.

"Come and get us!" he thunders into the open air.

And I think, "Yeah. *Hell*, yeah."

After Kraven's words are eaten by the tide, he waits. He waits so long I start to imagine there are bugs beneath my skin. That if I don't move—if I don't *do* something—they'll devour me alive from the inside out.

A small sound rings through the morning, the noise a stone makes when falling from a ledge to the jutting rocks below.

It sounds again. And again.

Something is coming.

Kraven shuffles back, and I match his steps. We breathe hard, waiting for them to show themselves.

A hand whips over the side of the ledge.

And a man, tall with lanky arms and legs, pulls himself up. He's wearing a steel-gray shirt, gray pants. If it wasn't for his dark skin, it'd be hard to tell him apart from the stone cliff he crawled up from. One of his pinkies is missing. I wonder how he lost it. Maybe it was from antagonizing a German shepherd as a kid, or from an Indian cooking class.

I lick my lips, nearly tasting the tension.

My legs move toward him before I even think about what I'm doing. I don't want to think. I just want to feel the crack of my knuckles against this guy's face. But something behind him stops me.

It's another arm, pulling another body over the edge. A woman. She stands upright, cracks her neck.

And then another arm. And another. And another and another and another.

Sirens appear, slithering onto their bellies and then rising up like cobras. They're mere humans who agreed to work for collectors. They don't have special powers or the ability to survive where we don't. I should take comfort in this. But there are too many of them. More than I want to count. I lean my head toward Kraven. "What are we going to do?"

"We?" he says, eyeing the sirens. "This is your fight." Before I can think, Kraven grabs the back of my shirt and hurls me toward them.

I land hard against the cold ground, frozen solid from winter's fury. I'm out here alone. They're surrounding me. I should be afraid. I should run back to Kraven and demand he fight alongside me. But this is what I want.

Release.

I jump to my feet and roar like the beasts they work for. "You want her? You've got to get through me first!"

They lunge at me.

⚜ 30 ⚜

INSIDE

I feel the crash of fists in my back, the splinter of a kick in my side. Teeth tear at my skin, and hands claw at my throat. It doesn't matter. I don't care. I'm tired of hiding from these people. Tired of running.

I remember Charlie the way I left her this morning, the way she looked at me with fear. I detest that. I detest seeing her afraid and being unable to ease it. Now I can. I grab the next fist I see and spin until I hear joints pop. Then I turn on the next siren, a girl my age. I grab her hair and throw her to the ground.

A siren twice my size wraps his burly arms around my chest. I use what Kraven taught me, throwing my heel back into his kneecap. The man collapses with a guttural groan. I leap over him and throw my elbow into a siren's nose. Blood sprays across his cheeks, and a smile lights up my face.

I'm doing well. Surviving. Taking them down one at a time. But the problem is that they keep getting back up. Their goal was to get past me to Charlie, and maybe to Aspen, but now they're focused on me alone. They're angry. And an easy way to alleviate that fury is to take me down.

They move like a flock of birds. One guy, the one who first stepped over the ledge, races toward me. The others follow his lead and fly forward. Together, they hit me like a wall. I land on my back, and rocks dig into my muscles.

I kick and flail—all arms and legs like an overturned beetle—but they easily overtake me. The first punch feels special, like I'll remember it a thousand years from now. But the rest blend together until the pain becomes all that I am. Even places they haven't touched scream out.

Then they stop. One at a time, they stop. Above me, their faces pull away until I see the blue of the sky again.

I try to get to my feet but nothing works. My body is broken.

Kraven moves toward the sirens. His lips curl back, and his eyes blaze, and he may be a liberator, but he looks like a monster.

The sirens seem to understand he's the bigger threat, considering I'm a bloody heap of tissue and bone. They charge toward him. I pull myself up as much as I can. I have to help. If we fight together, then we may have a chance to overcome them. But I know that's a lie. There are too many. All we can hope for is to send them back to their caves along the cliff wall.

The sirens close in. They're only a few feet away. Why isn't Kraven moving?

Move!

A shadow crosses Kraven's face and I see it—his rage. The temper he swallows every day. But he's not going to swallow it now.

The liberator curls in on himself, his arms wrapped around his stomach, head between his knees. A burning smell fills my nostrils.

And then he explodes.

His entire body opens like a thundercloud, and wings burst from his back. A glow wraps around his torso like the sun is pointing a finger straight at him. And he growls. He growls like a tornado and moves like one, too. Sirens scurry backward, but he storms after them, throwing them like they're made of nothing. They *are* nothing next to him.

I get to my feet, but my legs are shaking. I'm not sure whether it's from injuries or from watching Kraven. As I stumble back, I think of how I was terrified the collectors would find Charlie. That they would get to her. I think of how the threat of the sirens kept me up at night, of how I pictured them slinking through the cracks to steal her away.

But seeing Kraven blast through sirens, I know there is nothing to fear. Not now. Not with him here.

A daring siren rushes forward, undeterred by Kraven's wings. But the liberator just uses his wing like a battering ram and throws the siren twenty feet. When too many sirens charge him at once, he folds his wings around himself like a shield. Then he whips them open, and sirens fly up and out as if a bomb detonated at their feet.

The battle goes on for several minutes and all I can do is stand slack-jawed. I remember the way he fought the night the collectors took Charlie. But I didn't have the time to really focus then; I was too worried about getting my girl out of there. Now, though, all I can do is watch.

One by one, the sirens admit defeat and scamper toward the ledge. I manage to throw a few hits in as they flee to ensure they keep running. When I glance back, a single siren remains. He stands before Kraven, determined. His hands twitch, and I notice he's missing a finger. He was the first siren to appear, and he'll be the last to leave. Kraven rushes toward him, and the siren bends at the knees like he's going to leap over the liberator. When Kraven gets closer, the siren lunges. He doesn't leap, he spins.

He spins so quickly Kraven loses track of him, and so do I. When I spot him again, he's on Kraven's back. The liberator cries out when the nine-fingered man gets ahold of Kraven's left wing. He's tearing at it with his hands, his teeth.

The liberator whirls around and around, trying to grab at the siren. I rush forward, ignoring the ache in my body. I'm almost to him when Kraven jumps into the air and slams onto his back. There's a sickening crunch, and I can't breathe. I can't breathe because I'm afraid of what I'll see when Kraven rolls off him.

Slowly, the liberator slides to his right. The siren scrambles to his feet, and my airway reopens. I don't know why I was afraid of the guy being dead. I want them to be dead. *Right?*

I move forward to help Kraven subdue him. This is good, better than killing the dude. Now we can ask him questions, drill him until we know what the collectors' plans are. Why didn't I think of this before? Why didn't Kraven?

My hand grips the siren's biceps, but as soon as it's there, his arm is ripped from my grasp. Kraven has his hands around the guy's throat. The siren's eyes bulge. I take two steps in Kraven's direction, but he's too quick for me. He rushes toward the ledge.

"You don't belong here," Kraven snarls.

He's too close to the ledge.

Too close.

"Kraven," I yell. "Stop. We need him."

Kraven's wings snap open so violently I almost lose my footing. He squeezes tighter, and the siren fumbles at his hands. But that's wrong. Kraven taught us that never works. You have to be on the offense even when you're playing defense. The siren should tear at his nostrils. Gouge his eyes. He doesn't, though. The siren just keeps pulling on Kraven's hands, and now his face is turning purple.

"You don't belong here," Kraven repeats, quieter. I can hardly hear him over the ocean.

The liberator takes another step toward the ledge, and the siren nearly tumbles over. He tries to turn his head to see how far the fall would be, but Kraven clutches his neck too tightly.

I can't move. I can't speak. I'm afraid if I do, Kraven will drop him. And he can't do that.

He can't.

Big Guy would declare war on hell if a collector killed a human. So what would he do to one of his own? Someone that's supposed to work for him?

"You don't belong here." Kraven's voice is calm. "You belong in hell."

He throws the siren.

He throws the nine-fingered man who may have lost his finger on a fishing trip with his daughter. He throws him, and the siren's body seems to float in the air for a single moment, his face twisted with terror.

And then he falls.

The man is gone. *The human* is gone. Dead.

Kraven turns and looks at me, and my blood runs colder than the winter breeze. His eyes are black as night, and his hair is almost white against the sky.

I can't believe what he just did. What will happen to him? Will his cuff be removed? Will he be tossed into hell himself? But then I remember something Kraven said. *They're soulless.*

Does that make a difference? Does Big Guy only care about those he can still save?

I decide *yes*.

Kraven rushes toward me, and even though instinct tells me to flee, I hold my ground. When he gets within a few feet of me, I don't step back. Instead, I lift my chin to meet his gaze straight on. Kraven closes the distance between us and grabs my biceps. He drags me behind him as he heads toward the house, his wings still splayed open.

"Let go of me," I bark. "I'm not a child."

But he doesn't. He just keeps pulling me until we're inside the house, until we've woven through hallways and rooms and we're back in the training area. At that point, I jerk back. I don't care whether my arm pulls out at the socket, I won't be manhandled. If it's a fight he wants. I'm game. Even if I can hardly stand.

I rip my biceps from his grasp. He whirls around, and his wings sink behind his shoulders. A cracking, snapping sound tells me he's brought them back into himself. I open my mouth to fire out questions, but he cuts me off by grabbing my shoulders.

"What are you holding on to?" His voice crashes over me. "Say it."

I try to pull away but he won't let go. "Get away from me."

"Let it go!" he roars. "Let it go, or you won't save her."

"Get off me." It's all I can say. All I can think. "Get off me. Get the *hell* off me."

"Tell me what it is! Say it!" Kraven rears back, and before I comprehend what he's doing, his fist connects with my jaw. The world spins, and I'm falling. I hit the training mat and roll onto my side.

"Son of a bitch." I groan and clutch my face in my hands. I'm not sure whether Kraven is planning on hitting me again, and I'm not about to lie around waiting to find out. I get to my feet. My vision blurs before focusing. "You want to wrestle, Miami? That's fine. But you better be ready to breathe your last, because I won't stop until your broken cuff is in my hands."

A guttural sound rips from my throat as I lunge at him. He sidesteps me and circles an arm around my chest.

"Stop fighting me, Dante." He squeezes until my ears ring. "Let it go."

I try to throw my head back, but he cocks his own to the side. I end up head-butting his shoulder, which does absolutely nothing. My heel slams down, but he pulls his foot back. I was expecting he'd know this was coming. But I know he won't expect *this*.

I leap up and curl my knees toward my chest. Kraven is pulled off balance and crashes to the floor. He falls on top of me, and my face smashes into the ground. Doesn't matter. He's let go of me, and that's all I care about. I scramble away from him, then kick his face, hard. His nose crunches beneath my boot.

Once I'm upright, I jerk into a fighting stance. "Come on, Cyborg!"

A faint burning smell hits my senses, and my mind puts the pieces together. Burning smell equals wings. I'm not sure when I figured that out, but I almost wish I didn't know what was coming next.

I hobble toward the exit, my right leg dragging behind me. When I look over my shoulder, I see Kraven flying—*flying!*—across the room. His white wings spread out like a cloud. If I were looking at his wings alone, I might think he seemed peaceful. Innocent. But one glance at his rigid face, lips wet with blood, tells me I need to brace myself for impact.

Kraven slams into me, and we roll across the training mat in a heap. He lands on top of me and forces my shoulders back. My head hits the padding with a dull thump. It's the first time I realize how thin the blue mats are.

The liberator thrusts his face close to mine, so close I can see the pink of his gums as his lips peel back. "Let your demons go."

My heart hammers against my rib cage. All I can think about is getting him off me. Over and over I think about escape, because if I don't think about escape, then I'll think about what Kraven is saying, and I can't do that.

Kraven's chest inflates, and his words boom like a semi-sonic blast. "I said, *LET IT GO!*"

I snap. A thousand suppressed memories roll over me. I drown in them. "I can't!"

I'm not sure I've said anything at all until Kraven growls again.

"Why not?"

"I can't let go of my demons because I *am* a demon. Because I've *always* been a demon. I'm bad. There isn't something inside that I can let go of, because it's all I am."

Kraven jerks my shoulders up and slams me back down. "Tell me why, demon! How do you know?"

"Because they didn't care. Because my parents didn't give a *damn*. They said they loved me but where were they? *Where?!* They didn't want to be around me. That's how I know I'm bad, motherfucker, because even my parents didn't want to touch my ass."

There it is.

My darkness.

It's something I've carried around inside me since I was a child. Something I didn't dare talk about. My temples are wet with something. Tears, maybe. I don't know. All I do know is that I have to get out of here, or I'll suffocate. I throw my leg up and bring it right into Kraven's jewels. He falls off me and lands on his side, groaning

I get up and head toward the door. This time Kraven doesn't stop me. I feel the weight of what I just said sitting on my shoulders like a gorilla. All the memories I keep of my parents are the good ones. The time my dad finally took me on a trip with him. The time my mom made me meat loaf because I told her I liked it. But what about the others?

What about when my dad forgot my birthday year after year? What about when my mom forgot to pick me up from school when she promised she would? And I mistakenly believed her...again. I never stopped wanting them to pay attention, to notice me. And I hate myself for that. I *hate* it. I didn't want to love them. I didn't want to care what they thought.

But I did.

I believe they loved me. From a distance. When they had time. I try to tell myself that my dad cares now. He came to see me when I got cuffed as a liberator. And he left the ivory pendants for me and Charlie. That's something, right?

Whatever. It doesn't matter. Not anymore. I guess in the end, I returned their affection accordingly. After all, I made my father a corpse and my mother a widow.

You're welcome, Mom.

You're welcome, Dad.

Do you see what a good son I am?

I throw my fist into the wall beside me. The pain feels good, reminds me that I have pain all over—in my muscles, my bones, my eyes. But still the memories sit on my shoulders. They press me down until I can hardly walk. Press, press, press.

But I suddenly realize something, and when I do, I stop cold.

The weight isn't inside of me anymore.

ᛏ 31 ᛚ

YOU SPEAK OF WAR

As I make my way back to my room, the pain becomes unbearable.
Instead of focusing on it, I think about why Kraven took me outside.
The answer comes easily: to show me how much I need my wings.
And that staying here until I can summon them is worth the wait.

I take another step, and my ankle rolls. Another one, and my
knee buckles.

I'm falling.

Hours later, my eyes flutter open. The Mute Chicks stand over me.
Their hands knead my muscles, and their touch feels like a unicorn's
vagina. I groan deep in my throat, and one of the girls smiles. Her
cheeks redden, and I know I've embarrassed her, but I don't care as
long as she keeps doing whatever she's doing.

But they stop soon enough and move away, shuffling out the door
like they're eighty years old, even though one is probably in their late
twenties and the other is younger than me.

I pull myself up in bed and realize the hurt is mostly gone. I have
no idea how the Mute Chicks—who I'll henceforth call the Quiet
Ones, because it's a cooler name and I'm thankful and all—did this to

me. But it's like I didn't almost die this morning, more like I just got kicked in the face by a Clydesdale.

The Quiet Ones reappear through the doorway with Charlie between them. One of the girls strokes Charlie's hair while the other wraps her arm around her shoulders. Charlie seems comforted by their presence, and I suddenly understand why some liberators would choose to be *this* for her versus becoming a protector.

When Charlie is safely deposited in a chair near my bed, the women leave. Then it's just me and my girl.

"I can't believe he did this to you." Charlie's eyes are swimming with tears, but her mouth is pressed together in a tight line. She looks like she's ready to fight Kraven herself.

I realize she thinks every injury I have is from Kraven's hand. I measure my words carefully. "I'm learning how to better protect you."

Her entire body flinches. I said the wrong thing.

"I'm tired of people getting hurt because of me," she says. I expect her to repeat some version of this until she feels her point is made. But instead, she smooths her hair back and takes my hand. "But I know it's necessary. He needs me to be strong. This isn't about me. It's about mankind as a whole." Her eyes close. "And that means I'm going to have to think about everyone versus individuals I love."

Her eyes flash back open. "You may be hurt, Dante Walker. But I won't have you treating me the way you did this morning. You don't make decisions for me and Blue. And you don't make decisions for yourself that affect us, either. Do you understand?"

I'm almost as wary of upsetting Charlie as I am of Kraven's bottled-up rage. So I nod.

"Good." She leans over and touches her mouth to mine. The ivory pendant dangles from her necklace and tickles my chest as her hands explore the length of muscles in my back. A shiver races across my skin. Her lips hover over my ear, and she murmurs, "Valery is waiting outside."

My head falls back, and I sigh.

Charlie laughs and moves toward the door. "I'll be back. Don't go getting knocked around while I'm gone." She glances at me from over her shoulder. "The Silent Sisters are awesome, huh? They were putting all kinds of crap on you."

"I think you mean the Quiet Ones."

"Silent Sisters," she repeats with a grin.

That grin is so damn stunning.

As soon as Charlie steps outside, Valery bursts into the room all business and breasts.

"Nice cleavage," I tell her "Looks like you're really trying to make things easier on Max."

She ignores my comment and sits down. Her forehead is coated in a thin film of sweat, which I know can't be right, because girls like Valery would rather cut off their right arm than be caught perspiring.

"What's wrong?"

"What's wrong?" Valery says, her brow wrinkling. "What's *wrong*? Kraven never should have taken you"—she glances at the doorway— "*outside*. You could have been killed."

Understanding pours over me. Red was worried about me. I should hug her. I should get all serious and tell her I care about her, too.

But I just don't have it in me.

"You were scared I was going to get hurt," I say. "You love me. I mean, you are obsessed with me. Does Max know? Oh, man. I'm the reason you and Max aren't together right now. How did I never see it before now?"

Valery starts to get up but I grab her hand. My face softens. "Thank you, Red." I swallow and find that small function more difficult than normal. "Thanks for caring. If it had been you instead of me, I would have shattered Kraven's spine."

She smiles and shakes her head. It's the closest we'll come to admitting we like each other.

Outside the open door, I can hear Aspen and Charlie talking. They seem to be playing some sort of game. One will start a sentence, and the other will finish it. Then they'll laugh. I recognize Charlie's chiming laugh over Aspen's slightly deeper one.

"What are they doing?" I ask.

Valery rolls her eyes. "They've been doing it all morning. They can finish each other's sentences almost every time. It's pretty funny, actually."

I try to focus on what the two girls are saying, but Valery touches my arm, bringing me back to her. Her lips press together until they're nearly white, and then she stands and moves toward the lounge area.

"Hey, I need to talk to Dante without you guys here," she says to whoever is out there.

"Oh, so secretive," Annabelle says through a laugh.

Blue must make an offensive gesture because Valery yells at him and Annabelle laughs harder.

"Out, all of you," Red orders.

There's a shuffling of feet, and then Charlie's voice rings out. "I'll be back in a few minutes, babe. Want something to eat?"

A grin sweeps across my face. "How about a piece of my baby?"

"Disgusting," Blue says, though I'm surprised to hear the word isn't tinged with jealousy.

Valery watches them leave, then shuts the bedroom door. She sits back down. "What was he thinking? Do you know?"

I know she's talking about Kraven. "I wanted him to teach me how to summon my wings quickly, so that I could leave sooner."

Her eyes widen. "And did he?"

"No." I don't tell Red I went looking for the scroll. I'm sure she knows it's hidden at the Hive and that there's a decoy. I wonder how many liberators went searching for it and are walking around thinking they're the Secret Carrier.

Valery folds her hands in her lap like a Southern belle. "Dante, I've been meaning to ask. Do you know how to return to hell?"

My stomach drops. "Of course I do. I worked for hell for two years, didn't I?"

"So, how do you get there?"

Every muscle in my body tightens, reminding me there are still injuries to be healed. "That's not something you need to know."

Valery frowns.

"I don't want you anywhere near there," I clarify.

"I want to go with you."

Her announcement is like being submerged in icy water. "Out of the question. I'm going alone."

"But—"

"But nothing. I need you to stay here and help Kraven protect Charlie. This is my quest, Valery." What I don't tell her is how much it means to me that she's willing to come along. She has to know how dangerous it would be.

Red sits back in the chair. "Kraven said there were more sirens out there this morning than there were a few days ago."

My pulse quickens. "That isn't good." As Valery squirms, I decide to ask the question that's haunted me ever since I found out sirens existed. "Do you think the sirens will try and kill her themselves? Before, they were trying to get her to harm herself, but what about now?"

Valery's chest rises, and her boobs nearly make a full appearance. "I think Lucille is beginning to take more risks."

I smile at her continued use of Max's and my nickname for our ex–Boss Man. Maybe everyone will adopt the name. I'll be famous. Hashtag Lucille.

"I think he understands that harming an innocent human will trigger war on earth between heaven and hell," she continues. "But I also think he's gained confidence. He already has her soul. And if he can collect her body, too—the body of Big Guy's ordained human—then he may be ready to face the outcome."

"So you think Lucille sees Charlie as a symbol," I say, "and that by taking her body and soul, he's welcoming war? Like he's using her as an opening ceremony or something?" It's a thought I've had before, but speaking it aloud invites a wave of nausea.

"It's a war I think Big Guy would quickly accept." Valery rubs a hand along her neck. "I heard he was tempted to declare war after Rector killed Blue. But I guess ultimately his death was ruled an accident by Big Guy."

I think back and remember the surprise in Rector's eyes when the gun fired. But I don't believe his surprise meant he was remorseful. Not even for a second.

"And what about Aspen?" I ask. "Why is she so important? If you know, you need to tell me."

Red pulls on her earlobe. "I don't know, exactly, but I was told that liberating her soul was important to Charlie's plight."

"But how important?" I ask. "In a big way, or in a trivial way only Big Guy finds significant?"

"That I don't know." Valery meets my gaze and holds it, changes the subject. "Kraven wants three more days to train you. If he has really agreed to teach you how to summon your wings, it could be the difference between rescuing Charlie's soul and being captured."

Red wants the same thing I do, for Charlie to be safe, for me to liberate Aspen's soul, so I know she wouldn't push this if she didn't think the extra three days would truly help our cause. Reluctantly, I nod. "Three days. But then I descend into hell and steal back her soul, and nothing, and no one, will stop me."

A shadow appears from beneath the doorway seconds before it is flung open.

Valery gasps and releases my hand.

Aspen stands before us, green eyes blazing. She looks directly at me. "Take me with you."

✦⊰ 32 ⊱✦

MEANT TO BE

Aspen stands tall, awaiting an answer.

Valery rises from her chair. "What are you talking about, sweetie?"

"Cut the crap," Aspen says. "I overheard what you said. Those people, the sirens, they might hurt Charlie. And Dante wants to get her soul back from hell so they'll back off."

"It'll only buy us so much time," I interject. "If they lose her soul, they'll just regroup and form a new plan to collect it again. Or they may just give up and kill her for the fun of it."

Valery shoots me a *why are you telling her this* look.

I shrug. "She already heard everything."

"I'm going with you," Aspen says. "When you go down into hell to get her soul, I'm coming."

"Not happening," Valery says.

Aspen looks at me, and I open my hands. "You've been overruled."

"You didn't vote," she says through clenched teeth.

"Fine. You're not going." I study the determined set of her shoulders. "Why do you even want to go?"

"What else have I got to do?"

I try to hide my smile. "Not good enough."

Valery breaks in. "We're not discussing this. Aspen, you can't tell anyone what you heard here. Do you understand?"

Aspen ignores her and plunges on. "I want to go because I want to do something big with my life. Because I heard you say I was important and because I've always felt like I was *supposed* to do something important. Because Charlie is a good person, and she'll make the world a good place, and because I have a lot of wrongs to right." She pulls in a breath. "You came to liberate my soul, and this will complete your assignment. If I do this, then my soul will go to God, right? It'd be like I was risking my life for her, and for everyone, so that would have to be enough."

"Aspen, listen—"

"Also, I can fight," she says, her voice rising. "Better than you can. I'll do whatever you tell me to when we're down there, and if something bad happens, then I can help you escape." Aspen rushes to the bed and kicks the side of it. My head jerks up. Her face is flushed with fear and excitement, and I can almost smell the resolve rolling off her. "Because you said you wouldn't leave me. So I won't leave you. Or Charlie." She looks at Valery. "Or even you."

Valery meets my gaze, and it appears as if she's considering this. The thought ignites in my stomach. *I wouldn't be alone.* I don't want to be alone down there. Not in the least. But I can't allow Aspen to do this. She means too much to me already.

Looking at her now, at the fire in her stance, I see myself in her a thousand times over. She's confident, stubborn. It's why I can't let her go with me. One Dante Walker sneaking into hell is enough.

I open my mouth to tell her this, but she cuts me off again.

"You can't tell me no." Aspen points a finger at me. Her gloves are orange today. I wonder where she got them. "This could be why you were sent you to liberate me." She nods her head. "Maybe my mother was meant to leave. Maybe I was always meant to hate my father. Maybe I was supposed to befriend Lincoln and learn to fight and then meet Charlie Cooper and help you save her." Aspen's hand drops to her side. "If I save her, it'll make it better for my sister. And Sahara, she deserves that. So who are you, who are *either* of you, to tell me no? You want to know why I'm so important?" Aspen poses. "It's because I'm supposed to help rescue Charlie's soul. I know this. I can *feel* it."

Valery steps forward. "Okay."

"What?" I try to get out of bed and am relieved to find I actually can. "You can't tell her she can come. This is my journey. This is my—"

"Your *quest*. Right." Valery shakes her head like I'm an idiot.

"Quest is an awesome word," I mumble.

Aspen clears her throat, and I glance in her direction.

"All right," I groan. "You can come. But you'll have to train alongside Kraven and me. And let me tell you something, that guy is off his effing rocker. *Cyborg* my ass. More like Psycho."

A grin parts Aspen's mouth, but the gesture is short-lived. She wraps her arms around herself, nods once, and leaves the room.

"What are we doing?" I ask Valery when Aspen is out of sight.

Red holds a hand to her mouth. Through her fingers, she says, "I have no idea. But it could be good. Maybe she's right. This could be the reason Big Guy assigned you to her, the reason she's so vital to Charlie's path."

I sit on the edge of the bed. "It's almost like Big Guy assigned *her* to *me* instead of the other way around."

Blue's voice booms from the lounge area. "What's wrong? Aspen, talk to me."

Valery and I exchange a confused look before rushing from the bedroom. My muscles hardly ache as I move. It's so amazing, I almost forget about the panic in Blue's tone.

Aspen sits on one of the dilapidated couches, her gaze far away. Blue kneels in front of her as if he's praying at an altar. His hands hover over her thighs like he wants to touch her but isn't sure he should.

"Aspen," he whispers.

My chest tightens hearing the way he says her name. He doesn't rush it. It's more like he lets it linger in his mouth, tasting it. It's the same way I say Charlie's name.

Where is Charlie?

Aspen runs her hands over her long, dark hair. "It's okay. Everything is the way it should be." She finally lifts her gaze and meets my stare.

Blue stands and closes the distance between us in a flash. "What did you do to her?"

My mind buzzes. Is this right? Should I tell Aspen the deal's off?

I look at her again, and she nods. It's like she knows what's going through my head and is trying to assure me it's all right. I pull in a long breath. "I didn't do anything, Blue. Everything is fine."

"Bullshit. I'm tired of all the secrets." He points at Valery. "You carry some" —he jabs a finger into my chest— "and you carry some. And Kraven holds the rest. I'm tired of it. All of you say *no more secrets,* but there are always more."

I've never seen Blue's face so red. His head looks like an oversized strawberry. I move to squeeze his shoulder, but he bats my hand away.

"Don't touch me," he snarls. "You make everyone's life worse, *Dante.* You infect everyone around you, and I don't want your disease." Blue stomps toward the hallway as I try to breathe again. Because what he just said hurt worse than any siren's blow.

As he edges through the doorway, he passes Annabelle, Max, and Charlie coming in. Charlie takes one look at my face and rushes forward.

"Are you all right?" She wraps an arm around my waist, lets her fingers slide just beneath my waistband. "You shouldn't be out of bed."

"I'm fine." I press my lips against the top of her head.

Annabelle sits across from Aspen, and Max gawks at Valery's chest. "Hey, babe," he says to her. "I didn't know where you went."

A blush creeps over her cheeks. "You can't call me that."

"What, *babe*?"

She tries to look serious but can't help smiling when he waggles his eyebrows at her.

"What's going on with you two?" Annabelle asks.

"Everything," Max answers, moving toward Red.

"Nothing," Valery says, stepping back.

Annabelle crosses her legs and combs her fingers through her chin-length hair. "Looks to me like Valery's playing hard to get. Better not play too hard, or Max may go hunting elsewhere."

Valery's head jerks toward Anna. "What the hell do you know, Annabelle? You're lucky you're even here. I would've left you in Peachville if Dante hadn't insisted you come."

Annabelle gets up and acts like she's cranking something next to her hand. Her middle finger reels upward with each crank.

I'd laugh if there weren't so many hurt feelings rolling around here today. It's like we're a walking advertisement for anger management.

As Annabelle exits the room, waving her middle finger over her head like a flag, Charlie starts to go after her. I reach out and tug her back against me.

"Don't go," I say. "Please."

Charlie's brow furrows like she's not sure what to do. So I make the decision easier. Cupping the back of her head, I yank her closer until our mouths connect. Her lips move slowly at first, like her mind is elsewhere—probably with Annabelle. But soon enough she collapses against me, her fingers climbing up my back.

"Ew," Max says. "I wouldn't want to kiss that mouth. Who knows where it's been?"

Charlie breaks away like she's forgotten there was anyone else here. "I'll have you know I brush twice a day."

Max laughs at that, then looks at Valery. Red is working her bottom lip, and I can tell she's already wondering how to fix things with Annabelle. She sits across from Aspen, who's lost in thought again.

"She'll come back and I'll talk to her," Valery says, as if we asked.

A couple of hours later, Charlie is spooning tomato basil soup into my mouth, though I'm perfectly capable of doing it myself. Every once in a while she looks at the door. I know she's hoping Annabelle will come back like Blue finally did.

Blue stays in the lounge area out of sight, and I'm fine with that. I don't want to see him any more than he wants to see me. Charlie tries twice to go after Annabelle, but Aspen talks her out of it. She insists we've been in close quarters for too long. That we could all do with a little space. Each time, Charlie caves. But I'm not sure how much longer she'll be able to resist searching for her best friend.

My knee jerks nervously beneath the covers. Three days, three nights, and then we descend into hell. In the back of my mind, I hear a low whistling noise, the distinct sound only a demon makes. It's a noise Aspen and I will have to avoid hearing at all costs.

Charlie lays a hand on my knee. "You're going to spill your soup."

What I don't say is that I don't want soup. Who even eats soup for dinner? Senior citizens and runway models, maybe. But me? I need a good slab of steak and a baked potato. Hold the vegetables. Hold the garnish. Just bring me the rib-sticking shit.

The next time Charlie airplanes another spoonful of tomato grossness my way, I turn my head. Then I take the bowl from her and set it aside. The chatter from the lounge area dies until I'm certain everyone has crept off to bed.

Three days.

Three nights.

I wish I could spend every second of both with her.

There's only one thing I know of that will take my mind off what I'm going to do for Charlie, and that's Charlie herself. Every last part of her. I tug off the covers, swing my legs over the side of the bed, and guide her so that she stands between my knees.

My gaze meets her wide blue eyes, and I tell her, "I want you. Now."

33

CRIMSON ANGEL

I lift the hem of Charlie's shirt and press my lips to her bare stomach. Her head falls back, and her hair tickles my hands. I trail my way up her torso, slowly rising to my feet. When I'm standing over her, I stop and cup her face in my hands.

The last time Charlie and I were together, she was the one who took the lead. She showed me where she wanted to be kissed, how she wanted to be touched. But the thought of leaving Charlie, of knowing I may never make it back, makes me crave control.

I push my body against Charlie's until she's forced to walk backward. She releases a cry of surprise when her back hits the wall. I silence her with a kiss that borders on forceful. I listen for any sound that tells me she doesn't want it this way, but there's nothing to be heard.

My hands find her wrists. I pin them over her head and slide my other hand lower. Leaning forward, I kiss her neck. Then I bite the delicate skin there, soft at first, then much harder. Beneath my lips, I feel her throat vibrate with a small whimper.

"Tell me you want me," I say, my voice deep with lust.

Charlie is quick to respond. "I want you."

I spin her around so that her stomach pushes against the wall. My hand releases her wrists, and she reaches back to grab onto my thighs. I press against her harder, my hips connecting with her soft frame. My body swallows hers so easily.

"Take off your shirt," I command.

I give her only a few seconds before I make my next request. "Your jeans."

She does as I ask, her breath coming faster.

When she's stepped out of her jeans, she tries to turn and face me, but I keep her pinned there, my abs pressed against her back. My hands twitch, waiting to be released, and when I can't stand it another moment, I give them what they want. My fingers slide across every surface of her body until we're both aching to be together.

I step away and wrap my arm around her upper waist. My other arm circles beneath her legs, and I'm carrying her to the bed.

My lips never stray from her skin.

• • •

When I wake in the middle of the night, my chest is damp with sweat. I'd been dreaming about hell, about a blade biting into the flesh on my left arm and the clicking of demon nails. And about the devil's favorite torture devices, most of which include ice.

The bed creaks as I roll over, my arm searching blindly for Charlie.

But she isn't there.

My pulse picks up immediately. And by the time I've stepped into a pair of shorts the Quiet Ones gave me, my heart is pounding in my ears.

Something is wrong.

As soon as I know the answer—*Annabelle*—I'm rushing from the bedroom. I don't bother banging on Blue's door, I just throw it open. He bolts upright, eyes round with surprise. "Charlie is gone," I tell him. "I think something's wrong."

He answers the way anyone would after being awakened. "Whaa?"

"Get out of bed!" I back out of his room and find Aspen staring at me. "How can I help?" she asks.

That simple question provides such clarity that I could weep. Aspen is strong. She is fearless.

She is destined to help me steal back Charlie's soul.

"Go find Valery and Max," I order. "And Kraven. Tell them Charlie's not in her room and that Blue and I are looking for her." My hand sweeps through my mussed hair. "And tell them we haven't seen Annabelle since before dinner."

Aspen races from the room. I'm not sure how she'll find two liberators and one collector in this honeycomb of a house, but I trust her.

Blue appears after Aspen is gone. "You shouldn't involve Aspen," he growls.

I ignore his comment because now isn't the time. "You take a right down the hallway. If you don't find Charlie or Annabelle, meet me at the front of the house. The place with the three sets of doors."

We weave through the lounge and spill into the hallway. I'm about to turn left when Blue says, "They're probably just in the kitchen getting something to eat."

I can tell he doesn't believe that, so I just keep walking.

After twenty minutes of searching, there's no sign of the girls. I tell every staff member I see to bring Charlie and Annabelle to the entrance if they see them, but when I get there, I only see Blue. The way his face contorts tells me he hasn't had any luck. I nod toward the first set of doors, and together, we start trying different ones. The doors aren't locked from the inside, which seems like a gross security fail, but I decide Kraven must have his reasons.

I have no idea how Valery memorizes the order when the doors are always being repainted. For a moment, I consider trying to find the hidden door at the back of the mansion, the one Kraven took me through yesterday morning. But I decide if Charlie and Annabelle went outside for whatever idiotic reason, they would have gone this way.

After more than two dozen unsuccessful attempts, Blue and I finally land outside. The moon is full overhead, casting enough light so that I can easily see. As we spread out, our shoes crunching over patches of snow, my heart climbs into my throat. I start thinking about the sirens, about why they've been stalking out here in the cold instead of trying to break in. Are they waiting for the collectors to recruit more of them? And why aren't the liberators doing anything besides training? I hate that we're practicing defense when we should be all offense.

Then I think of something else, something that makes my breath catch.

Maybe the sirens are waiting for Charlie to come to them. Wouldn't that be easier? It's not like she'd stay inside the Hive forever. Sooner or later, she'd go outside—to take a walk, to see the ocean up close.

To find a missing friend.

Before I know what I'm doing, my legs are pumping beneath me. I abandon trying to be quiet and call out her name. "Charlie! Charlie, are you out here?"

Blue follows my lead, and why wouldn't he? He doesn't know about the sirens on the cliffside. He knows it's safe inside the Hive, and that the outside is uncertain, but he doesn't know how many of the collector's soldiers cling to the rocks above the sea.

"Annabelle?" Blue hollers. "Charlie?"

A scream rips through the muggy night air.

Blue and I look at each other for one brief moment. Then we're running. My arms whip up and back, and I sprint like I'm competing in the hundred-yard dash, like every hundredth of a second means the difference between success and failure.

Blue and I round the house, and I see a shape spread out along the ground. As I get closer, I make out short dark hair splayed over pale skin. *Annabelle.* She's still so far away. It'll take time to get to her. Too much time.

I see someone standing near Annabelle's still body. Their arms are open wide, and they're walking fast toward Anna.

"Stop!" I shout. "If you touch her, I'll kill you. I'll *kill* you."

By some miracle, the person stops moving. I run faster. Faster. Blue is at my heels. We're only a few feet away when I see who's walking toward Annabelle.

It's Charlie.

Her hands are covered in something dark and wet. She drops to her knees.

As Blue rushes to Annabelle's still form, I race toward Charlie. I reach out to touch her, but she stops me with a stare. Her eyes are wild and ferocious, and I'm not sure what she'll do if I get any closer.

She raises her palms to the sky like she's making an offering. She looks like an angel.

An angel painted in blood.

The blood is everywhere. It drips from her fingers. It covers her chest. It's in her hair. Along her neck. There's even a splatter of dark-colored dots peppering her left ear.

I don't care where the blood came from. The Quiet Ones will fix it. They'll make Charlie better. And they'll make Annabelle wake up.

My arms snake around Charlie, and she stares at me like she's not sure who I am.

I guide her toward Annabelle. Blue has to get her. He's got to help Annabelle, and we have to get both of them inside. Now.

Blue turns toward me, but I can't see the expression on his face. If he looks grief-stricken, I will hit him. Annabelle has to be okay. She has to. Blue wraps himself around Annabelle and starts to stand. I hear Anna groan, and I'm so relieved, I think my knees may buckle. But they can't. I have to be strong. Strong enough for me and Charlie both.

I follow behind Blue as he walks Annabelle back toward the front of the house.

My heart hammers in my chest, and all I think is, *Get inside—get inside—get inside.*

The four of us have only made it ten feet when I hear Charlie mutter something.

I try to ignore it. I can only focus on one thing right now, and that's getting us out of here before the sirens climb up from their grave.

Charlie speaks again, and this time I hear her. I hear her, but I don't want to.

She repeats herself over and over. I try to shush her, but when I do, she raises her voice.

"I killed him," she says. "He's dead, and I did it."

Blue doesn't take another step even though I'm telling him to hurry the hell up.

"It was a siren, I think. It must have been." Charlie holds her hands out again. "I didn't think it would kill him."

"What?" Blue asks, his arms still holding Annabelle upright. "What killed him?"

Charlie smiles. I know it's a nervous gesture, but it sends a chill up my spine all the same. "He was crouched in front of Annabelle. He wouldn't get away from her. He was going to hurt my best friend." She shakes her head. "I wasn't going to let that happen."

"Blue, *move*!" I yell.

He remembers we're outside and turns back to his burden. For every two strong steps he takes, Annabelle takes one labored one. He's all but dragging her behind him, and that's fine as long as it gets her closer to safety.

Charlie keeps talking beside me. "It's like he was waiting for me," she says, her voice devoid of emotion. "So I let him come. I ran away from Annabelle so he'd chase me and get away from her. And then I turned and faced him." Charlie puts a hand to her chest like she's feeling for something that isn't there. When she pulls her palm away, there's a bloody handprint left behind. "I stabbed the horn directly into his eye. And his eye…it just burst. So then I tried to stab him in the other eye. But I missed and got his throat. After that, I just kept going at his face until he stopped—"

"You did what you had to do," I say, cutting her off. My arm grips her waist so hard I know it must inflict pain. But I can't loosen my grasp. I may never take my hands off her again.

"Do you hear that?" Charlie asks. She sounds like a child, like she's asking about ice cream instead of demons buried by the dark.

I spin around and see what she heard—the shadow of a man creeping slowly toward us.

"Blue," I say, instilling as much calm into my voice as I can. "I want you to take Charlie and get the two of them inside."

His gaze meets mine. He opens his mouth like he's going to say something, but I already know.

"We're cool," I tell him. "We're always cool. Now go."

When I crane my head back around, I find that the siren is now racing forward. I fill my lungs and then start running in his direction, too. It's just one siren, just one, and behind me is my world.

We're only a few feet apart when I realize his eyes aren't on me. They're set on the people fleeing toward the house. He snarls, and his shoes pound the earth. He's so close now. Close enough that I reach out to grab him. But I miss. I made a mistake. I misjudged how fast he was going, and now he's past me and crashing toward Charlie like a bolt of lightning.

"Blue!" It's the only word I can get out.

Blue jumps into action. He lets go of Annabelle and leaps in front of Charlie. His arms spread out behind him, pushing her back.

But the siren speeds past Blue and Charlie both.

I suddenly understand who he is headed for, who he was *always* headed for.

And now it's too late.

⅗ 34 ⅖

MY REASON

The siren—not much older than me—takes Annabelle's head in his hands. His voice comes out rough, like the sound a truck makes driving over pebbles. "I'm going to snap her neck. And you're going to watch."

Charlie comes alive in an instant. The blood is forgotten. The body she left behind—gone. Now there's only Annabelle. She shoves Blue from behind, and he's so startled, he tumbles to the ground. "I know what you want," she says, her head held up high. "I'll go with you."

The siren smiles, and the sight raises goose bumps across my skin.

"Charlie, don't move," I say, slinking toward her. "Don't take another step."

But she's not listening. She wants this. She's waited for a moment when she could protect those she cares about instead of the other way around. And now she won't be denied. Charlie moves closer, and the siren's grin widens.

"Rector is going to be so pleased," he says, licking his lips.

My pulse pounds at my temples at the name. Rector. The head

collector. The same collector who got too close to my mom, who forced Charlie to forfeit her soul, who *accidentally* killed Blue.

"Get back," Annabelle mumbles to Charlie, barely conscious. It's the first time I've heard her speak, and her words, the life in them, fill me with courage.

I'm almost to Charlie when the siren says, "You're all Rector wants, so I guess it doesn't matter what I do with this one."

He means Annabelle.

He's going to kill Annabelle even though Charlie is within his reach.

But in a flash, the siren is airborne.

He's flying through the air, and Kraven is standing in front of Annabelle like a wild dog. His wings spread out, and he roars with unbridled fury. He turns once and takes Annabelle's face in his hands. His eyes search hers.

Then he's soaring toward the siren, his wings brightening the night sky.

The siren screams so loudly, my ears ring. I don't know what Kraven is doing to him, and I don't care. There's a quick snapping sound, and the screams stop. Seconds later, Kraven is touching down in front of Annabelle. He glances around, searching for any other source of danger, but there's nothing to see.

Except for the blood covering Charlie's body.

Annabelle's knees buckle, and Kraven sweeps her into his arms. He leans his head down and presses his cheek against hers. And then, as if he remembers we're watching, he pulls away.

Valery, Max, and Aspen come rushing around the corner of the Hive. Max gets to us first. "Is everyone all right?" He sees Charlie. "Holy crap."

I seek out Aspen and find she's staring at me. She nods. "We can't wait any longer," I tell Kraven, my gaze still on Aspen. "So if you have any secrets to share, now's the time."

Kraven moves toward Blue and passes Annabelle into his arms. Then he grabs my shoulders and jerks my chest against his. "I'm going to take her."

"Dude, back off." My muscles clench. "What are you doing?"

Kraven holds me in place. "Have you not liberated a soul recently? You can't take it with you down *there*. Now hurry up; more sirens will be here any moment." He glances around like he can't believe they aren't here already, like this may be some sort of trap.

A wave of understanding washes over me. Grams. Kraven wants me to give him her soul so he can turn it in to Big Guy. Makes sense. The fact that I'd forgotten this detail makes my face burn. I close my eyes and try to pass the soul into him, but I can't.

"Stop trying to give it to me," he barks. "I have to take it from you. That's the only way it works."

How am I supposed to know this crap? I was never taught how to steal souls, though that didn't stop Rector from figuring it out. I quit trying to do anything, and when I do, I feel a slight tickle along my chest. I'm not sure if that means anything. When Rector took Charlie's soul from me, I didn't sense much of anything. If I had, maybe I would have known what had occurred. "Did it happen? Do you have it?"

"What's going on?" Charlie asks from beside me. She's still dazed but seems to be doing better. She and everyone else are staring at Kraven's wings. Even the people who'd already seen them once before are speechless.

Kraven doesn't answer either of us. He just darts toward Blue and takes Annabelle back. Guess I'll take that as a *yes, I took her soul.* "Go now, Dante. Quickly. I have to get them inside."

"He can't go now," Valery says. "He promised you three more days. Doesn't he need that to learn—?"

"Red, this can't wait," I say. "You know it can't."

"What is everyone talking about?" Blue says. "And why are we doing it out here?"

"Max, will you lead us?" I say.

"No!" Valery barks. "You don't need him."

Max steps to my side. "Of course, man. If you insist on being an idiot, I won't let you do it alone."

"He can't go back there," Valery insists. She's talking to me but grabbing onto Max's shirt. Tears fill her eyes, and her cheeks bloom red.

"Blue, take Charlie inside right now," Kraven demands. Though Blue's face is filled with confusion, he does what Kraven asks. At first Charlie holds tight to my waist, shaking her head *no*. But as Blue begins to pull her away and I begin to push, she starts shouting. I know Charlie doesn't know exactly what's happening. But she knows enough. She knows I'm going somewhere and that it can't be some place good.

"No, no!" she cries. "You can't go. Not after what happened. Not after what I did."

"Charlie, it's okay." A lump forms in my throat. "They'll watch after you."

"But where are you going?"

I glance over my shoulder at the cliff and the ocean beyond it. Blue's right, we can't stay out here much longer, but I'm afraid if I go back inside, I'll never leave. "Charlie, you have to trust me. Go back inside the Hive before the other sirens—"

"I won't go until you tell me where you're going," she snarls. Charlie is slowly becoming hysterical. Blood drips from her shirt onto the ground, and her eyes are wide with fear. "Tell me. Tell me!"

I pry her fingers from my shirt as tears sting my eyes. Charlie's bottom lip trembles.

My heart.

It may never beat again.

Aspen comes to stand beside me. "Are you ready?" I ask her in a whisper. She pulls in a deep breath and takes my hand. Her glove feels slick against my palm.

Seeing this, Charlie goes apeshit. Blue wraps his arms around her waist as Charlie throws herself toward me. "Her? You're taking *her*?"

As Charlie writhes against Blue, I can't help but be amazed. I can't believe she ever thought I'd want her to change. This beautiful, peaceful girl. Look at her go. She's thrashing like a rabid beast. Fighting for what she wants.

No, I never wanted her to change.

But she has.

"I lost my Grams," Charlie says. "I won't lose you, too." Her face is twisted with misery. It's only been a few days since Grams passed away. Each night, I see it in the way Charlie sleeps—broken and filled with nightmares. But during the day she pushes it down so we won't know, so we won't feel sorry for her. Not now, though. Now the pain is right there, raw. So close it's like I could reach out and grab it.

Her words sting, but I won't stay. Because I love her—*I love her*—but this is about saving her life. And it's about saving the lives of others, too. I don't want to care about other people, those humans whose faces I've never seen and whose names I've never learned. But I do. I care because Charlie taught me how to care. And now I have to do what's right.

Even if it means leaving her.

Even if it means I may never return.

I release Aspen's hand and take Charlie Cooper's face in my hands. My chest breaks open. "My sweet angel," I whisper. "You are my pain. You are my reason. I love you. I love you."

Our lips connect. I taste the salt of her tears, the tang of siren blood on her mouth. I kiss her as if it might be the last time.

And then I let go and turn away.

I start walking.

Max and Aspen follow, and Charlie starts to sob.

"You love me?" she cries. "You *love* me! You said forever, Dante. Forever means you can't leave. You can't. You said forever!"

I can still hear her screaming as she's dragged inside the Hive. With every step I take, my body burns hotter. My hands shake, and I clench my teeth. I want to run to her, to dry her tears. But I just keep walking. I must.

Forever.

35

GOOD-BYE, FRIEND

Twelve hours later, after a grueling flight, little sleep, and bad food, Max, Aspen, and I wait on a private runway for our car. We may have left the Hive without a dime between us, but Max had his phone. And though Valery is none too pleased that Max came along, she did agree to make us accommodations once he explained what we needed.

I'm still thinking about the things Charlie said when a black sedan pulls up. I hope she knows I'm doing this for her.

Inside the car, Aspen shifts in the leather seat, bringing me out of my head. She works her necklace between her fingers and watches me. She's waiting for some kind of direction, but I have nothing to give her.

"So," she says. "Alaska."

I shrug.

"I thought it'd be somewhere hot." Aspen glances at Max, hoping she'll have more luck digging information out of him. But he doesn't look at her. He's lost in thought, and I don't have to guess who he's thinking about. Or what color her hair is.

I don't want to talk. I just want to let my stomach eat itself. But

Aspen has done something phenomenal. She's volunteered to go on this soul-stealing mission whether it's a good idea or not, and I feel like I owe her my attention.

"We'll be there in a couple of hours," I say. "It takes time to drive in this kind of weather."

Aspen looks outside the window. Snow flurries lash by us in a strange war dance. The road is barely two lanes wide, and I can only really see the tracks where other tires have driven. Before long, that'll be gone, too. Then we'll be on snowmobiles.

"I would have thought we'd be somewhere hot," Aspen repeats.

Exactly, I think. *That's why we're here instead.*

Before long, the driver stops the car. He gets out and pops the trunk. Then he gets back in and hands us thermal wear and heavy jackets. As he tosses a red beanie to me, I wonder how much he knows about what we're doing out here.

Next to nothing.

They never know anything. But then again, that's the luxury money affords you. Pay someone enough, and they won't ask questions. Sometimes I see a familiar face, but the end result is always the same: car, snowmobiles, no questions.

When Max and I step outside, the snow bites at my exposed skin. There isn't much of it considering I'm wearing two layers of heavy-duty winter clothing, snow goggles, a stocking cap, and gloves. Aspen finishes changing in the car and steps outside. Though the wind howls, I can still hear her gasp from the sudden change in temperature.

"It won't be for long," I yell. Then I nod toward the three red-and-black snowmobiles. Max shakes hands with one of the snowmobile drivers. Aspen and I stomp over as the guys pass us and jump inside the sedan, the chains on the snow tires clinking as the car pulls away. I give Aspen a quick rundown of how to work the snowmobile. She nods her head and hugs her arms around her waist.

Max checks something in the storage area behind the seat and gives me a thumbs-up. I know what he was checking for, but I don't want to think about it. Not yet.

I glance at Aspen and cock my head forward. She gets on her snowmobile and tugs on a helmet. I can see her body shaking, but I'm not sure whether it's from the cold or something else.

After pulling on my own helmet, my right thumb squeezes the throttle, and we're off.

I lean into turns and barely notice the numbness snaking over my body. I don't have to ask for directions. Neither does Max. We'd know the way with closed eyes and frostbitten balls. Every time I catch Aspen driving in my peripheral vision, my stomach flutters. *This was a mistake*, I can't help thinking. *She shouldn't be here.*

But then I remember what she said at the Hive, about this being the reason I was assigned to her, the reason she's so important to Big Guy. So I focus on that. And I think about Charlie. I try to keep them both suspended in my mind. It helps.

At least until I see it—

The entrance to hell.

Max and I turn our snowmobiles to the right and ease off the throttle. Then we dismount and head into the forest with Aspen at our heels. The first time I had to find the tree, the white spruce among all the others, I imagined I'd never make my way back to it. There are no distinguishing marks. Nothing that says, *I am the one to take you there.* But trust me when I say once you know it's the one, it's hard to unknow it.

Snow climbs to just beneath our knees, and we're breathing hard by the time we arrive. With tall trees coated in frothy white powder and the ground glittering beneath our feet, it really does feel like Christmas. Guess it's high time to spread a little holiday cheer in hell.

"Is this some kind of joke?" Aspen shouts over the wind. "Are you guys going to bury me out here?"

I toss a smile her way even though I'm not feeling it. I remember the first time I returned to this place on my own. It was like having a dentist appointment that you know would be painful and going, anyway. It's like that times a million.

We stop in front of the tree. It's easily eighty feet tall and reminds me of a Christmas tree every time I see it. I'm sure Lucille finds this wildly amusing. Aspen gazes upward and runs her hand over the sharp needles. Her fingers extend out from orange gloves.

Did she sleep with them on last night?

I think about telling her she should take my gloves so she doesn't get frostbite. But she won't need the warmth for much longer.

Max reaches into the back of his pants and pulls out a short blade. It's what he was checking for on the snowmobile. Valery remembered everything Max asked for. Though I bet this part of the instructions made her particularly nervous.

My best friend hands the knife to me. Just like the tree, it isn't anything special—a four-inch blade with a wood handle.

Blood surges through my veins as I angle the knife toward my inner arm. Aspen gasps.

"Wait," Max says. "How are you going to do it?"

I let the knife drop to my side and put a hand on his shoulder. "You and I, we know every corner. It'll be easier than you think because no one would ever dare try what I'm going to do. Lucille's arrogance is his Achilles heel."

Max knows this is true but doesn't want to let it go. He pulls me into a hug so quickly I almost stab him in the leg. I throw my free arm around him, and my chest aches. My best friend has done so much for me. He's risked his cuff to leave the collectors and be with me and Red, and he's risked it again by coming here. I wish I'd made more time to hang out with him over the last few days. I only hope I can show him how much I care about our friendship when I get back. *If* I get back. I may talk a big game, but I know I may never see this part of earth again. And that includes Max.

"Get off me, leech," I tell him, wiping a hand across my eyes. "Just wait with the snowmobiles. We'll be back before you know it."

Max studies the snow beneath his boots.

When I bring the knife to my arm this time, I don't hesitate. I drag the blade across my inner left forearm until a dark trail of blood rises up. Turning my arm over, I let the blood drip onto the base of the tree. Then I hand the knife to Aspen.

"Left arm," I tell her. Even this part I want to protect her from. But I know I have to let her do this without help, because it'll only get worse from here on out.

Aspen closes her eyes, grits her teeth, and copies what I did. Then she turns her arm over. Her blood sprinkles across the snow, staining it red. Max backs up and holds my gaze.

Beneath the tree, the ground splits apart.

There's a loud rumbling as a black hole spreads out from the roots. It swallows the blood-stained snow as a flesh offering and yawns open. I rush to Aspen's side and pull her away from the black void. She's holding her chin high, but I see the way her hands clench into fists.

"You can stay," I tell her. "Max can take you back."

"No," she says. "I'm doing this." I don't know where her resolve stems from, but I accept her answer and move away. Aspen peers over the lip of the opening and sees the descending stairs. "It's an actual place," she says. "Hell is here on earth."

"Of course." I ease myself down onto the first step and turn toward her. "Last chance, Aspen. You don't have to do this."

Her gaze shifts to Max before landing back on me. Determination rages in her eyes, so I offer my hand, and she steps down beside me.

Max moves closer. "I don't know how much longer I can do this," he says unexpectedly. "I can't be a collector while she's a liberator. At some point I'm going to have to take a risk like you guys are."

I don't know why he's telling me this now. But it's almost like he wants me to know on the off chance that I don't come back. I glance at his cuff. He means he wants to remove it. He wants to break off the dargon and see if Big Guy accepts him so that he can be with Valery.

"Not yet, champ," I say. "Wait until I get back. Then we can do it together."

The line between his eyes relaxes. He smiles.

I lift my hand in a wave.

He flips me off, and I laugh.

Then he turns and heads back toward the snowmobiles. There are so many unsaid things between us. He, more than anyone, knows what Aspen and I are about to face. I watch him walk away, bringing his knees up high to avoid stumbling in the snow.

Aspen squeezes my arm, and I turn my attention to the stairs.

"Are you ready?" I ask.

Aspen lets go of me and begins the descent. I follow after her. The ground closes over our heads. Snow drops down as the earth seals tight, sizzling against the ground.

When I hear the first moan of agony, I know it's real.

I've come home to hell.

⊰ 36 ⊱

WELCOME TO HELL

Aspen and I shed our heavier clothes as the temperature rises. Everyone assumes hell is the hottest place they can imagine. It isn't true, though hell certainly isn't cool, either. Within a few seconds, sweat pricks my forehead and arms. I seriously wish I could sport shadow down here; it would make things a lot easier. Of course, I guess it doesn't matter if Aspen is with me. I also regret not bringing a weapon. I know what Kraven said about losing my cuff, but right about now I'm fretting over things much worse.

We take the stairs down for what feels like an eternity. I try to keep my eyes on the steps in front of me instead of the walls. Aspen hasn't noticed what they're made of, and I hope she never does. But at one point, as we're finally nearing the bottom, she slips. Her arms flail, and she catches herself against the walls.

"Watch it," a gravelly voice says.

Aspen almost screams. I have to cover her mouth to stop her. "Shhh," I tell her. "No matter what you see, no matter what happens, don't scream."

I spin toward the wall. "And *you*. You're not supposed to talk unless you see something unusual."

Aspen's eyes widen when she sees the faces. Hundreds of them stick out from the walls like they're masks. There isn't much light in the stairwell, but it's enough to make out that they're human.

"She nearly pushed me back through," the face complains. "You know how hard it is to get a spot."

I imagine the bodies trapped between the walls, shoving their faces through so they can see who comes and goes. The faces don't actually protrude. It's more like the wall bends to their shape so that each one looks bluish-black, just like the stone that locks them inside.

"Shut up," I order. "You're not hurt."

"It's Dante Walker," a face nearby whispers.

"Ooh, Dante is back," another says.

"Who's the girl?"

"Dante is bringing the king a live one."

"I knew he'd come home!"

Their voices blend together like a warped song. It almost drowns out the sound of the moans, ever present.

Aspen's trying to make herself as small as possible. Her cheeks are scarlet with fear, and she's trying to look everywhere at once. "This can't be real. I just—"

"I know." I grab her hand and force her to keep moving. Near the bottom of the stairs there's a soft glow. Aspen must think it's the flicker of a light or a torch. But it's neither. "Remember, no matter what happens, no screaming." I look ahead and consider what waits there. "The collectors are the only ones who will definitely recognize I shouldn't be here. The others may not know."

The others. The demons and tortured humans. *Those* others.

I decide not to clarify and instead lead the way. As we move forward, I say a silent prayer to Big Guy that the collectors aren't here, that they're all above ground recruiting more sirens or sealing souls or whatever.

Aspen and I step down from the last stair and walk into a circular room. Red dirt covers the floors, and a green glow washes the area. The ground shakes, and I grip Aspen's hand tighter.

"What's that sound?" she asks, her voice shaking.

Before I can answer, a bear the size of a barn pads into the room. The familiar green hue radiates from his eyes. It burns bright as he studies us. Aspen stumbles backward as the bear rises up on his hind legs and roars. The sound is deafening. It shakes the bones beneath my skin, and my eardrums feel as if they've ruptured.

Hello, old friend.

The bear, coated in thick black fur with teeth the size of my arm, drops down onto all fours. He kneels and opens his mouth wide. It's so wide, a human could walk into his jaws if they only hunched down.

And that's exactly what we'll do.

"We have to go in there," I say.

Aspen's face twists with dread. "Inside his mouth?"

"It won't be for long," I clarify. After we'd left the Hive, Max and I tried to prepare Aspen for what she should expect in hell. But she wouldn't listen. She said if she knew too much, she'd be tempted to back out. So I only explain what I have to, when I have to.

Together, Aspen and I approach the bear's mouth as we would the entrance of a cave. Saliva drips from his teeth like rain falling from the side of a house. We wait just outside his jaws, and his pink tongue rolls out like a red carpet. As soon as we step inside, the snakes come. I'll give them credit; they waited longer than they usually do, coiled in the pockets of the bear's cheeks.

At first, Aspen kicks at the serpents, trying in vain to free her legs of them. But they come faster, more and more until we are covered. They twine around our wrists like bracelets and squeeze our middles until it's hard to breathe.

I can tell Aspen is dangerously close to breaking The Rule.

A snake with black scales and an orange head sinks its fangs into her neck. She cries out but stuffs a fist into her mouth to block the sound. She shakes her head back and forth.

My muscles clench. I don't want her to be here. I don't want anyone to know this is where I came from or to experience this level of terror. But I try and push the thought from my mind and focus on the end goal: get to the soul storage room and get out of here.

"Aspen," I say, keeping my voice as calm as I can. "The snakes won't hurt you. Just keep walking toward the bear's throat. We have to go into his belly."

"Oh, God," Aspen wails, tears streaming down her face.

She keeps walking.

Darkness swallows us, but I know it won't last long. I can hear Aspen whimper. She's strong, so strong that her legs carry her forward even though she's blinded by fear. Aspen may think she's failing me, but she's doing as well as I could've possibly hoped.

Slime drips down my back as we stoop low and continue through the bear's massive throat. Beside me, slick pink ridges quiver when I touch them.

"Aspen, do you trust me?" I ask.

Aspen hesitates. When she speaks, her voice is choked. "I trust you."

I tickle the bear's throat with my fingertips. I want to get this over with. The mammoth animal works his tongue so that we're thrown side to side.

"What are you doing?" Aspen hollers.

I would tell her to keep it down, but it doesn't matter. Not in here.

The bear swallows.

We slip down his throat like it's a water park slide. Aspen grabs onto my leg, and we tumble head over heel. My heart pounds against my rib cage. Not because of what's happening—I've done this too many times to be afraid—but because I know how Aspen must feel, how her mind must scream for release.

We land hard, and I pull Aspen to her feet.

She wipes her gloved hands over her eyes and tries to hide the fact that she's been crying. I don't know why. She just got swallowed by an oversized bear, for crap's sake. I think she's allowed a few tears.

I take her shoulders in my hands. "Are you okay? We've got a few more rooms to pass through, not too much longer. This place is an unending labyrinth, but I know the way. Can you make it?"

Aspen's eyes widen as she takes in her surroundings. "What is this place?" Her face holds a child-like fascination. My stomach lurches; that fascination will soon change to something very different.

"The Hall of Mirrors," I answer.

The room is a perfect square and filled with reflective objects. An intricate chest, a suspended chandelier, musical instruments, picture frames, scattered furniture, children's toys, stairs leading to nothing—they're all mirrors. An uncertain smile slides across Aspen's face. "It's so beautiful," she says, turning to me. "How is it possible?"

Light radiates from an unknown source, illuminating our bodies and bouncing off the mirrors. It's a pristine palace. A house of wonders.

But it's also a place of nightmares.

Aspen picks up a sphere and tosses it between her hands. It's amazing how quickly she goes from tearful to confident curiosity. But then she looks closer at the globe. Her eyes narrow, and her features harden.

"What am I seeing?" Alarm colors Aspen's voice.

"It isn't real." I rush to her side but stop when the images begin bouncing from the mirrors. My mom stands with her back to me, laughing. My father watches, blood dripping down his cheeks. I move toward the center of the room, stepping over glass tiles that play an endless reel of Max being torn open. My mind repeats what I just told Aspen, but it's hard to believe what I'm saying because it's all right here.

This room is always hard. No matter how many times I pass through it, my head throbs. My muscles tighten.

I can't breathe.

Aspen drops down onto the floor and covers her head. She's in the fetal position muttering about her father. Her back rises and falls too quickly. I've got to get to her before her heart gives out.

But it's hard when Charlie's face stares back at me, her eyes gouged out.

"You have to believe it isn't real," I say to Aspen, and maybe to myself, too. "You have to believe it isn't real, or we'll never get out."

I drop onto the floor and watch Max being dismembered beneath my hands. Then I lunge at Aspen. I yank her into my arms and whisper in her ear, "Think about Sahara. Think about Lincoln. Remember why we're here. This isn't real. It's in your head. Believe what I'm telling you. You have to, Aspen."

Several seconds pass before her head lifts. She looks around the room, and though her face is contracted in pain, she says, "It isn't real."

The moment she speaks those words, I believe them, too.

The room changes colors. It's red. There are human bodies everywhere, shielding their eyes and screaming for the images to stop. Aspen never knew they were there. But I did.

Beneath us, the floor cracks into a million pieces.

Aspen freezes and I see him—a collector—standing in the Hall of Mirrors, arms folded across his chest.

The floor shatters, and we fall.

⊰ 37 ⊱

WE ALL FALL DOWN

I've memorized this fall. I know the way the gravel will dig into my muscle when I land. But it doesn't lessen the blow when I hit the ground.

Aspen smacks onto her side and rolls to the left. I land flat on my back. The breath is ripped from my lungs, and if I could, I'd lie still. But I can't. Not after who I saw. "You're all right," I tell Aspen, helping her up. I'm not sure if she is or not, but I need her to be, so I keep tugging on her arm. She stands and looks overhead. The shattered floor is now a stained-glass ceiling. Light slinks in through the jigsaw pieces, casting a riot of blues, greens, and purples across the area. The heavenly colors do nothing to soften the smell.

"Oh, my God," she groans. "What is that? It smells like…"

"It's decay." My blood hammers behind my temples as I search for him. He's here. He must be.

There's a narrow bridge connecting the dark platform we're on to a similar one on the other side. We have to cross over to get where we're going. I contemplate not telling Aspen about the collector—about Patrick—but I must. This isn't something she'd want to be in the dark about.

Aspen is running her hands over her long, dark ponytail when I say, "They know we're here."

Her head whips around. "How do you know?"

"There was one back there. In the Hall of Mirrors."

Aspen glances around like she's searching for him. "It could be only one," she says, but the way her brow furrows tells me she doesn't believe that. "How fast can we get to the soul storage area?"

In response, I grab her hand, and we dart toward the bridge. The pine boards creak and sway beneath our feet, and far below, black oil bubbles and pops. Moans fill the air, and I know what they are, but we have to keep moving.

The bridge sways wildly, wider and wider, and I order Aspen to run.

The demons. They're coming.

They're climbing up the posts that support the bridge, nails digging into the old wood. If Aspen sees them, she'll scream. And once that happens, the demons will scream, too. There's a rule in hell: no matter how much pain you're in, no matter how many horrors you face, you can never scream. If you do, they'll come for you. And you will be punished.

The creatures are close. Their stench makes me light-headed, but I have to keep pumping my legs.

"If it isn't the infamous Dante Walker," a voice shouts. It isn't a scream, but it's dangerously close.

A shiver races down my back as I turn around, hanging onto the rope handrail for balance. Patrick, the collector, stares back at me, a shit-eating grin smeared across his face. I trained Patrick a couple of years ago. He's a good soul collector and has a decent left hook, if memory serves. He's a scrapper, a small guy who's quick and eager to please. Patrick would like nothing more than to hand-deliver me to Lucille.

I gauge how far Aspen and I are from the other side and know we could make it there before he does. In fact, once the demons crawl over the side, they may even take him down. They're slow and stupid, but they have strength in numbers. But if he runs fast enough—and God knows he's a fast fucker—he'll make it across, too.

Not if I hold him up, though.

My eyes lock with Aspen's. "Run."

Then I turn and race toward Patrick. The bridge rocks, and I almost tip over the side twice, but I keep moving. Patrick accepts the challenge and storms in my direction. I don't know what his goal is. Maybe to toss me to the demons so I'm trapped. Then find Lucille and lead him here.

We both run hard, realizing we have seconds before the demons ascend. As we get closer, I anticipate he'll go for my chest. Maybe even my face. But instead he drops low and barrels into my legs.

I smack onto my back with a grunt. Patrick dives on top of me like a Doberman, all snapping teeth and lean muscle. He goes for my throat, and I let him. My thumbs dig into his eyes, and he bites down to keep from screaming. Taking advantage of his pain, I bring my knees up. I kick out, and his body flies backward. He's upright in a flash, racing toward me with wide brown eyes.

He stops.

Crawling over the side of the bridge is a demon.

Its body is shaped like a human's, but it's all wrong. The angles are too sharp, and the spine is too curved. Black-and-yellow scales cover the creature's torso, and talons grow where fingernails should be. The demon's beady black eyes fix on me. Its mouth drops open. A low whistle emanates from its throat. The sound could be from a young girl strolling through a park with a boy's face in her mind. It's a sweet, innocent noise, but coming from this creature it's chilling.

This thing, this *creature*, used to be a person.

The demon moves toward me, toenails clicking against the bridge. Behind it, Patrick scurries backward. He smiles. This is exactly what he wanted. I contemplate what action to take. If I flee, the demon probably won't catch me, but I'll lose sight of Patrick. And it's better to have your enemy in view than hidden in the shadows. So I'll fight it. I'll toss it back into its bubbling grave and then toss Patrick in after him.

But I've got to hurry, because more demons are coming.

The creature is bigger than me, but not nearly as quick. And that's what I'm counting on. I rush toward the monster but stop when a *thump-thump-thump* comes from behind.

Aspen rushes past and charges toward the demon. The heel of her hand rams into its mutated nose, and the creature hisses and falls back. She doesn't give it a moment to think. Aspen ducks when the monster swipes a clawed hand at her, then she drives a closed fist into its side. She hits it again on the opposite side.

"Oh, man!" Patrick says from a few feet away. "Boss Man is going to love her."

My mind buzzes as I try to pull her away, but she brushes me off and keeps fighting. This time she rears back and thrusts her foot into its stomach. When the demon hunches over with a sickening gurgle, she kicks it in the face. The demon recovers quickly and attacks. It drags a single claw across her bicep, and somehow Aspen doesn't scream.

She just gets angry.

Her fists fly faster than I can follow. She's totally kicking its ass, and though I don't want to leave her alone with the creature, I know this frees me up to take care of Patrick.

I set my gaze on the collector. Then I brush past Aspen and tackle him to the planks. He grabs the rope handrail over his head and uses it as leverage to kick me away.

I'm back on him in a blaze, sweat covering my brow. It's sweltering in here, and the *smell*. I ignore both and fling myself on him. Taking a cue from Aspen, I throw my fist into his sides, then land a blow straight into his shining teeth.

Once I'm standing, I pull him up with me. And then I underestimate him, forget how fast he is on his feet. He reaches out and grabs a handful of my hair. My scalp stings as he rips me forward and then past him. I fly toward the edge of the bridge and just manage to keep from falling by grabbing onto the handrail. The bridge sways like a drunken sailor, and it's everything I can do to stop myself from tumbling over the side.

I look back at Patrick. He grins from ear to ear. Then he lifts his leg up. I understand what he's about to do a moment before he does it. He's going to kick me off the edge. And that's going to be it.

But the collector stops cold, his knee still raised, when he hears the whistling sound over his shoulder.

The demon rises up from behind him like the moon. It lowers its black shiny head until their cheeks are pressed together. They almost look like lovers. Patrick is shaking and turns a shade of white that seems impossible.

The demon wraps his arms around Patrick and then kicks off from the side of the bridge.

They are gone.

Falling toward the thick oil.

The collector may be there an hour, a day. Or he may stay for eternity. It just depends how hard he fights, and for how long. Maybe he'll let go of his humanity entirely and become one of them. The same way I think Rector has begun to do.

Once I hear the splash of his body hitting the oil, I join Aspen in her battle against the demon. Together, we are able to shove it back toward the dark liquid blanket. Aspen glances around, her breath coming fast.

"Is he gone?" she asks.

"For now," I answer. "How's your arm?"

She grips the place where the creature cut her. "I'll be fine. What now?"

"Stick to the plan. Get to the soul storage room and get out of here. Handle obstacles as they come." We race toward the end of the bridge as more demons claw their way over the side. Thankfully, they'll never make it to us in time. We near the door, and I tell Aspen, "Remind me to thank Lincoln for teaching you how to fight. You're an animal."

She grins. "That was a lie."

"What?"

"He didn't teach me how to fight. I taught him."

I slow down and stare at her. "How did you—?"

"Dante. The door. Do we need a key or…?"

I shake my head. "Right. No, we just go through." The door swings open beneath my hand, and we step into the next room. Aspen immediately falls back with fright, but I push her forward. We must close the door behind us, or the demons will keep coming.

Aspen's hands fly to her ears, and she looks at me, eyes dancing with fear at what she sees.

❧ 38 ❧

FIRE DANCER

Around the circular room are twelve fireplaces. They are ten feet tall and ten feet wide. Inside them, humans are bound by their ankles. Flames shoot up from stacks of wood at their feet and lick their skin. The moans are louder here than almost anywhere else. Every once in a while someone lets out a scream. When that happens, the fire burns blue. It engulfs their entire body and singes their hair. The demons don't come when they scream. The fire takes care of that.

The smell of burning flesh and smoke fills my senses, and even though I've smelled it a hundred times, I almost heave.

With my chin, I motion toward an empty fireplace. It burns just as bright as the others, but there aren't any bodies in this one. "That's where we're going."

"Inside there?" Aspen gasps. "With the fire?"

"We just have to walk through it," I say, as if this is somehow better.

Aspen's gaze turns to the burning bodies. "Can we do anything for these people?"

I shake my head. "It's too late for them."

She bites her lip and cringes. I wonder if it's the sound they're making, or the smell, or perhaps the sight of them that bothers her the most. She looks back at the empty fireplace. "Will it hurt?"

I want to tell her no. I want to protect her from all of this. But I can't. "It will," I answer honestly. "But only as you pass through it. Once we're on the other side, your wounds will heal."

She squats down, and her gloved hands touch the ground. It's like she's lost the will to stand. "How much farther?"

"We're almost there." I grip her shoulder, and she stands back up. Then she grits her teeth.

"Let's go, then."

We clasp hands and approach the flames. They seem to bend toward us, eager for a taste. "Ready?" I ask.

"Could I ever be ready for this? For any of this?"

I almost laugh. Almost.

"Quickly!" I order. We dart toward the hearth, and within seconds we're engulfed. The scent of my own flesh burning fills my nose, making me gag. Aspen's hair is on fire, flaming orange. Her mouth is open in a perfect circle of black, but no sound comes out. Pain radiates through every nerve in my body. It's so intense, I think I'll collapse.

I forget about Aspen. I forget about Charlie. There's only agony, slicing open my skin and filling it with blinding heat. The skull buckle on my belt melts and drips silver onto my shoes. My right ear peels off and falls to the ashes below, a hunk of charred meat. The sizzling sound I heard before is now cut in half. My vision blurs, and I know the fire is eating my eyes, sucking them from their sockets like the pimento in a stuffed olive. The misery is too much. The fire is too greedy, too hungry. I've done this before, but I can't do it again. I can't take another single step after this one.

It's over.

We fall to the floor on the other side of the hearth. Aspen wraps her arms around herself and rolls on her back, but our skin has already repaired itself. Even my clothing and belt buckle look untouched. That's the beauty of hell. Your body is never destroyed. That way, the pain can always continue.

"You're okay," I say, brushing the ashes from her hair. It's black again. Not red or orange or any other color that makes my stomach churn. "We're so close."

Aspen coughs into her open hand, but nothing comes out. Her lungs are perfect. Untouched. She slowly comes to a stand. I offer her my arm, which she refuses. A pang of guilt rushes through me, but I push it down. I can't think about how horrible it is that she's here now. If I do, I won't be able to concentrate on anything else.

We're in a room that's a perfect square. The walls and floor are made of charcoal-gray concrete, and it doesn't seem that threatening. There aren't giant bears or snakes or demons or even fire. It's just a room. But we all have our weaknesses. And this has always been the one I hate the most.

The walls start moving.

They push Aspen and me away from the edge of the room. She spins to look for the fireplace, but it's gone.

Soon, the ceiling is moving, too, sliding down toward the floor with a rumble.

"What's going on?" Aspen says, twirling like a ballerina to see the walls inching closer. I can tell right away this is different for her. She knows what's happening, and her body is already writhing with terror.

"We can pass through them," I say with as much conviction as I can muster. "You have to believe it, though. Just like with the Hall of Mirrors."

Aspen's lips curl back with panic. "I can't do this, Dante. Make them stop."

I know exactly what she means. There's only one thing that makes my mind threaten to shut down, and that's being boxed in. I take her face in my hands. "Listen to me," I say. "This won't hurt you."

The walls grind closer. The ceiling is five feet above our heads. She closes her eyes and shakes her head.

"Aspen, stop it," I say. "Look at me."

Aspen grabs onto my wrists but doesn't open her eyes. "I can't do this anymore," she mumbles. "I want to leave. I want to go home."

I put my mouth close to her ear. "I want you to remember the time you and I were in Sahara's room. Remember Lincoln painted his nails black and Sahara wanted to be spun in a circle? You couldn't lift her, but I could. I can lift you now, but you have to believe I can."

Aspen's green eyes flash open. They swim with tears as she holds my gaze. "You said you'd never go away."

"I never will."

Aspen tilts her head to the side. "I don't want to die. Not without telling him."

Confusion crashes through me, but there isn't time to think on it. The roof comes down and touches the top of my head. I let go of Aspen's face and fumble for her hand. Squeezing my eyes shut, I tell myself that I am made of air. I am nothing. I am nothing, and the wall is nothing, too.

The ceiling passes over my head and shoulders. I am left untouched, sliding through the cement like a ghost. Aspen bends down, and tears slip down her cheeks. I lean down to keep hold of her hand.

"Aspen, you're not really here," I yell. "You are back in your room with Sahara."

The ceiling creeps downward.

"You are at Lincoln's house, laughing at his paranoia."

Aspen smiles up at me, though she can probably only see my legs.

The rest of my body is invisible, buried in the concrete that isn't really there. At least not once you stop believing in it.

I think fast, my brain whirling with what to tell her.

"Aspen," I say gently. "You are with Blue. You're telling him how you feel, and he's holding your hand. He's asking you to come with him. All you have to do is stand up and pass through the ceiling. And he'll be there."

Aspen's gaze moves to our connected hands. I'm losing my grip on her. She swallows and seals her eyelids tight. Then she stands up. Her body slides through the cement like a hot knife through butter.

We are both on the other side. The ceiling is gliding down our legs. I step up onto it, and Aspen does the same. Then we are being lifted up instead of pushed down.

"So," I say, titling her chin up to look at me. "Blue, huh?"

She releases this nervous laugh and shrugs. "I almost died. Cut me some slack."

"You *thought* you almost died," I clarify. "If the ceiling had come down on you, it would have crushed you, yes. But then it would have just repeated the torture over and over. No biggie."

Aspen manages a small smile. "What a way to spend a birthday."

My heart skips a beat. "What did you just say?"

"It's my birthday," she says.

As Aspen and I are lifted higher and higher toward the next room, the soul storage room, my blood freezes in my veins. It's Aspen's birthday. Her *birthday*. Eighteen years ago, Aspen Lockhart was born.

And eighteen years ago today, so was Charlie Cooper.

⨟ 39 ⨠

I KNOW YOU

I gape at Aspen as we are lifted high into the air. All around us is blackness. A void. This is the final step before we get to the soul storage room.

Every muscle in my body tenses as I anticipate what we'll see. Will the collectors be there? Will Rector?

But more than that, I can't stop thinking about what Aspen said. That it's her birthday. It can't be a coincidence that she and Charlie share the same date of birth, the same age. Lucille assigned me to collect Charlie Cooper's soul, and then Big Guy assigned me to liberate Aspen Lockhart's soul.

There must be a connection between the two girls, but I'm not sure what it is past their birthday.

A square of light flickers into view overhead, and before long, we are lifted through it. The concrete beneath our heels comes to a stop. Aspen gasps, and a hesitant smile touches my lips.

"Even in hell, souls are beautiful," I say.

Aspen grins at me, and the gesture lifts my spirit. The shelves are aligned one after another. They stand forty feet tall, and each one has thousands of cutouts for the souls they hold. The shelves almost make the place seem like the world's largest library, where each soul is a book—a story of someone's life. Of course, these stories would lead to nightmares.

The souls glow like a million fireflies, winking as we pass wall after wall of them. It's cool in this area of hell. Not to the point where I shiver, but in the way you'd expect a cavernous room to be far beneath the earth's crust. Breathing in, I relish a thick, musty scent similar to rain. This room feels euphoric after the ones we've passed through.

"This place is amazing," Aspen says, her hand resting over her heart. The light casts playful shadows across her face, catching on her mouth and eyes and even the diamond in her nose.

"It's hard to think these people deserve to be here." I touch a finger to one of the souls. It twinkles beneath my touch like I've tickled it.

Aspen stops and meets my gaze. "You didn't deserve to be here."

My hand drops to my side. "Yeah, I did."

"No, I don't believe—"

"I lived for myself, Aspen," I say, my tone tightening. "And I wasn't a nice person. It's harder than you think to find favor in heaven. People down here, people like *me*, we worked every day to make ourselves happy. And we never worked for Big Guy. We wouldn't have. He expects his followers to do for others, not just themselves."

Aspen studies me, turning over what I said in her mind. "You're different now."

I let the conversation go and move past her. "We need to find Charlie's soul."

"How?"

I walk along the pristine hardwood floor, wondering the same thing. "I'll recognize it."

I hope.

Aspen moves in a different direction, and within a few seconds, I don't hear the sound of her footsteps.

"Aspen?" I call out.

"I'm over here," she answers. "Just looking around."

"Don't go too far." Despite the lowered temperature in this room, sweat still coats my brow. I don't forget where I am for a single second. If one collector knew we were down here, the others probably do, too. The question is, how many of them are here?

When I remember the determined scowl on Patrick's face, I pick up my pace. My feet move faster as I pass rows of luminous souls. I approach a towering shelf that feels...different. My hands twitch as I move down the aisle, searching for what made me hesitate.

But there's nothing that screams to me. It's more like a whisper.

I shake my head and decide it's not here. If it were her soul, I'd know it like a bat to the skull.

Aspen's voice resonates through the hall. "Dante!"

Her tone isn't alarmed. It's more *surprised*. I leave the aisle I'm in and rush in the direction of her voice. When I find her, she's stooped over something. Her back is arched like a question mark, her dark ponytail caressing her cheek.

"It's a letter or something," she says as I approach.

I move closer until I can see what she's referencing.

It's a scroll.

The *second* scroll

It's enclosed in a glass case like we're in a freaking museum. I debate telling her what I know about the scrolls, which is pretty much zilch. And that this could be a fake like it was at the Hive. Not that seeing the real one did me any good. I look closer to see if there are any words on this scroll—

But something stops me.

It isn't a whisper. It's a *scream*.

And it's coming from the next aisle over. Aspen doesn't seem to hear it, which means it's only in my head. This could be it. I move away from Aspen and toward the place that calls out to me. As I approach, the sound overwhelms my body and causes my legs to shake.

I turn the corner, and there it is. There's a carved column that stretches to my abs, and above it floats an iridescent ball. It glows and spins like a child's toy. My breath catches as I near the ball. Inside there's a soul, and it's the most remarkable thing I've ever seen. It glimmers as I approach, almost as if it remembers the night I collected it.

Behind me, I can hear Aspen calling my name. She's talking about the scroll, but I don't give a rat's ass about that thing. Not when Charlie's soul is singing to me. I move closer and reach out my hand.

Is there an alarm?

Will the ball hurt me if I touch it?

It doesn't matter. I can't stop myself from reaching out—

"Dante, this thing is really freaking me out," Aspen says.

I'm so close to Charlie's soul, so close I can feel the warmth it radiates even from inside the orb.

Aspen's words continue to reach me, though I'm hardly listening. "This thing is saying that there are—"

Wait, what?

I jerk my hand back from Charlie's soul as a current of energy courses through me. "Aspen, are you saying you can read the scroll?"

"Uh, yeah. I've read it three times. It's freaky as shit."

Though every part of me aches to take Charlie's soul, I hurry toward Aspen. I come to stand beside her, positive that this is another faux scroll. But when I see it, the hairs on the back of my neck rise.

There aren't any words.

I place my hand on the glass case and narrow my eyes. "Are you sure you see words?"

Aspen glances at me like I'm crazy. "What, are you blind? It's right there."

"I see the scroll," I say. "I just don't see any words."

Aspen takes three steps back from the case. "Stop messing around."

I turn and look at her. Aspen's green eyes are round with worry. But there's something else there, too—excitement. "The first time I read it, I sort of knew it was true."

"What does it say?" I ask, my pulse pounding.

Instead of answering, she stands stock-still, staring over my shoulder. I follow her gaze.

A collector steps out from the shadows.

40

WICKED LITTLE ROSE

I recognize him immediately. It's the same collector who has haunted my dreams ever since the night he struck Charlie and killed Blue.

"Rector," I hiss.

The collector bows his shaved head in acknowledgement. A close-lipped smile stretches his mouth as he brushes off the front of his navy-blue starched shirt. Always with the formality, from his clipped words to his militaristic air. Rector waves his hand forward, and Kincaid steps beside him. The two of them now stand ten feet in front from me, and Aspen is an arm's length behind me.

"Is that it?" I ask.

Rector's grin widens. "Patrick is here, too. Everyone else is working above ground."

"Actually, Patrick is drowning with the water demons," I say.

His smile falters, but not for long. "No matter. You are here, and that is all we need."

"I brought a friend," I say.

Rector rolls his shoulders. "I see that."

"She and I are going to kick your ass, old man. Then we're going to take Charlie's soul."

Beside Rector, Kincaid laughs. "Nice plan you got there."

Kincaid is the newest collector on my old team. He pulls on his short blond ponytail like he's prepping to tango. His nose is too big for his face and his eyes too small. He has a birthmark along his right cheekbone. It's like a beacon for my fist.

Aspen steps close to me and puffs out her chest. "You don't know who you're messing with."

"I think we do," Rector says, his dark eyes searching her face.

Aspen sucks in a breath. The way she does it seems like I'm missing something important. "Are you the one who stole Charlie's soul from Dante?"

Rector folds his hands together like we're moments away from enjoying tea and crumpets. "Dear child—"

"Don't you dare call me that. I'm not your daughter, asshole."

Oh, smack! Rector done hit a nerve.

"Let me try again," Rector says. "The two of you are not leaving here. But I do have a proposal."

Fury builds in my chest. A proposal? From *him*? Screw that. I suddenly remember with painful clarity the way this dick hurt my girlfriend. I remember that he's the reason everyone I care about has been put in danger. He took Charlie's soul from me, but tonight I steal it back.

"Hey, Rector," I growl. He glances in my direction. "Let's play instead."

I lunge. My mind splits open as I tackle him to the ground. Thoughts of Charlie flash in my head each time my knuckles crack into his jaw. Kincaid lands his heel directly into my side, but it does nothing to tear me from the collector beneath me. Kincaid raises his leg again for another blow—

And Aspen is on him.

She leaps onto his back and wraps her legs around his waist. Her hand covers his eyes. Kincaid stumbles around blind as Aspen uses her other hand to grip his right ear. She rips downward, and Kincaid roars.

Rector wraps his hands around my throat, but I remember everything Kraven taught me. Instead of trying to pull his hands away, I go straight for his eyes. They squish beneath my thumbs, and he jerks his head back. He releases my throat, and I bring my knee up between his legs.

Rector curls into himself and I shove him to the ground. Then I spring on top of him. He manages to rise onto his hands and knees before I land on his back like I would a horse.

"Giddy up, shithole," I yell.

Aspen laughs from where she's fighting Kincaid, which makes him furious. He rushes toward her, blood gushing from his ear and down his neck. He almost grabs her around the middle, but Aspen leaps to the side. She's a snake one moment, a rabbit the next. She'll throw her weight into one of his vital organs, then hop out of his grasp. Aspen seems to know she can't take on a man if he falls to the ground. So she stays upright no matter what. I've seen her stumble more than once, but she shoots back up like a life vest beneath the sea.

Under me, Rector drops to his stomach and rolls quickly to his right. I don't expect the maneuver, and I lose my hold on him. He pulls himself up and lands a fist directly into my gut. I groan and cover my stomach. Wrong move. Kraven would have told me to ignore the pain and protect myself at all times.

Rector's hand whips across my face.

Holy crap. The dude just backhanded me like a dirty-ass pimp.

Anger bubbles inside of me until I fear I'll explode. A snarl builds in my chest. Rector must sense the change because he takes two quick steps back. I race at him like a Mack Truck, and he seeks cover behind a row of souls. I'm almost to him when I notice the row rocking back and forth.

I stop cold and try to retreat. But it's too late. The towering shelf comes crashing down. From the corner of my eye, I catch sight of Aspen reaching out to me. Seconds later, Kincaid takes advantage of her diverted attention and tackles her to the ground.

The shelf lands on me, and I'm out.

• • •

When I come around, Rector is standing over me. "That is it? A few seconds? I thought you would be out for at least a day or so, Mr. Walker."

Aspen chokes on a sob. The sound is half sorrow, half relief. Kincaid has his arm around her waist. I know she could escape his hold, but she must have decided that Rector is too close to my body. That he could do too much harm to me if she struggled now.

Rector rubs his hands together as pain spreads through my legs. The shelf has fallen on my pelvis, pinning me to the ground. I try to push it off and cry out when the enormous shelf doesn't move a hair. All around, souls pepper the floor, twinkling like white Christmas lights. Numbness bites at my stomach as I fall back and stop struggling.

Rector squats down. I contemplate driving my fist into his knee, but just the thought of attempting it sends a fresh wave of agony over my lower half. The pain becomes a living, breathing thing; it eats away at my muscles—at my mind—like a virus.

"It took so little to take you down," Rector says, his nose wrinkled.

I lock eyes with Aspen, and even though I'm filled with fury, my pulse slows. She's waiting for my direction, but she won't want to hear what I have to say. She could fight her way past Rector and Kincaid, I think, but she'd have to leave me behind, and maybe Charlie's soul, too.

"You know, I figured you might try something like this," he continues. "But I never thought you'd be stupid enough to bring *her* with you." Rector draws himself up and walks toward Aspen. She brings her gloved hands up and assumes a defensive stance, even though Kincaid tries to hold her in place. "Such a wicked little rose." Rector brushes the side of her face, and for some reason, she lets him. Though her quick breaths tell me she won't tolerate his touch for long. "Such beauty. But your thorns sting, don't they?"

"Take your hand off me, old man," Aspen spits. "And help me lift that shelf off Dante."

Rector lets his hand fall away. He grins. "Or?"

"Or I'll kill you."

"Aspen," I croak, "get out of here."

"Not happening," she responds, her eyes locked on Rector. "Not without you. And not without Charlie's soul."

In a flash, Rector snatches the chain from Aspen's neck. It breaks with an audible *chink*.

Aspen's face goes slack with shock. Rector loves to do this, to take what's important from those he's harassing. I'll never forget that the last time we met, he had my red sneaker on his gnarly feet and my father's penny in his palm.

Aspen's eyes narrow like she's decided something. "Take it. I don't want that noose anyway."

Rector's smile widens. He reaches for her gloves.

Aspen becomes enraged.

She bites at his shoulder and growls. But Rector manages to peel them from her hands as Kincaid restrains her. I'm surprised Aspen doesn't do more damage, but then I notice her injured arm again and wonder just how bad it is.

"Don't take them," Aspen pleads. "Please give them back."

My heart twists, and my mind threatens to click off. I try again to lift the shelf, but the blackness comes on stronger. I have to get out from under here. I have to end Rector.

"Hold still," Rector orders me without turning away from Aspen. "And you, my wicked little rose, have been a very bad girl." He holds her palms up to examine them closer. "Seems someone thought you shouldn't be such a wild thing. Can't say I disagree." Rector nods to Kincaid, and the younger collector falls to the ground, bringing Aspen with him.

Rector pulls back his leg and slams it into Aspen's side.

She screams.

⇥ 41 ⇤

THE SUMMONING

The sound of Aspen crying breaks what's left inside of me. "I'm going to slaughter you, Rector," I roar. "I'm going to break you in two."

"Strong words for a liberator taken down by a shelf," he responds before throwing his fist into Aspen's stomach.

Aspen writhes against Kincaid, and her screams rattle my head. Kincaid wraps his arms and legs around her body tighter, locking her in place.

Rector hits her again. And again.

Visions of the night Rector did the same thing to Charlie dance through my memory. And though I love Charlie, seeing him do this to Aspen doesn't hurt any less. She is my friend, the sister I never had.

She is a piece of me.

And each time Rector makes her cry out, my spirit is crushed a little more.

Soon there's nothing left but darkness crouched within my chest. It floods every part of my body, and raw rage provides me a burst of adrenaline. I shove against the shelf with everything I have, and it moves—a little at first, and then more.

This gets Rector's attention. "I was not going to kill her, you know. She just needed to be tamed a bit." Rector brushes off his black slacks and runs a hand over his shaved head. "Are you trying to get a little breathing room down there?" He chuckles, and the sound raises the hairs on my arms. "Dante, do you know how sweet it felt to collect your girlfriend's soul? I could almost taste her inside me."

My rage burns brighter.

The pain in my legs and hips is forgotten.

"What I really cannot wait for is the girl herself." Rector sucks on his bottom lip. "She is so deliciously innocent. I dream about the moment our soldiers bring her in. Once we have her here, I'll make her mine, you know. I'll make her my princess."

My hands curl into fists and red fills my vision.

Kill him—kill him—kill him.

"I can't wait until the first moment our lips touch," he continues. "Until I lay her down in my bed and show her what it means to be a demon's bride."

I can't take it a moment longer.

I use every bit of strength I have left and shove the shelf as hard I can.

It isn't enough.

Rector kicks me in the ribs, and I bite down to keep from screaming. My energy is gone. Aspen is pinned to the floor. And Rector is standing over me like a tornado, as if every movement makes him stronger.

I close my eyes and listen to my heart *whomp-whomp* in my ears. The sound of my pulse seems to beat her name.

Charlie.

Charlie.

Charlie.

The darkness ebbs away as I picture her face in my mind, her bright, eager eyes and the swell of her pink lips. The way she looked the first night we were truly together, and the zooming noise she made while spoon-feeding me tomato soup. The sight of her in that sexy ballerina-inspired dress, and the way she fought against Blue to come with me here, blood staining her chest. She is my reason for breathing, the only reason I would trek back into hell.

Since the first day I met her—her cheeks reddening like strawberries—I knew she was different. Her laugh made me want to smile again, and her touch had me questioning everything. She's the girl who fed her lunch to raccoons, who dug Skittles out of her pocket. She was unfashionable and socially awkward and easily the biggest nerd I'd ever met. And I fell madly in love with her. Even now, as every minute passes, my entire being aches for her more. To watch the way she radiates kindness. To see her smile. To kiss her.

A burning smell fills my nose.

I don't recognize the scent at first, but when I do, my eyes snap open. Rector looks the same, so I know it isn't him.

It's me.

Like a crash of lightning, something Kraven said strikes my very core: *"You have to call on the purity inside of you."*

But nothing inside of me is pure.

Nothing except my love for Charlie Cooper.

Pain rips through my body. I twist side to side in agony, and my back arches off the ground. My muscles tear apart, and my teeth grind together so tightly I'm sure there's nothing left of them but dust. Something pops in my chest, and then I'm splitting open. My skin is tearing apart, and I'm going to die. I'm going to die because I don't know how to control this, and instead it's controlling me.

Everything stops.

The pain ceases, and the ringing in my head quiets. I'm standing upright. Rector is backed against the wall, horror shadowing his face. Kincaid has released Aspen, and the two of them cower near the floor. Everyone stares at me, eyes wide and mouths open.

Instinctually, I flex my back and feel a weight shift behind me. It's the same way I move my arm, a simple command from my mind. But this isn't an arm. Or a leg. Or even an open hand.

It's a wing.

I curl the right one around my body so that I can see it, and I gasp. It isn't waxy like Rector's was, and it isn't sterile white like Kraven's. Instead, it's something in between. An ocean of black feathers covers my wing, so dark they're almost blue. I pull the left one in front and inspect it. They are the same. When I understand what this means, that I have accomplished the impossible, an incredible, unbridled power rushes through my veins.

My glare finds Rector.

My wings crash open.

And a growl rips through my throat.

Rector closes his eyes, and his face tightens with concentration. I know he's trying to summon his own wings, but I'm not going to let him. I race forward and whip my left wing across my body. Then I swing it out and throw Rector ten feet from where he stands. He lands on his side and rolls three times. When he tries to lift himself back up, he stumbles and grunts in pain. I relish the sound.

In the blink of an eye, I'm on him. I use my wings to lift him upright, then circle my feathered appendages around his body, restraining him in a circle of black. His arms fly out, searching for something. But there's only me. *Pow!*

I pound my clenched fist into his gut and his rib cage and the line of his jaw. From the sound of it, Aspen is tearing Kincaid a new one outside our boxing ring. I take a step back and thrust my wings against Rector's chest. When I yank them open, he flies through the air and slams into a soul shelf. The shelf teeters back and forth but doesn't fall.

Without hesitation, I charge toward him again. I hold Charlie's face in my mind as I kick him one, twice, three times in the side. Then I think about the things he did to Aspen and lose myself to fury. My fists crash into his face so many times that my knuckles begin to slip against his flesh. I shake the blood off my hands, thankful that we're immortal, that the cuff around his ankle means the torture is never ending.

Rector lies on the ground in a heap. I glance over to where Aspen is landing another kick on Kincaid's knee. He falls but quickly regains his composure. I'll hand it to him, he's persistent.

"Hey, Aspen," I say, nodding toward Rector. "Want to get some payback for earlier?"

Aspen moves away from Kincaid and toward me. Kincaid wipes the sweaty blond hair from his forehead and narrows his beady eyes. His face looks like it belongs on a WANTED poster.

Aspen studies my wings warily. "I didn't know you could…"

"Yeah," I say, "Me, either. Not really."

She gets closer, and Kincaid makes a movement like he's going to tackle her from behind. I wag my finger at him. "Calm down, anus. You and I are going to play next."

Kincaid raises his hands like he wants none of that.

I reach out to Aspen, who flinches. Our eyes connect. "It's okay. I'm still me," I whisper. Then I take her face in my hands. "Are *you* okay?"

Her gaze travels over my wings and then down to the floor where Rector groans. She nods.

I wave my hand toward him. "My gift to you."

Aspen's mouth tightens into a thin line. She looks one last time at my wings before turning her attention to Rector. I, on the other hand, spin around and stroll toward Kincaid.

"Want to dance?" I ask. Kincaid shakes his head. "Too bad."

I hit Kincaid exactly six times and wing-slap him once before he drops like a bag of stones. His eyes roll back in his head. He's not dead, of course, but he won't be causing us any more problems.

Aspen is down in Rector's face, whispering something to him. He clenches his jaw, but the ashen color on his face gives him away. I couldn't be more proud of Aspen if she grew testicles.

I nudge Kincaid with my foot and confirm he's down for the count. Satisfied with my handy work, I head toward Rector and Aspen. Aspen sees me coming and straightens. Rector spits blood onto the floor. He swishes his tongue around his mouth before spitting out a tooth.

"That's unsightly," I say. "People have no manners these days."

Aspen wraps her arms around her waist and winces.

"Are you sure you're all right?" I ask, my tone softening.

"She is fine," Rector answers for her.

I kick him. "I wasn't talking to you, asswipe." I nod toward Kincaid. "See that sack of shit over there? Your collector buddy? He struck out. So it's just us three, big boy. And soon it's just going to be you. Because me and Aspen here? We're going to take Charlie's soul and skedaddle."

I grasp Aspen's hand and move away from Rector. I'm playing Mr. Tough Guy, but deep down I feel like collapsing. When I saw Rector and Kincaid, and maybe even when I first spotted Patrick, I figured we may not make it out of here. I draw my wings back into myself like it's nothing, like I've done it a million times. It doesn't hurt the way it did to bring them out, which is something. I notice suddenly that my long-sleeved T-shirt is still intact. I guess the initial burning singed through my clothing.

Aspen sighs next to me. When I glance at her, she's smiling. We're both in shock at our success. I want to scoop her up into a hug and laugh but decide to wait until we've blown this joint completely.

We're only a few steps away from Rector when he speaks.

"Did you think it would be so easy?" he asks. A chill races over my skin. "Did you think I would let you both waltz out of here with Charlie's soul?"

I cross the distance between us. "What else you got, Rector?" I snarl. "Stop screwing around and just bring it, because Aspen and I will take on anything. So let's see it, champ."

Rector sits up a little straighter and grins. Blood trickles from the corner of his mouth. "As you wish." Rector fills his lungs. "Come on, my sweet children! Come to me!"

Aspen and I scramble backward, retreating as quickly as we can from what appears before us.

❖⧙ 42 ⧘❖

A CHOICE

Demons pour into the room. The whistling sound they make engulfs my senses. There are so many of them, too many to defeat. My mind spins, deciding whether to try and fight regardless.

Beside me, Aspen clutches my arm. I glance at her, at the crease between her green eyes. Understanding passes between us. We won't make it out of here. I expect to get angry, for that anger to fill every crevice in my head. Instead, I am awash with guilt. I allowed Aspen to come with me on this futile quest.

And I'm the reason she may die tonight.

Demons creep closer as Rector struggles to stand. At last, he's successful. I don't know what to do. I'm not sure there's anything *to* do. Rector has won. He's wanted to destroy me ever since he learned my name. And now he has me cornered. So it surprises me when he limps toward Aspen like I'm not even in the room.

"My wicked little rose," he says to Aspen. "Don't be upset. You brought them here with your screams, after all."

"Stop calling her that," I bark.

"No," Aspen whispers.

I squeeze her hand. It wasn't her fault. The demons would have come eventually, the scent of our perspiring flesh guiding their noses.

Rector ignores me. "As I was saying when we first met, I have a proposal."

"Screw your proposal." I step in between him and Aspen. I may not be able to defeat the demons, but I can kick his ass one more time before they attack us.

"Let him talk." Aspen's spine is straight, and her chin is raised. She looks like a goddess.

"Smart girl," Rector says.

I stare him down for a few more seconds, then move aside. Right now, I just want to make things better for Aspen, so if she wants to hear what he has to say, then I'll oblige.

"Start talking, old man," Aspen says.

Rector folds his arms across his chest and grins. "My proposal is simple," he says to Aspen. "Dante can leave and take Charlie's soul with him. But you will stay behind."

My fist connects with Rector's jaw. He hits the ground.

The demons stir. Their overgrown toenails click against the floor, and they raise their giant heads and hiss. The yellow-and-black scales smeared across their bodies remind me of bumblebees. One near the front flicks out its forked tongue. The demons are waiting for an order to strike, their glassy eyes taking in everything. If Rector weren't here, I have no doubt they would have already overpowered us.

I step away from Rector and shield Aspen with my body. She shoves me to the side, but I don't miss the way she grips her injured bicep.

Rector looks up from the ground like he's not altogether surprised to be there. "Despite that very rude gesture, my offer stands."

Aspen sobs quietly. I grip her shoulders. "I'll never let that happen. I told you I'd never walk out on you, and I won't. Do you understand?"

"This isn't your choice," she mutters.

"The hell it isn't."

Aspen shrugs my hands off and gulps in air. "What will you do to me?"

She's talking to Rector, but I don't want to hear the sound of his voice. "Don't say a damn word to her."

He ignores me. It takes everything I have to keep from knocking the rest of his teeth out. "You won't be harmed," Rector replies. "But I do think you'd make an excellent collector one day."

Aspen bolts upright. They glare at each other, and the pair seems to have a silent conversation. After a moment, Aspen breaks off her stare and pushes herself against my chest. I'm thrown off by this. It takes me a moment to respond, but then I wrap my arms around her.

Of course Rector would want Aspen as a collector after seeing how viciously she fights. He's misinterpreted her strength as hidden sinfulness. But why would he trade Charlie's soul for a future collector? It doesn't matter, I decide. I'll never let him have her.

"Shhhh," I say near her ear. "Everything is going to be okay." I lower my voice. "When I give you the signal, I want you to run like you've never run before. Don't stop until you get outside. Find Max and get out of here."

Aspen steps away from me. Tears streak down her dirty cheeks. "You're like my brother, Dante. I love you like a brother." She turns and faces Rector. "I'll stay."

"No!" I roar.

Aspen tries to take my hand, but I jerk away from her. "You're not doing this."

Rector nears Aspen. I try to block his path, but Aspen goes to him. The collector meets my gaze. "I keep Aspen, body and soul. In exchange, I give you your life and Charlie's soul. She has made her decision. Now go."

My stomach heaves. My eyes sting, and suddenly the room is spinning. "I can't…"

"Go," Aspen says, echoing Rector. "Return Charlie's soul."

I move toward Aspen, but she pushes me away. The stinging in my eyes is now blinding me. "I can't leave you," I say, tears dripping down my face. "I can't."

"This isn't your decision to make, Dante." Aspen's voice is cold, like she's already out of reach.

I jab a finger at her. "I won't let you do this."

"It's done."

"Damn it, I said *no*! You told me you'd do as I asked down here without question. You promised!" I'm furious, but I don't care. She has to listen to me. I won't leave her here.

Aspen closes her eyes. When she looks at me again, there's only resolve to be seen. She's not changing her mind. And I can't make her leave without getting us both killed.

"Aspen…" The word is a plea.

"You set out to make me a better person," she says, a gentle smile gracing her mouth. "Turns out you're a damn fine liberator. That, or I always had it in me to change." She rubs a hand over her eyes. "You tell Sahara…you tell Sahara I did this for her. When she's older. When she understands. Tell Lincoln he was a good friend. My *best* friend. And tell Blue… No, don't tell Blue anything."

I nearly choke as I say, "How am I supposed to do this? How am I supposed to just leave you?"

"Valery said I was important. They all said I was important. This is why—my life for her soul," she says. "I'm staying for Sahara. And for Lincoln and Blue and everyone else who deserves a chance at a peaceful world. Now leave, Dante."

"Aspen, please—"

"Leave!" she screams.

A ball of ice forms between my shoulder blades. Aspen's face is red, and her hands are clenched. I turn away. I'm still not sure I can do this, but I'll take the opportunity while I have it to get Charlie's soul.

Rector and his demons don't try to stop me as I head in the direction of the floating orb. Inside is the ball of light. With every step, my body yearns to be closer. Charlie's soul is like a beacon, calling me to it. I stop when I'm an arm's length away. My heart pounds against my rib cage, and my back arches involuntarily, pushing me forward. The way my body reacts, it's like it's greeting her soul, like they're old friends. What's more, her soul itself has pressed against the orb as if it, too, is eager to be reunited.

This time I don't question things. I touch both palms to the ball, and it bursts like a bubble made of dish soap. As soon as the orb is gone, her soul shoots toward me. The moment it touches my chest, my arms fly open and my head falls back. A crushing sense of *rightness* consumes me. The demons are gone. Rector isn't here. And Aspen is safe in her bed.

All that's left is me and this bliss.

Gently, I touch a hand to my chest, and my knees nearly buckle. With Charlie Cooper's soul inside me, I am fulfilled. I am whole again.

Before I lose this sense of resolution, I stride toward Aspen. I pull her into a hug. "I understand now that we must all make sacrifices," I say. "But I will be back for you, Aspen. I'll return and blow this entire place apart with the strength of God himself to save you."

Aspen collapses against me and cries into my shoulder.

"Are you sure you want to do this?" I ask her one last time.

"I'm sure," she whispers. And then, "Come back for me."

I hold her head in my hands and know this is it—this is where I do the thing I said I wouldn't ever do. I have to leave Aspen. I put my mouth near her ear so that only she can hear what I say next. "Your father may never know how amazing his daughter is, but I do."

Aspen covers her face. Then with one hand, she pushes me away. "Go, Dante. Go now."

I do as she asks. I turn from her—from my friend, my sister—to leave. But not before socking Rector in the stomach one last time. He falls to one knee.

"One day, Rector, it'll just be you and me," I say.

Then I run.

As a token of good faith, Rector gives me a thirty-second head start before sending the demons after me.

✦⮑ 43 ⮐✦

LIGHT

Thirty seconds is longer than I thought Rector would give me. He said he'd let me leave with Charlie's soul, but Rector is nothing if not a liar. I bet as soon as he ushered Aspen from the room and she was out of earshot, he made the order.

I'm able to move through hell faster without Aspen. I know the ins and outs and which areas to avoid, like the ones leading to Lucille. Though everything in me screams to return to Aspen's side, I also know I'm lucky that Rector is egotistical enough to want to handle this himself. Because if Lucille knew I was down here, I'd be a human Popsicle by now.

I run faster, but the whistling sounds increase. The demons are slow, but there are so many of them. And once they're worked into a frenzy, they crawl out of invisible cracks, calling out to one another in their terrible language.

One appears in front of me in the Hall of Mirrors. I am able to spin around it and hurry past. No harm done.

As I near the end of the mirrored room, three demons reach for my legs. The entrance to the bear's stomach is within sight but still too far away. I fall to the floor when one of the demons grabs ahold of my shin. My heel smashes into its teeth, forcing it to release me.

I'm up, racing toward the throat without looking back. I don't want to go into the darkness, but I don't have a choice. So I keep running. I keep running even when the slickness causes my feet to slip. My fingers dig into the fleshy tissue for support, and the bear doesn't like this. His throat works, the clenched muscles making it hard for me to claw up.

Halfway to the top, a demon lunges on me. I tumble backward. At the last moment, I spot the bear's tongue and latch on. I dangle over the open throat like a rock climber, the demon clutched onto my ankle. It outweighs me, and there's no way I can hold on for long. I raise my free leg, and with all my strength, I ram my heel into the demon's face.

The demon falls. I move toward the bear's teeth. I zigzag through the spaces between them and almost pierce myself on the tip of his canine. When I land outside the bear's mouth, the creature snaps at me. He wants his meal back. I roll to the right and spring back up. Then I race toward the stairway where protruding faces will watch my ass retreat to the earth's surface.

But when I get to the foot of the stairs, I stop cold. On every single step, blocking any possible escape, is a demon. Together, the snapping jaws and warped bodies look like an army. It's such a devastating sight that I nearly return to the bear and ask him to swallow me back down and keep me in his gut this time. The faces protruding from the walls yell greetings to me, chattering about the demons on their stairs, but I barely hear them.

I'm so close.

Only a few hundred steps stand between remaining in hell and returning Charlie's soul.

There are too many demons, though. Too many to attempt any kind of plan. Too many to dream of living through this.

As the demons slink toward me, I cover my chest with my palm and close my eyes.

I breathe in.

I breathe out.

I savor the feeling of my lungs expanding, of my heart beating. Every nerve in my body demands an answer to this problem. But I don't have one. It's over. When Lucille finds out I'm here, he'll remove my cuff. And if I'm lucky, I'll slip into an eternity of nothingness quickly.

It's sad, really. The end. I've fought so hard for life, whether it's as a human or a collector or a liberator. I just wanted more time. But even I know when the clock is about to stop ticking.

And this is it.

I wish I could kiss Charlie one more time. I wish I could bring her to a nice restaurant for the world's best crab cakes. I wish I could take her on a Ferris wheel ride just to hear her laugh. I wish I could buy her a Valentine's Day card and a vase of sunflowers and a beagle puppy she picked out herself.

I wish I could slip an emerald ring onto her beautiful hand.

I wish I could lift the veil from her smiling face and kiss her soft lips and tell the whole world that she is my wife.

I wish I could feel the kick of a child in her stomach and know it is ours.

As the demons slither closer…and closer…I know I will never have these things. But I will settle for this—I will settle for giving my life for Charlie Cooper.

I open my mouth as wide as it will go and release the most bone-rattling battle cry I can summon. Then I call to my wings. They rise from my back like a black sun, the pain filling me up. With Charlie's name on my tongue, I charge toward the demons.

I am hit and bitten and clawed so many times I lose count. The pain wraps me in a cocoon until it is everything. I hold my own for as long as I can, picking demons at random and taking them to the ground. My wings are a more powerful weapon than I anticipated, but in this closed space it's difficult to use them.

Still, I fight like a champion. Like someone who might just defeat a horde of devils to save the girl he loves. It's the worst part—hope. Even when I realize that I'm drowning in demons, that they are crawling over me like fire ants, I still hang onto the idea that I could make it out. I know it's untrue. I acknowledged as much before I ever launched my attack. But it's still there, hanging on like a loose tooth.

When a demon bites down on my shoulder, and I feel the joint separate, I know it's over. A warm current seeps from my chest and into my limbs. It enters my mind and whispers words of reassurance. I will die a final death or suffer for eternity, but either way, it is okay. It is okay because she was mine for a little while.

Inside my head, I send her a message. One I know she'll never hear. *I love you, Charlie. I would have fought a thousand hells for any part of you. My angel.*

When I open my eyes, all I see is a swirl of black and yellow, of teeth and saliva. And I know I'm losing my grip on reality, because between the demons' bodies, I spot the ghost of the girl I love.

Her shirt is stained with red and her face is shadowed with rage and she doesn't look like the person I remember.

She looks like an assassin.

Clenched in her palm is a knife. She tosses it to her right hand. "You want me?" she screams.

The demons turn their gruesome heads toward her.

"Come and get me!"

Charlie rushes down the stairs like a militia of angels are at her side. She slices the throat of the first demon she sees and cries out as the red-black blood washes down her hands.

It's her. It's *truly* her.

The sight of Charlie Copper, of my only love, lifts me from my agony. And even though many of my bones are broken and I can hardly see out of my left eye, I climb to my feet. I don't understand how this is happening, how she's really here. But I can't question it for long because the demons are moving toward her too quickly for me to hesitate.

My pulse races as I push past one demon after another. They don't try and stop me. They're too curious about this small girl and her glittering knife.

I leap in front of Charlie, wanting so bad to touch her, to make sure she's flesh and blood. Instead, I launch a new attack. I fight as best I can with my right arm, since my left swings uselessly at my side. With the motivation of keeping Charlie safe behind me, I'm able to hold them back. My girlfriend slashes at demons' outstretched arms with her blade, and I'm impressed by how viciously she does so.

Despite the odds, Charlie and I are able to take a step toward the surface. And then another. And another. Once again, hope dances in my peripheral vision, just out of reach. But it's there, and that's all I care about.

"Charlie, keep moving toward the top." They're the first words I've been able to speak. I don't know if she responds; the whistling sound is too loud. I step back and collide into her. A moment later, she moves away. We do this a step at a time, back-to-back. Charlie whips her blade across the few demons farther up the stairs, and I fight the ones below us. We don't take any out, but we hold them back. And that's enough.

The faces in the walls watch us retreat. Some seem happy to see our progress, others appear infuriated. We ignore them and keep battling. After what feels like hours, we near the top. Only a few dozen steps remain between us and the world above. It's then that I realize only one of us is getting out of here—that one of us will have to hold them off while the other flees.

My heart plunges to my feet.

Charlie came here for nothing. I was never going to make it out alive. But seeing her one last time, watching her fight to save *me*, it reminds me who I'm dying for. It reminds me that this is the way it should be.

"Charlie." I yell. "When I say 'go,' I need you to run past the demons. Don't stop until you've reached the top."

"I won't leave you," she cries, her back still pressed to mine.

Her words make me want to spin around and press my mouth to hers. "You're not leaving me. I'll go when you go."

Charlie doesn't respond, and I pray she'll do as I ask.

I grab the closest demon to free the path in front of her. "Run!"

She runs.

She runs for several seconds without looking back. Just as I'd hoped, the demons don't chase her. Instead, they turn their attention to me.

Good-bye, angel.

Charlie turns. Our eyes meet, and unadulterated sorrow crosses her face.

Then her expression changes. Her eyes widen so that she almost looks crazy, like she's lost her mind to fear. I shove the demon in front of me aside so I can see her face one last time.

She races toward me.

"No " I holler. "Keep going!"

But she doesn't stop. She flies down the stairs like she has wings of her own.

My heart hammers in my chest because I feel it—I *feel* that something big is about to happen.

Charlie Cooper reaches the demon closest to me and lays her hands on it. She screams so loud, I'm sure my eardrums must burst.

An electric white light forms beneath her palms. "Get *back*!" she roars.

The demon soars through the air.

It lands a hundred feet below and doesn't move. The other demons study Charlie for a moment. Then they retreat. They click down the stairs to get away from whatever power just came out of her hands. The faces in the walls pull back one by one and disappear from view. *Pop-pop-pop!*

I watch the demons' flight for a split second, my head spinning, then grab Charlie's hand and scramble upward, out of hell and into the afternoon sky. She gasps when my black wings spread out against the snowy backdrop, a storm of feathers arching over our bodies.

Her eyes roll back in her head.

I catch her when she falls.

KISS YOU IN THE DARK

As Charlie sleeps and the Quiet Ones dress my wounds, Valery explains again what happened. Charlie had eavesdropped on Red's and Max's discussion about what he needed to get to hell's entrance. Then she jacked Valery's credit card and went after me.

I guess there's a loophole when the men you hire to transport you to hell don't ask questions.

But I'm still pissed at Max. I don't believe Charlie was as "crazy in the face" as he describes. *Apparently,* she jumped off her snowmobile, found the knife, and threatened to kill herself if he didn't tell her how to find me. Once Charlie descended, he says he called Valery for reinforcements.

Max is my best friend, and he cares about Charlie, but I guess I don't blame him for not wanting to be tortured for eternity because my girlfriend wanted a joyride in hell.

Valery hasn't left Max's side since we've been back at the Hive. Though they still aren't allowed to be married, the way she looks at him says she's happy that he didn't enter hell with me or even Charlie, and word on the street is that Big Guy is pleased with the potential

Max has shown. This doesn't resolve Valery's and Max's relationship issues, because those two won't be pleased until they're allowed to be together entirely. But it's a start.

Blue hasn't said a single word to me since I returned, but he did punch me in the face. After Valery told him what Aspen chose to do, and that I left her behind, I expected nothing less. To be honest, I savored the feel of his fist. It felt deserved.

Annabelle has stayed by Charlie's bed for the two days she's been asleep. The two of us have grown closer, and she's been the one to comfort me when I think about Aspen, which is always.

When the Quiet Ones finally inform us that Charlie is waking up, we all rush in to see her—Max, Valery, Kraven, Blue, Annabelle, and me. As soon as her eyes open, I reach for her hand.

She smiles.

My heart splits open.

"They promised me you were okay," I say, swallowing a lump in my throat.

Charlie glances around, taking in each of our faces. "Where's Aspen?"

I bite the inside of my cheek, and Blue glares at me. Valery fills her in as Kraven stands in the doorway watching. When Charlie has heard everything, tears stream down her face. It reminds of when we mourned Blue's death. I can only hope Aspen's story ends as well.

"It's my fault she went down there," Charlie says. "It's my fault she's still there."

"It's no one's fault," Kraven retorts. Then he raises the question no one else dares ask. "Charlie, what happened down there? What happened with your hands?"

She studies them. When her eyes widen, I know she remembers. "I don't know," she whispers. "It was like…instinct."

Kraven nods. But I know he's just as clueless as the rest of us.

I lean over and kiss Charlie, and even though everyone is watching, it doesn't seem like there's anyone in the room but her. When finally our mouths part, I say, "I have something for you."

Kraven has already explained to me that Charlie's soul can't be returned to her body. But it *can* be turned into heaven. Kraven and I stand close together, and I tell Charlie, "Watch."

We press our chests together.

Kraven's face strains.

Nothing happens.

When he hasn't pulled away after several seconds, I say, "Can we move this along, buddy? I know you like being this close and all, but it's starting to make me uncomfortable." Kraven releases me and shakes his head. A chill explodes inside my chest and the floor seems to drop out from beneath me. I know what he's saying by giving up, but I don't *want* to know. "Why are you shaking your head? Take her soul. Take it!"

The liberator glances at Valery, then back at me. "Are you sure you collected her soul?"

"Of course I am," I say, my tone stiff with panic. "I recognized it right away. It's like my body knew—" I stop talking and the room spins. Everything suddenly makes sense.

Charlie's soul isn't inside of me.

It's my own.

That's why Rector let me walk out of there. Now that I work for the other side, Lucille doesn't really care about keeping my soul. In fact, I bet my soul just lingering down there disgusted him. Maybe he would have kept it out of spite, but once Rector saw an opportunity to get my hopes up and crush them, he took it.

Anger shoots through my limbs. I feel like a ticking time bomb, like I will detonate if I ever hear Rector's name again. Squeezing my eyes shut, I whisper, "I stole back my own soul. I only thought it was

Charlie's." My hands clench at my sides. "I've ruined it all. Everything. I never should have left Aspen down there."

"It's okay, Dante." Charlie reaches for me. The tilt of her head says she's devastated about Aspen, but that she's also relieved that I'm safe.

That makes one of us.

Valery steps forward. "Maybe it was Aspen's destiny, Dante," she whispers. "Maybe that's why she was so important. No other collector or liberator harbors their soul. With your soul back in place, there's no telling what you can do." She reaches out to me. "Perhaps you'll be able to protect Charlie better this way, and that…that's important."

"No!" I growl. "Aspen being here is more important than my soul." My mind spins in circles and lands on the one thing I haven't thought about since returning to the surface. "She could read the scroll."

"What?" Kraven moves toward me. "*Who* could read the scroll?"

"What scroll?" Charlie asks.

Blue and Annabelle look equally confused.

Kraven races from the room. He's back within minutes, the scroll in his hand. He looks at Valery. "There are still no words."

Valery reaches out, and Kraven hands it to her. She bites her lip in frustration. Then she walks over to the bed and lays the scroll on Charlie's lap.

"What are you doing?" Kraven asks. "The message can only be read by the kings."

"Maybe not," Valery snaps.

Everyone holds their breath as Charlie scans the gold sheet of paper. She looks up and asks with a shaky voice, "You really can't read this?"

Valery gasps.

"What does it say?" Kraven asks, his entire body quivering with anticipation.

Charlie looks back at the scroll. The walls quiet their creaking. The ocean stops whispering. We all wait for Charlie Cooper to read us our fates. "It says," she whispers, "that there will be a great battle on earth between heaven and hell. It says the victor will rule the earth and all those who live upon it." She narrows her eyes at the bottom of the page. Her body recoils from the scroll like she doesn't want to say the last part.

"What is it?" Blue asks. "What else does it say?"

Charlie meets my gaze. "It says the battle will be won by two girls born on the same day, in the same year. Two girls—a savior and a soldier."

The world tilts, and I'm falling. I catch myself on the edge of Charlie's bed.

"Oh, God," Valery says, "Charlie is the savior and…and…"

Blue grabs a nearby lamp and launches it across the room. "And Aspen is the soldier!" he roars, pointing a finger at me. "She's the soldier, and you left her there. You *left* her!"

"Blue, stop," Charlie begs. But he's already gone.

I cover my face, remembering when Aspen said it was her birthday. When she told me it was she who taught Lincoln how to fight, and not the other way around.

There it is—the reason Aspen Lockhart is so important. She wasn't meant to help rescue Charlie's soul from hell. And she wasn't meant to return my own soul to my body. She was destined to stand beside Charlie in a war between heaven and hell, and now she's locked beneath the earth.

I raise my hand like I'm asking a question, but honestly, I'm not sure what I'm doing.

Everyone looks at me.

"It's okay, right?" I run a hand over my forehead, thinking. "We'll go down and get Aspen. All of us. And then we'll be ready for this battle, if it ever happens."

Valery's gaze lands on Kraven. He shifts uncomfortably.

"What?" I ask. "What else are you hiding?"

"Not hiding. It's just…" Kraven clears his throat. "All liberators must complete training."

I laugh. What he said is just too ludicrous. Beside me, Charlie reaches out her hand. I press our clasped hands against my thigh. "You're crazy if you think I'm waiting more than a day to go back for her," I tell Kraven. "We're going. We can't leave her there. You heard what the scroll said. Plus…plus she just can't be in hell. She's our friend. She's been with us—"

"Dante." Valery moves toward me.

I shake my head. "I'm not listening to this. We're not training while she's in hell. I won't sit here and—"

"Dante!" Valery's tone shocks me into silence. She straightens her green dress and touches a hand to her chest. There's something else she knows, something she's about to say but I don't want to hear it. I don't want to freaking *hear* it. She says it, anyway. "Our king handed down orders."

She glances at Kraven for support.

"Well, what is it?" I growl.

Valery looks at Annabelle and then at Charlie and finally at me. "He has declared war on hell," she says. "We're going to war."

• • •

Later that night, when everyone is asleep and Charlie is in my arms, I think about what Valery said, that Big Guy has declared war on hell. The liberators will fight. And I'll get my chance to settle the score with Rector once and for all. But what of Lucille? Will he fight, too? And if so, how will we ever defeat him?

I stroke a finger across Charlie's cheek and watch her chest rise and fall gently. She's safe beside me. I take one of her hands and inspect it. Such power radiated from these hands, power she never knew existed. I place her arm next to her side and smile to myself. The *savior* is dreaming and working her bottom lip as if she's talking.

My angel, the savior. How many times did she tell me she loved me as we lay here, buried in these blankets? Too many to count, and way too few to satisfy either of us.

I brush my lips against her ear and whisper, "Forever." I hope she hears my words in her dream world. With my head back on the pillow, I push myself closer to her small sleeping body and kiss the back of her neck.

Charlie and Aspen are destined to do great things—a savior and a soldier.

And me?

I'm only what Charlie—and Aspen—need me to be now. Fire rages through my veins as I think about protecting these two girls. About what I'll do if either are hurt.

I no longer belong to hell. And I do not belong to heaven.

I am not a collector.

And I am not a liberator.

I am a warrior.

Acknowledgments

Thank you first to Laurie McLean for loving Dante Walker as much as any agent could (or should?). I'll be forever grateful to you for launching my career as a writer.

Thank you to Liz Pelletier, Heather Riccio, Jessica Estep, Stacy Abrams, and the entire team at Entangled Teen for loving Dante's bad boy ways. You guys rock.

Hugs to Wendy Higgins, Brigid Kemmerer, and Trisha Wolfe for reading early versions of *The Liberator* and for laughing at Dante's antics.

Thank you to my entire family—the one I was born with, and the one I married into—for the endless love and support. A big shout out to Peggy, Hassan, Kristi, Nancy, and Tommy for pushing *Dante Walker* books into people's hands.

Love, love to my grandma, Jo Ford, who is part of my family but deserves special attention for believing her granddaughter can do no wrong. Sometimes it feels like no one understands me the way you do. Thank you for teaching me that it's every girl's perfect right to be pampered shamelessly.

To Angee, Gianina, Laryssa, and Jaga—fabulous friends who ask about my books every time I see them.

Huge thanks to Felger & Friends Hair Salon— especially Teresa

Gomez, for the fabulous airbrush makeup, and Tyse Kimball, for working wonders with my hair—for making me feel like a rock star for *The Liberator* release party.

To the V Mafia, and to all of Dante's fans, thank you for everything. Without you and your continued enthusiasm, my job wouldn't be half as fun. I adore you guys.

And finally, always, to my husband, Ryan. You totally came up with Dante Walker (no, you didn't), and I love you for that (I love you for other things, but not that). I can't imagine my life without you, boo. You're the only husband who'd watch his wife put on a play with stuffed animals and question the character's intentions with a serious face. I love you…forever.

Read on for a sneak peek at Melissa West's epic sci-fi romance Hover
Available in stores and online now!

On Earth, seventeen-year-old Ari Alexander was taught to never peek, but if she hopes to survive life on her new planet, Loge, her eyes must never shut. Because Zeus will do anything to save the Ancients from their dying planet, and he has a plan.

Thousands of humans crossed over to Loge after a poisonous neurotoxin released into Earth's atmosphere, nearly killing them. They sought refuge in hopes of finding a new life, but what they became were slaves, built to wage war against their home planet. That is, unless Ari and Jackson can stop them. But on Loge, nothing is as it seems...and no one can be trusted.

CHAPTER 1

"What is that?" I ask, pointing to a dark triangular building in the distance. My tone is formal, focused, just as it always is when we're discussing the city's breakdown.

Emmy shifts beside me. Emmy has been my sole healer at the Panacea, the Ancients' version of a hospital, for nearly a month now. She is more personable than the other healers, who often appear exhausted or angry. I've been trying for weeks to understand the need for healers beyond their ability to maintain life on the Ancients' planet, Loge. They cultivate the land, nourish it. On Earth we might have called them corporeal Mother Natures. But when it comes to Ancients needing healers, I'm at a loss Ancients have xylem running within their bodies, similarly to how humans have water. Xylem itself has healing properties, so why the need for healers? Something doesn't add up, yet each time I press Emmy on it, she gives me a distant look and responds with short answers that give me next to no insight into anything beyond the fact that my questions make her uncomfortable. This one is no exception.

"That be the Vortex," Emmy finally says, her speech different than the other Ancients I've encountered. It's intentionally choppy, like she can't be bothered to use complete sentences. She washes her hands together nervously as though they were under a faucet of water and she wanted to make sure the soap touched every inch of flesh. "RESs train there."

I nod. I know very little about the RESs, beyond that RES is short for Republic Employed Spy, and that Jackson is one of them.

I think to the night he revealed himself to me in my room. I was petrified. I had lost my Taking patch moments before, breaking one of the only formal rules of the Ancient/human treaty. The Taking patch was a small silver eye covering, created by the Chemists on Earth, to not only block our vision, but immobilize us, while the Ancients came into our rooms at night to Take our antibodies so they could acclimate to Earth. We weren't allowed to see them, an act punishable by death, and there I was, my eyes closed tightly as I waited for my Ancient to come and offer up my punishment. Only the punishment never came. I opened my eyes to find Jackson Locke hovering above me. *Jackson Locke.* My greatest competition for top seed in Field Training. Everything became so hectic after that moment. He told me about our refusal to allow the Ancients to coexist with us, as promised in the treaty, that soon a war would begin. He begged me to help him stop it. Before I truly knew what I was getting myself into, before I even allowed myself a second to think it through, I had agreed. And now…here I am, half human, half Ancient. A girl lost among strangers, linked to the enemy. Though, now, I no longer consider them the enemy. Maybe I never did. Something has changed within me. I never would have imagined humankind could be as brutal as we became in those weeks leading up to the release of the neurotoxin. The cylinders of Ancient organs. The testing chambers full of dead Ancient children. And then once we had released the neurotoxin and poisoned our own people, the execution chambers built to disingrate our remains.

I have no idea what the Ancients stand for, what morals ground them or what passion propels them, but I now know that deep within the human concept is something dark, selfish, and completely willing to do whatever is necessary to support the idea of humanity. Because that's what it is, an idea. True humanity would never behave as we have behaved.

I glance over to Emmy, and then back to the triangular building. Each day we do this. She comes in with the intention of checking on me and stuffing me with these circular healing foods called bocas, but we always end up by the window, staring out over Triad, the largest city on Loge, while I ask question after question. I try my best to hide my true intent, but my efforts are futile. Emmy knows, what I'm sure most here know. I am not one of them. I do not trust them. And I will do whatever is necessary to protect the other humans from them. After all, it's all but my fault they are here. If I would have gone to Dad about Jackson, if I would have confided in him, none of this might have happened.

My mind drifts to the days that led up to the release of the neurotoxin, to Jackson and how uneasy he had become. Why didn't I see it? We had spent weeks together, growing closer with each passing day. An intensity had built between us, a dependency on the other, that was unlike anything I had ever experienced. It was as though we were the only two people who understood what was happening, and through each other, we found comfort. More than comfort. My chest tightens at the thought of his lips on mine, his body pressed so closely to mine I could feel his heart beating in rhythm with my own. But even after all that, I never pushed him for details. Instead, I stood by helplessly as our Chemists released a poisonous neurotoxin into Earth's atmosphere, killing thousands. Of course, they couldn't have known how many humans had been healed by Ancients over the years, effectively exposing them to Ancient xylem—effectively turning them *into* Ancients. They couldn't have known. I couldn't have known. So why did I feel so guilty?

I didn't ask for any of this. I didn't ask for Jackson to seek me out for help. I didn't ask for him to heal me, turning *me* into an Ancient. And I certainly didn't ask him to bring me to Loge, which cemented my guilt in place. Because while I was here, healing, those I cared about were on Earth, abandoned.

The constant ache in me to hear their voices, their reassurances that they're okay, is enough to drive me insane.

The main door to the Vortex opens, and I crane my neck to get a glimpse inside. Two Ancients exit, but from this distance, I can't make out anything inside.

"Do you think the humans are in there, Emmy?"

She sighs. "I don't know, child. Not my matters."

"But have you seen any of them? I mean, surely some have come here for treatment, right?" I glance at her, hopeful.

She shakes her head, looking conflicted.

At this point, I have more questions than I can possibly hold within my useless brain, which brings me back to the Vortex, and my true intent on pressing Emmy to tell me everything she can about Triad—I have no idea where the other humans are being held.

"Emmy?"

She averts her eyes, and I feel a common frustration bubbling up within me. "Fine." She knows. She just refuses to tell me.

I've been at the Panacea for three weeks. Three weeks of tests and analysis and enough bocas to feed all of my hometown of Sydia, and still, I have yet to see a single human. Not injured in the Panacea. Not dancing in the fields that cradle the city like a blanket. None. Not one. Which means either Zeus is keeping them somewhere…or they're all dead.

I study the Vortex, its almost black exterior, and imagine it full of men and women training, like Jackson, to pretend to be human on Earth, to kill humans by Taking them to death. A shiver creeps down my back. That has to be where the humans are being held.

"Come child, eat." Emmy holds out a bowl of bocas, purple on the outside, sunshine yellow on the inside. They taste like oranges, but look like grapes. "Young-one be here soon for assignation. We need to get you ready."

The assignation. There are four sectors in Triad of which one can be assigned to work—the factories, the schools, the military, or the government. The healers on Loge possess the ability to cultivate the land and heal living creatures by zeroing in on the inner workings of the person, animal, or plant and "fixing" whatever isn't working just right. That ability also allows them to look at that living thing's purpose. So, the top healers in Triad conjure together with Zeus to give an analysis on all Ancients once the Ancient turns sixteen. This analysis is known as the assignation, and the results determine which of the four sectors of Triad the individual will work. Most everyone goes to the factories, but advance intellect can often sway an individual towards military or government, which are the sought after jobs in Triad. Emmy tells stories of her kids pretending to be RESs, running around in disguise. It's prestigious. A mark of honor.

And the very last thing I want to be here.

The RESs are responsible for the attacks on Earth that led to the release of the neurotoxin. We may have killed thousands of our people by releasing the neurotoxin, but they killed thousands just to prove they could. Becoming an RES would be the ultimate betrayal. But in the end, I'm not sure I'll have a choice. It will all come down to Zeus. And if I have learned anything in the three weeks that I have lived in Triad, it's that what Zeus wants, Zeus gets.

I can still hear Emmy's words, mere days after Jackson brought me here to save me from the neurotoxin that was poisoning me to death. "Not young-one," she had said. "Old-one." And I knew, the words pounding into my head like a migraine until one single name appeared—Zeus. Zeus wanted me to become an Ancient. The question is…why?

The curtains to my private room sway, and I wait anxiously for Jackson to enter but no one emerges. Jackson and Emmy have been the only two people that I've seen since coming here. Though, I really shouldn't call them people. They aren't, even if they look as human as I do. But that's not why I call them people. I call them that because it makes me feel like I'm not really on another planet, just another country, like any day I could hop a hovercraft and fly home.

I've realized it's familiarity that grounds us, and without it, the mind drifts into dangerous territory. I've only considered death once, when the nightmares mixed so thoroughly with my thoughts that all I wanted was a little relief. Now, I'm medicated with one of their concoctions to make sure I don't drift again. I hate what it does to me, the constant humming in my brain as though I can't be trusted to think or act by myself. Emmy says she'll take me off it soon. Every day she says it will be soon. I'm starting to wonder if *soon* means something different here.

Aside from Emmy, Jackson comes by every day—and every day I try my best to avoid talking to him. I think to how quickly I trusted him. I've thought it through a thousand times. Why? Was it that I felt like I knew him? Because I did in a way. I had known Jackson—or the Jackson I thought he was—since we were kids. Seeing someone year after year, growing up together, gives you a sense of comfort, like you're predisposed to trust simply because you remember what the person looked like six inches shorter. I don't know. Sometimes I think I'm just trying to make sense of my decisions, justify them, because the truth is, after weeks now of nothing but my own guilty thoughts, all I can come up with is hope.

The attacks were increasing. Everything felt so intense. I didn't need him to tell me that a war was coming—anyone with a brain could sense it. I needed to believe that we could stop it, that there was hope. And no one knows what it's like to trust on hope alone until they've been so deep in horror that there is nothing left *but* hope. That's where I was, maybe where I still am—in horror—but there is no worry of me trusting on hope again. I made that mistake once… and he let me down. Now I'm stuck here, waiting to learn what Zeus has planned for me.

"How you feel today, child?" Emmy asks after a while of silently staring down at Triad in motion. It's like watching clockwork move, everything and everyone so robotic I have to wonder if they are programmed.

"Good," I finally say and she smiles, taking my hand in hers. She has a youth about her, despite her outward appearance. Her hair is white, outside of an orphaned blonde strip in the front. Her face has creases around her eyes and mouth that suggest she's laughed more often than she's cried. I've never seen her laugh or even smile, which makes me wonder how long it's been since she felt the happiness that created her lines. She doesn't look at me, likely afraid I'll ask her, yet again, to explain what she had meant about Zeus. Questions about Triad she can handle, and does to appease me, but Zeus is another topic altogether.

I glance down at the bowl of bocas and prepare for how I'll ask her. "Emmy," I start.

She peeks behind her, making me wonder if Zeus's shadow follows her around. "I told you, no talk of him. Now, young-one be by soon. Eat. Food brings—"

"Healing. I know. Emmy, please…"

"Not my place. Now rest." She pats my hand one last time, leaning in to hug me, and says, "His eyes are everywhere here, his ears in the walls. Be careful, child." She straightens, pulls out the band of beads from her pocket that I've seen her reach for when she gets worried, and laces them through her fingers again and again, her look distant.

As soon as she leaves, I return my attention to the city. I find myself standing by my window for hours each day, surveying Triad, hoping to see something new that gives me an idea of where the humans are, but each day the sun sets with me knowing nothing more than I had learned the day before. Now, the sun rises from a wall of green foliage that lines the city, separating Triad from whatever lies beyond it. Within the wall, there are rows and rows of houses, neighborhoods perhaps. I imagine what they are doing in their homes. If they are eating dinner now or playing games or watching some version of a T-screen.

From the neighborhoods, a large bridge stretches over a river into a city that covers the rest of everything visible. Building after building, all with green roofs, all different sizes and as rustic looking as the Panacea. It's simple looking. But also beautiful, unlike anything I've ever seen before. Every day, I stare, mesmerized, until my eyes drift to the furthest edge of the city, to the rock-like building that stalks forever to the sky. There are no visible windows or doors in this building, giving it a look of complete power and terror. I remember asking Emmy what it was and her responding with only, "His." I didn't ask for clarification, I knew what she meant, and we ended up watching it together that day. Her eyes full of worry, mine of wonder.